Powerless

Powerless

LAUREN ROBERTS

SIMON & SCHUSTER

First published in Great Britain in 2023 by Simon & Schuster UK Ltd

Text © 2023 Lauren Roberts
Cover © 2023 Lauren Roberts
Cover images © Shutterstock, Depositphotos,
moonchild-ljilja, DeviantArt, resMENSA
Cover design by Seventhstar Art
Map © 2023 Lauren Roberts
Map design by Jojo Elliott

3 5 7 9 10 8 6 4

Simon & Schuster UK Ltd
1st Floor, 222 Gray's Inn Road
London WC1X 8HB

www.simonandschuster.co.uk
www.simonandschuster.com.au
www.simonandschuster.co.in

Simon & Schuster Australia, Sydney
Simon & Schuster India, New Delhi

A CIP catalogue record for this book
is available from the British Library.

PB ISBN 978-1-3985-2948-9
eBook ISBN 978-1-3985-2950-2
eAudio ISBN 978-1-3985-2949-6

Printed and bound in the UK
using 100% renewable electricity
at CPI Group (UK) Ltd

www.laurenrobertslibrary.com

MIX
Paper | Supporting
responsible forestry
FSC® C171272
www.fsc.org

For every girl who has ever felt powerless.

Izram

The Bowl A...

The Shallows

North

N

E

S

CHAPTER 1

Paedyn

Thick, hot liquid runs down my arm.

Blood.

Funny, I don't remember the guard nicking me with his sword before my fist connected with his face. Despite being a Flash, he apparently couldn't manage to move faster than my right hook to his jaw.

The smell of soot stings my nose, forcing me to clamp a grimy hand over it to stop a sneeze from slipping out.

That would be a very pathetic way to get caught.

When I'm sure that my nose won't alert the Imperials lurking beneath where I'm hiding, I return my hand to the filthy wall my back is currently pressed against with my feet planted opposite me. After taking a deep breath that nearly has me choking on soot, I slowly begin my climb upwards once again. With thighs burning almost as much as my nose, I force my body to continue shimmying while stifling the sneeze.

Climbing up a chimney isn't exactly how I thought I would be spending my evening. The small space has me sweating, swallowing my fear before scrambling to the top of the cramped corridor, eager to replace grime-caked walls with a starry night. When my head finally peeks over the top, I greedily gulp down the sticky air, then climb up and over, immediately bombarded with a new concoction of smells far more unpleasant than the stench of soot clinging to my body, my clothes, my hair. Sweat, fish, spices, and I'm quite certain some sort of bodily fluid, blends to create the aroma that surrounds Loot Alley.

Balancing atop the chimney, I strain my eyes on the shadowed roof to inspect my sticky arm. I'd nearly forgotten to examine it without the usual biting pain that accompanies a sword slash to remind me.

I rip off a strip of cloth from the sweaty tank that clings to my body, dabbing at the gash with it.

Adena's going to kill me for ruining her stitching. Again.

I'm surprised when I don't feel the familiar twinge of pain as I rub at my arm with the rough fabric, impatiently sopping up the stickiness.

And that's when I smell it.

Honey.

The same honey that belongs to the sticky buns oozing out of the many pockets in my ragged vest and dripping down my arm – mistaken for blood. I sigh, rolling my eyes at myself.

It's a welcome surprise, nonetheless. Even honey soaking my clothes beats trying to wash blood out.

I take in a deep breath and look out over the crumbling, rundown buildings cast in shadows by the flickering lampposts dotting the street. There's not much electricity here in the slums, but the king generously spared us a few lampposts. Thanks to the Volts and Scholars using their abilities to create a sustained power grid, I have to work exceptionally hard to stay in the shadows.

Farther from the slums, the more the rows of shops and homes slowly improve in condition and size. Shacks turn into homes, homes turn into mansions, leading up to the most daunting building of all. Squinting through the darkness, I can just barely make out the looming towers of the royal castle and the sloping dome of the Bowl Arena that resides beside it.

My eyes flick back to the wide street stretched out before me, scanning the surrounding sketchy buildings. Loot Alley is the very heart of the slums, pumping crime and trade throughout the city. I trace the dozens of other alleys and streets jutting off from it, getting lost in the maze that is the city before offering a sigh and small smile to the familiar street beneath me.

Home. Sort of. Technically, a home implies that one has a roof over their head.

But stars are far more fun to stare at than a ceiling.

I would know, seeing that I used to have a ceiling to stare at every night, back when I had no need for the stars to keep me company.

My traitorous gaze sweeps across the city to where I know my former home lies wedged between Merchant and Elm Streets. Where a happy little family is likely sitting around the dinner table, laughing and discussing their day with one another—

I hear a thump, followed by the murmuring of voices that drag me from my bitter thoughts. Straining to hear, I can just make out the muffled, deep voice that belongs to the guard I so kindly relieved of his duties a short while ago.

'—came up right behind me, quiet as a mouse, and then . . . then the next thing I know, I get a tap on the shoulder and a fist to the face.'

A very irritated and very shrill female voice echoes up the chimney. 'You're a Flash, for Plague's sake, aren't you supposed to be fast or something?' She takes a deep breath. 'Did you at least get a look at his face before you let him rob me? Again?'

'All I saw were his eyes,' the guard mumbles. 'Blue. Very blue.'

The woman huffs in irritation. 'How helpful. Let me just stop every person on Loot to see if their eyes match your vivid description of very blue.'

I stifle my snort as something creaks from the other end of the room, followed by a chorus of muffled footsteps. From the groan of rotting wood shifting beneath several new pairs of boots, I immediately deduce that three more guards have joined the hunt.

And that's my cue.

I hop off the chimney and grab onto the raised ledge of the roof, swinging my legs over the side to dangle above the street. Blowing out a breath, I let go and bite my tongue against a yelp as gravity yanks me towards the ground. With a soft thud I drop ungracefully into a merchant's wagon brimming with hay. The stiff straw pokes through my clothes like one of Adena's pincushions, and a cloud of soot and hay rises on the night breeze when I jump out onto the street.

Passing the time by plucking straw from my tangled hair, I begin my journey back to the Fort, weaving through beat-up merchant carts, all abandoned for the night, feet dancing over trash and broken trinkets. Looters slumped against alleys or tucked in between buildings whisper among themselves as I pass.

I feel the weight of the dagger tucked into my boot and relax at the comfort of the cool steel as I pass groups of fellow homeless huddling together for the night. I can see the faint shimmer of purple forcefields shielding some, while others don't even have an ability strong enough to allow them to sleep peacefully, which is the exact reason they call the slums their home.

I keep my steps swift and sure as my eyes sweep back and forth across the alleys, never letting my guard down. The poor don't discriminate. A shilling is a shilling, and they don't care if they jump someone worse off than them to get it.

Several guards cross my path as I zigzag down streets, forcing me to slow down to steer clear of them. Every shop, corner, and street has been bestowed the gift of leering, white-uniformed law enforcers. These brutal Imperials have been stationed everywhere along Loot Alley by decree of the king due to an increase in crime.

Clearly has nothing to do with me.

I slip down a smaller alley, making my way towards the dead end. There, tucked in the corner, is a mangled barricade of broken merchant carts, cardboard, old sheets, and Plague knows what else. Before I'm even halfway to the pile of garbage we call home, a face obscured by wild shoulder-length curls pops up over the Fort.

'Did you get it!?'

Untangling her long legs from where she sits, she effortlessly stands and phases right through the three-foot wall of our trash barricade without a second thought, and then she's bounding towards me with so much hope in her eyes that you'd think I've offered her a real roof over her head and a warm meal. And though I can give her neither of those things, I do have something far better in her opinion.

I sigh. 'I'm offended you doubted me, Adena. I thought you'd have a little more faith in my abilities after all these years.' I sling my pack from my back and pull out the crumpled red silk from within, unable to suppress my smile as a look of awe settles on her face.

She greedily claws the silk from my hands, running her fingers through the soft folds of the fabric. Peeking up through the curly bangs hanging in her hazel eyes, she looks at me as though I've just singlehandedly eradicated the Plague rather than steal fabric from a woman not much better off than we are.

Like I'm the hero and not the villain.

Adena's smile could rival the sun over the Scorches desert. 'Pae, you and your sticky fingers work magic, you know that?'

She throws her arms around my neck, pulling me into a crushing embrace that causes more honey to ooze down my vest and pool in my pockets.

'Speaking of sticky fingers . . .' I peel myself from her hug to fish around in my pockets. I retrieve six smashed sticky buns, only slightly unappetizing with the hay now decorating them.

Adena's eyes go wide at the sight before snatching one from my hand just as greedily as she did the fabric. She turns mid-bite and strides right back through our fort without a second thought, plopping herself down on the colorless, rough rugs that lie on the inside of the barricade. She pats the spot beside her expectantly, and unlike her, I ungracefully leap over the wall before I can take a seat.

'I bet Maria wasn't too happy about her shop being looted. Again. Poor thing should really up her security,' Adena says between bites, a crooked smile joining the crumbs on her face.

Despite my robbing the woman at least once a month for the past several years, she's still only managed to conclude that I am a he. At least she's trying.

'Actually,' I say with a shrug, 'she had two more Imperials stationed around her shop than normal. She must be getting tired of all the stolen sticky buns over the years.'

Adena narrows her hazel eyes at the sight of my smile. 'Thank the Plague you didn't get caught, Pae.' As soon as the familiar phrase slips past her lips, my jaw sets instinctively while hers falls open mid-bite. She visibly cringes, her brow crinkling and throat clearing. 'Sorry. Bad habit.' My fingers drift to the thick ring on my thumb, spinning it mindlessly while I muster a weak smile. This topic is one we typically try to avoid, though it's my fault the subject became suddenly awkward to speak of in the first place.

All due to a moment of weakness that I wish I wasn't so relieved about. 'You know it's not the words that bother me, it's—'

'It's the meaning behind them,' she cuts in with a smile and a shockingly accurate imitation of my voice.

I nearly choke on my laugh and a piece of sweet dough. 'Are you quoting me, A?'

By way of answering, she takes a bite of sticky bun before declaring between mouthfuls, 'And it's not the Plague that makes you sick, it's what came after.'

I nod slowly while absentmindedly tracing the rug's worn pattern beneath us, the feeling familiar beneath my finger. The idea of thanking the Plague that killed thousands of Ilyans makes me lose my appetite for even sticky buns. Thanking the thing that caused so much pain and death and discrimination.

But all anyone cares about now is who the Plague didn't kill. The kingdom was isolated for years to keep the sickness from spreading to the surrounding cities, and only the strongest in Ilya survived the disease that altered the very structure of humans. The fast became exceptionally faster, the strong became unbeatable, and those who lurked in the shadows could become the shadows. Dozens of supernatural abilities were bestowed upon Ilyans alone, all varying in strength, purpose, and power.

Gifts given as a reward for surviving.

They are Elite. They are extraordinary. They are exceptional.

'Just . . .' Adena trails off, poking at her sticky bun while struggling to form words for once. 'Just be careful, Pae. If you get caught and aren't able to talk yourself out of it—'

'I'll be fine,' I state far too casually, ignoring the worry that washes over me. 'This is what I do, A. What I've always done.'

She sighs through her smile, waving a dismissive hand. 'I know, I know. You can handle yourself with the Elites.'

I feel that rush of relief once again, making me feel both guilty and grateful that she truly knows me. Because not all those who survived the Plague were fortunate enough to be gifted with abilities. No,

14

the Ordinaries were just that – ordinary. And over the next several decades following the Plague, the Ordinaries and Elites lived in peace.

Until King Edric decreed that Ordinaries were no longer fit to live in his kingdom.

It was over three decades ago when sickness swept through the land. Due to the outbreak of what was likely a common illness, the king's Healers used the opportunity to claim that Ordinaries were carrying an undetectable disease, saying it was likely the reason they hadn't developed abilities. Extended exposure to them became harmful to both Elites and their powers, and over time, the Ordinaries were dwindling the abilities Elites are so protective of.

I fight the urge to roll my eyes at the thought.

My father believed that was bullshit, and I think no differently. But even if I had proof of the king lying through his teeth, it's not as though a girl from the slums is in any position to be believed.

But the king couldn't allow his Elite society to be weakened or worse by mere Ordinaries. Extinction was not an option for the extraordinary.

And so began the Purging.

Even now, decades later, tales of the bodies that scattered the sand under the scolding sun are casually passed around campfires, scary stories whispered among children.

Sticky fingers close over mine, the honey coating Adena's hands as sweet as the spreading smile she shares with me. My secret is stowed in the glint of her eyes, in the loyalty lining her expression. I've spent so much of my life resigned to the fact that nothing would ever be real. Every friendship false, every kindness calculated.

'Hide your feelings, hide your fear, and most importantly, hide behind your facade. No one can know, Paedy. Trust no one and nothing but your instincts.'

My father's gentle voice is oddly jarring as it echoes in my head, reminding me that every part of my life *should* be a lie and the girl sitting before me *should* be as deceived as the rest of the kingdom.

Selfishness only stole my sanity for a single night, but that was all it took for me to endanger the both of us.

'Alright, enough talk of the Plague,' Adena says cheerily, scanning the alley before adding, 'and your . . . situation.'

I don't bother stifling my snort. 'It seems that two years haven't been enough time for you to practice subtlety, A.'

I doubt she even heard me. Doubt she can focus on anything other than the fabric now gliding between her fingers. With hazel eyes scanning over sewing supplies, Adena abandons our previous conversation to ramble about what pieces she'll be making with the new silk. Her warm brown hands dig through scraps of fabric in the flickering lamplight, beginning to fold edges, pin corners, prick fingers, curse relentlessly.

We fall into the type of easy conversation that only comes after spending years surviving on the streets together, making it easy to interpret Adena's garbled words around the pins pressed between her lips. I roll over, finally falling quiet as I watch her steady fingers and furrowed brow, too engrossed with her work to sleep.

A stabbing pain in my side has my drooping eyes flying open, drowsiness forgotten. The jagged stone jutting up from the alley floor has me groggily grumbling, 'Mark my words, I'm going to steal a cot one day.'

Adena rolls her eyes at me, just as she does every night I make the same empty promise. 'I'll believe it when I feel it, Pae,' she singsongs.

I've rolled over about a dozen times before a scratchy, balled-up blanket collides with my head. 'If you don't quit your squirming, I swear I'll sew you to the bloody ground,' Adena says with all the sweetness of a sticky bun.

'I'll believe it when I feel it, A.'

CHAPTER 2

Kai

A ball of fire skims past my face, nearly singeing my hair off. I barely have the time to duck when I feel a second wave of heat rippling towards me.

Plagues, Kitt's in a lovely mood today.

Dancing on the balls of my feet, I watch as another sphere of fire comes hurtling in my direction as the familiar feel of adrenaline floods through me. I throw up a shield of water, hearing the fire hiss before it melts into nothing more than a thick cloud of steam. Kitt squints, attempting to see me through the smoke before his eyes widen when I suddenly collide with him. We tumble to the ground as I pin him down, raising a flaming fist aimed at his face.

'Yield?' I can't keep the smile from twitching my lips. He coughs out a laugh, his gaze flicking between my face and the blazing fist raised beside it.

'If I say no, are you really gonna punch me, little brother?' Despite the fire burning mere inches from him, Kitt's green eyes glint with amusement.

'I'd think you would know the answer to that by now.' I smile slightly as I cock my fist back farther, posing to strike.

'Alright, alright, I yield!' Kitt sputters. 'But only because I wouldn't

want poor Eli to have to set another one of our broken noses.'

I chuckled darkly at the thought of seeing the look on the royal physician's face if we were to stumble in with yet another broken bone. After standing to my feet, I offer a hand to Kitt who's still sprawled on the ground.

The smile he gives me doesn't quite reach his eyes when he finally says, 'Plagues, Kai, you're better with my powers than I am.'

'And that is why *you* will be ruling the country,' I say simply, 'while I'll be fighting on the battlefield, distracting the enemy with my dashing good looks.'

'Are you saying I couldn't distract the enemy with my own dashing good looks?' Kitt asks through his deep laughter, feigning offense.

'I'm saying that we are only half-brothers, so I'm afraid that means you only have half my charms.'

Kitt barks out another laugh. 'By that logic, I suppose you only have half my brains then.'

'Thank the Plague for that.' The words are barely out of my mouth before he's shoving me with a grin.

We walk the worn path between the dirt training circles that reside on the castle grounds. Imperials in training and other Elites of higher status continue their sparring as we pass, most using abilities while few use weapons.

Heads turn towards us, their eyes burning my skin mirroring the sun beating down on us from above. Ignoring the stares, I breathe in the training grounds' familiar scent of literal blood, sweat, and tears before grabbing a sword from a weapons rack and tossing one to Kitt, who's expression can only be described as exasperated.

'You know I've always enjoyed fighting with weapons more than abilities,' I say in answer to his pointed look as I mindlessly test the balance of my blade.

Kitt saunters farther into the muddy ring, all but rolling his eyes. 'Yes, I'm well aware of how much you love to beat down on me with a sword.' I rotate my wrist, swinging my blade as we begin circling each other. 'It does happen to be one of my favorite hobbies, yes.' I advance suddenly, swinging my sword down hard against his and sending a jolt up my arm. 'See, isn't this fun?'

Kitt grits his teeth against my strike. 'Riveting.'

I fall into a familiar trance, letting my feet dance around the ring as we spar, getting lost in the rhythm. My mind clears. My body hums with energy. I've always felt most alive when I fight. It's what I was made to do, what has kept me sane over the years of training and tutoring.

A dimwitted king is a dead king.

Father's words ring through my mind, having been drilled through my skull after every complaint about my tedious lessons as a boy. Though, I won't have to worry about being a dead or dimwitted king, seeing that I won't be a king at all. And after arguing just that to Father, he kindly created a new saying for me to live by.

A dimwitted Enforcer is a defeated empire.

Encouraging.

A sharp pain sears up my forearm, dragging me from my thoughts with a jolt.

'Better get your head in the game, Kai, or I might actually beat you.' Kitt has a look of triumph on his face that I intend to wipe off. 'I wouldn't want my future Enforcer slacking on the jo—'

Before he can even finish his remark, I'm pushing his sword to the ground and pinning it under my own before swiveling behind him. In one swift motion, I kick my boot up, sliding a dagger from it to settle the sharp tip against his back.

'I'm sorry, what was that, Your Majesty?' I release my hold on him, and he turns as I sweep into a mocking bow while tucking the dagger back into my boot. That earns me a solid shove that nearly has me staggering, one I return in kind while Kitt chuckles.

His dirty blond hair is far more dirty than blond at the moment, splattered with chunks of mud from rolling around in the ring. Our shirts have long been abandoned in the summer heat and, like me, sweat slicks his tanned chest.

It's almost comical how obvious it is that we're only half-brothers. Other than our physical differences, I lack Kitt's caring like he lacks my callousness. He's patient, personable, and fit for the throne like I'm fit for the battlefield.

A king where I am a killer.

'Kai, are you even listening to me?' Kitt looks equally concerned and amused as he snaps his fingers in front of my face. 'Plagues, how much blood did you lose?'

I follow his gaze to see rivulets of red trailing from the wound on my arm, blood weaving between my knuckles and dripping from my fingertips. 'Well, looks like Eli won't be getting the day off after all, thanks to you.' I glance up at Kitt, expecting a remark only to find his gaze fixed on something across the grounds. 'Now look who's not paying attention.'

My eyes stray to the figure strutting towards us, training leathers clinging to her every curve and lilac hair whipping in the wind. 'Oh, look. Bitchy Blair,' I breathe under my breath before she reaches us, causing Kitt to choke on a laugh.

'Hello, boys.' Her voice is like ice, cold and smooth. 'How's the training coming?' Her gaze sweeps lazily over the both of us before returning to our faces with a slight smirk twisting her lips. 'Getting ready for the Trials, Kai?'

'Not that I need to prepare.'

A slow smile creeps onto her face at that. 'I would think the future Enforcer would want to make a good impression on the kingdom by winning.' She's suddenly very interested in her nails, feigning nonchalance.

I run a hand through my hair with a bored sigh. 'And I plan on doing just that.'

She gives me a smile that's anything but sweet. 'I would hope so, seeing that you're the best Elite in decades. Or so they say.'

Plagues, here we go.

Kitt takes a step forward and puts a hand to his chest like he's been wounded. 'Ouch, Blair. I'll remember that comment when I'm king.'

'Aw, did I wound your pride, Kitt?' She offers him a fake pout before turning her attention back on me. 'Besides, I personally think I'll be winning the Trials.'

I huff out a humorless laugh before peering down at her small form. 'And what makes you so sure you'll even be competing?' I say this knowing full well that she will, in fact, be in the Trials.

With a flick of her wrist, a dagger flies from the weapons rack in response to my comment. Before I can blink, it's suddenly suspended in the air and digging into my jugular.

'As the daughter of the general,' she steps towards me until there are mere inches between us and whispers, 'I think I have a pretty good shot of getting into the games. Don't you?' She giggles even while pressing the floating knife to my throat, further proving her point.

The buzz of dozens of powers pounds through my blood, all belonging to the other individuals training in the courtyard. I force the other abilities to fall silent, focusing on Blair's power and the feel of it humming beneath my skin, urging me to grab hold of it. She's a powerful Tele, and her demonstration with this dagger is the least of what she can do with her mind. I reach out to that tingling feeling that is her ability and let it wash over me, claw to the surface.

And then I become it.

Just as I did with Kitt's Dual power of fire and water, and just as I can do with any one of the abilities surrounding me.

My smile is cold as I flip the floating dagger in mid-air, pushing it against the tough leather covering her heart with nothing but my mind. 'Well, then you better get training,' I say quietly before loosening my hold on her ability, letting the dagger fall to the ground with a thud. I don't bother saying anything more before I turn and stride towards the castle.

Kitt falls silently into step beside me, seemingly just as lost in thought as I am as we make our way back through the castle gates. With the Trials only two weeks away, it seems I'm no longer able to blissfully ignore their existence and my role within them.

The smell of roasting chicken and potatoes wafting from the kitchens is enough to steal my attention. I shoot a glance at the abnormally quiet Kitt before turning to stride through the kitchen doors.

'Afternoon, ladies.' I flash a quick smile at the cooks and servants milling around the kitchen as they prepare dinner. 'Miss me?' I croon, lifting myself up onto a hard counter and leaning back on my palms. I catch the eyes of a few servant girls before they redden and turn back to their work, exchanging giggled whispers with one another.

The heat of the kitchen hits me like a wave, washing over me and coating my already slick skin—

My skin.

I run a hand through my hair before running it down my face, unbothered by the realization that I've been walking around without a shirt after abandoning it in the filthy ring – a habit even Father hasn't been able to break.

Kitt's head pops around the corner, a grin splitting his face. 'I thought I smelled my favorite dish. You're such a sweetheart, Gail.' He strides over to the cook stirring a pot full of creamy potatoes over the sweltering stove, her dark skin glistening with sweat.

She can't help but smile at the look lighting Kitt's face. 'Oh, don't think I did this for you, Kitty. Mashed potatoes happen to be my favorite as well.' She smiles, patting him on the cheek before turning to continue her stirring. Her eyes meet mine from where I sit atop the counter before darting to my arm and the wound I'd forgotten was still bleeding there. With a shake of her head, she says sternly, 'You better not get blood on my counter, Kai.'

I crack a smile at that. 'This wouldn't be the first time.'

She shakes her head at me again, fighting a smile all the while. Gail's been slipping us extra food and treats since we were boys running around the castle with half our clothes on – which we clearly still do. She's witnessed far more than one fight unfold in this very kitchen over who gets the last of her sticky buns.

'You two haven't visited me in a while,' she says, adding seasoning to her potatoes. 'Getting sick of me, hmm?'

'You, yes. But never your food.' The words have barely left my mouth before a glob of potatoes comes flying at my face. I don't have the time or energy to duck before the mash joins the matted mud and dirt.

'Never a dull moment with us, is there?' Kitt muses from where he's leaning against a ledge, watching as I pull at the potatoes clinging to my hair.

I hop off the counter and stride over to the cook, giving her a peck on the cheek. 'Always a pleasure, Gail.' I reach around her to grab an apple from its basket as I say, 'I look forward to our next food fight.' After tossing one to Kitt, I rub my own apple on my pants before taking a bite.

'Prince Kai?'

I stiffen, sigh, and turn towards the voice behind me. A young boy looks up nervously, his hands fidgeting with the hem of his shirt. I raise my eyebrows, my impatience evident.

'The king requests your presence in the throne room.'

CHAPTER 3

Paedyn

The wheel of a merchant's cart rolls over my toes. I bite back a yelp but don't bother biting back my rather rude retort directed at the oblivious man who's mindlessly crippling people with his cart.

Well, today's off to a great start.

I slept fitfully last night, tossing and turning as I faded in and out of my recurring nightmares. Flashes of my father dying while I can do nothing but hold his hand, climbing up a chimney only to find the top boarded up, and Adena, the only person I have left in this world, being dragged away from me screaming.

Sometime between my numerous nightmares, Adena made a feeble attempt to shake me awake. I rolled over groaning, trying to cling to the little bit of blissful sleep I managed to steal. I may be the thief, but I'm regularly robbed of rest.

Persistent per usual, Adena then switched her strategy, deciding to pelt me with rough scraps of fabric until I finally raised a white cloth in surrender.

The sun, lazy as ever, is slowly struggling to peek over the run-down buildings, casting Loot Alley in morning shadows while I make my way down the cobblestone path. As the street comes alive with the hustle and bustle of merchants haggling while beggars plead with

anyone who spares them a glance, I easily blend into the chaos that surrounds the slums.

My hands itch to snatch some food to quiet my grumbling stomach and to bring back for Adena. My eyes flick across the street in search of my next unfortunate victim to rob when—

Something's not right.

Fourteen. There are only fourteen Imperials lining the street.

But there should be at least sixteen today.

I would know, seeing that I've memorized their rotations.

I spot Egg Head and Hook Nose in their usual spots outside of Maria's shop, along with several other Imperials with equally accurate names. With the white, leather masks obscuring half their faces from view, it's rather difficult to come up with creative nicknames for the bastards, so I pride myself on the few I've invented.

Normally, the prospect of fewer guards would be a relief, and perhaps it's my Psychic abilities kicking in, but the sight worries me.

My stomach growls angrily, impatient as ever.

Food first, funny feeling second.

I zigzag through the crowd with ease, swiping apples from the cart that ran over my toes, the revenge as sweet as the crisp fruit I bite into. Leaning against the crumbling wall of a shop, I spot what looks to be a young apprentice haggling with a tradesman. I watch as he fixes the merchant with a glare before throwing down several coins and snatching up a bundle of what can only be black leather. My eyes skim over the shillings as they roll on top of the cart, counting them quickly to find far too many coins there for leather.

He's in a hurry. That's why he's willing to pay double what he should rather than take the time to negotiate a cheaper price. And he has the money to spare.

The perfect target.

I step onto the street and head for the boy now quickly shoving through the crowd while I pull at the leather strap holding my hair out of my face and off my neck. It falls down my back in a cascade of messy, silver waves while I curse the sweltering heat that already has my neck sticky with sweat. Letting a curtain of hair fall over my shoulder and into my face, I morph myself into the perfect picture of innocence.

'Make them underestimate you. Make them overlook you until you want to be seen.'

It's been so long since I've heard my father's voice that the soft sound of it threatens to slip from my memory and drift into death with him.

The thought shatters when we collide.

I stumble, scrambling to grab hold of the unsuspecting apprentice as I let myself fall. Gathering a fistful of his shirt in one hand, I slip the other into his vest pocket where I saw him grab his coins. I can feel six shillings there and resist the urge to grab all of them before only palming three.

Greed is not an easily tamed emotion, but I force myself to leave the other coins, knowing that he's likely smart enough to feel the lack of weight in his pocket if I take them all. And I don't need to add any more scars to my back for getting caught.

But right as I'm about to pull out my hand and ramble an apology for nearly running the boy over, my fingers catch on the inside lining of his vest. No, not just the lining – a secret pocket. I feel a folded piece of parchment within, and on an impulse I can't explain or justify, decide to palm that too before sliding my hand out and shyly looking up into the apprentice's face.

His brown eyes are wide as I stare up at him through the strands of hair blowing across my face. I arrange my expression into that of utter embarrassment and quickly uncurl my fist from his shirt.

Blowing a strand of hair from my eyes, I take a step back to put some space between us. 'I am so sorry, sir!' I force myself to sound breathless, embarrassed, harmless. 'I'm quite certain I am the only person in all of Ilya who is capable of tripping on air!'

Go on. Underestimate me. Overlook me.

He runs a hand through his curly hair and chuckles. 'No worries. Guess you have quite the talent then.' He wears a smile, but his gaze lingers a little too long for my liking. So, I offer him a grin and a nod of my head before turning on my heel and vanishing into the crowded street.

The sugary scent of sticky buns wafts down the busy alley as I stroll past Maria's shop and sidestep into one of the many small alleys branching off Loot. The note I nicked grows damp with sweat as I grip it in my palm. What could possibly be written on this little piece of paper that warrants it to be so hidden?

I intend to find out.

Flattening my back against the grimy brick wall, I unfold the edges of the paper to reveal a scribbled note:

Meeting begins quarter past midnight.

White house between Merchant and Elm.

Bring the supplies.

I stare at the note, blinking in confusion while my heart races in anticipation.

That's my house.

Well, that was my house.

I can tell by the slant of the letters and the smudging of the ink that whoever wrote this was likely in a hurry to hide the note from prying eyes.

Prying eyes like mine.

Dozens of questions flood my mind, each one more confusing than the last. Why on this Plague forsaken earth are meetings being held at my house?

Former house. You left it, remember?

And to meet there in the middle of the night with supplies—?

The leather.

I trip over the uneven cobblestone, ripping me back to reality and the realization that I've been pacing this whole time. I shove the crumpled note back into my vest, mind still reeling as I step out onto the busy street now bathed in sunlight. I shake my head, trying to clear it as I push through the throng of people bartering, gossiping, and cursing.

Beginning to wind through the merchant carts once again, I fall into the familiar rhythm that is my honest occupation – thieving. My mind wanders as I work, leaving me to wonder whether Adena is having any luck selling her clothes on the other end of the long street.

I steal, she sews.

And that's been our lives for the past five years. I was barely thirteen and utterly alone in the world when Adena quite literally ran into me. Well, she phased right through me. I'll never forget the look on the Imperial's face as he sprinted after her, screaming about stolen pastries. And without a second thought, I didn't hesitate before sticking my foot out into his path. As soon as I got a glimpse of the guard's face meeting the pavement, I was chasing after the gangly, curly-haired girl who ran right through me.

An uneasy alliance was born that day, one that was supposed to stay that way.

My hand freezes mid-air, hovering over a plump grapefruit when a chilling scream cuts through the mayhem of Loot. I twist around, fruit forgotten, searching through the throng of bodies to find the source of the noise. My eyes scan the crowd before snagging on a small, slumped figure crumpled against a wooden pole stained red at the center of the street. An Imperial hovers over the small boy, whip in hand, looking disgustingly pleased with himself as he stares down at the child. I know that look all too well. I've been that bleeding child far too many times.

He got caught.

I wonder what it was that he stole, what it was that could possibly justify such a beating. Some fruit? Maybe a few shillings from a merchant? I remember slumping up against the wooden pole, shaking with the pain caused by each crack of the whip while I bit my tongue to keep from crying out. The pain fades, but the scars remain as a reminder to do better.

The young ones always get caught. They're needy. They haven't learned to control their greed or live with their hunger yet, making them easy targets for the Imperials to use as an example.

There's nothing you can do for him.

I have to beat those words into my head to ensure my feet don't find their way to the boy. Because I tried once. Tried to step in and help a little girl who reminded me of myself. So scared, and yet, so determined to never show it. When she looked up at me, the fire in her gaze reflected my own. In the end, my attempt to help only ended with extra lashings for the both of us.

I grimace and quickly turn away from the gruesome scene only to get a mouthful of starchy, crumpled uniform when I slam into the lowlife wearing it.

The Imperial stares down at me, amusement flickering in his eyes surrounded by that white mask. Though he looks to be at least ten years my senior, blond hair sticking up at odd angles, he takes his time lazily trailing his gaze over my body. I bite my tongue before I can say something he'll likely make me regret.

Imperials aren't known to be gentlemen when it comes to young girls – or to anyone for that matter – and I don't intend to find out if he is the exception. 'So sorry, sir. I seem to be madly clumsy today,' I say, planning my escape into the crowd.

A clammy hand wraps around my wrist and spins me back around. I summon every bit of strength I have to suppress the fighting instinct that screams at me to knee him in the groin and bash his head into the stones beneath our feet.

'Why in such a hurry?' His toothy grin and black eyes send a shiver down my spine, and the foul stench of alcohol on his breath only adds to my unease.

I smile and force myself to be polite as I shake out of his grasp. 'Just trying to run some errands before the market gets too crowded, that's all.'

'Hmm,' he grunts, eying me skeptically. 'Say, what's your power, girl?' I fight the urge to stiffen as he continues with a grin, 'By decree of the king, I'm to question anyone I feel . . . should be questioned.'

He loves being in control. Having power.

'I'm a Mundane,' I say simply, stating my tier on the Elites' food chain to prove that I am of little threat and importance to him. 'A Psychic.' I look him right in his black eyes as I say it, willing his black heart to believe me.

'Is that right? I've never met a Psychic before.' He chuckles darkly and takes a step towards me, bending his head close to mine so I get another whiff of the alcohol clinging to him. 'Prove it then.'

I'm growing quite tired of that demand.

I meet the Imperial's eyes, refusing to give him the satisfaction of thinking I'm concerned, though my pounding pulse proves otherwise. 'I'm sensing anger and . . . regret from you. You've . . . You've just split up with your wife. Well, actually, she left you.' The look of utter shock on his face brings a small smile to my lips. 'And if you really want me to be specific, because, well, you told me to *prove* it, it's because you . . .' I stop mid-sentence, squeezing my eyes shut while pressing fingers to my temple, putting on a convincing show. ' . . . You cheated on her? Wait, I'm getting something else . . .' I peek up at his face, now red with rage, as I continue rubbing my temple. 'You . . . you want her back. But she doesn't want you—'

I'm prepared for the backhand before I feel the sting of it across my face.

Blood flies from my mouth, and I keep my head turned away from him as he growls close to my face, 'Bloody witch is what you are. Get out of my sight, Mundane.'

I spin on my heel and smile, blood pooling in my mouth and dribbling down my chin. I force myself to stumble back into a cart, snatching some fabric hanging off the edge from behind my back. I turn around quickly, clutching the bundle to my chest as I tear off a corner with my teeth to wipe up my bloody mouth and chin. I'll use part of the fabric as a napkin, and the rest can go to Adena. Two birds with one stone. Shoving the remaining cloth in my pack, now stuffed full of food, coins, and other stolen goods, I head back towards the Fort all while replaying the last five minutes over in my head.

It wasn't hard to get under the Imperial's skin, and I knew once I had, he'd slap me silly and let me scurry away. This wouldn't have been the first time I've let that happen. And proving my *Psychic* abilities was hardly difficult considering that the evidence was written all over him.

The thin tan line on his now empty ring finger was my first clue that he was formally married. Then, there's the fact that he moved his wedding band to his other hand rather than pawning it off for money, telling me that he still cares for his ex-wife and is probably still pining over her. The disheveled hair, crumpled uniform, and smell of whiskey on his breath further prove that he is obviously a single man who no longer has a wife to make him look presentable.

Men would likely go extinct without women to coddle them.

As for the part where he cheated on his wife, well, that was more so an educated guess based on the way he looked at me along with the *stellar* reputation the Imperials have made for themselves. Clearly, the assumption hit a nerve before he hit me.

The midday sun beats down on me as I make my way back to the Fort to meet Adena for lunch just like always. I take my time meandering down Loot, gnawing on an apple while hunger gnaws at me.

The salty smell of fish basking in the sun atop merchant carts hangs in the air. Children scuttle in front of my path, laughing as they chase each other down the street. The sound of voices haggling and cursing is like a chorus to me, a tune I'm all too familiar with.

A large, colored banner catches my eye as it begins to rise above the crowded alley, strung between two shops by a Crawler. He scurries up the wall as though there's glue on his palms and feet, allowing him to climb up the smooth shop with ease. As he secures the rope connecting the banner to the wall, I turn my attention to the words scrawled on the green tapestry in large, black lettering:

THE SIXTH PURGING TRIALS IS ABOUT TO BEGIN
REMEMBER THE PURGING. THANK THE PLAGUE.
HONOR TO YOUR KINGDOM,
YOUR FAMILY, AND YOURSELF.
YOU COULD BE THE NEXT VICTORIOUS ELITE.

I snort loudly, nearly choking on a chunk of my apple. Although the Purging Trials are nothing to laugh about, I can't help but find it comical that they are meant to be a *celebration*. In honor of the Great Purging over three decades ago, the Trials were created to showcase the people's supernatural abilities and bring *honor* to the only Elite kingdom.

I wouldn't say murdering innocent people brings honor to me, my kingdom, or my family – not that I have any left to bring honor to. And yet, every five years, young Elites are chosen to compete in these games for both the glory and enough shillings to build your own comfy castle while you try to escape the trauma the Trials caused you.

But the part that has me shaking with both laughter and rage is that the lesser Elites, those with Defensive and Mundane abilities, are made to believe that they have a chance of winning these twisted Trials. I feel suddenly numb as I look at the excited faces surrounding me, all crowding under the sign, grinning and pointing.

We are the first to die.

The Elites who compete aren't *chosen*, but rather, born into their fate. It's always those of royal blood or of higher status on the Elites' tier of power. I scan the crowd, eyes skipping over the smiling faces of Mundanes who are only thrown into the Trials for entertainment after the king allows us to pick who we wish to *represent* us.

Despite the king insisting that the killing of fellow Elites in the arena is *frowned upon*, it's no secret that Death itself is a contestant in the Trials. Dying teenagers apparently make things exceptionally more entertaining, and if the Elites won't do the killing, the king will pull the strings in the arena.

I push through the throng of people gathered under the sign, all talking over one other about who will represent Loot and what they would do with the prize money.

There have been very few times in my life when I haven't envied the Elites. But at the thought of competing in the Purging Trials, I've never been more thankful to be nothing and no one of importance.

Completely Ordinary.

CHAPTER 4

Paedyn

'Are you gonna eat that?' Adena is eying the half-eaten orange on my lap while I sit leaning against the alley wall behind the Fort.

'Have at it.' The words have barely slipped past my lips before she leans over, her curly hair blowing in the soft breeze as she snatches the fruit and pops a slice into her mouth.

The Imperial with the impressive backhand left me the lovely gift of a split bottom lip, making it difficult to choke down food. 'How'd you do today?' I ask while mindlessly spinning the thick, silver wedding band on my thumb.

The cold steel of my father's ring bites into my skin, comforting me like it always has. I suppose I'd have my mother's too if it weren't buried with her when I was a baby. Illness, Father had said. She was an Ordinary, after all, and the lot of us are apparently weaker, diseased humans.

But he married her anyway. Loved her despite it. Protected her. Kept her secret just as he did mine.

Adena sighs, and I'm brought back to the present when she says between bites of orange, 'Can't complain. Oh, I sold that top I had been working on for ages! For three whole shillings, too! You know, the green one with the deep neckline and scalloped hem?' I give her

the same confused look I always do when she starts speaking in her sewing language. 'Ugh, you're hopeless when it comes to clothes, Pae.'

I glance down at my battered tank beneath the olive-green vest atop it. Everything changed the day Adena made me the pocketed vest, knowing that it would serve me well as a thief. That was the day an uneasy alliance began to blossom into an easy friendship.

Adena taps a finger against her lips, considering something. 'I bet if you had on the right outfit, everyone would be too busy staring at you to even notice you're robbing them.'

I snort. 'I'd rather not have people staring while I'm committing crimes. That seems a bit counterproductive.'

I snatch up my dagger and tuck it into my boot, brushing my fingers along the swirling, silver handle. It's the only other keepsake I have from Father besides his ring – both of which I never go without. I'm admiring the intricate handle for the hundredth time before jolting when I suddenly remember something. 'Be careful today, A. There are fewer guards out than usual for some reason, and I don't like it. Just . . .' I struggle to find the right words. 'Just keep an eye out for anything out of the ordinary, okay?'

She looks slightly unsettled by this news, but the narrowing of her hazel eyes is playful. 'Is this your Psychic juju warning you of potential danger?'

'Yeah, we definitely need to work on your subtlety,' I sigh, shaking my head at her with a smile.

I stand to leave, groaning as I stretch out my sore body. Adena gathers her clothes, all varying in different sizes and colors, and reluctantly waves goodbye before heading back out onto Loot in the hopes of selling more items before sundown.

I step out into the crowded street now bathed in late afternoon sunlight and head towards the buzz of the marketplace. I start off easy. First, nicking some fruit and fabric before growing bored and moving on to bigger and better items. Wallets, watches, and shillings are what I'm really after this evening.

I spy a man with dark blue hair and a glittering watch adorning his thick wrist before quickly deciding to make him my next target. Peering down the packed street, I spot a few others with abnormally

34

colored hair dotting the crowd, evidence that a genetic-altering Plague comes with more perks than just supernatural abilities. Though, even with the mop of silver hair atop my head, I still wasn't gifted a power to accompany it. It takes me far too long to escape the blue-haired man after stealing his watch. Not because he caught me, no, but because he wouldn't stop *talking to me*. After stumbling into him and slyly slipping the accessory from his wrist, it was clear the poor man was dying to spew gossip with anyone willing to smile and nod at him.

I'm about ready to head in early and call it a decently successful night when a tall figure, completely clad in black, strolls onto Loot. He walks with an air of confidence, so at odds with the hunch that the homeless have adapted in the hopes of drawing as little attention to themselves as possible.

But this man . . . this man is making it difficult to look away.

He wears a loose black button-down, tucked into slim black pants and separated by a simple belt. His collared shirt is halfway unbuttoned, billowing open in the breeze to expose part of his tanned chest. His facial features are fuzzy from this distance, but his tar-black hair falls over the top of his forehead in messy waves. With his hands buried in his pockets, his long strides carry him deeper into the market, looking cool and collected.

He's not from here. I can see it in the way he looks around as if taking it all in. It's likely he is an Offensive, an Elite of higher status or noble blood who rarely sets foot into the slums. I can see in the way he walks, in the shine of his shoes, that this man will be carrying far more than a few measly shillings. I squint, trying to get an idea of where he might have slipped his silvers.

There.

Swinging against his leg, attached from his belt with a strap, hangs a pouch that many Ilyans use to carry change. Specifically, the confident ones, seeing that an unguarded pouch is easy pickings for a thief. Easy pickings for me.

My last, unlucky target for the night.

It's a good thing he's so bleeding tall, or I would have lost him in the swarm of people. I watch women of all ages crane their necks as he passes, trying to get a better view of the handsome stranger before he melts into the mass of people. I shove through the crowd and tail him until he steps out of the main path between merchant carts and onto a less crowded street. I shake out my hair, letting the long waves fall limply over my shoulders as I cut down a street, heading to cut him off. The back alley I zigzag through spits me out onto the same one the stranger strolled down – and now I am heading straight for him.

I keep my eyes glued to the ground when we collide.

Following my usual routine, I let myself stumble backward from the impact, fighting against every instinct screaming at me to plant my feet and stand my ground. Strong arms wrap around my waist to keep me from falling, leaving his money pouch open and exposed to lowlifes like me. I grab hold of the front of his shirt, acting as if I did so as a reflex to keep my balance. Really, I just needed a reason to have my hands so close to his body without looking suspicious.

The starving boys from Loot don't feel like this.

The thought dissolves when I reach my hand into the pouch at his hip, my fingers deducing that there are at least twenty shillings casually hanging from this man's belt. He must be very confident in his abilities to walk around Loot with so much . . . well, loot.

I'm tempted to rip off the pouch and run, knowing full well he'd catch me in about three long strides. But, not knowing when I'll quite literally run into an opportunity like this again, I refuse to leave without at least half of what's in his bag.

But he'll feel the weight difference if I take half.

My mind is reeling.

Then distract him.

With all this plotting happening within a matter of moments, I quickly and quietly clutch half the coins in my fist before carefully pulling my hand out of the pouch as I steady myself against him. Then, I slowly tear my gaze from his partially exposed chest where the edge of a dark tattoo peeks out behind the folds of his shirt.

My eyes finally meet his.

It's like looking into a storm.

His eyes are the color of thunderclouds settling over Ilya, of smoke puffing from the chimneys overhead, of the stolen silver coins clenched in my fist. His black, long lashes are in total contrast with his steely gray eyes, now sweeping across my face. Shock raises his dark brows, tightens his sharp jaw, emphasizes his strong cheekbones.

We stand there, staring at each other.

I'm suddenly, acutely aware of every place he's touching me. His strong arms are still wrapped around my waist and half holding me up, though his gaze feels like a caress in and of itself. I clear my throat as I remove my fisted hand from his shirt, revealing crumpled, fine fabric beneath before moving to step out of his hold.

His lips twitch, allowing me to glimpse a dimple on his right cheek. He slowly slides his arms from my waist, releasing me as his hands catch on the rough bottom of my vest.

Calluses. He's a fighter.

Not that I need to be a Psychic to figure that out, seeing that his physique makes that fact obvious. With the thought of him being a trained fighter and double my size in mind, I nonchalantly pull my hands behind me to hide the evidence of my crime. The coins slide silently into my back pocket as I take a deep breath, trying to pull myself together.

'Do you always fall into the arms of handsome strangers, or is this a new thing for you?' His question displays that dimple again when a grin settles on his face, revealing white, straight teeth.

'No, only the cocky ones.' I smile coolly while he looks at me like I'm a puzzle he's trying to decipher, amusement playing all over his face.

Distract him.

He chuckles and runs a hand through his ebony hair, only managing to make the waves messier. Gray eyes search mine as he says, 'Well, looks like I've made quite the first impression then.'

'Yes,' I say slowly, 'though I still haven't decided if it was a good or bad one yet.'

Keep his mind off the money and his focus on you.

He shrugs, shoving his hands into his pockets – the perfect picture of cool indifference. 'I caught you, didn't I?'

Now it's my turn to laugh. He cocks his head slightly to the side as he peers down at me, the corner of his mouth tilted up. Leaning in, he adds, 'Maybe you should consider that detail before you decide, darling.'

Plagues, a pretty boy with pretty words.

Dangerous.

His smoky eyes sweep across my face, once again looking at me as though I'm an intriguing riddle. I refuse to fidget under his gaze as I take a step backward towards the busy street.

'I'll keep it under consideration, *darling*.' I draw out the last word, mimicking him with a grin. His smile widens, displaying dimples on both of his cheeks. I force myself to ignore them as I add, 'And thank you for saving me from eating cobblestone. I seem to be cursed with clumsiness.'

'Well, your clumsiness found me, so I'd hardly call it a curse,' he says simply, now leaning against the wall, hands in pockets.

I smile, unable to suppress the eye roll that accompanies it. I glimpse his grin one last time before spinning on my heel and walking back onto Loot Alley, disappearing into the crowd.

My mind is reeling, replaying the observations I made of him as I make my way down Loot. The scars splattering his arms and the raw knuckles from a recent fight intrigued me the most, and it's almost a shame I won't discover the story that accompanies them. The thought of an Offensive Elite wearing scars almost brings a smile to my lips. Proof of weakness.

I grab the coins in my back pocket, letting them clink in my palm with a triumphant smile.

I doubt he'll be missing these.

CHAPTER 5

Kai

The collared shirt I throw on is scratchy and uncomfortable, making me suddenly miss the days when I was young, and it was socially acceptable to run around half-naked.

Though, that's never stopped me from doing it now.

After slipping on one of my only pairs of shoes not currently caked in mud, I stride over to the door. I pass messy shelves that threaten to tip from the weight of far too many books, my desk that is currently covered in documents I'm avoiding, and the four-poster bed jutting out from the wall, the cause of several stubbed toes and incessant swearing. Sighing, I close the door on the comfort of my room, wishing desperately that I could dive onto my bed and sleep through dawn. Alas, duty calls, and it's best not to keep him waiting.

I shove my hands into my pockets as I stroll down the white halls leading to the throne room. Late afternoon sunlight streams through the windows lining the corridor, causing the ornate paintings on the walls to glitter in the golden light. Far too soon for my liking, I round the corner and nod to the guards standing outside the throne room before pushing open the heavy doors.

'Ah, Kai. It's about time.' Father's deep voice echoes down the vast length of the throne room. Its walls are decorated with large, wide

windows draped in dark green silk – Ilya's kingdom color – accompanied by the sculptured molding crawling up the walls and onto the ceiling. Currently, a long wooden table resides in the middle of the polished marble floor where the king occupies the chair at the head.

'Good, you put on a shirt.' He sighs but I see a slight smile in his eyes. 'I considered telling the servant to add that detail to the message he gave you.'

'Oh, don't worry, Father, I won't make the mistake of showing up to the throne room without a shirt. Again.' I memorize the hint of a smile on his face, not knowing the next time I'll see it. The next time I'll earn it.

He's a brutal man, a Brawny who is strong physically as well as mentally. He's stern, stubborn, and set in his ways, so seeing him offer even the faintest of smiles has me involuntarily returning a faint one of my own. Our dynamic together has always been *difficult* to say the least, but in moments like these, it's easier to ignore our unpleasant past.

He clears his throat along with any emotion on his face.

And there's the father I'm so used to.

'I have a mission for you as the future Enforcer.'

'I live to serve,' I answer flatly.

I live to kill.

My life means the end of someone else's.

The types of *missions* Enforcers get sent on are anything but heroic. I've had dozens over the years, all part of my training to become the future executioner, commander of armies, and right-hand man to the king. Everything from battle strategies and executions to interrogations and torture fall into my line of work as the expected Enforcer.

All glimpses into my bright future.

'My informants know of a family harboring an Ordinary near Loot Alley,' Father continues, sounding slightly bored. 'I need you to investigate and eradicate the problem.'

Eradicate equals execute.

After the Purging, when the Ordinaries were banished to the Scorches to protect Ilya from their disease, the king decreed that any remaining Ordinaries found in the kingdom would be executed.

Three decades ago, he offered them a chance to survive if they could cross the Scorches and reach the cities of Dor and Tando on the other side where they would be no harm. But the king's mercy only lasted that day of the Purging, and I now deliver death on his behalf.

'Of course,' I say, running a hand through my hair and over my set jaw. The action doesn't go unnoticed.

'Kai.' He looks at me, almost *gently*. I haven't seen that look since I was a boy, and even then, it was a rarity reserved for the few times I pleased him during my training. 'No one envies the job of the Enforcer. It's brutal. It's bloody. But the Plague has given you a rare gift. Your ability as a Wielder is very powerful, and you'll serve this kingdom well one day.' He pauses before adding, 'I've made sure of that.'

He has indeed.

Training has been my whole life, my whole purpose. Rather than having a single ability to manifest and master, I've spent years learning how to control dozens. But I honed my body as much as my abilities, becoming a weapon myself. How to use and kill with every weapon at my disposal has been ingrained into my brain – a reflex I have refined.

But I can't take all the credit. No, it's the king who made me what I am today. The king who took it upon himself to aid in both my physical and mental training. After learning my weaknesses, he ensured they were eradicated. And while I've learned to block out most memories of the training I endured as a boy, I can do nothing to ignore the image of my father's cool face paired with the same chilling words I've heard all my life.

'If you cannot endure suffering, you are unfit to dole it out, Enforcer.'

I've fought in battles, initiated interrogations, and conducted torture all while Kitt sat in on countless meetings, devised treaties, and spent his days beside a kinder king than the one I know.

His days consisted of education, tutoring, and far more pleasant time spent with the father he loves so much. As the heir, Kitt's always been guarded, protected, and even getting him out into the training yard with me when we were boys was no small feat.

When I look back at the king, his green eyes are already pinned on me. Kitt's eyes. After Father's first wife died while giving birth to his son, he married the daughter of a trusted adviser. Unsurprisingly, he quickly fell in love with my mother's caring and kindness, her bravery and beauty. I look like her, with my dark hair and light eyes, just as Kitt takes after Father, both green-eyed and blond.

I clear my head, tucking thoughts of the past away until the next time I'll allow myself to dwell on them again. My voice is dull when I finally ask, 'When do I leave?'

Those exact words poke at a memory, reminding me how naïve I was when I asked them before my very first mission. Not knowing that I would become a murderer that day. Not knowing I would watch a man crumple to the floor in a pool of his own blood.

'At dawn.'

Dawn comes far too early for my liking, and before I know it, I'm making my way to the stables.

The large, white barn casts an even larger shadow in the early morning sunlight. Each wall is lined with stalls where the horses nibble on hay, looking up at me curiously.

My gaze slides over the two Imperials standing to my left, accompanied by three horses saddled for the journey ahead of us. I grit my teeth. The king pulled two guards from the rotation on Loot Alley as a safety precaution, though I'm more than capable of handling this on my own. But it seems that in a single night, Father has suddenly grown to care for my well-being. It's only taken nineteen years and the fact that I am now valuable to him.

I shake my head and mount the horse closest to me, swallowing my pride enough to admit that it's wise for Imperials to be with me in the case of a banishing.

The trip to Loot is a long one, and we pass the time in utter silence. Streets slowly turn to slums as we head farther into the city, and I could smell the large market alley before reaching it.

The familiar scent of fish, smoke, and other mysteries welcome me as we head onto Loot. The echo of our horses' hooves clopping down the uneven cobblestones bounces off the walls of rundown shops lining the street. A few early risers dart out of the way, making room for us as they point and whisper.

We turn left down a smaller street jutting off the main alley and head for a small, wooden shack. I hop off my horse without hesitation and stuff the reins into the gloved hand of an Imperial, letting him deal with securing the animal.

If they must be here, they might as well be useful to me.

I stride to the door, slipping a hand out of my pocket to knock. I hear a thud from inside, followed by the sound of heavy footsteps before the door swings open, creaking on its rusty hinges.

A huge, burly man with a thick beard and even thicker hair stares at the scene before him. I'm surprised he can fit through the door frame. His blue eyes widen under his bushy brows as he looks between myself and the two Imperials now flanking me.

'Prince Kai . . . ?' The man looks astonished and flustered all at once. 'Hi, er, what an honor!' His falsely cheery voice carries down the street, likely waking his neighbors as he reaches out to offer a handshake.

His grasp is firm and calloused, much like my own. 'Nathan, correct?' He nods, and I continue, 'I had a few questions to ask you about an Ordinary found here in Loot. I'm sure that's not a problem.' I watch him closely, searching for any indication that he knows what I'm talking about. Nothing. His face remains utterly expressionless. 'Mind if we come in?' It's not a question and he knows it. I already have my foot over the threshold before he steps away from the door.

The house is no bigger than my bedroom back at the palace. On one side of the room, small beds are pushed together and lined crookedly against the wall. The kitchen resides in the other half of the room, equipped with a rundown sink, a chipped wooden counter, and a large table surrounded by two wide-eyed boys and a woman. A large, faded rug joins the two sides of the room, the only decoration and splotch of color in the house.

Nathan clears his throat. 'This is my wife, Layla.' She smiles warmly, her white teeth contrasting against her dark skin as she eyes the Imperials shifting on their feet behind me.

'And these are our boys, Marcus and Cal.' Nathan points at each of his children, naming them off. Marcus keeps his eyes pinned to the table, not daring to look at me, while his younger brother, Cal, is far too curious to keep his eyes from darting to mine.

I reach out with my power, making sure none of them are the Ordinary hiding in plain sight. My Wielder ability is especially helpful as the Enforcer, making my job far easier and far more efficient.

Nathan is a Brawny, and I'm not the least bit surprised, seeing that he's a mountain of a man. I can feel Layla's power as a Healer bubbling in my blood like champagne while Marcus and Cal both possess Mundane powers – Marcus with the lie detecting ability of a Bluff, and Cal as an Enhancer with his heightened senses.

'You know why I'm here,' I say coolly. 'Have you seen or heard anything about an Ordinary hiding around here?'

'No, sir, we haven't.' It's Layla who says this, her soft voice steady.

My eyes sweep over the house again, stopping on the sink. Bowls still sticky with porridge are piled within it, waiting to be cleaned.

Five.

Five bowls when there are only four mouths to feed.

Interesting.

'Well, then you won't mind if I take a look around?'

Once again, not a question. I casually stroll through the small house, stopping every once in a while to examine something more closely. I feel the eyes of both my Imperials and the family burning into my back as I take my time perusing the home, hands casually in my pockets.

Nothing seems out of the ordinary.

I'm about ready to call this a dead end and a waste of my time when I step in the middle of the patterned rug, now faded from years of trampling feet. A creak sounds beneath my shoes. I stop and shift my weight, listening for the sound again. Sure enough, wood groans once again beneath the rug.

Interesting.

Though Nathan's face remains expressionless, the blood has drained from it, leaving him ghostly pale. 'Lift the rug,' I say dryly to the guards, never taking my eyes off the family. And that's when I spot an emotion I'm all too familiar with, the one that tends to accompany my presence.

Fear.

As the rug rolls back, I spot the outline of a trapdoor, blending in

44

almost seamlessly with the rest of the dirty, wooden floorboards.

The thud. This is what I heard closing when I was outside.

A sob escapes Layla when I kneel and swing the trapdoor open, revealing a cramped, dark space beneath. There, tucked in the corner and hugging her knees, sits a little girl. When she looks up at me, the fire in her eyes matches the bright red of her long hair.

Plagues, she's so young.

She can't be more than eight years old, but the girl doesn't fight me as I reach down and lift her out of the damp box. I set her on the floor where she stares defiantly up at me, not a trace of fear on her small face splattered with freckles.

I feel for any sort of power coming from her, just to be sure. Nothing. There is nothing extraordinary about this girl – because *she's* Ordinary.

Strangled sobs begin filling the room.

'No, no, no!' Layla's shaky screams echo off the walls. 'You can't take her! You can't! She's my daughter, please!' The Imperials step between me and the raging family, but I push past them, annoyed. The boys are both sobbing now, hugging their mother's legs while Nathan looks stunned, silent tears slipping down his cheeks and into his matted beard. 'Calm down and tell me where the hell she came from and how long you've been harboring her.' My voice is low and stern, cutting through the chaos. The little girl standing before me looks nothing like this family with her freckles and flaming red hair. Not to mention that both Nathan and Layla are Elites, meaning the two of them could never produce an Ordinary.

'She . . . she's been here for three years.' Layla's voice trembles, sobs racking her small frame. 'We f-found her on the streets, so we took her in. We wanted a daughter. I couldn't have any more kids . . .' she trails off, wiping at her face. 'I'm one of the few Healers in the slums, and she seemed healthy, strong. So, when we found Abigail, we . . . we finally got to have a little girl.'

Abigail.

I wish I didn't know. Wish I didn't have to add another name to the endless list of those unfortunate enough to cross my path, unfortunate enough to cross the king.

I heave a sigh.

Here it comes.

'You know the law.' More choking sobs fill the room, forcing me to raise my voice. 'By decree of the king, all Ordinaries are to be executed. As for anyone harboring said Ordinaries, they are to be banished to the Scorches—'

I'm in the middle of reciting the same rehearsed lines I've said dozens of times when a large, solid body charges at me. The blank stare he wore just moments ago is long gone, replaced by a hatred that contorts his face in fury. Nathan hits me around the middle and runs me into the wall, knocking the air from my lungs while bashing the back of my head against the hard wood.

That's gonna kill like the Plague tomorrow.

I distantly hear a scream tear from Layla's throat, along with the Imperials' heavy footsteps as they run over to intervene. 'No!' I shout at them, ducking under a punch aimed at my nose while the guards halt, confused. 'I'll handle him myself.'

He throws another punch, this one intended to break my jaw. I dodge just in time to see his fist connect with the wooden wall where my face was, sending splinters flying when his hand breaks straight through.

My fighting instincts take over, and I don't even bother reaching out to use Nathan's power. With his fist still buried in the wall, I duck under his outstretched arm and pull out his wrist, twisting his arm behind his back to press it beneath his left shoulder blade. He grunts in pain before kicking back at my kneecap, hard. Pain sears up my leg as he spins out of my hold, raising his supernaturally strong fist.

Ignoring the pain in my knee, I drop and sweep my leg in a wide arc, connecting with his ankles and sending him sprawling onto his back. Then I'm on top of him, pinning his arms down with my knees as I finally let his Brawny strength claw to the surface, knowing I won't be able to keep him down without using his own power against him. He thrashes, baring his teeth at me.

'Shut up and listen to me,' I pant. 'We can do this the easy way, or the hard way. And personally, I'd prefer the easy way.'

'She's my daughter!' he bellows, a look of anguish in his eyes as he tries to tear me off him.

'Well, clearly, you have no regard for my feelings, because you want to do this the hard way.' I sigh, cock my fist back, and connect it with his jaw. His head snaps to the side, stunning him long enough to let me speak. 'If you don't cooperate, even your wife won't have the ability to heal your broken body once I'm finished with you. So, I suggest you thank me for not killing you right here in front of your family and do exactly as I say.' Nathan stills beneath me, the fight seeming to drain from his eyes. I shift, crouching beside him to stare down at his defeated form. 'Now, get the hell up before I change my mind,' I murmur before standing to my feet. When he doesn't budge, I add, 'Patience is about as foreign to me as mercy, so I wouldn't press your luck.'

At that, he scrambles to his feet and steps in front of his huddled family, blocking them from me. Shielding them from a monster. I keep my eyes locked on the sight of them, taking in the tears spilling down their cheeks and sobs slipping past their lips as I bark orders to the Imperials.

They hurry to heed my commands, tying up the prisoners as I casually add, 'Keep to the side streets. Clearly, I'm in a good mood today. Feeling merciful if you will,' I huff out the words. 'So I'd rather not have an audience.'

The Imperials grunt their agreement, smiling slightly at my idea of *mercy*. Within a matter of minutes, Nathan, Layla, and their two boys are tied and shuffling behind the horses. They twist their heads around, hatred burning in their gazes as they eye Abigail tied and firmly held in my grasp.

They know what happens now. My reputation is rather renowned, stories of the murderous monster murmured throughout the streets.

This is the part where I kill the Ordinary while the Imperials escort the criminals to the Scorches where they will likely follow her into death. With its blistering heat by day and freezing temperatures by night, it's no simple feat to make it to the other side of the desert where the cities of Dor and Tando lie. Not to mention that I've just sentenced this family to try and do just that with no supplies, no food, no water, and no hope.

It's a far more painful death than their Ordinary daughter will suffer. 'Please! I'm begging you, please spare her!' Layla is shouting at me between sobs as she shuffles over the cobblestones behind the horses.

'She's just a child—'

An Imperial reaches behind from where he sits atop his horse and strikes her across the face, cutting off her plea. 'Shut up, *Slummer*.'

I rip my eyes from the scene, pulling the girl away and down the street. Her feeble attempts to wiggle out of my grasp would be comical if it weren't for the humorless situation we find ourselves in.

She's eerily quiet for a child being dragged to her death. Most Ordinaries are screaming by now, pleading and bargaining for their lives. But her struggle is silent, her stare piercing. I keep my eyes locked on the empty alleys we head through, wondering how familiar one must be with hiding everything they are in order to hide their emotions even while facing death.

I steer us down a shadowed alley, not yet touched by the faint sunlight beginning to paint the kingdom golden. The Ordinary – *Abigail* – squirms, attempting to twist out of my grip for the dozenth time. I look down at her, amusement coating my voice as I say, 'You are a persistent little thing, aren't you?'

She huffs, causing her flaming hair to flicker around her face before she sends a solid kick to my shin. I would have been impressed with her form if it weren't for my growing frustration. I drop to a crouch in front of her so her angry green eyes can meet mine. Only when she lifts her leg to swing it at me once more do I say softly, 'I wouldn't do that if I were you.'

She blinks, and right when I think she's heeded my warning, she stomps on my foot before trying to pull her arm out of my grip with no luck. And then she's squealing, flailing in an attempt to get away from me.

'Alright, well, we can't have that.' I slip a knife from my boot as I murmur, 'You are not going to make this easy for me.'

At the sight of the dagger, she swallows, suddenly still. 'Just put it in my heart,' she blurts with her eyes pinned on the knife, voice delicate in the way that only a child's can be. 'I heard Momma say it's quicker that way.'

'Did she now?' I ask quietly. 'There are other quick ways as well you know.'

And I know every single one of them.

I watch her flinch as I bring the blade closer to her, watch her eyes widen as she finally allows herself to feel the terror she's been desperately trying to hide. Then she takes a deep breath that sounds like something akin to acceptance before squeezing her eyes shut against the face of a monster in front of her.

The dagger slices, cutting easily. The girl—

Abigail.

—sucks in a shaky breath.

After a long moment, a teary green eye peeks open. She blinks as the bindings slip from her raw wrists and land at her feet. Her gaze skips from her unharmed heart to my face before landing on the dagger in my hand. 'Aren't you gonna put that in my heart?'

My lips twitch. 'Listen closely, Abigail. I cut your bindings, so now you have to do me a favor in return. I need you to stay quiet and stop struggling.' I search her face before adding, 'Understood?'

I don't wait for an answer before I once again begin leading us down streets and alleys. She must have understood me well enough because she now walks stiffly in silence, making no move to break out of my hold.

When the Scorches come into view, so do the two Imperials standing at the edge of it. They pay no attention to the family they are supposed to be watching head into the desert, now blurry figures dotting the sand. I peek my head out behind an alley wall, watching as the Imperials talk idly. Before long, they're shrugging and spinning on their heels to head back down the street.

Typical.

I was counting on the guards' predictable laziness and failure to finish tasks. And I hadn't wanted the banished family paraded through the streets like they typically are, because then I would have a crowd to witness my treason.

Once they've passed us, we slip onto the street and head for the sand. The family is far ahead, and since I'm feeling rather lazy myself, I reach out to grab hold of one of the Imperials' Flash ability. He'll be out of my range soon, so I hurry to pick up the girl and dash into the desert.

We've nearly made it to the family when distance has the Flash's ability slipping away from me. Nathan startles at the sound of us behind him and spins, eyes wide when they land on Abigail in my arms.

Layla is running towards us and has the girl wrapped in her arms in a matter of moments with the whole family encircling the two of them. They sob as I step aside, feet shifting in the scolding sand that has begun spilling into my shoes.

And then they turn towards me, eyes burning hotter than the sun beating down on us. Nathan only offers me one word, low and laced with hatred. 'Why?'

I slip out my dagger and cut the bindings around his wrists in one swift movement, meeting his gaze as I say, 'I don't kill children.'

Hypocrite.

As if that is not exactly what I'm doing. In fact, I'm only prolonging the inevitable. But at least they will all get to be together in the end – a mockery of mercy that I only bestow upon children.

I move down the line of stunned prisoners, cutting their bound hands free. I look them each in the eyes, most still glossy with tears, before turning to the little girl. The Ordinary.

Abigail.

I walk towards her slowly and lower myself to one knee, sinking deep into the hot sand so we're eye to eye. Though she doesn't say a thing, her eyes speak volumes. She's only a child, and yet I see a devastating amount of determination behind her gaze.

Perhaps you may not need powers to be powerful.

I reach into my pocket, pulling out a small pocketknife from within. Its white handle is engraved with golden swirls, but its small blade is sharp. I hold it out to her.

'Every girl deserves something equally as pretty and deadly as they are,' I say, urging her to take the knife. She eyes me warily before stretching out a small hand to pluck it from my palm. 'Use it wisely.'

I run a hand through my hair as I stand to my feet with a sigh. 'In accordance with our laws and by decree of King Edric, I hereby banish you from the Kingdom of Ilya for your acts of treason.'

With that, I watch as Nathan puts an arm around his wife who in turn reaches out an arm for her children to huddle into.

They turn as one.

And I watch as they walk to their doom.

CHAPTER 6

Rai

Despite my swollen knee screaming in protest, I force myself to walk evenly. By the time I make it back onto Loot Alley, late afternoon has cast the street in a warm glow. I always enjoyed it down here. There's nothing regal about the slums of Ilya, and yet, it's refreshing in a way the stuffy palace never could be.

My eyes sweep back and forth as I weave through the throng of people bartering, cursing, and shopping. I allow myself a moment to take in the sights and smells of Loot — neither of which are very pleasant. Everything down here is dull, leached of color. The banners, the food, the people. By midday, the street always smells of sweaty bodies and questionable food.

But despite it all, Loot is buzzing with *life*.

The crowd pushes and pulls me in different directions like a human current, and I fight to escape the wave of people. I finally break free to head down a smaller, less crowded alley where homeless crouch against walls, some begging for money while others use their powers to entertain themselves. Though the slums are mostly home to the Mundanes, I spot the occasional Defensive Elite sprinkled among them. The purple glow of forcefields engulfing a few catch my eye, as well as a Shimmer manipulating the light around him into a darting

beam, occupying both himself and a stray cat.

I keep walking as I look around, paying no attention to the path before me.

And apparently, neither was the person who slams into my chest with a grunt.

Instinctively, I reach out to steady the individual before they fall over from the impact, my arms wrapping around their waist. *Her* waist. The body I'm holding undoubtedly belongs to a female, though the mass of long silver hair brushing against my arms is proof enough.

She's small but strong, leaner than most of the scrawny girls from the slums. I can feel it in the curve of her waist where my hand fits comfortably, though it's evident that malnourishment stripped her of most of the muscle she evidently once had.

Her palm is pressed to my chest where a thick ring hugs her thumb, and after a few seconds of my studying her while she attempts to steady herself, she heaves a shaky breath before meeting my gaze.

It's like drowning in the ocean.

Her eyes are the color of the Shallows Sea's deepest corner, a clear sky as it begins to drift into night, the subtle shade of a forget-me-not. And like the hottest flame, her eyes are blue and full of fire. Her high cheekbones lead up to equally strong, dark brows, now slightly raised as she takes me in.

Her ocean eyes widen, and I watch a faint flush rise to her cheeks when she realizes how closely I'm still holding her against me. She drops her hand from my chest and, like the gentleman I am, I slide my hands from her waist with a smile tugging at my lips.

'Do you always fall into the arms of handsome strangers, or is this a new thing for you?' I say, watching as a smirk that could rival my own lifts her lips despite the bottom one being split open.

Interesting.

'No,' she answers, sarcasm dripping from her every word, 'only the cocky ones.' She holds herself with a certain confidence that tells me there was once a time when she did not. And just like that, I am suddenly, annoyingly intrigued.

She clearly has no idea who I am. Perfect.

I laugh at her remark and run a hand through my hair, doing little to tame it. She watches me closely, intensely, seeming to be just as interested with me as I am with her.

I drown in her blue eyes. Every time our gazes meet it's like ice meeting the hottest fire, like gray mist rising on the deep blue ocean. I look away briefly before saying, 'Well, looks like I've made quite the first impression then.'

'Yes, though I still haven't decided if it was a good or bad one yet.' Her lips twitch into a slight smile, the type that makes a man's head turn just to get another glimpse of it in the hopes it was meant for him. And that small, precise gesture alone tells me I'm not the first she's practiced it on.

My hands stray to my pockets, and I shrug indifferently as I lean against the grimy alley wall. 'I caught you, didn't I?'

She laughs, the sound warm yet sharp. Playful yet pained, as though happiness isn't habitual for her. Her head tips back slightly, silver waves falling nearly to her waist as she looks up at me, eyes crinkled with laughter.

I lean in slightly, daring to close some of the distance between us. 'Maybe you should consider that detail before you decide, darling.'

And with that, I'm suddenly curious, suddenly wondering what power she possesses. So I reach out to her ability with my own.

Nothing. I feel nothing.

I study her face as I try again and again to sense her power. Normally, this would be the part where I either throw the girl over my shoulder and carry her to the dungeons to be further examined, or I simply kill her on the spot due to the mere suspicion of her being an Ordinary.

And yet, I don't move.

You're tired. Injured. It could be a mistake.

Before I have time to decide her fate, she takes a step back towards the crowded alley. 'I'll keep it under consideration, *darling*.' She gives me a small smile, holding my gaze while continuing to back away. 'And thank you for saving me from eating cobblestone. I seem to be cursed with clumsiness.'

'Well, your clumsiness found me, so I'd hardly call it a curse.' My grin only grows when she rolls her eyes at me before spinning on her heel and heading back towards Loot. I finally allow myself to skim my eyes over her, taking in the fitted black pants and olive vest currently covered by silver hair. Nothing about the way she walks gives me the impression that she sleeps on the streets, though her ragged clothes and busted bottom lip tell me otherwise.

I run a hand over my face, realizing I've been staring after her for far too long. So, I turn and begin heading down another small alley, now quiet in the setting sunlight, my thoughts occupied with the fact that I may have just let an Ordinary walk free.

But I'm not distracted enough to miss the four large shadows rising up on the alley wall beside me. 'Listen,' says a gravelly voice belonging to one of the men behind me. 'All we want is that pretty pouch of coins on your belt. Hand it over, and no one needs to get hurt.'

I huff out a sigh, pressing the heels of my palms into my eyes.

This day just keeps getting better and better.

And that's when I feel it.

With my attention finally on the coin pouch at my side, I suddenly notice how much lighter it feels than before—

Before her.

Why that little—

A shadow shifts on the wall, lurching towards me. I spin around, ducking under the man's punch before landing one of my own to his stomach. With a grunt, he doubles over coughing while I take in the others.

Two Brawnies, a Blazer, and a Crawler.

Only the most desperate Defensive and Offensive Elites find their way to the slums to beat down beggars for the few coins they have. With that in mind, I let the Blazer's power seep into me, let the flames flick over my fists.

Another Brawny comes charging at me with a smile.

They're always so cocky. And that's coming from me.

I crouch low right before he collides with me, his momentum sending him rolling over my back to land hard on the cobblestone. My flaming fist connects with his jaw and the sickening stench of burned flesh stings my nose.

I look up to see the Crawler scaling the wall, intending to drop on top of me and pin my body to the ground. As he leaps from where he clings to bricks, I drop the Blazer's power and take on the Brawny's. My now supernaturally strong fist meets the Crawler's stomach in midair, and he's thrown backward against the wall before falling to the ground with a thud.

The Blazer stalks towards me, his mouth curled into a snarl.

He chucks a ball of fire in my direction, and I leap to the side to avoid it – not quickly enough. I curse colorfully as fire scorches the outside of my bicep, burning my flesh and slowing me with the pain.

My mind is racing nearly as fast as my heart. I can't get close to him when he's forcing me to play defense and dodge his fire, but I know if I start throwing it back, we'll most definitely burn a street down.

I am not in the mood for this.

I let the Crawler's power quite literally crawl to the surface before grabbing hold of it. Dodging balls of fire as I go, I run up the side of the alley wall and along the building until I'm parallel with him. In one swift movement, I leap from the wall, tackling him to the ground before quickly switching powers to raise a flaming fist at his face.

'Y-you're Prince Kai,' he stammers. 'The . . . the future Enforcer.' Being so close, he's finally recognized me and my ability, now clearly regretting his decision to jump the prince.

'Unfortunately for you, I am.' I cock back my blazing fist and— A piercing pain cuts through my skull like a dull knife.

The Blazer's power flickers out, and I'm unable to do anything but clutch my pounding head, panting from the pain. I've grown very familiar with torture over the years, but this is like nothing I've ever endured.

Through the haze of agony clouding my vision, I see a tall figure step into the alley. His hand is raised towards me, face grim, thin lips pulled downward in a scowl.

Silencer.

Impossible.

My thoughts scatter, leaving nothing but pain to ponder.

The Silencer smothers my power. Smothers me. They can do more than just strip you of your ability, making you no more than an Ordinary. He's incapacitating me. My mind, my ability, my body.

My vision goes blurry, spots swimming before my eyes.

Fight it.

I can't. I'm going to pass out. Die. Both. And there's nothing I can do to stop it.

Fight. It.

I slump to the ground, my head slamming against the stones.

If Father could see me now . . .

I'm fading fast. Even with all my training, I've never felt so weak, so powerless, so out of control. I take one last look at the man leaching me of my strength. I hadn't realized we'd drawn a small crowd until I see faces swimming in my vision.

They have no idea who I am.

An unsuspecting audience to watch me drift into darkness.

Or worse, maybe they do know who I am. Maybe they're celebrating at the sight of the monster finally being put down, put out of his misery.

And then something catches my eye.

I blink away the blurriness long enough to see something glint in the light behind the Silencer – the sun reflecting off a mass of silver hair.

CHAPTER 7

Paedyn

dena is going to collapse from shock. Then she'll squeal, and I'll cover my ears. I've never stolen so many coins from one person. Not that I've had the opportunity, seeing that most of us in Loot don't even have more than a dozen silvers to our name, let alone casually carry them around.

My mind is reeling as I slowly make my way down Loot, now cast in shadows as the sun sinks behind the crumbling buildings.

I shake my head in astonishment and take my time strolling through the market, allowing myself to admire my accomplishment. Several merchants are already packing up their stands, closing up shop for the night. Kids scuttle around the street chasing one another, earning dirty looks and shouts from the shoppers still milling about.

I cut down an alley, close to where I robbed the unsuspecting young man, and start heading back to the Fort.

I can't wait to see the look on A's face—

I stop suddenly, eying a small crowd gathered farther down the street. *Must be a Veil.*

It's no surprise that the power of invisibility can inevitably aid someone at sleight of hand, using their ability to make cards disappear at will by simply holding them. I admire their deceitful

little shows to earn some shillings.

I'm about to head the other way when I hear gasps coming from the crowd, echoing off the crumbling buildings. Not the typical *oohs* and *ahs* that are present during magic tricks, but scared gasps of shock and surprise. When my curiosity gets the better of me, I find myself behind the throng of people, wedging between sweaty bodies and pushing my way to the front of the crowd. When I raise my eyes to the scene before me, I gasp, cupping a hand to my mouth.

It's *him*.

I saw him less than ten minutes ago, and yet his shirt now clings to him with sweat as he prepares to strike the man pinned beneath him with a flaming fist. Three other bodies litter the cobblestone behind him, slowly staggering to their feet before stumbling away.

It's clear what happened here, obvious that these men had the same idea I did upon seeing the pouch hanging from the stranger's hip. But they chose a much more violent way to get the coins – well, whatever is left of them.

I see the stranger say something to the man before he raises his fiery fist, ready to strike.

And then, something is suddenly, terribly wrong.

He's clutching his head, and I watch his cocky expression crumple into utter agony when a figure steps out from the shadows. I can only see his back, but he's tall and lean, raising a thin hand at the stranger gasping in pain on the alley floor.

That's impossible.

The crowd around me seems just as confused and awed as I am. With his hand still outstretched, the Silencer takes small steps towards the black-haired figure now slumped on the ground.

He's crippling his power. He's crippling *him*.

I can see the stranger still trying to fight, trying to hang on to consciousness. The sight is suddenly so startlingly familiar, so sickening that I nearly stumble into the man beside me.

This stranger and the man who raised me look nothing alike, and yet, the image of one crippled on the ground seems to bleed into the other. I suddenly feel like that little girl again, standing idly as my father died beneath me.

I look around, eying the gawking crowd. No one budges. Even with their fancy powers, no one makes a move to help. Either too afraid to do so or too heartless to help.

I know how this ends. I've lived it.

When I look back at the stranger, it's my father I see. Taking a deep breath, I take a step forward.

I won't stand by idly again. I couldn't save my father, but I'll honor him now by saving someone from the same suffering he endured.

I'm probably going to regret this.

I creep to the edge of the crowd and begin slinking up behind the Silencer. I can practically feel the audience's attention shift to me, the throng of people silently watching. Crouching low behind the man, I spot a large, loose rock lying on the cobblestone and snatch it up.

Here goes nothing.

I draw up to my full height right behind him and silently raise the rock, intending to connect it with his skull—

No such luck.

He pivots, his black eyes boring into mine. With his attention on me, his crushing hold on the stranger drops, and I hear him gasping for air on the ground.

The Silencer lifts his slender hand towards me, his shoulder-length hair whipping in the breeze. He's trying to Silence me.

I almost smile. No such luck.

Nothing happens, of course, considering I have no power for him to smother. He looks at his hand, then back at me, confused. The sight is almost comical, and that split second of hesitation is all I need.

I grab his wrist, twisting his arm at an odd angle before driving my knee into his stomach. I hear the air whoosh out of his lungs as he clutches his arm to his body. And with that, my adrenaline kicks in, itching for a fight.

It reminds me of all those late nights and early mornings with my father. Hours of training in the makeshift dirt ring behind our home.

'*Both your mind, as well as your body, need to be trained. Conditioned,*' he'd say as I dodged his punches, all while answering his dozens of questions that tested my observation. I wielded any weapon we could get our hands on while my father trained every part of my being – my mind, my body, my *Psychic* ability.

Until one day he wasn't there to train me anymore. Wasn't there to protect me anymore. Wasn't there to continue teaching me how to protect myself anymore.

The Silencer recovers quickly, throwing a punch with his good arm and jolting me from my thoughts. I duck under it and aim a right hook at his jaw. His forearm flashes up to block my blow, forcing my arm down before grabbing it and spinning me so my back is pressed against his chest. And then the crook of his other arm is trapping me in a chokehold.

I gasp for air, trying to remain calm. I fight the urge to claw uselessly at the arm crushing my windpipe and instead whip my head back, connecting my skull with his nose and earning a sickening crack followed by the sound of gurgling blood.

Blood.

There was so much of it coating the floor of our small house resting between Merchant and Elm Street. Coating me, my father. I haven't been back since that night I ran. That night the king plunged a sword through my father's chest.

The Silencer's hold around my neck loosens as he stumbles back, clutching his nose. But I'm not done yet. Not even close.

I slip the ring from my thumb and slide it onto my middle finger before sinking my fist into the Silencer's cheek, ignoring the sting in my hand. Dropping his hands from his gushing nose, he swings at me again, but I already knew it was coming.

He always takes a step with his left foot before he punches.

I block the blow and grab his shoulders as I bring my knee to his stomach once again. Before he's even caught his breath, I have his head in my hands, driving his already broken nose down into my awaiting knee.

I channel all my rage into each blow.

My rage at the king who slipped into my father's study where he sat in his cushioned armchair, reading late into the night.

Another right hook to the Silencer's jaw.

My rage as I vividly remember the sound of my father's cry when the sword tore through his chest, tearing me from sleep.

I send a kick to the Silencer's groin.

My rage as I saw my father sliding out of his beloved armchair and onto the ground, slipping in his blood.

I drop and sweep my leg in a wide arc, knocking the Silencer to the ground.

My rage as I held my father's hand, screaming and begging him to wake up.

I sat there all night, pants soaked with blood, trying to puzzle out what could possibly justify killing him. But the king doesn't need a reason to kill, he needs a reason to let people *live*.

I beat down on the Silencer, barely aware of what I'm doing as my mind reels.

I was numb. My hand clamped around my father's cold one, holding it while I rocked back and forth, sobs shaking my body. I brushed his brown hair from his eyes, straightened his bloody clothes, whispered about all the memories we shared while begging him to come back to me so we could make more.

I was completely and utterly alone in the world.

And when sunlight poured through the windows, shedding light on the gruesome scene, I couldn't stand to be in my own home – not that I could afford to keep the house at thirteen years of age.

I tried to bury him. Tried so hard to drag him outside and give him a proper goodbye, give him the honor he deserved. But I was so small, and he was so large, so heavy, so *dead*. I slipped and slid in the pool of my father's blood, unable to budge his body. So, I pulled the wedding ring from his finger, pushed it onto my thumb, and ran.

The same ring I'm now using to sink into the Silencer's cheek.

If Father could see me now . . .

I hover over him, my rage finally beginning to fade as his black eyes widen. Blood streaks his face, gushing from his mouth, nose, and the other scattered cuts I've given him. I slide my dagger from my boot as something flickers in his eyes.

Fear.

He fears what he cannot control.

And in this very moment, that something he cannot control is *me*. I bring the hilt of my dagger down hard against his temple, knocking him out cold. Still crouching over him, my gaze finds the gray one pinned on me. Emotions flash across the stranger's face as he takes me in, takes in what I've done. Shock, awe, confusion, and amusement of all things, flicker across his face. I tear my eyes from him, returning my knife to my boot as astonished murmurs rise from the crowd. I turn, stunned to find a mass of people staring. Merchants, women, and children gawk at the scene, all whispering and pointing. Three Imperials suddenly push through the crowd, hastily throwing people out of their way.

I stiffen, preparing for some sort of punishment. Maybe a few more lashes to decorate my back with.

But they charge right past me, right past the unconscious Silencer, and drop to their knees before the stranger.

That's . . . interesting.

And apparently, I'm not the only one who thinks so. The hum of whispers from the crowd grows louder, allowing me to catch bits and pieces of their hushed conversations.

'—Silencer here in Ilya—'

'—it's Prince Kai who fought off four men—'

'—fought the Silencer without using a power!'

I freeze, heart pounding, barely breathing.

Prince Kai.

I'd never seen the man. Never thought I would.

Never thought I would steal from him either.

But I've heard enough about his reputation. How he's supposedly the strongest Elite in decades. How he's the future Enforcer, said to be callused and calculating, yet charismatic and charming when he wishes to be – when he chooses to play the part.

I've heard how he's a rare and powerful Wielder, able to sense another's power and use it himself so long as they are close enough to him.

The Deliverer of Death, they call him.

The prince usually stays in the comfort of his cushy palace, so it's likely that no one recognized the stranger as anyone of importance. And when he does leave the castle, well, the people he visits don't typically live to tell the tale.

I slowly turn towards the Imperials huddling around the prince and watch as he shoves past them, irritated by their smothering. He barks an order, telling them to take the Silencer to the dungeons as well as clear the crowd from the street. The prince exudes authority and power with every step, every word. Imperials scurry to obey him as they round up the mob of people and push them back out onto Loot.

His eyes find mine.

Even with his countless injuries, he strides towards me, pushing the limp from his walk. A predator stalking its prey.

And that's my cue.

I try to slip into the crowd unnoticed, hoping to be washed away in the current of bodies. Hoping he will forget that I saved him and let me leave quietly.

No such luck.

A calloused hand grips my arm before spinning me around to pin me against the alley wall. He presses both my wrists against the brick with strong hands before leaning in towards me.

I writhe in his grip, but he doesn't budge. I'm not sure what I was expecting him to do, but it certainly was not this. Maybe offer a polite thank you – not an interrogation against a grimy wall.

I would have never saved him if I knew who he was. What he is. What he does. I huff in irritation, sending silver hair blowing into my eyes and obscuring my view of his piercing gaze. 'Is this how you treat all the people who save your life or is this a new thing for you?' I grind out the words through clenched teeth, mocking his first ones to me.

'I wouldn't know, seeing that no one has ever saved me before.' There's the ghost of a smirk on his face, offering me a glimpse of that annoying dimple.

'Well, let me enlighten you. When someone saves your life, a polite thank you will suffice.'

'Maybe,' he sighs and leans in closer, 'but not for those who steal from me.'

I think my heart stops beating. The prince knows I stole from him. The prince. The future Enforcer. The Deliverer of Death.

I'm dead as the Plague.

But my fear is quickly replaced by a much more welcome emotion – anger. I'm angry with myself for helping the prince who kills like it's nothing and grants his father's wishes like he is everything. I'm angry for finding him *not* repulsive since the very kingdom he's so loyal to makes me sick with its twisted values and beliefs. He is the future Enforcer, the executioner of innocents, of Ordinaries, of *people like me.*

Feeling reckless and rather emboldened with death a mere breath away, I say, 'So he's pretty *and* he has a brain. The ladies must love you.' The smile I give him is anything but sweet. 'You know, you might make a good thief if it weren't for the fact that you were so easily fooled by one.'

He's smiling. Amused. Arrogant as ever. 'You do realize who you're talking to, right?'

'A cocky bastard?' I say innocently before biting my tongue. I clearly have a death wish.

But to my surprise, he tips his head back and barks out an authentic laugh, the sound rich like the chocolate I occasionally steal and deep like the Shallows Sea.

'I've been called worse,' he murmurs after composing himself, his hands still clamped around my wrists. Then the amusement fades from his eyes, quickly replaced by cool consideration. 'Despite you robbing me, I suppose I should thank you for your help.'

I almost laugh at that. Apparently, saving his life is comparable to simply *helping.*

'Although, I am curious as to why the Silencer couldn't smother your power. Along with why I can't seem to sense one from you.' He's eying me like he did in the alley when I stole from him. Like I'm a puzzle he's trying to piece together.

I blink up at him as realization rams into me.

He has the rare ability to sense another's power and use it himself . . .

He tried to sense my power in the alley. Only to find that there was none.

I'm dead as the Plague.

I look up at him, filtering the fear from my expression despite my

65

frantic thoughts. I shrug my stiff shoulders, hoping the action looked far more casual than it felt. 'I'm a Mundane. A Psychic.'

'A Psychic,' he echoes, disbelief dripping from every word. 'Tell me, what is it that you can do?' He pauses. Shrugs. 'I've never met a Psychic before. Call me curious.'

I swallow the hysterical laugh threatening to bubble out of me. The future Enforcer isn't curious, he's calculating. But he must be rather amused by me, otherwise, I'd likely be dead by now.

'My power is a sort of . . . *sense*,' I say easily, reciting the rehearsed line. 'I can only sense strong emotions from others, getting flashes of information because of it.'

I look into his eyes, willing him to believe me. Hoping he'll accept the answer and move on with his life. Hoping that he will let *me* move on with my life.

He looks to be fighting a smile. 'Is that right?'

'And why would it be wrong?'

His eyes flick between mine for a long moment. 'Why is it I can't sense or use your power then?'

I swallow, trying to seem as though I'm not struggling to come up with a believable lie. 'My ability is unpredictable. Even I can't control what I see or when I see it. That, combined with the fact that my power has little strength as it is, must be why you and the Silencer can't pick up on it. It's a mental ability.' I shrug. 'I must be able to guard my head from those trying to get into it.'

I hold my breath, waiting for his answer.

Except that he doesn't give me one. He simply stands there, staring at me. I huff before blurting, 'Go on. Ask anyone in the slums about me and my power. Better yet,' I lean forward slightly, 'you can ask your Imperials. I had a lovely conversation with one of them just this morning.'

His eyes narrow slightly before he slowly releases my wrists and takes a step back. 'Maybe I will.' Then the bastard smiles. 'But I'd still like to witness these Psychic abilities of yours for myself. Prove it.'

If I had a shilling for every time someone said those words to me, I wouldn't even bother stealing anymore. He crosses his arms over his broad chest, eyebrows raised expectantly as he elaborates, 'Read me.

Or whatever it is you say you do.' Then he leans in, gaze glittering with amusement. 'Impress me, darling.'

'My power isn't some party trick for your entertainment, but I'll play along, *Prince*.' I give him a sarcastic smile before my eyes dart over his body. 'I'm not even sure I'll be able to pick up on anything with how unpredictable my ability is.'

'Is that so.'

I ignore his mocking tone of voice and think of the calluses on his palms and the dozens of scars marring his arms.

Well, obviously he's a fighter. You don't have to be a Psychic to figure that out.

I know I need to tell him something worthwhile if there is any hope of being believed. Any hope of surviving this conversation. He'll kill me without a second thought for simply the suspicion of being an Ordinary. 'May I see your hand?' The words are a demand disguised as a question. I hold my palm out expectantly, eyes flicking from his face to the hand at his side. Only the best performance will do for the prince.

His expression is annoyingly neutral, never taking his eyes off mine as he places his hand in my own. 'You know, I've never met a thief with manners. And it seems you're most definitely not the exception.'

I huff at that, ducking my head to turn my attention to the large, calloused hand in my own.

'Is there a reason you insist on holding my hand?'

My gaze snaps up to his cool one. 'Don't worry, I'll try to resist kissing your knuckles, Prince.'

At the mention of his knuckles, my eyes sweep over them while his laughter washes over me. They're red and raw, not only from this fight but also from one prior. Blood trickles down his fingers from the reopened scabs, though he barely seems bothered.

'You were in a fight,' I say. 'And—'

His scoff cuts me off. 'I told you to impress me, not state the obvious.'

'I'm not talking about *this* fight,' I sigh, dropping his hand to gesture around us while simultaneously fighting the urge to punch that stupid grin off his face. 'I'm talking about the fight *before* this one.'

I watch him closely, noting that nothing about his expression indicates whether I'm right or wrong.

Plagues, he's not going to make this easy for me.

My gaze drops briefly to his shoes. From this close, they don't look as shiny as I once thought they were when I spotted him across Loot. In fact, they don't look shiny at all.

Sand.

His once polished, black shoes are now covered in a thin dusting of sand, barely visible. As though he's been walking through the . . .

Scorches.

And there's only one reason why a prince, specifically the future Enforcer, would set foot in the Scorches at all.

He banished someone. And that same someone put up a fight.

I'm reminded of the two Imperials missing from rotation today, and it all begins to fall into place.

The prince needs guards to drag prisoners to the Scorches. Triumph begins to bloom in my chest, but I stamp it down. Something's not right.

Normally, the town would be gossiping for days about who was banished and why. The *criminals* would have been paraded through the city, drawing a crowd to watch them walk to their death. But I haven't heard a single word uttered about this. Odd, considering they usually flaunt the banishes, use them as examples, show them off to warn the kingdom of what happens when you cross the king.

He didn't want anyone to know about it.

In a matter of seconds, I have all the information I need.

'You were somewhere . . . hot. Sandy.' I squeeze my eyes shut before adding, 'The Scorches.' I peek up at him to find his eyes searching my face. 'You banished someone. Or . . . a group of someones.' At this, he stiffens, ever so slightly. His cool facade cracks. And in that small action alone, he's just confirmed that I'm correct.

And that I shouldn't know any of it.

'But . . .' I pause. 'You don't want anyone to know that do you?' I can't suppress my small smile as he peers down at me, looking both impressed and confused.

'And what emotion are you sensing all of this from?' he asks quietly. I blow out a breath before taking a wild guess at what the future Enforcer could be feeling, if the man has emotions at all. 'Is it . . . guilt I'm feeling? Worry?' He seems to still at that, giving me silent conformation that I must be at least partially correct. 'Was that *proof* enough for you, Your Highness?'

I am well aware of the dangerous game I'm playing. And yet, I can't seem to forfeit my feelings of hatred for him and everything he stands for.

But the smirk that lifts his lips tells me that he likes the game too. 'Plenty. Well,' he exhales, shoving his hands in his pockets, 'like you so kindly pointed out earlier, I should thank you, again, for helping me, darling.'

'Paedyn.'

His dark brows raise slightly in question. 'My name is Paedyn, not darling.'

'Paedyn,' he echoes with a small smile, testing out the word. His deep voice makes my name sound so rich, so regal, as if I'm the one with royal blood pumping through my veins.

We stare at each other for a moment, his icy eyes sweeping over my flushed face and doing nothing to cool it. 'You know, I can enlighten you on another way to thank someone for saving your life.' I pause, suppressing a smile. 'Repaying your debt.'

He tips his head back and laughs darkly. 'Did you not get enough silvers when you robbed me the first time?' I shrug as he continues coolly, 'Need I remind you that you said a simple thank you would suffice?'

'Yes, a thank you would *suffice*. Not satisfy. And, well, that was also before I knew who you were.'

He begins backing away all while reaching into his pouch to pull out a coin. With a flick, it's flying towards me. I barely have enough time to throw out my hand and catch it as he says, 'Something to remember me by.'

He's several steps from me now, though his eyes are still locked on mine. 'Oh, and darling?'

'*Paedyn.*'

'You were right.'

He takes another step backward.

I huff out a sigh. 'I'm not sure I should even listen to what you're about to say since you didn't address me by my name which is—'

'Paedyn,' the sound of my name from his lips cuts me off, 'the ladies do love me.'

And with a wink, he turns and strides out of the alley.

CHAPTER 8

Paedyn

'What. The. Plagues. Happened?!' Adena's vigorously shaking me by the shoulders, making my teeth rattle. As soon as I got back to the Fort, confused by the events of the day and very content to go straight to sleep, Adena pounced on me and demanded every detail.

'What? How do you . . . ?' I'm stumbling over my words, wondering how she could possibly know that today was any different than the hundreds prior.

She cuts me off, eyes wide with excitement and unanswered questions. 'Everyone's talking about it! The whole market is buzzing about the silver-haired girl who fought off a *Silencer*!' I stare at her, dumbfounded. She barrels on, her words fast and breathless. 'And the *prince*?' She all but squeals. 'You saved the *prince*?!'

'Well, he doesn't seem to want to admit it, but yes, I saved the prince's ass.' This time, she does squeal. 'But only after I stole from him.'

Her mouth flies open. It's so dramatic that I can't help but laugh. 'You *what*?'

'In my defense,' I say, hands raised in innocence, 'I didn't know it was him.'

'Pae, the prince . . .' Concern clouds her gaze, and she blinks about

a dozen times before saying, 'He's a Wielder. Could he . . . Could he sense you didn't have a power—?'

I cut in before any more color can drain from her face, quickly explaining the events of the last half hour. Adena's eyes are wide, her curly bangs clinging to her lashes as I fill her in on everything from robbing the prince to fighting the Silencer. After she learned of the lie I'd spun for the future Enforcer, we talked quietly until the shadowy alley was swallowed in darkness.

'Okay, but is he really as handsome as everyone says he is?'

I give her a flat look that I doubt she can see but know she can sense. '*That* is the question you're dying to ask after everything we just talked about?'

'That wasn't an answer,' she singsongs.

I lie down on the rough carpets, stifling my groan with a scratchy blanket. Choosing to keep my mouth shut gives Adena all the answer she needs.

She squeals, and this time, I stifle *her* with a blanket.

Dawn creeps over the rooftops, and I mimic it from below and tiptoe along the streets.

Blending into the utter chaos that ensues every morning on Loot, it normally isn't hard for me to slip around unnoticed while slipping watches from shoppers' wrists, or coins from unguarded pockets.

But not today.

Today, I'm not invisible. A thief's worst nightmare.

Eyes. Dozens of them, all pinned on me as I pass. I hear them whisper to one another, pointing and gawking.

A few begin clapping as I walk down the aisle of merchant carts, staring at me in awe. There are dozens of familiar faces in the crowd, having grown up surrounded and surviving by the same people. *Friend* is too strong a word for anyone who isn't Adena, but I've been building my reputation as a Psychic for years, earning respect and witnesses to my abilities.

The crowd seems to part for me, leaving a wall of people watching on either side.

'The Silver Savior,' I hear a man whisper before others echo his words.

I stop, almost stumbling when my feet seem to stall. There, once blocked from my sight by crumbling shops, hangs another banner now in clear view.

THE PEOPLE OF ILYA HAVE CHOSEN
INTRODUCING YOUR CONTESTANTS
FOR THE SIXTH EVER PURGING TRIALS:

KAI AZER

ANDREA VOS

JAX SHIELDS

BLAIR ARCHER

ACE ELWAY

BRAXTON HALE

HERA COLT

SADIE KNOX

My eyes scroll down the list of names quickly. And then my heart skips a beat. Maybe a dozen.

Because the final name scrolled in large letters for all to see is far too familiar.

PAEDYN GRAY

CHAPTER 9

Kai

Blood seeps through my shirt. Some of it mine, though most of it belongs to the Silencer – which is what I still have to call him since the bastard refuses to even give up something as insignificant as his name. Even despite how *persuasive* my actions can be.

In short, I've been torturing the man for hours. I've made zero progress, and my small amount of patience is now nonexistent. I'm annoyingly amazed at how much torture this man can tolerate, although, I suppose that pain becomes a familiar thing when you are continually inflicting it upon others. You become numb to it.

The Silencer and I are starting to sound very, very similar.

The dungeons below the castle are dark, dirty, and riddled with death – so at odds with the light, lush castle above. Cells line the walls, some filled with prisoners, others filled with the remains of previous ones.

The Mute lining each of these cells is the only reason I'm still standing before the prisoner, inflicting my own kind of unimaginable pain upon him. Since the material was created with the help of Silencers before the Purging, it's become extremely rare, forcing the king to hoard it. The Scholars used Transfers with their ability to place power into objects, putting the Silencers' smothering strength

within materials. Over the decades, this limited supply of Mute has been used to craft cells, cuffs, and shields around the stands within the Bowl Arena.

Other than the Mute cell, I'm also accompanied by my father's loyal Silencer. Because, ironic as it is, Silencers can silence each other, assuming one of them is stronger. So, I work while the solemn Silencer stands by, and the one at my feet screams.

Without the protection that the Mute and Silencer offer, I'd likely be rolling on the floor in agony. Again. I can't stop replaying the scene in my mind, remembering the pain splitting my skull. The utter helplessness as I lay there, completely at the mercy of a mere man.

But then she showed up.

Paedyn.

A Mundane. A Psychic, a fighter, a thief. And yet, the only one willing to help for whatever reason. The only one *able* to help.

Or so she says.

Although I'm skeptical, her demonstration was impressive. She shouldn't have known about the Scorches, the banishment, the fight – any of it. And seeing that I don't know a single thing about Psychics, nor have I ever encountered one, I can't exactly prove her wrong. There are dozens of powers I have yet to witness, considering that my training consisted of mostly Offensive abilities. Father made sure I never wasted my time, stooped so low as to learn the powers of lesser Elites.

But even in my haze of pain, the glimpses I caught of her fighting were captivating. *She* was captivating. Yes, she was skilled, but what intrigued me most was how much emotion she channeled into each blow. The passion packed in each punch; the rage rolling off her.

I take one last look at the bloodied, slumped man in the corner of his cell before turning to my father's Silencer. 'I'm done here, Damion. You're free to go.'

Wiping my bloody hands on my already bloody shirt, I step out of the cell to stride down the long hallway of the dungeon, passing glaring prisoners as I go. I make my way up the stone stairs leading to the main floor of the palace and nod to the Imperials stationed beside the heavy metal door at the top.

The king will be expecting an update of what I've learned from the interrogation, which happens to be absolutely nothing. I steel myself for the unpleasant conversation we are about to have.

Far too soon, my feet find the worn rug that covers the floor of his study, a victim of being paced and trampled on for years. My eyes roam over the large desk and cushioned chairs before settling on the two individuals sitting near the stone fireplace.

Relief washes over me at the sight of my brother. His blond hair is messy, like he's been running his hand through it for hours, mirroring Father's ragged look.

'Well, someone's been . . . playing with the prisoner for quite some time now.' Kitt's tone is dark, but his eyes brighten when they land on me.

I sigh before settling into my usual cushioned seat beside Father. Crossing an ankle over my knee, I casually confess, 'And after all this time, you'd think that I would have learned something useful.'

The thud of Father's papers hitting the table is a sound I've come to associate with disappointment. 'What seems to be the problem?'

'He's being . . .' I pause, searching for the right word. 'Difficult.' It's the best I can come up with, earning a snort from Kitt.

Father looks less amused. In fact, he doesn't look amused at all, and he never really has when it comes to me. 'Then make him *less* difficult, Kai.' He pinches his fingers to the bridge of his nose and closes his eyes, the action making him look older, wearier. 'Either make him talk or kill him. I have no desire to keep the Silencer alive if he has nothing to offer us.'

I glance at Kitt, his face grave, void of its usual amusement as he watches Father. When the king is distraught, Kitt is devastated.

'It's that damn Resistance,' Father growls, his hand dropping from his face to reveal a grimace.

'Do you really believe this Silencer is in line with the Resistance?' Kitt asks, concern written in the creases around his eyes.

'Why else would he try to take a prince? My son?' The king shakes his head, staring blankly at the flickering flames in the fireplace. 'They're trying to attack me in any way they can. I thought I took care of them. Purged the Fatals so they couldn't harm us, overpower us.' He takes a deep breath before continuing. 'Apparently, I thought wrong. Some remain, and they've joined *them*.

'We need to put an end to this little *Resistance*,' Father spits before downing the rest of the alcohol in his glass. 'They may want Ordinaries to live, but in doing so, the Elite race and power will eventually *die*. Ridding my kingdom of Ordinaries is a sacrifice that must be made for the good of the people. But they are too damn *selfish* to see that. Kai,' his gaze is piercing when it lands on mine, 'make this Silencer wish he were dead before bestowing that mercy upon him.'

'Oh, I was already planning on it, Father.'

I'm drenched in sweat.

Not an uncommon occurrence when training.

My bloody shirt is long gone, and the sun beats down on my back as Kitt and I circle each other in one of the dirt training rings. We go through our normal routine of sizing one another up and spewing nonsense before actually making a move to fight. The familiar pattern calms me, eases my restless mind for the time being.

We dance around the ring, swords flashing, laughing as I nick him on the cheek with the sharp tip of my blade, an action he returns in kind. The swords are soon discarded, replaced by our powers. Kitt easily hits targets with fireballs before dousing the burning wood with water. I, on the other hand, find myself indecisive and antsy: a terrible combination. I filter through the abilities of those surrounding me, attempting to choose one to train with. The rings are full of dozens of Elites, all filthy from fights and slumped from sparring. I jump from a Flash's power to a Veil's before switching to a Shell, though I've never especially liked the feeling of my skin turning to stone.

I can't seem to focus and that only frustrates me more.

I hear the *whoosh* from behind before feeling the familiar wave of heat that radiates towards my back. I drop to the ground, barely avoiding a stream of fire that would have singed off my hair.

'What has you so distracted?' I turn to see Kitt grinning crookedly at me. 'Hey, I almost got you there. Wouldn't be so pretty with that mop of hair singed off your head, now, would you?'

I can't decide if I want to laugh with him or ring his neck – a common predicament I find myself in.

'I guess beating you in the ring today was too easy. Now I'm bored.' I shrug and grab some throwing knives from a weapons rack before beginning to pelt them at a tree a few yards away.

'Hmm,' Kitt hums. Even with my back to him, I can hear the smile in his voice when he says, 'Can't stop thinking about the girl who saved your life, huh?'

By way of politely answering, I spin and throw a knife at my brother. It just barely skims past the side of his head, sinking into a target far behind him with a thud. He blinks at me. 'Touchy subject, I take it?'

I push past him and rip the blade from the wood. 'Now, what would give you that impression?' I shrug casually. 'She clearly wants nothing to do with me.'

I like a challenge.

'And besides,' I add, clearing the thought from my head, 'it's not like I'm ever going to see her again.'

Kitt's response is quickly drowned out by the sound of our names being yelled across the yard. We turn in unison, watching as a lanky boy bounds towards us. I see the flash of a white smile against dark skin before he disappears, simply winking out of existence. Before I even have time to blink, he's standing right before us with a goofy grin splitting his face.

I curse under my breath. 'If you pop up like that again, I'll make good on that threat to stake you to the ground.'

'What our brother *means* to say,' Kitt cuts me an amused look, 'is "hi, Jax, how are you?".'

The boy before me is only fifteen and growing like a weed. He's gangly, clearly still trying to figure out how to work his long limbs. I don't know when he suddenly started growing up, and quite frankly, I don't like it. The small boy who lost his parents in a shipwreck is now the tall young man we've adopted as the little brother we never asked for. But after all these years, Jax hasn't just grown in height – he's grown on us.

'I'm good, Kitt. How nice of you to ask!' That crooked grin only grows when he looks at me, brown eyes blinking innocently. I hook an arm around his neck and pull him against my chest to scrub a fist over his short hair.

He sputters, trying to shove away from me while I ask, 'Aren't you going to ask how I'm doing, J?'

When I finally release him, he turns to face me, rubbing his head with a grin. 'My bad. How are you doing today, Kai?' He says this all with mock sincerity, and I can't help but smile.

Kitt cuts me off before I can tease him further. 'He's in a mood,' he sighs before dropping his voice to murmur, 'Careful, Jax, he's been playing with the knives again.'

I brush past them to pick up said throwing knives, needing to do something with my hands. 'I am not,' I spin and throw a blade into a target, 'in a mood.'

Jax leans into Kitt's shoulder, whispering, 'That's what he *always* says when he's in a mood.'

'Excellent point, J.'

'Plagues,' I mutter, 'the two of you together is unbearable.'

They continue talking while I continue to pelt the target with knives. Better than throwing them at a person, so clearly, I'm not in a *terrible* mood. I'm about to let another blade fly when a flash of color catches my eye.

I hadn't even noticed Blair was training on the other end of the courtyard, but there she is, lilac hair blowing in the wind while she spars with Sadie. Well, a dozen Sadies, seeing that she's a Cloner.

They circle each other before Blair is suddenly surrounded by a barricade of bodies, all tall and chestnut-haired. It's chaos. Blair tosses a copy of Sadie through the air with her mind only for another one to jump on her back, trying to bring her to the ground. It's almost comical to watch, except that I know firsthand how deadly their powers can be, know what it's like to possess them.

I look over to Jax and Kitt, their eyes pinned on the fight as I move to stand in line with them. Before long, Blair is strutting between the rings with Sadie following behind. Blair's pale skin is in complete contrast to Sadie's dark complexion, opposites of each other in every way.

Despite the two of them having grown up together, they couldn't be more different. Since Sadie's father is an adviser to the king, her family lives with the other nobility that are deemed important enough to reside in that designated wing of the castle.

They stop in front of us, Blair tipping her head as she says, 'Boys.'

Kitt slings an arm around Jax's shoulders before nodding at each of the girls. 'Blair. Sadie.'

Sadie offers us a small smile, genuine but reserved in the way she's always been. 'I wanted to congratulate you two on making it into the Trials.'

Right. They announced the contestants today.

It's no surprise that I'm in the Trials. The kingdom and I have been aware of my fate since I was a young boy. The future Enforcer must prove himself, and the Trials force me to do just that. My next mission is to win the competition, and if I don't—

I freeze, Sadie's words finally sinking in.

'I wanted to congratulate you two . . .'

I throw a confused glance at Kitt, certain this must be some sort of mistake. The Trials have always been my fate, not his. The future king rarely stepped outside the castle walls, let alone into a bloody arena where Death could claim him. Father would never risk the life of his heir like that, but he certainly has no problem risking me and my reputation. 'Yes, at least two of the brothers will get to be together,' Blair says with a smirk, her eyes flicking from me to – No. Not him.

'W–what?'

His voice is filled with awe, his brown eyes wide with wonder.

Jax.

He looks between Kitt and I, a smile spreading across his face. 'I did it! I'm in the Trials!' He's practically jumping off the ground in excitement, resisting the urge to Blink around the rings out of excitement. I meet Kitt's gaze, and his knowing frown matches my own.

This is going to make the Trials far more difficult. Now, I'll not only be protecting myself, but also a little brother who nearly faints at the sight of blood.

But we say nothing to discourage Jax, pasting on smiles to replace the frowns pulling at our faces. Competing in the Trials is a high honor that only a few are granted, and Jax deserves to celebrate despite our sudden stress over the situation.

'Well, it looks like we are all rivals now,' Blair says with a smirk, letting her words sink in. Not a very sly way to inform us that both herself and Sadie will also be competing.

We all stare at each other, Sadie silent and Blair smirking. Kitt clears his throat, cutting into the conversation. 'Do you know who else is competing?'

Sadie nods, pulling a crinkled flier from one of her pockets. Kitt skims the names quickly before sighing. 'Yep. There are only three names I don't recognize. Must be Defensive or Mundanes from the city.'

He hands me the flier, and I quickly scan the list.

My eyes snag on a particular arrangement of letters before my breath snags in my throat.

There, at the bottom of the list, lies a name I've thought of far more than I care to admit.

It's *her*.

CHAPTER 10

Paedyn

I might have stood there for hours, gawking up at the banner displaying my name in giant letters, if not for the mass of people gawking at me.

They chose me.

Or in other words, they chose me to die.

And all because I saved that prick of a prince.

A tap on my shoulder shakes me from my stupor.

I stiffen at the sudden smell of starch and heave a sigh before turning slowly to face the Imperial. He's young. My eyes flick between his messy red hair and brown eyes boring into mine, completely unbothered by my obvious disdain for his kind. He offers me a small, shy smile.

Unsettling.

In all my years, I have never met a kind Imperial, and I doubt he is the exception.

'You're Paedyn Gray, correct?' He gestures to the sign above us with a wave of his hand.

'Who wants to know?' I blurt.

'Er,' he rubs the back of his neck, 'the king? I'm here to escort you to the palace where you will be staying until the Trials are over.'

The unspoken words hang in the air between us. *Or until you die.*

'Now? Right now?' I hate how high and breathless my voice sounds, but I can't stop the panic rising up my throat. 'But the Trials don't begin for another two weeks.'

He almost looks apologetic, and I hate it. 'The contestants always head to the palace two weeks in advance for training, interviews, and of course, the first ball.'

How could I forget how showy the Trials are?

His head whips around, red hair rippling like flames as he searches to see if anyone is watching. Then he leans in slightly, his next words a murmur. 'I can only give you about . . . hmm, five minutes or so before we have to leave.'

I don't hesitate before bounding down the street as fast as my legs can carry me.

Adena.

I skid to a stop in front of our little alley and swallow the lump in my throat at the sight of her tucked behind the Fort, humming while she sews. I take it all in as I stride towards her. Every piece of garbage we scavenged together to keep us warm at night. Every scrap of clothing piled beside her as she works. Every curly piece of hair escaping the messy bun at the nape of her neck. Her dark brows furrowed over hazel eyes in concentration.

Will I ever see her again?

I try to push the thought from my head as I sink to the ground and pull her into a crushing hug. She gasps in surprise before quickly discarding her work and squeezing me tight. 'Happy to see you too?' She laughs into my hair and pulls away, concerned by my sudden show of affection. 'Are you . . . okay?'

I meet her eyes, memorizing the specks of gold flecking them. 'I'm leaving, A.'

'W-what?' The look on her face is equally scared and skeptical.

'They are sending me into the Trials. The people want me there, apparently.' I'm rambling. 'For entertainment purposes, of course.' I offer her a weak smile, but nothing can stop the look of horror from spreading across her face.

She brings a soft, brown hand to her mouth as she breathes, 'Oh, Pae . . .' She trails off, not knowing what to say, what to do. 'But you . . . You don't have an ability—'

'It's gonna be alright,' I say, trying to convince her as well as myself. 'I'll be—'

'Don't you dare say you'll be *fine*,' she huffs as anger temporarily swallows her fear. 'Pae, the Trials are deadly enough, but if they find out about what you *aren't* they will—'

'Kill me,' I finish for her. 'I know.' The fear floods back into Adena's eyes, crashing into her so hard I worry she may crumble. A sad, small smile lifts my lips as I take her in. I'm leaving the only person who knows me, the only person I can truly trust. She's been a constant in my life, an anchor that I'll be drifting without.

But this is for the best. It's safer for her without me here. 'I can do this,' I say softly. 'I was *made* to do this.'

Adena nods numbly, knowing this already. Knowing how my father began training me when it became apparent to him that his little girl was an Ordinary doomed for death.

She knows how at the age of five, my life changed before it had even begun. Father sat me on his lap, whispered that I was different, that I had to pretend to be something I wasn't if I wanted to grow up with him by my side. It was our own little game, he said. A game of pretend. A game in which he'd already chosen the perfect role for me to play for the rest of my life.

'What's a Psychich, Daddy?' That question is still so vivid in my mind, though it was over thirteen years ago when I'd asked it.

Father had just chuckled softly, a seemingly simple sound that I wish I could have memorized. 'A *Psychic*, Paedy, is a fancy word for someone who's observant. A power that can be faked with years of practice. Something you don't have to be gifted with, but a skill you can learn.' At that, he'd bopped the tip of my nose with his finger. 'And I'm going to teach you. That way, we can always be together.'

If only death had any regard for promises.

I'm suddenly pulled into another suffocating hug. 'Come home to me, Pae. Please?' Adena's voice is muffled against my hair. 'You're all I have left, you know.'

I wish more than anything that those words weren't so terrifyingly true.

When Adena's mother fell ill, it was likely my father who tried to treat her. Healers are uncommon around the slums, and the people needed him as much as they loved him. But even Elites have their limits, while it seems Death knows no bounds. And since Adena never knew her father, he could have been the hazel-eyed merchant I robbed this morning for all we know.

A pained laugh slips past my lips. 'And you are all *I* have left, A.'

'Good.' She sniffs and pulls back to look at me. 'Then you better find a way to make it back to me. If anyone from around here can make it out of those bloody Trials, it's you.' The look she gives me is defiantly determined. 'At worst, you lose and come home. At best, you win the damn thing.'

I huff out a laugh at the absurd thought. 'I'll try my best for you, A.' After swallowing the lump in my throat, I add, 'I'll visit you. I promise. I'll find a way. Walk if I have to.'

She smiles, giving me one final hug before waving as I head down the alley. Standing to her feet behind the Fort, she shouts, 'This is not a goodbye, only a good way to say bye until I see you next!'

It's the same cheesy line she's said for years, and yet, this is the first time it's sounded like a goodbye. 'You're my favorite, A!' I call back to her, voice breaking without my permission.

'And you are mine, Pae!'

Smiling, I finally tear my eyes from her and begin hurrying down Loot, considering running away from the Imperial, the Trials, *everything*. But the reckless thought is gone as quickly as my feet are pounding against the cobblestone. I'll be hunted down and killed if I run. At least with going to the Trials, I have a fighting chance at survival. Sort of.

Panting, I make it back to the Imperial who is now joined by a small girl assessing me timidly. 'Ready to go?' he says, looking between the two of us. I humor him by nodding, despite having no choice in the matter.

We head down Loot in silence, passing crowds of people as we walk, all clapping and shouting their congratulations at us. As we near the end of the long street, I see a dark coach awaiting, paired with an Imperial sitting atop the driver's bench with his white uniform nearly blinding in the sun.

Our redheaded Imperial opens the door for us before he too joins the guard on the bench. The girl scrambles in and I follow, peeking my head out the door for one last look at Loot Alley before the coach seals me inside, separating me from my former life.

Cushioned black seats await us, and I'm almost too busy admiring the fanciest thing I've ever seen to notice the boy sitting across from us. His brown hair is neatly styled on his head, just above his dark green eyes that are currently pinned on me. By the condition of his clothing, I can tell he comes from a nicer area of the slums and likely falls into the Defensive tier of Elites.

The coach lurches forward, and I cling to the wall. I already don't like small spaces, let alone small places that *move*. I steady my breathing, forcing myself to calm down before I look back at the bored boy.

'Hi,' I say, trying to ease the tension. 'I'm Pae—'

'I know who you are,' he cuts me off, immediately deciding that staring out the window is far more interesting than our conversation. 'You're the girl who *saved* Prince Kai.' His tone suggests that this is not, in fact, precisely what happened. As if dozens of people didn't *see* it happen.

I open my mouth, allowing words to spew out before I can think better of them. 'Correct. And clearly you don't have a reputation, or I would have heard of you by now.'

His eyes snap to mine, nostrils flaring. 'I'm Ace. Ace Elway.' He says this proudly, straightening the collar of his shirt as he continues, 'I'm an Illusionist. Rare. That's why I'm here.' His smile is as cold as his eyes. 'And I'm going to need those twenty thousand shillings to finally get me out of these *slums*, so I'm sure I'll be making quite the reputation for myself soon enough.'

I've never encountered an Illusionist, but I've heard enough about them to know he's dangerous, even as a Defensive.

'And who are you?' he asks the girl beside me. 'What can you do?' She glances between the two of us, looking as if she wants to disappear. And I almost laugh when she does.

She's there one second and gone the next. I stare at the empty seat beside me before her form reappears, materializing in a matter of moments.

Veil.

'I'm Hera,' she says shyly. Her deep, brown eyes meet mine as she brushes a strand of silky black hair behind her ear. Something about the action seems vaguely familiar, making me wonder if she's one of the popular Veils that perform street magic.

'I'm Paedyn,' I say over the rumbling of the coach rolling over uneven cobblestones.

'What's your power?' she asks curiously.

'Psychic.' I shrug casually. 'I mostly sense strong emotions that give me flashes of information. It's not much, but it's all I've got.'

Liar. You haven't got anything.

'Really?' Her eyes go wide, probably shocked that someone with such a weak Mundane ability could make it into the Trials, let alone defeat a Silencer.

'It's an uncontrollable mental ability, and the only reason the Silencer wasn't able to get into my head when I *saved* Prince Kai.' I toss a pointed look at Ace. 'I guess that's why people want me in these Trials at all.'

Ace the Ass snorts. 'They only want you in the Purging Trials to watch you die, Mundane.'

I stare at him, and after a long moment, a small smile tugs at my lips. 'Oh, most definitely. But at least they will be watching me at all.'

CHAPTER 11

Paedyn

Silence is the only sound for the remainder of the ride, leaving the window beside me to be my only source of entertainment.

We pass dozens of streets crowded with smiling strangers, all waving and gawking. Some cheer and run next to the coach as we pass, trying to get a glimpse of us before we roll away to our dooms.

As we get closer to the palace, the houses grow larger, finer, and the streets are no longer riddled with homeless shuffling about. I spot the tips of the daunting towers before the whole daunting palace comes into view below them. It's huge. Even with its gray stone and cold exterior, it's breathtaking. Grassy hills and vibrant gardens filled with brightly colored flowers I didn't even know existed surround the castle walls, softening the intimidating structure.

I hear the clopping of hooves hammering against smooth stone as we head into a courtyard, passing a large fountain residing in the center with white statues scattered around its perimeter. When the coach finally slows to a stop, I peek through the window to see a large, stone staircase leading into the palace, surrounded by beds of flowers.

The Imperials hop from their cushioned perch and open the doors to the coach, allowing warm sunlight to pour into our small

compartment. I practically tumble out in my hurry to escape the cramped coach and the company inside. Once my feet are on solid ground again and swallowed by open air, I take a deep breath, inhaling the sweet scent of flowers and sunshine.

The other two stumble out to stand beside me, both wide-eyed and staring. A voice startles us from our gawking when the red-haired Imperial clears his throat and says, 'Follow me.'

We file up the stone steps behind him, passing dozens of Imperials lining the staircase. When we reach the top, two more guards step out and join the redhead leading us before walking through the giant doors.

If the outside was beautiful, it pales in comparison to *this*. Every wall is ornately decorated with glittering paintings and intricate molding that climbs up the walls and clings to the ceiling. Everything is dazzlingly white with the occasional pop of emerald that dots the hallways we trudge down, showcasing Ilya's kingdom color.

I'm too mesmerized by the sheer size and beauty of this place to even realize that the redhead is speaking to the three of us. '—rooms are this way, in the East wing of the palace.' He gestures to the many hallways that I'm assuming are filled with equally embellished rooms.

He suddenly spins on his heel to turn and face us, forcing me to skid to a stop before I nearly crash into his chest. 'The next two weeks will consist of training, meeting the other contestants, interviews, and the first ball. And every week between each Trial will follow the same routine. An Imperial will be assigned to you for the remainder of your stay here, and they will escort you to and from anywhere you need to be until you are acquainted with the castle.'

One of the Imperials standing behind us moves beside Hera, while the other takes his place next to Ace. 'Well,' the young Imperial claps his hands in front of him with a sigh, 'we will show you your rooms and let you get situated.'

When Hera and Ace have rounded the corner at the end of the hall, I turn to my personal Imperial. 'So, you'll be keeping an eye on me then?' 'Lucky me.' He chuckles and turns, motioning for me to follow. 'I'm Lenny, by the way.'

'I never thought I'd say this to an Imperial, but it's nice to meet you,

Lenny.' Clamping my mouth shut before anything else I shouldn't be saying spews out, I pick up my pace and try to catch up with his long strides.

'Yeah, well, I don't blame you. Most Imperials can be . . .' He rubs the back of his neck, searching for the right word.

'Pigs?' I mutter before I can think better of it.

He cuts off his laugh with a quick clearing of his throat. 'Yeah, they have me do a lot of the talking around here. I guess I'm not as intimidating.' I swiftly look him up and down, unable to help but agree. His messy red hair combined with the explosion of freckles splattering out from under his mask diminish any hope of looking threatening. He stops in front of a door near the end of a long hallway before pushing it open and gesturing inside.

I bite my tongue to keep from gasping at the sight of the most beautiful room I've ever seen, filled with bookcases, a dainty vanity, a writing desk, and . . .

A bed.

An *enormous* bed. After sleeping on jagged cobblestone for five years, the thought of getting to sleep on *that* is overwhelming. I blink in amazement as I finally take a step inside. The carpet is plush beneath my feet, and I spin to see a bathroom peeking out behind a door to the left. I stride towards it, fighting my smile when I see a pristine, porcelain bathtub, sitting atop golden legs.

Hot, running water.

An equally shiny toilet and sink sit on the white, marble floor to complete the set. I slowly step out of the bathroom, still staring at the bedroom before me. Out of the corner of my eye, I can see Lenny watching me, amused by my awe. 'I hope you find your room to be . . . satisfactory?'

'Oh, it'll have to do, I suppose.' I plop onto my bed as I say it, sarcasm dripping from the words.

'Well, I'll let you get comfortable, seeing that you'll be spending a lot of time in here,' he says, turning to step out the door.

'What do you mean by that?'

He rubs his hand over the back of his neck with a sigh. 'You'll find out soon enough.'

Lenny was right to tell me to get comfortable. I've been trapped in this room for two days.

It's become my personal gilded cage, locking me in with luxuries. The guards stationed outside my door don't deem me important enough to grumble more than a few words about following orders by keeping me confined to my room. So I've scoured every inch of the chamber, occupying myself by thumbing through books, soaking in hot baths, devouring delicious meals.

And yet, I've never felt more anxious.

The inside of my cheek is sore, the result of incessant biting in an attempt to calm my nerves. And despite sleeping in a soft bed for the first time in years, I'm restless. I haven't spoken to anyone since my first day here, haven't even been told what the hell is going on. I've been left to pace the padded floor, worrying over who my opponents are and what they can do.

Mind games, that's what this is.

The king likely finds this comical. Loves the idea of us anxious, restless, and trapped in our rooms until he says otherwise. This is meant to set us on edge, make us antsy.

A knock at the door has me pausing my pacing.

Lenny's head peeks around the door frame, a sheepish grin on his face. 'So . . . how are you, Paedyn?'

I blink at him. 'How am I? *How am I?*'

He creeps farther into the room, his next words slow. 'Okay, so, I'm getting the feeling that you're not . . . great.'

My laugh is bitter. 'You could say that. It's been *two days*. Where the hell have you been?'

'The king likes to keep the contestants completely isolated for the first couple of days,' he says stiffly. 'But, good news, you'll be having dinner tonight with the other contestants, along with the king and queen.'

I swallow. After forty-eight restless hours, I'm suddenly going to meet the contestants that have plagued my thoughts, and the king who has plagued my nightmares.

'I'll be back shortly to escort you to dinner,' Lenny says, turning towards the door. 'If you need anything, just holler. I won't be far. Oh,' he glances at me over his shoulder, 'and you might want to change before dinner.'

When he's gone, I slip into the bathroom and fiddle with the various knobs on the tub until hot, steaming water begins pouring out. Within minutes, I'm stripped and soaking in the now foamy water, thanks to the unnecessary amount of soaps and salts I dumped in. I scrub my hair and body vigorously, leaving my skin red and refreshed.

I haven't felt so clean in years.

My mind wanders to my many worries, the warm water doing little to soothe me. The Trials consume my thoughts, reminding me of the power I lack and the little protection I possess. Not to mention that if the Trials don't kill me, being discovered as an Ordinary most definitely will.

I soak in the bubbly water until it grows cold like the baths I'm so used to. When I finally muster the strength to force myself out of the tub, I'm shivering as I slip on a green silk robe.

I make my way back into my room, opening the white doors of the giant wardrobe across from my bed to stare at the dozens of colors and patterns, all hung neatly on a rack. Attire for every type of occasion is casually hanging there, all at my disposal.

Adena would die if she saw this.

I stare blankly at the clothes, then down at my ratty ones lying forgotten on the floor. I haven't the slightest idea of what is appropriate to wear to this dinner and I would rather not make a fool out of myself before the Trials have even begun.

Remembering that Lenny said to *holler* if I needed anything, I intend to do just that. I'm sure the Imperial has witnessed several of these meals and will have some idea of what the expected attire is.

I stride to the door and wrench it open, looking down as I tighten the tie of my robe. I do, in fact, holler, 'Lenny, what the hell am I supposed to wear—'

And then I look up.

My eyes meet wide, bright green ones. I've never seen the man standing before me; I would have remembered. His messy, dirty blond hair looks slightly damp as if he too just got out of the bath. He has simultaneously strong, yet delicate features, with his straight nose and soft lips. His hand is raised, still posed to knock on my door.

He recovers faster than I do. 'Wardrobe problems?' His mouth twists into a playful grin, and something about it seems so familiar, and yet, not at all.

'Clearly,' I say with a small smile. His eyes quickly sweep over me, and only then do I remember that I'm wearing a robe. I pull it tighter around myself, fighting my flush.

He clears his throat. 'Well, no need to worry. Your maid, Ellie, will be in soon to help you dress and prepare for dinner.'

He speaks with an air of authority, as though he is used to giving orders. Despite his plain clothes – slim black trousers and a tighter, green shirt that shows off his lean figure – I know right away that this man is no servant.

A contestant?

At the thought of having a maid wait on me, I quickly say, 'That won't be necessary. I can take care of myself, thank you.'

His gaze travels from my still dripping and tangled hair to the silk robe I clutch closed. 'Clearly,' he says, mimicking my response to him only moments ago with that oddly familiar grin on his face.

I look down at myself and nearly laugh. 'Okay, perhaps a maid will be necessary after all.'

He laughs softly before gesturing to the room behind me. 'I just stopped by to see if everything was adequate?'

I find myself almost laughing once again. 'If *this* is adequate, I can't even imagine what is considered exquisite around here.'

His eyes search mine. 'Then remind me to show you the gardens sometime.' He offers me a nod. 'I look forward to seeing you at dinner, Paedyn.'

I blink at him.

'Strange,' I say slowly. 'I don't remember telling you my name.'

'Oh, you didn't need to.' That crooked grin is teasing his lips once again. 'I make it my business to know all the pretty girls who save my little brother.'

Plagues, he's—

'I'm Kitt by the way.' He flashes me a grin before turning to stride down the hallway, leaving me shocked and staring.

Prince Kitt. As in 'future king of Ilya' Kitt.

What is it with me running into royals?

I had never seen the future king before, and I'd definitely never thought I'd meet him in a robe. He's the heir to the throne, the next ruler who is ready to follow in his vile father's footsteps. Between him and his brother—

His brother.

That's why his smile looked so familiar.

I've seen a variation of it on the other prince's face, though Kitt's was bright and boyish while Kai's was cockier, colder.

I watch as a small, dark-haired girl steps shyly up to my room with a timid smile tipping her lips. 'Good evening, miss. I'll be your maid while you're here at the palace, and I'll assist you with anything you may need.' Her voice is soft and delicate, but her rehearsed words are steady.

'Please, call me Paedyn.' She looks at me warily, but I press on. 'Plagues, a couple days ago I was sleeping in some garbage, so trust me when I say you shouldn't call me *miss*.'

She fights a laugh at that, nodding slowly in agreement. 'Great,' I sigh, 'now that that's settled, can you help me figure out what it is I'm supposed to wear tonight?'

She smiles shyly at me, looking relieved. 'That, I think I can help with.'

We spend the next half hour filtering through outfits before settling on something relatively plain by the palace's standards, though it's still the nicest thing I've ever worn.

With half the wardrobe emptied onto the floor, we've decided on a pair of shiny black leggings paired with a silky, dark green blouse. It's relatively low with drooping sleeves I already know will be accidentally dipped in food. I slip a small dagger into the back band of my pants, and the flat blade against my back is cool and comforting.

After lacing up high boots, Ellie motions me over to the vanity where she begins playing with my hair, trying to make the damp mop look presentable. 'So, mi—' She clears her throat and tries again. 'So, *Paedyn,*' she emphasizes my name with a small smile, 'do you have any idea what the Trials will be like?'

'Not a clue.' I give her a pleading smile through the mirror. 'I was hoping you would, though, seeing that I'm sure you overhear a lot in the palace?'

Her next words are little more than a murmur. 'All I know is that this year is supposed to be . . . different.'

'Different?' I echo. 'In what way?'

She shrugs, fistfuls of my hair grasped in her hands. 'I dunno. Just different somehow.'

I struggle to see how a Trial could be *different,* seeing that each one is as bloody and brutal as the last. But the little information makes me feel even more unprepared for what is to come, and I try not to dwell on the unease curling in my gut.

Ellie soon gives up on my hair with a huff, deciding to let it lie limply down my back. She then adds powder to my face before smearing a bit of black onto my lashes. 'There,' she says, studying me. 'No more looking like you slept in garbage.'

I snort. 'Plagues, aren't you coming out of your shell.'

She reddens before a knock on the door has her scurrying up to answer it. Lenny looks down at her and smiles, only causing her flush to deepen.

'Ready to go, Paedyn?' He drags his eyes from Ellie to meet mine.

When I meet him in the hallway, we begin our walk down the intricately decorated halls. As we zigzag through the maze that is the castle, I try my best to make a mental map of the layout.

One left, two rights, another left . . .

We are soon back in the large entry hallway that stretches to the even larger doors we first entered through two days ago. Lenny leads me to another pair of floor-to-ceiling doors a little farther down the wide corridor as he murmurs, 'The throne room. This is where you'll be having your meals with the other contestants.'

Before I have a chance to spout off questions, he nods to the guards standing nearby, silently ordering them to push open the looming door.

And at first, no one seems to notice me.

They are all sitting around a long, wooden table at the center of the marble floor, so at odds with the delicate beauty of the throne room. As for the Elites surrounding it, they talk comfortably to one another, seeing that many of them likely grew up together.

I take a deep breath and begin walking slowly towards the table. Eight pairs of eyes flick in my direction, looking me up and down as I make my way over to them.

Of course I'm the last one to show up.

I pull out a chair at the end of the table next to Ace, reluctant to sit beside him, but relieved to be seated so everyone can stop staring.

Except that they don't.

I feel their gazes and look up, unable stop words from tumbling out of my mouth. 'So, what's for dinner?'

I let out a sigh of relief when the girl sitting on the other side of Ace snorts and leans over the table to look at me. Her bob of wine-red hair shines in the late afternoon sunlight streaming through the window, competing with the shiny silver hoop in her nose. 'I keep asking the same question!' Her honey eyes seem to glitter with mischief. 'I'm Andy.'

'Paedyn,' I say, offering her a small smile.

'Well, if we're making introductions,' a deep voice carries from the other end of the table, 'I'm Braxton.' I look up to see a huge, dark-skinned boy tipping his head towards me.

Brawny.

I nod at him as a higher male voice calls out, 'I'm Jax!' I look down the table at him, taking in his shy smile. Names are now being shouted across the table. Other than Hera and Ace who came from the slums, it's obvious that everyone else is well acquainted.

'I'm Sadie.' I turn towards the voice to see a girl with warm skin studying me. Her stare is assessing, curious. The girl beside her tips her chin up and clears her throat, drawing my attention her way.

'Blair. Pleasure to meet you, Paedyn.' She spits out the words like they leave a vile taste in her mouth, all while looking down at me like I'm something sticky on the bottom of her boot. I get the immediate impression that this girl wants nothing to do with Mundanes, let alone anyone who calls the slums their home. Her lilac hair spills over her shoulders, contrasting against the brown eyes glaring at me. She's stunning, yet startlingly cold.

'The pleasure is all mine, Blair,' I say coolly. The hungry look in her eyes makes me feel as if *I'm* going to be her next meal.

And then a deep and annoyingly amused voice comes from the end of the table, directly across from me.

'And I'm Kai. But you already knew that.'

CHAPTER 12

Kai

She's here.

Kitt was howling with laughter when he discovered exactly who Paedyn Gray was, though, a flick of one of my knives shut him up real quick. But even while raising his hands in surrender, he couldn't stop babbling about how funny the whole situation was.

And he's right. It *is* laughable. The Psychic girl who unwittingly saved a prince she clearly couldn't care less about is now rewarded for it by being forced into Trials that could kill her.

And now she's sitting right in front of me.

After washing my body of the sweat and blood that accompanies a long day of training and torturing, I made my way to the throne room. Soon after, Braxton shuffled in, followed by Jax who's still bouncing with excitement.

The rest of the familiar group followed shortly after, along with a boy and girl I hadn't recognized – the ones from the slums. The seats around the table filled up, leaving the two at the head for the king and queen and one beside me for Kitt.

But right as we all get comfortable and begin idle conversations about the same regurgitated topics we've spoken of for years, something happens.

She happens. She walks in.

Taking the seat across from me, not even glancing in my direction, she says, 'So, what's for dinner?'

She speaks confidently, even as her fingers fidget, spinning the ring on her thumb.

Interesting.

Introductions are quickly exchanged between Andy, Braxton, Jax, Sadie, Blair, and the newcomers Ace and Hera. And yet she still hasn't even bothered to look at me.

That just won't do.

'And I'm Kai. But you already knew that.'

That finally gets her attention. The corner of my mouth twitches with the ghost of a smile when her eyes lock with mine. Her lashes are darkened with makeup, contrasting against the bright blue of her gaze. Soft, silver waves tumble over her shoulders and into her face, and I have the sudden and annoying urge to push the strands out of her eyes, if only so I can see them better.

'Yes, unfortunately, I did already know that.' Her soft smile is in total contrast to the sharpness of her gaze.

Our eyes snap to the large doors when they groan open, my attention now fixed on Father and Mother striding through them. No, the *king* and *queen* striding through them, looking every bit the part. They glitter in the sunlight that streams from the huge windows surrounding the throne room, light reflecting off their crowns and jewels as they make their way to the table. I'm used to this formality, the king in a fine suit while the queen shimmers in an elegant dress. Father looking stern and severe, while Mother looks serene with her shining smile.

Kitt follows behind them, looking casual and yet every bit the future king. His gaze finds mine before flicking to Paedyn with a knowing smile on his lips. He takes the seat beside me as the king pulls out one of the heavy wooden chairs for his queen.

'Welcome to the sixth ever Purging Trials,' he booms down the table.

Mother sweeps a strand of black hair out of her eyes, saying, 'And congratulations to all of you for making it here.'

'It is an honor to be chosen,' Father says. 'An honor to your kingdom, your family, and yourself.' He repeats the words that have been drilled into my head since before I could understand them. 'I suggest you spend your time wisely to prepare for the Trials. You never know what might be thrown at you.' His eyes land on me, silently and less than subtly reminding me of my mission to win. 'I would urge you to use your remaining time before the first Trial, as well as each week in between the next ones, to train.'

And to watch your opponents train.

I can almost see the unspoken words in his eyes. Knowing how your competition fights, learning how to read their movements and maneuvers, could be the difference between life and death.

'As well as practicing your dance steps!' Mother says warmly, as she's always enjoyed the balls far more than the bloodshed of the Trials.

Father smiles at his wife. It's a genuine gesture, the kind he only gives away to her. 'Enough talk of the Trials. Let's eat.'

And with that, the procession of servants begins, all carrying steaming trays to the table. Dozens of dishes piled high with food are set before us. Seasoned turkey and heaps of beans are being shoveled onto plates. Gail herself brings out a tray of gooey sticky buns, setting them before Kitt and me to tease the two of us. I give her a quick wink as she walks away, rolling her eyes at me before bustling out of the room.

Kitt and I talk idly as we pass trays of food around, shooing away servants when they offer to serve us. I'm in the middle of piling turkey onto my plate when my eyes snag on Paedyn, sitting rigidly across from me. Her jaw is locked tight as if she's trying her hardest not to let it fall open. Curious, I look down the table at Hera who is wearing a similar look of awe on her face. Even Ace, who seemed to be the better off of the three, can't help but silently stare at the amount of food placed before us. My gaze slides back to Paedyn who's too busy blinking to bother eating. I can only imagine what is going through her head. Probably something along the lines of how disgusted she is at the amount of food we waste while she barely had enough to survive. As I look at the masked anger growing on her face, something tells me she'd rather go hungry tonight.

And that won't do.

Just because we are competing against each other doesn't mean I want to beat her by default due to her starving to death. So, I stab a piece of turkey with my fork, reach across the table, and plop it onto her plate.

Her eyes snap to mine, her face a cross between annoyance and shock. 'Do you like beans?' I ask casually, and when she doesn't answer, I pile them onto her plate anyway. 'Well, I guess I'll find out.'

I lean over the table, adding potatoes to the growing pile of food on her plate as I murmur, 'Are you going to make me spoon-feed you too, or can you handle feeding yourself?' With that, I smile at her in a way that will undoubtedly make her want to throw her beans, and a punch, at my face.

Her eyes burn like blue flames, practically scolding me with a glare. But just as I suspected, she reluctantly picks up her fork and shoves some beans into her mouth with her gaze pinned on me. I lean back in my chair, grinning. She could see it in my eyes that I would, in fact, spoon-feed her if she didn't start eating, and there was no way in hell she was going to let that happen.

The next several minutes are filled with the sounds of clinking silverware and scattered conversations. Blair turns towards Kitt and me, talking about Plague knows what. In general, Kitt is a far better man than I am, and especially so when it comes to her. He talks casually while I offer my attention to the food in front of me instead.

Father's voice suddenly cuts through the din of conversation. 'So,' I look up to see he's staring at Paedyn, intrigued, '*this* is the girl who saved you in the alley?'

Only after robbing me.

I can feel everyone's eyes flick towards us, all listening in on the conversation. Paedyn gently drops her fork and stares at the king with so much intensity in her gaze that she briefly reminds me of Blair. There is a certain emotion clouding her eyes as she looks at him – an emotion she is trying to hide. I don't have time to try and decipher it before she schools her features into neutrality with the blink of an eye.

'Yes, I did save his life. Isn't that right, Your Highness?' She turns her attention towards me, her smile turning into a challenge.

'So you do know my title after all.' Sarcasm coats my words while a smile toys at the corners of my lips. 'You know, I wasn't sure. Because back in the alley you were calling me something very, very different.'

Her smile is all teeth. 'I'm sure whatever I called you was warranted.' A pause. 'And accurate.' A smile. 'And deserved.'

Cocky bastard.

Her eyes, her smile, her tone – all of her screams the two words. Screams the title she's bestowed upon me.

'And what was your title, again? The Silver Savior?' I huff out a quiet laugh. 'Fitting. I know how much you love *silvers*.'

Paedyn's cool smile falters at the meaning behind my words. She's annoyed. I'm amused.

Mother's feelings clearly mirror Paedyn's, because she shoots me a look before saying, 'Thank you, Paedyn, for helping Kai. It did not go unnoticed by us, or the people, seeing that they wanted you in the Trials.' Paedyn dips her head and smiles softly at her, though it doesn't quite reach her eyes.

At the sound of my father's voice, her smile wavers. 'I must say, I've never met a Psychic before.' He looks at her curiously. 'Your powers are . . . intriguing.'

Paedyn relaxes and laughs lightly. 'Yes, well, my father said it's a rare, yet small gift that not many Mundanes possess. I suppose the most useful part of my ability is that I'm not affected by the Silencers, as well as your son, it seems.' A strand of silver hair falls into her eyes, and she tucks it behind her ear absentmindedly as the rest of the table returns to their previous conversations, apparently bored with listening in on this one.

'Ah, yes, your father. Adam Gray was a great Healer. A very educated man,' Father says thoughtfully.

Paedyn goes rigid in her seat. 'You,' she clears her throat, 'you knew my father?'

'Yes, I did. He would come to the palace during fever season to help our own court physicians when there were too many patients to attend to.'

Paedyn nods. 'Yes, I remember him doing that every winter.'

Their conversation is cut short when the servants pour back into the room to clear the dishes. They weave around the table, grabbing plates and silverware before disappearing back into the hallway, leaving a spotless table in their wake.

Father and Mother stand as one. 'Get some rest, Elites. Your training begins tomorrow.' With the king's final words, they turn and stroll out the grand doors.

A beat of silence passes before chairs are scraping on the marble floor, and everyone is standing to their feet. Three Imperials are heading towards the new Elites, ready to escort them back to their rooms.

I watch as a young, redheaded guard saunters up to Paedyn with a grin. And suddenly, I'm stepping between them before I can stop myself. 'I'll take it from here.'

He looks at me, confused. 'Sir, I am to escort—'

'I'm aware. And I'm perfectly capable of making sure she gets to her room, don't you agree?'

'Yes, Your Majesty.' And with that, he tips his head towards Paedyn before striding from the room.

I glance at her myself, the look of confusion on her face mirroring the boy's. And then I turn and stroll out the doors, not waiting for her to catch up. She huffs before the quick click of her heeled boots begins echoing behind me.

'Why the sudden urge to be a gentleman?' she calls dryly from behind. I stop and spin on my heel, watching her as she walks towards me, my gaze briefly flicking over her.

'Don't get used to it,' I say with a quick smirk. 'My room just happens to be across from yours, so I might as well be a gentleman just this once.' I shove my hands into my pockets as we begin walking again, this time with her at my side. 'And why would a prince be staying in the contestants' wing of the palace?'

'Well, in case you haven't noticed, I too, am a contestant in the Trials.'

She huffs out a humorless laugh. 'Yes, I have happened to notice. But I thought the prince was supposed to have some grand room stocked full of servants who wait on him hand and foot?' Her question is accusing, lovely words laced with venom.

'Oh, don't worry, I have one of those too,' I reply coolly, hearing her scoff beside me. She's only partially right. I do have a grand room, though I refuse to let servants wait on me. 'All the contestants are to have the same living conditions before and during the Trials. That way, no one can accuse anyone else of being favored or having the upper hand.'

We stop outside her room where she turns to face me fully. She looks like she might laugh again, but when she speaks, her words are bitter. 'Just because we are all staying in similar rooms, doesn't mean others don't have the upper hand.'

I'm quiet as I consider her for a moment. If I were a Mundane thrown into the Trials, pitted against some of the strongest abilities Elites can have, I doubt I would feel any differently. Her power isn't something she can wield as a weapon like the rest of us. She's forced to rely on her own strength rather than the strength of an ability.

I suddenly think of how she fought the Silencer, so skilled and so sure of herself. Perhaps she has a better chance of surviving these games than she gives herself credit for.

I watch her gaze trail over my shoulder to the door I'm currently blocking. She opens her mouth to say something, drawing my attention to the healing split in her bottom lip.

On an impulse I couldn't seem to ignore, my fingers catch her chin and lift her face up towards mine. She's too stunned to move, and I take advantage of it. 'I would have thought you could avoid a direct hit like this. Guess you're not as skilled of a fighter as I thought.' I shrug and tilt her head towards the light, casually examining the angry cut in her lip.

Oh, but she's no longer standing there stunned, still, and silent.

In one swift movement, she grabs my wrist from under her chin and twists it outward with a jerk, sending a shooting pain up my arm. Then she's gripping my shirt and shoving me against the wall. Her free hand finds the dagger strapped to my hip and slips it out, settling the sharp blade against my throat.

'Would you like to find out just how skilled of a fighter I am?' She looks up at me coolly, amusement dancing in her eyes at the situation I'm currently in. She loves the sight of the prince pinned against a wall. And not just any prince: the future Enforcer.

I lean against the cool stone, laughing darkly as I slip my hands casually into my pockets. That only has her pressing the blade harder against my throat, threatening to draw blood.

Vicious little thing, isn't she?

'Careful, Highness. I wouldn't want to spill royal blood.' She's mocking me and it's an adorable attempt.

I lean towards her, letting the sharp steel of my own blade bite into my throat, drawing a thin line of hot blood. 'Careful, darling. You forget that spilling blood is what I do best.'

We stare at each other.

She's eying me with an expression I can't quite read, but she recovers quickly, diverting the conversation with ease. 'One of your Imperials did this to me.' She uncurls her fist from my shirt and gestures to her lip. 'Speaking of, did you ever ask him about me? I'm sure he had much to say.'

I had, and he did. After speaking with each Imperial assigned to the morning rotation, one mentioned his recent encounter with the Psychic. The man's disdain for Paedyn was more than obvious as he recapped what she had sensed from him.

And yet, he failed to mention how he'd hit her.

Perhaps I'll relieve him of one of his hands, so he never has the opportunity to lay it on a woman again.

'I spoke with him, yes,' I say quietly. 'Though it seems we may be having another conversation in the near future.' Her eyes flick over my face, making me feel abnormally and annoyingly anxious under her gaze. I clear my throat and look down towards the knife she still holds steadily against my neck. 'I thought we established that you *do* know who I am, correct?' The corner of my lips twists upward as I say it, remembering our encounter in the alley. When I had *her* pinned against a wall.

'I do,' she says, so close to me now that I can study all the different shades of blue in her eyes. 'I've said it before, and I'll say it again. A cocky bastard?'

I laugh, only making the dagger sink farther into my flesh.

'Besides, it doesn't matter who you are.' Her gaze drops to the floor briefly before fixing back on me. 'We are competing against each other now. No *favoritism*, remember? You said so yourself.'

Fine. I'll play along.

I slip a hand from my pocket and reach around her back, slowly, holding her gaze all the while. She looks at me, confusion written all over her face, though her hold on the knife is firm. She and I both know she won't actually slit my throat, so I'm not the least bit worried as I continue to wrap my arm behind her until my fingers brush against the cold handle of a dagger tucked into the band of her pants.

I knew it was there, saw the sun glint off the silver hilt when she stood from the dinner table, turning her back to me.

Smiling down at her, I slide out the dagger slowly, my fingers briefly brushing against her lower back. I think I hear the faintest gasp slip past her lips as I press her own knife to her throat, mirroring what she's doing to me.

'You're right. We are competing against each other now.' I laugh softly. 'Guess I better start trying then.'

We watch each other for a long moment. Her gaze is unwavering, reminding me of the still ocean, the calm before the storm. 'Mark my words, Prince, I will be your undoing.'

I lean in, ignoring the knife against my throat as I murmur, 'Oh, darling, I look forward to it.'

Far too much time passes. And then—

Slowly, surprisingly, she drops the knife from my throat.

I too lower my – her – dagger and place it in her expectant, outstretched hand. She moves to pull away, to leave me and this conversation, but I catch her wrist. She stills at my touch, and my eyes lock with hers as I guide her hand, and the knife clutched within it, to my chest. The blade lined with my own blood meets the fabric of my shirt, and her knuckles brush my chest as I wipe her dagger clean.

'So much for not spilling royal blood,' I sigh.

She exhales slowly. 'It was going to happen sooner or later.'

'So, I should get used to this?'

'You should expect this.'

I smile. 'Then I look forward to our next encounter.'

I wink and she rolls her eyes before slipping my dagger back into its sheath and returning her own into the band of her pants. And then she's brushing past my arm and heading for her door.

'Always a pleasure,' I say, striding to my own room across the hall.

'Unfortunately, I'm afraid I can't say the same.' I see the flash of a grin before she steps into her room, swinging the door shut behind her.

As soon as I'm on the other side of my own door, I'm pacing around the room that just so happens to be right across from hers. My fingers stray to my neck, feeling the sticky warmth of my blood there.

This girl might be the death of me. Literally.

CHAPTER 13
Paedyn

weat rolls down my forehead and clings to my lashes.

I am so out of shape.

After three long days of training, my body is sore and screaming at me to stop. My years of living on the streets have taken their toll, leaving me weaker than I realized despite my regular running from Imperials and scaling chimneys.

I lower my head and bring the hem of my dirt-stained tank to my eyes, huffing as I wipe the beads of sweat from my face. I'm filthy. And sadly, it's the most normal I've felt since I arrived at the palace.

A tall, padded tree looms before me, the indentations from my fists still visible in the rough cushions wrapping around the trunk. I've been in the training yard for hours now, along with the other contestants all doing various exercises or sparring against one another.

The yard is nothing like the crude, muddy ring I grew up training in. I turn and lean against the padded tree, sweeping my gaze across the dozen large rings dotting the grassy yard where most of my competition is currently residing.

Wide, wooden racks filled with weapons and shields, all new and waiting to be used, accompany each of the rings. I've never seen

anything like it. So many weapons at my disposal. So many weapons going to waste.

My eyes skim over the training yard. Everywhere I look, my fellow competitors are exercising, stretching, sparring, and just as dirty and drenched in sweat as I am. They all seem to avoid training with their abilities for the time being, likely waiting to put their powers on display until the interviews.

Just the mere thought has me anxiously spinning the ring on my thumb. This time tomorrow, we'll be showing off to the kingdom of Ilya while trying to win their favor. From the little I've learned from Ellie, the interviews are how the people choose who they want to support in the Trials. It's a time for the Elites to display their strength, talk themselves up, and try to earn the people's votes.

And that is exactly what I need to do: win the people over. They play a vital part in these twisted games, and the more votes a contestant gets, the more it boosts their score.

I sigh and breathe in the humid air, smelling of fresh grass, dirt, and more than a hint of sweat. I'm relieved to be training, to be doing something with my hands to keep my mind from wandering to dangerously detrimental thoughts. Such as the Trials and the possibility – the likelihood – of my impending death.

I'm yanked from my thoughts when my eyes land on tanned skin. With the afternoon sun beating down on us, the boys have long abandoned their sweaty shirts. And it's annoyingly . . . distracting, to say the least.

Kitt and Kai circle each other in a ring, smiling as they exchange words, seeming to be sparring verbally before they begin doing so physically. The brothers look comfortable, content in this moment together.

Though the future king isn't a contestant in the Trials, that doesn't seem to stop him from training and eating with us as though he is one. I've kept my distance from both the brothers and my other competitors, though the tension between all of us only grows with each passing day.

My gaze wanders back to the boys, tracing the identical dark tattoo swirling just above their hearts. Even from this distance, I can make out Ilya's symbol of strength etched into their skin.

The crest itself is simple, consisting of thick swirls all connected in a sideways diamond. It supposedly represents the different powers and how they all work together, while also representing the four landmarks that surround Ilya. There's Plummet Mount to the North, the Shallows Sea to the West, the Scorches Desert to the East, and the Whispers Forest to the South — all coming together to create a diamond around the city.

I blink and tear my eyes from the brothers before turning back towards the tree, suddenly feeling the urge to hit something again. I spin and land a solid kick into the thick pads, resounding in a satisfying *thunk*. Sweat rolls down my body in rivulets, even after stripping down to my thin tank, now damp and clinging to me uncomfortably. My slim, black pants are hot to the touch under the cooking sun, and I roll them nearly to my knees, tempted to tear the damn things off.

I hammer blows into the matted tree until my knuckles are red and raw before leaning my sweaty forehead against the cushion, panting slightly. The mat stifles my groan before I force myself to make my way to the closest weapons rack.

My fingers dance along the beautiful throwing knives lying innocently on the rack. The smoothness, the sheer sharpness of these knives has me itching to throw them. I turn my attention to the target ten yards ahead of me and begin burying several knives deep into the rough wood. I fall into a rhythm, letting my body relax with each knife I let fly. I feel focused. I feel dazed.

I missed this.

I let my mind wander, watching as the knives meet their mark. Suddenly, I'm standing in my backyard again, throwing small, measly blades into the rough bark of a tree. My father paces behind me, drilling me with questions. Questions about my surroundings, about things I should observe in seconds, even while my mind focuses on the blades sinking into their target.

I can almost hear my father's footsteps in the dirt behind me.

The familiar whoosh of a knife cutting through the air has me ducking instinctively, feeling the whisper of a blade above my head before looking up just in time to see it sink into the target.

110

A beautiful throw.

But I'm far too pissed to admire it. I draw up to my full height and whirl on my heel, eyes locking on the gray ones a few yards away.

He's the perfect picture of innocence: hands already in his pockets, hair ruffling in the breeze, and a lazy smirk on his lips. 'Good reflexes, Gray.'

That cocky son of a—

'What the *hell* is wrong with you?' I stomp towards Kai, closing the distance between us in a matter of seconds. 'What if I didn't duck, huh?'

He shrugs. *Shrugs.* 'Then, I would've had less competition to worry about.'

'So, you're admitting that I'm a threat to you?'

'I never said that.'

'But you implied it.'

'Don't flatter yourself.'

My chest heaves as I hold his gaze. A single dimple makes an appearance when he looks down at me, the corner of his mouth tilted in amusement. And with that, the urge to hit him only grows.

'I knew you'd duck, Gray,' he murmurs, his lips twitching with the use of my last name. A shiver runs down my spine despite the sun beating on my back when he leans even closer to whisper something in my ear.

But I never find out what it was he wanted to say.

A prick of pain pierces my ear, and I jerk in shock. I hear the thud of a knife hitting the target behind us and look up over Kai's shoulder to see Blair, hand outstretched. A smirk twists her red lips but her dark eyes flick between Kai and me.

I reach a hand to the shell of my ear where my fingers are quickly coated with sticky blood. She sent the knife flying into the target, but not before it left its mark on me.

She cut me. On purpose.

A muscle feathers in Kai's jaw, the only indication of his temper. He remains hovering over me, refusing to turn towards Blair while half blocking me from her with his body.

'Territorial, are we, Blair?' I say, looking from Kai to her blazing

111

gaze. She clearly didn't like the fact that the prince was giving someone else attention, even if that attention was him throwing a knife at my head. Maybe she's into that.

She ignores my question, voice smug. 'Just thought I would mark my target before the Trials begin.'

And then she spins on her heel and struts away, leaving me staring after her. I swallow, feeling smaller and weaker than I ever have before. Blair's display was a reminder of how easy it would be for any of these Elites to end my Ordinary life.

She marked me.

'You're getting blood in your hair, darling.'

My eyes snap to Kai still looming over me, now assessing my wound with his piercing gaze. I reach up, intending to tuck the hair behind my bloody ear when his hand catches my wrist.

'Don't,' he sighs, his calluses brushing my skin as he pulls my hand in front of my face and nods at my bloody fingers. 'Unless you wish to add more blood to your hair?'

I try not to gape at him, and that only makes his grin grow. 'Why are you . . . ?'

'Being a gentleman?' he finishes for me, sighing as though he doesn't quite know the answer himself. 'Let's just say I happen to know how difficult it is to wash blood out of hair, so I don't envy your current situation.' His eyes wander over my stinging wound and the blood I can feel dripping from it. Then he drops my wrist before gingerly tucking hair behind my ear, muttering, 'You're making a mess, Gray.'

I blink at him, vaguely wondering if a wound this shallow made me lose enough blood to have me hallucinating. Something must be horribly wrong because the future Enforcer just *gently* tucked hair behind my ear so it wouldn't get any bloodier than it already is.

'Turn around.'

The command snaps me back to reality.

There's that lovely future Enforcer.

His brows rise expectantly, waiting for me to obey the order. Instead, the words that fall out of my mouth are, 'And why would I do that?'

His voice is flat. 'Because I told you to.'

'And that is supposed to mean something to me?'

I am playing a very, very dangerous game.

He cracks a smile. 'Fine.' And then he's suddenly stepping behind me, muttering, 'Stubborn little thing.'

Rough fingers brush against the nape of my neck.

My breath catches as he casually pulls my hair into his hands, combing the strands out of my face and away from my bloody ear. 'What are you—?' I stop short, feeling the pattern he's gently weaving. 'Are you . . . *braiding* my hair?'

'Why do you sound so surprised?' he asks simply, unaware that my mouth is hanging open in shock. His voice is full of that cocky challenge as he says, 'What, do you need me to teach you how to?'

'No, I don't need you to teach—' I pause, taking a breath. 'How do you even know how to braid?'

He huffs out a laugh that stirs the hair at the back of my neck. 'You say that like it's supposed to be difficult.'

We're quiet for a moment, and the brush of his fingers traveling farther down my back has me stilling. I clear my throat. 'I thought you told me not to get used to you being a gentleman?'

I can practically hear the smirk in his voice when he says, 'And I still stand by that statement.'

'Then why are you doing this?'

He heaves a sigh. Fingers fall to my arm, and I almost jump at the sudden skim of his calluses. They stop on the strap wrapped around my wrist before slipping it off to begin securing my hair.

'There,' he says, stepping around to stand in front of me as he flicks the long braid over my shoulder. Then he gives it a tug, admiring his handiwork with a smile that displays his dimples.

I look down at the braid and stifle a snort at the sight of several strands sticking out. 'I thought this *wasn't* difficult for you?' I laugh as I say, 'You do know that *all* of the hair is supposed to make it into the braid, correct?'

'Odd way to say thank you, but I suppose that is the best I'll get from you.' He leans in closer, lips lifted into a mocking grin. 'Perhaps if you won't let me teach you how to braid, you'll consider letting me teach you some manners.'

I nearly choke on my scoff at the thought of the future Enforcer teaching me *manners*. His eyes skim over my ear before he takes a step away, slipping his hands into his pockets. 'You should get that healed up before the interviews tomorrow,' he says casually, nodding to my wound. 'We wouldn't want Blair's mark on you to scar.'

The sudden bite in those words has me stunned for a moment as I study him in the growing silence. 'No,' I finally manage, 'we wouldn't want that.'

His gaze sweeps over me again before he turns, tossing a smirk over his shoulder. 'Good luck tomorrow, Gray.'

I don't bother fighting my smile. 'If I had any manners, I would wish you luck as well, Prince. But you already informed me that I don't.'

He laughs, and the sound snakes down my spine as he continues to stride away. Without him to distract me, my ear stings furiously as I begin my trek back to the castle with one thought occupying me.

He never answered my question.

CHAPTER 14

Paedyn

The cool steel of my father's ring does little to comfort me as I spin it on my thumb.

Gentle fingers are gliding through my hair, pinning and pulling at the messy strands. Between Ellie's soothing touches and the plush vanity bench I'm currently slumped on, my drooping eyelids threaten to pull me back into restless sleep despite my reeling mind. Ellie must see the worry and weariness written all over my face because she offers me a sympathetic smile in the mirror.

'How are you feeling? You know, about the interviews?'

The constant spinning of my ring never slows though my nerves never calm. 'Well, I have no idea what to expect. And if it goes poorly . . .' I trail off as Ellie nods at me in the mirror, not needing me to finish that thought.

'Don't overthink it. You'll be fine,' she assures while continuing to pin up my hair. 'Besides, the people can't stop talking about the *Silver Savior*.'

The Silver Savior.

I nearly laugh at the name I've been bestowed. If they really knew why I was able to stop the Silencer, they wouldn't be calling me a savior anymore. In fact, they wouldn't be calling me anything, because

I would just become another dead Ordinary who doesn't deserve a name, a title, a memory.

An elegant low bun sits at the nape of my neck when Ellie finishes, sparkling pins holding it in place while silver ringlets surround my powdered face and darkened lashes.

After much deliberation, we settle on a sleeveless, light blue dress. Elegant, but not too flashy. 'You'll want to make a good impression, and I think this one will do the trick,' Ellie says with a smile. As soon as I've slipped into it, I'm being dragged over to the mirror so Ellie can admire her handiwork. Between the hair, makeup, and blue gown hugging my body, I almost look like I *belong* here. Like I haven't been sleeping on the streets for the past five years of my life.

A knock on the door startles me enough to stop staring at my reflection. 'You ready in there?'

Lenny is waiting outside the door when Ellie pushes me into the hallway, sneaking a shy glance at him before retreating into my room. He gives me an easy smile before leading us back to the main, massive doors of the castle and into the sunbathed courtyard beyond.

We're not alone. Most of the other contestants are tensely milling about while the rest slowly file out of the castle. Soon, Imperials are shuffling by, joining the group of us standing idly.

'What's going on?' I breathe to Lenny, still standing beside me.

'We,' he gestures to his fellow Imperials, 'are escorting you all to the Bowl.'

My eyes drift to the looming structure sitting innocently nearby. I'd never been to any of the contestants' interviews before, so I've never had the pleasure of packing into the arena stands alongside thousands of other Ilyans. It's been granted its unoriginal name due to the sloping, bowl-like shape of the large stadium that I never thought I'd step foot in. The group sets an easy pace as we make our way to the Bowl, Imperials flanking us on all sides. It's less than a mile from the palace, and I'm completely content to study my surroundings as we walk the gravel path. Twisted, drooping trees loom over us, oddly enchanting with the way the sun streams through their leaves to cast the ground beneath them in dappled light. Vibrant white and light pink flowers dot the branches while several of them flutter down, scattering the path with petals.

I let myself fall to the back of the group, watching my competition as they stride in front of me. All the boys wear some variation of slim pants and colored button-downs while the girls wear sleek but simple dresses.

Braxton and Sadie speak in hushed tones with hesitant smiles, while Andy keeps sticking out her foot to catch Jax's ankle, sending him stumbling while she snickers. My eyes sweep to Hera, quiet as she looks around in awe at the tunnel of trees enclosing the path. Ace, on the other hand, has his nose so high in the air that I doubt he can even see what's in front of him.

Finally, my gaze trails to the two tall figures striding at the front of the group. Kitt and Kai chuckle quietly, a seemingly common occurrence when the two of them are together. Once again, the future king blends in with the contestants, making me briefly wonder if he *wishes* he was a part of these twisted Trials.

Blair wedges herself between the two brothers, laughing at something one of them said. Both her lilac hair and shimmery navy dress gleam in the sun, giving the illusion of a constant spotlight following her. She uses any excuse to touch the boys, making her anything but subtle. She knows what she wants, and it's clear that it is one of them. I almost admire her resilience.

I walk quietly while watching the pink petals fall from the trees, drifting to the ground on a gentle breeze—

'I see you found something to wear.'

The deep voice beside me makes me jump, and I curse under my breath at the sudden sight of the future king beside me. He's chuckling at the stunned look on my face, and I fight the urge to shove him for startling me like that. I take a deep breath before meeting his green gaze, the color matching the leaves hanging above us – matching the color of his father's eyes.

The king's eyes.

The sudden realization has me faltering. I force myself to swallow my disgust towards this man and the corrupt kingdom he will rule in his father's likeness. Taking a deep breath, I remind myself to be civil, polite.

Play the part.

'Yes, but I can't take all the credit.' I look down at my light blue dress, billowing in the soft breeze. 'I have Ellie to thank for this.'

'Ah, yes.' The future king's grin is teasing, startling me. 'Ellie, the maid you insisted you didn't need?'

'That's the one,' I reply dryly. 'You know, I thought she liked me, but it seems she wants to torture me with these shoes.' I can already feel my feet beginning to blister in the too-tight, strappy sandals Ellie insisted I wear.

He laughs again, a bright and contagious sound that manages to make me uneasy. 'I don't envy you or the blisters you'll likely have.' A small smile curves his lips as he gestures to me. 'But it suits you nonetheless.'

'Thank you . . .' The words come out sounding more like a question than I intended.

I always assumed the future king would be cold, calculating – more like his brother at the very least. But Kitt seems to be quite the opposite, which confuses me, considering who his father is and what his future holds.

Lost in thought, I look up to see the giant silhouette of the Bowl looming closer, awaiting us at the end of the tree tunnel. It's enormous. Other than the castle, I've never seen a structure so large.

I feel something land on top of my head and practically jump out of my skin. Kitt barks out a laugh as he reaches over and plucks the thing from my hair, making me flinch. The action doesn't go unnoticed, and his brows crinkle with concern.

I'm not playing the part very well.

Wiping my face of the anxiety I'm sure is written all over it, I try to manage a weak smile as I stare down at the pink flower he now twirls between his fingers. I glance up, catching sight of several petals clinging to Kitt's messy hair.

'You know,' he says softly, plopping the flower back on top of my head, 'this also suits you.'

I take a deep breath and force a stronger smile. 'I could say the same about you,' I say, pointing at his blond hair full of petals. He returns my grin as he runs a hand through it, doing little to rid his hair of the flowers creating a crown atop his head.

'Well, now we're matching,' he says simply, his eyes watchful. I look away, still feeling his gaze roaming over my face as I try my hardest to look calm, collected.

'You look . . .' He pauses, trying to find the right word. 'Anxious.'

So much for calm and collected.

I offer him a quick smile that doesn't reach my eyes. 'Well, let's hope anxiety suits me as well.'

'Is it the interviews that have you nervous, or is it something else?' His words are soft, curious.

Concerning.

My gaze slides to his before quickly looking away at the sight of the king's eyes staring back at me. 'Just the interviews, and the possibility that I'll make a fool out of myself.'

'You'll be fine. Especially after your . . . incident with my brother in Loot.' He gives me that charming grin of his. 'You know the people are still talking about you.'

I'm about to respond when my face is suddenly bathed in sunlight. I hadn't realized the tunnel of trees had ended, leaving me blinking rapidly in the blinding light.

But the sun is gone as quickly as it came. The group quiets when we step into the shadow cast by the Bowl. We make our way into one of the many large, cement tunnels leading into the arena, our footsteps echoing off cold stone walls until we are spit out onto the lowest level of the stadium.

My head swivels back and forth, eyes wide as I take it all in. Wrapping around the entire oval arena are dozens of wide rows covered in concrete benches that climb up the side of the Bowl. My eyes sweep over the thick glass encasing each section of the stands.

No, not glass.

Mute.

I've only briefly learned of the rare material invented by the Scholars, let alone seen it myself. By means that are far too complicated for me to understand, this glass look-alike prevents the Elites within the stands from using their powers, so as not to interfere with the Trials.

I tear my eyes away from the odd phenomenon and continue perusing the Bowl with my wide gaze. Though we stand at ground level beside the bottom row of benches, the sand-packed arena lies below us. I walk over to the thick, metal railing at the edge of the path and look down. It's easily a fifteen-foot drop to the arena floor below us, packed with sand.

The Pit.

And that is where the Trials will take place while hundreds of Ilyans watch from the stands encircling us.

The Imperials begin herding us along the path until we come to a stop beside a wide room jutting out into the pathway, surrounded by thick glass. Peering inside, I can see three large and luxurious chairs, all sitting on a polished wood floor and looking so at odds with the gray, cold concrete covering the rest of the Bowl.

The king's box.

So this is where he sits comfortably and watches us die.

To my surprise, the Imperials begin pushing us into the glass room, one by one. We all file into a line and watch as Kai strides to the far corner. I crane my neck to see him lift a hidden latch from the floor, swinging open a trapdoor before jumping down easily.

A hand on my shoulder urges me forward.

Where are we going?

I walk through the stuffy room and make my way to the hole in the floor that awaits me. The room beneath is cast in shadows, making it impossible to see how far down the floor is.

I sigh before stepping off the edge and into the darkness.

My feet hit the ground with a soft thud. After estimating that the drop was nearly seven feet, I'm thankful that the ground beneath my sandals is plush. But with the shifting mat beneath me and my bent knees to lessen the impact of the drop, I can't help but stumble forward into something solid.

No. Not something. *Someone.*

Strong arms wrap around me before I feel the rumble of deep laughter coming from the broad chest I slammed into. Large hands are placed firmly on my hips and as my eyes adjust to the darkness, I can just make out the familiar curve of a smirk on Kai's lips as he looks down at me.

'Sloppy footwork, Gray. I'd hate to be your partner on the dance floor.'

I push against his chest with my palms, and he reluctantly releases me, laughing darkly. 'Well then the feeling is mutual.' I'm flustered and I hate it. 'And I have fabulous footwork, thank you very much—' I clear my throat, averting my gaze before adding quietly, '—when fighting.'

He's right, once again. And once again, I hate it. I *am* a disastrous dancer. I may be able to dance around in a brawl, but that skill doesn't extend to the ballroom.

He laughs again, but before he has the chance to make some sly comment that I would most definitely make him regret, Kitt drops down beside me.

'Toying with your competition, Brother?' I can hear the amusement in his voice as he walks over to a large lever on the wall and jerks it upward. The lights above us flicker and hum to life, painfully reminding me of home and the few buzzing lamps that scatter Loot Alley.

'I can't help but toy with the competition that's fun to play with,' Kai replies with a sloppy shrug.

I'm about to say something I likely shouldn't when our conversation comes to a halt as the rest of the Elites quite literally fall into the room. Looking around, I find the space filled with plushy chairs and couches along with an assortment of snacks sprawled out on a long table, making it clear that we are waiting here until the interviews start.

Everyone mills about the room, dropping into chairs and grabbing food. I feel a brush of a hand on my shoulder and startle, spinning around to meet a pair of amused, honey eyes hiding behind strands of wine-red hair.

'Jumpy, aren't you?' Andy quirks a brow.

'Yes, well, I thought you were Kai and was preparing to break your nose.'

She snorts loudly. 'Understandable. My cousin's an ass. Kinda.' She jerks her head towards Kai, but the smile doesn't fade from her face.

'Your . . .' I blink. 'Cousin?'

'Yep. He's lucky enough to be related to me.' She smirks, her nose ring winking in the dim light. 'They both are.'

'So, you grew up in the palace too? With them?' I nod my head towards the boys who look to be mercilessly teasing Jax.

'Yeah, unfortunately.' She shakes her head and chuckles. 'The number of fights those two have gotten into over food . . .' She trails off, smiling to herself. 'Anyways, I'm what they call a *handy* back at the palace. My dad and I fix anything that needs fixing in the castle, and trust me, those two have broken a lot over the years.'

Eventually, we find our way to one of the couches and plop down, talking hesitantly. We're polite with each other, content to have a civil conversation while still being very aware of the fact that we are competitors.

The thundering sound of hundreds of stomping feet quiets us all. The rumble fills the arena above, making my stomach twist. They're here. Hundreds of Ilyans – thousands, even. All here to watch the interviews, the show. Here to choose who they want to support, who they want to live.

I'm not sure how long it takes for the parade of footsteps climbing up the rows to quiet. But the voices don't. They chant and cheer, waiting for the contestants to show themselves. The Imperials beckon us back towards the trapdoor where I suddenly find myself in another line, waiting my turn to pull myself out of the room and back into the glass box above us.

I hadn't even noticed the future king beside me until he reaches up to pull something from my hair. I don't even have time to flinch before he's holding a flower in front of my face – the one I had forgotten was tangled in the silver strands.

'Although I think it suits you, maybe you shouldn't do your interview with this on your head.' He gestures to the flower with a smile. 'You might attract a lot of attention. Especially from bees.'

Play the part.

That's what I must keep telling myself. Because every time I look at him, all I can see is his father, and a man who will one day rule over a corrupt kingdom. And yet, despite my disgust, I force a smile to my face. 'Thank you. For saving me from both embarrassment and bees.'

Braxton steps beneath the exit, and I'm thankful for the excuse to look away from the future king. The Brawny doesn't even need to jump to grab hold of the lip before easily pulling himself off the floor and through the trapdoor. One by one, the boys help themselves up into the room above until only the two princes remain.

They help the girls up with ease, practically lifting Hera through the opening. Blair takes advantage of the situation, using it as an excuse to have the boys' hands all over her. After Sadie politely asks for a boost, I'm left alone with the brothers.

I look up through the trapdoor, assessing my jump when Kai steps behind me, ducking his head so his chin nearly rests on my shoulder. 'Too stubborn to ask for my help, Gray?'

'No,' I say coolly. 'Too strong to need it.'

His next words are murmured close to my ear. 'That's what I like to hear.'

The heat of him vanishes when he steps to the side, gesturing to the trapdoor above with a smile twisting his lips.

I jump, my fingers curling around the edge of the opening as I dangle in the air for a moment. I've never been more grateful for the many years I've had to practice scaling buildings. I pull myself up, ready to swing my legs over—

'This damn dress,' I huff. It's stiff, the fabric hugging my hips making it impossible to move freely.

'Go on.' It's Kai's taunting voice I hear behind me. 'Ask for my help, Gray.'

I roll my eyes at the wall in front of me. 'Stubborn, remember?'

I hear Kitt chuckle before I feel hands brushing my legs. Startled, I look down, eyes landing on a bent head of messy black waves. Kai is gripping the bottom seam of my dress, his eyes flicking up to mine.

'May I?' His voice is soft, tone amused.

I swallow, roll my eyes once again, and nod against my better judgment.

And then he's ripping my dress.

He tears the fabric easily, creating a slit up the side of my thigh, freeing me from the tight confines of the fabric. His rough fingers briefly brush my skin as he says, 'I am more than willing to rip your dresses for you, Gray. To help, of course.' Kitt snorts while Kai smirks. 'You only need to ask.'

'Why ask when you're so eager to offer?'

123

Kai's laughter follows me as I finally pull myself up, arms burning with the strain. When I stand to my feet inside the glass box, I'm relieved to find the chairs are still empty. The thought of seeing the king after the way he so flippantly spoke about my father as if he wasn't his murderer makes my blood boil. Before that dinner, I'd never had to fight the urge to shove a fork through someone's jugular.

I take a deep breath before stepping out onto the pathway. The crowd roars.

Here we are.

The Imperials lead us to a small opening in the railing opposite the box, where stairs have been placed for us to get into the Pit below. My feet hit the hard sand of the arena as the crowd cheers, sounding as though the Trials have already begun.

We walk across the large floor of the Pit, stopping in the middle where a makeshift stage rises a few feet off the ground. Ten plush chairs line the back of it while two more are centered in front. The Imperials usher us onto the stage where we take a seat. My gaze catches Lenny's, and he gives me a reassuring nod before stepping into line with the other Imperials.

'Welcome, fellow Ilyans, to the sixth ever Purging Trials!'

The crowd roars as I snap my head towards the high, female voice. She turns to face us, brown eyes bright with excitement and full, red lips curved into a smile as she takes us in.

Tealah.

Ironic that her bright teal hair matches her name. I'd never seen the young woman who conducted the interviews for the previous Trials, but I've heard enough about her unique appearance to identify her.

'Oh, but this is no ordinary Trials!' She beams at the crowd, flashing her white teeth. 'For the first time in Purging Trials history, we have a future Enforcer competing.' I can almost feel the thousands of eyes shift in Kai's direction. He's clearly used to this attention, appearing completely relaxed as he reclines in his chair.

Tealah continues, 'And because of that, this year's Trials will look a little . . . different.'

The crowd goes wild.

Ellie's words echo in my head, mirroring the ones Tealah just spoke. *Different.*

All because there is royal blood competing? All to make things more difficult for the future Enforcer?

I don't have time to ponder it more before Tealah says, 'Are you ready to meet your Elites?' She flattens her hand to her chest as she speaks, causing her words to carry across the arena. Her ability as an Amplifier allows her to project her voice, as well as the voices of others, so long as she is touching them. A Mundane power, yet useful in this line of work.

The crowd cheers and stomps, mimicking the rumble of thunder. 'Why don't we meet Jax first? Jax, sweetie, would you come sit up here with me?'

Jax plops down in the chair angled towards Tealah at the front of the stage with a shy smile on his face. He fidgets, one of his long legs bouncing on the ground as she pelts him with idle questions about his life and the Trials.

'Er, I like sparring with Kitt. Mostly because he lets me win sometimes. Kai . . . not so much.' The crowd erupts in laughter at Jax's response to what he likes most about training for the Trials. He smiles sheepishly at Tealah, his grin widening when he shifts in his seat to spot Kai's quick shrug.

'Isn't he just adorable?' Tealah flashes a smile at the crowd before asking, 'Tell me, Jax, how old are you again?'

Tealah's hand rests on his shoulder, amplifying his answer. 'Fifteen.'

Plagues, he's so young.

'Fifteen and already bestowed the honor of competing in the Trials!' Tealah exclaims, looking towards the crowd for approval which they offer in the form of stomps and cheers. 'And remind us again of your power?'

He clears his throat. 'I'm a Blink.'

'How fascinating! Tell us more for those who haven't witnessed this ability.'

'Well,' he straightens in his seat, 'I can teleport anywhere that I can see, in a . . . well, in a blink.' He smiles as the audience laughs.

'Alright, Jax, one more question before you show us what you can do.' Tealah looks suddenly serious as she says, 'What are you expecting from the Trials?'

Jax's head tilts to the side thoughtfully. 'Well, I'm not sure what the Trials will consist of, but no matter what, I'm expecting to honor my kingdom, my family . . .' He pauses and tosses a glance at Kai. 'And myself.'

The stadium explodes in applause at hearing the motto of the Purging Trials. Tealah stands and guides Jax down the steps of the stage and onto the packed sand of the Pit in front of us.

'The floor is all yours, Jax!'

One second, Jax is grinning at the audience, and the next he's gone. I spin in my seat to see where he went, only to find him standing right behind Kai, a mischievous grin on his face. He ruffles his hair before vanishing, leaving the prince sputtering.

Jax continues his little routine, Blinking from one spot to the next, causing the crowd to gasp in surprise at each new place he appears in. After a few minutes, he Blinks back to his original seat, right between Kai and Braxton, where the former doesn't hesitate to trap him in a headlock and mercilessly ruffle his hair.

Tealah continues her own routine of questioning the contestants before letting them loose to show off their abilities, following the same pattern.

It's nothing but a talent show. A showcase of who is the strongest.

Braxton smashes and hurtles stone statues that have been scattered across the stadium for him. After Ace's interview, where he spoke as though he'd already won the Trials, he strode down into the Pit, pompous as ever. The illusions he casts look so real, so easy to mistake for reality. He made fire flare, burning across the sand in a trail of flame, managing to even smell of smoke. And then it was gone in a flash as quickly as it had appeared, leaving nothing behind.

Sadie, being a Cloner, displayed her power by creating ten copies of herself and striding them through the stands. Each duplicate offered quick waves to the crowd before filing back to her seat.

Blair followed Sadie's interview, being annoyingly sweet towards Tealah and the crowd, though I don't miss the sharpness return to her voice when talking about winning the Trials. She stepped out onto the packed sand and gently lifted Tealah right off the ground using her power of Telekinesis, informing me that her strength lies mentally rather than physically. In fact, the blade that sliced my ear only yesterday was likely thrown by her power, not her hand.

Hera was shy, squirming in her seat and only talking when necessary. I could practically see her sigh in relief when she was finally free to show off her ability and avoid talking to the audience. She vanishes, and after a moment, Tealah vanishes too. The crowd applauds, left staring at the empty air where they once stood.

Andy was the most entertaining by far, unashamedly telling embarrassing stories about her childhood with Kitt and Kai. The crowd loved her, laughed at her every word. But when she stepped out onto the floor of the Pit to display her power, my gasp was swallowed up by the crowds. Right before my very eyes, she transformed into a tiger. Then a falcon. A wolf. All of them the same wine color of her hair. And then, after casually switching between multiple animals, she transformed back into her human self, her lilac dress somehow still perfectly intact.

Tealah chooses Kai next, leaving me for last.

Great.

With Kai smiling at her, Tealah looks flushed and flustered. It's clear he's slipped on his charming mask as he jokes and interacts with the crowd. When Tealah asks him about what he's expecting from the Trials, his answer is the same as all the other contestants before him: Honor to my kingdom, my family, and myself.

When the prince finally finishes, he flashes a grin at the blushing Tealah before stepping right off the stage to showcase his power. Well, everyone else's powers. He goes right down the line of contestants, using each of their abilities and wooing the audience with them. Their powers seem easy to him, familiar, the result of many years of training.

When he comes to the end of the row, his eyes meet mine. His head cocks slightly to the side as he takes me in, gray gaze wandering over my face. I can't imagine how much it must rattle him to not be able to use my *ability*, and the thought brings a small smile to my lips as I look down at him.

Then Kai is back in his chair, and I'm striding towards my doom. 'And lastly, we have Paedyn Gray!' Tealah's voice echoes through the arena as she pats the seat beside her expectantly.

Play the part.

CHAPTER 15

Paedyn

My palms are slick with sweat. I sit down in the seat beside Tealah and smooth out the skirt of my dress, if only for an excuse to wipe my sweaty hands on the smooth silk. I look up into the audience, and my breath catches. I'm embarrassed that I hadn't observed them before, but now I can't seem to tear my eyes away.

The king and queen and . . .

Kitt.

They stare down at me from their snug, glass box. The king and his heir sit close together, their similarities striking me like a blow to the chest. Their sandy hair and emerald eyes mirror one another, looking so alike that my hatred for one begins to bleed into the other.

'So, Paedyn, tell us about your incident with Prince Kai!' My eyes trail back to Tealah's, nearly blinded by her gleaming white teeth and vibrant hair. She leans towards me and places a soft hand on my shoulder, projecting my voice for all to hear.

'Well, according to Prince Kai, there's not much to tell. But if you ask me, I think he's a little embarrassed that a girl from the slums had to come to his rescue.' The words tumble out of my mouth before I can stop them.

Plagues, I need the people to like me and mocking their prince is probably not the best way to—

Laughter.

To my surprise, and saving grace, the audience finds me amusing. I peek over my shoulder at Kai and watch the ghost of a smile grace his features.

So, maybe I can bash their prince after all. I can work with that.

'Not afraid to tell it like it is!' Tealah laughs softly before moving on to the next question – the one I'm sure many are wondering. 'So, tell us again how is it that you were able to fight off the Silencer? I mean, it's clear you can hold your own in a physical fight, but how come the Silencer didn't affect you?'

I take a deep breath, knowing that this detail is very important for everyone to understand, to *believe.* 'Well, Tealah, I'm a Psychic. It's a mental ability that allows me to sense strong emotions from others and get flashes of information. And because of that, I have the power to guard my head, keep it safe from people like the Silencers.' I smile slightly before adding, 'And apparently, people like Prince Kai, since he can't use or sense my small ability.'

'How fascinating! I must say, I've never met a Psychic before!' Her eyes are wide, looking very intrigued with me, as I'm sure the rest of the crowd is.

'Yes, well, despite it being a Mundane ability, it does seem to be quite rare.' I smile brightly as if I'm not lying through the teeth I'm flashing at her.

'Alright, Paedyn, tell us about your life in the—' she stutters, almost saying *slums* before choosing to say, '—in Ilya?'

I contemplate lying some more, saying how it wasn't that bad, how it was easy living in the slums. But it seems I suddenly have the urge to be honest.

'You mean, life in the *slums*?' She blinks at me, surprised by my blunt correction. 'There's not much to tell. Life on the streets isn't much of a life at all.' I look her right in the eyes before turning to face the hushed crowd. 'These past few years, hunger and cold have been the only constant in my life. But it's not just me. There are dozens of others who sleep on the same hard cobblestone I did. Dozens of others

130

who will do anything for a single shilling.' I pause and take a breath. 'Living in the slums is survival of the fittest. So, in a way, I'm more prepared for these Trials than anyone.'

Tealah stares at me in shock, clearly not expecting that answer. Then something like pity gleams in her brown eyes. I hate it. I don't want her or the crowd's pity. I want *change*.

She quickly moves on to more light-hearted questions about training and my fellow contestants. 'Who do you think will be your biggest competition?'

'Hmm.' I tuck a strand of hair behind my ear, contemplating my answer.

'Perhaps Prince Kai? Seeing that he has the ability to use any power?' Tealah offers.

'Not mine, remember?' I laugh lightly and so does she. 'He won't be a problem. In fact, we'll see how far he makes it in these Trials without me there to save him.' I smile sweetly as the crowd roars with laughter, practically feeling Kai's eyes burning a hole into the back of my head.

'Alright, Paedyn, last question. What do you expect to get out of the Trials?'

My mouth opens, intending to spew out the practiced motto of the Purging Trials like everyone else had. Like I'm *supposed* to do. But when my eyes lock on the glass box above me, lock on the current and expected king, words fall out of my mouth before I can bite my tongue.

The *wrong* words.

'Survival. I expect to survive this.'

I can feel thousands of eyes pinned on me.

Tealah manages a slow blink while wisps of teal hair blow across her face in the soft breeze. Finally, she clears her throat and stands stiffly to guide me down the stage.

'Alright then,' she tries to act natural as she says, 'show us what you can do!'

Now I'm blinking at her.

How the hell am I supposed to do that?

'Um,' I look around the stadium as I say, 'why don't you choose a random person from the crowd, and I'll . . . I'll read them.'

What the Plagues am I talking about?

Tealah smiles and nods, clearly happy to go do something. I watch as she climbs the steps out of the Pit and begins walking down the rows of people, smiling and waving as she goes. After a few minutes of contemplation, she finally points to a young girl seated a few rows above. The poor girl looks concerningly confused but cautiously stands before making her way down into the Pit, guided by Tealah.

When she approaches me warily, I realize she can't be much older than I am. Her short brown hair paired with the freckles splattering her face grant her a constant look of innocence. I smile and reach out to take her hands, wanting to make a show of this.

'Don't worry. I won't bite,' I say softly when she takes a slight step back. I offer her what I hope is a warm smile, and with that, she slowly holds her tan hands out to me. Grasping them gently in my own, I quickly observe her before squeezing my eyes shut.

I have everything I need.

I think of the tarnished chain around her neck, paired with the faded, large ring hanging from it that was just barely visible behind the folds of her shirt. I'd kept my father's ring after he died too, only I wear mine on my thumb. 'I'm sensing . . . grief. You,' I squeeze her warm hands, taking a deep breath, 'you lost a man that was very close to you. A while ago. Your father?'

I open my eyes to see her mouth hanging open. 'Yes,' she says quietly, even with Tealah's hand on her shoulder to amplify her voice. 'Yes, he died four years ago.'

'I'm so sorry for your loss. I know what it is like to lose a father.' I keep my eyes locked on hers, though I desperately want to glare up at the king in his shiny box.

A collective gasp echoes through the crowd, amazed that I could know such a personal detail.

And they want more.

Tealah selects person after person to come down into the Pit, each one more excited to be *read* than the last. I spout random and personal things about them, things that a stranger shouldn't know.

'You just found out you are pregnant—'

132

'Your father is a blacksmith—'

'You stole the shoes you're wearing—'

Every time, both the person I read and the crowd above us are in awe.

They gasp, clap, and cheer – a completely captivated audience.

Plagues, if I knew people liked this so much, I would have charged for readings on the street.

A lanky young man now stands before me, a grin lighting up his face as he stares down expectantly. Closing my eyes, I recall the faint ring of dirt clinging to the right knee of his pants as he walked towards me. That, combined with the subtle outline of a small box in his coat pocket and the happy glow on his face means I come to my conclusion in a matter of seconds.

'I'm sensing joy. Because . . .' I release one of his hands to press my fingers to my temple. 'You just got engaged. Today.' I open my eyes just in time to see his mouth fall open.

'Yes! She's right! I just proposed less than two hours ago!' He spins to face the crowd, a wide smile on his face as the audience goes wild.

'Congratulations!' My shout is swallowed by the cheering crowd as he practically skips up the stairs to return to his seat. With that, I spin on my heel and head back to my chair, not waiting for another person to come striding down for me to read.

'Here,' Tealah sweeps an arm behind her, gesturing to us, 'are your contestants for the sixth ever Purging Trials!' Her voice echoes across the stadium only to be quickly drowned out by the crowd.

The contestants around me stand, and I do the same. We wave and smile at the crowd, watching as they chant, stomp, and pump their fists in the air.

I feel sick. I feel used.

This is all a game to them.

But if I want to stay alive, I have to play my part. I have to play *them*. Being a pawn in their game is the price I have to pay to survive. Make them believe I like this, and in turn, they will like me.

So I straighten, holding my head a little higher as I smile a little brighter.

I am no one's pawn.

CHAPTER 16

Kai

Blood clings to my hands, my clothes, staining everything a sickening red. Torturing tends to be a messy occupation, and despite how many years of practice I've had, it never seems to get any easier. Or cleaner.

Unlike Kitt, who has been trained since childhood to be poised, just, and kingly, my training has consisted of more *hands-on* work. Battle strategies, assassinations, and the art of torture made up much of my education. And due to this unique and extensive training I've received, I am very good at what I do.

Except, it seems, when it comes to the Silencer cowering on the dungeon floor before me. It's been days. I've beaten this man to a bloody pulp, and what have I learned in return?

Nothing.

To say that I'm pissed would be an understatement. The only useful word I've gotten him to slip past his lips, besides the splitting screams and pleas, is what I'm assuming is his name.

Micah.

I sigh, crouching down to hover over his broken, bloody body. His long hair, matted with blood, falls into his deep brown eyes. They widen when they meet mine, making him look so young. He can't be

more than a few years my senior.

'Now, correct me if I'm wrong,' I say, deceptively soft, 'but I don't believe you're mute.' I grab his jaw and pry it open to reveal the blood pooling in his mouth, over his tongue, staining his teeth scarlet. 'But I could easily make that happen. I could carve out your tongue.'

I drop his head to the stone floor and stand to leave, aware that I'm already late for dinner. Slamming the door to the cell behind me, I offer Damion a curt nod. He gives me a slow bow of his head in return before following me down the long hallway of cells.

Our footsteps echo off the stone walls as we make our way up the stairs and into the bright, sun-filled hallway above the dungeons. I deftly head to the throne room even while my mind wanders.

The Trials are quickly approaching with only four days separating us from the first deadly game. These past few days have followed the same routine of training, eating, talking, and torturing. And well, toying with Paedyn. She's been my main source of entertainment as of late. *She's* entertaining. With her wit and stubbornness and obvious annoyance with me—

Stop.

I push thoughts of Paedyn from my mind as I stride through the large doors of the throne room. My hands find their way to my pockets, casual despite how very aware I am that my navy shirt splotched with blood does not quite fit the dress code for dinner.

The servants have already brought food to the table, which everyone sitting around it is greedily enjoying. Heads turn when they hear my shoes on the polished floor, several pairs of eyes flicking from my face to the blood clinging onto my clothes. I ignore their stares, seeing that I was too tired to change and too hungry to care.

'Ah, Kai. Glad you could make it.' Father sounds peeved, per usual, as I take my seat.

'Honey,' Mother says quietly, leaning towards me, 'you look a little . . . well, bloody.' She cringes as her eyes roam over me, assessing her son.

'Occupational hazard, Mother.' I give her a small smile, the sweet one I reserve for only her. She nods hesitantly before trying to relax back into her chair.

I barely listen to the quiet chatter carrying on around me. I'm finishing the last of my beans when an incessant tapping has me looking up.

Strands of Paedyn's silver hair fall around her face in loose curls, the rest of it tied back into a messy knot at the nape of her neck. Her eyes are pinned to her plate, her thumb and silver ring tapping a steady beat against the wooden table.

And then those ocean eyes slide up to mine.

I tip my head towards her drumming thumb. 'Is there something on your mind, Gray?'

She looks me over as if noticing my presence for the first time. 'Is there something on your shirt, Azer?' Her eyes skim over my clothes before widening slightly. 'Is that . . . blood?'

I'm sure I imagine the flash of worry on her face, the look of concern when she thinks it may be my own blood staining the shirt. 'Careful, darling. You almost look as if you care.' I give her a lazy smile, and she gives me a lazy eye roll.

My gaze snaps to Mother when her gentle voice cuts through my thoughts. 'I hope you all have begun pairing up for the first ball!'

I glance around the table. Only the three who haven't previously lived in the castle look slightly confused. Hera, Ace, and Paedyn haven't grown up watching these balls, haven't even *been* to a ball. I envy them.

'As is tradition,' Mother continues, 'the contestants will partner up for the balls that are held before each Trial. And since there is an odd number of you, whoever does not have a partner will be paired with someone, don't worry.' Her smile somehow grows wider as she says, 'So choose your date and get practicing your dance steps.'

Kitt shifts beside me, and I see him quickly glance in Paedyn's direction. I run a hand through my hair before turning my attention back on my food, needing to focus on something.

Since the girls outnumber the boys, it's likely that Kitt will be paired with whoever doesn't have a partner. But that won't stop him from asking one of them if he wishes to.

It's clear that Paedyn intrigues him. But even if Kitt wasn't going to ask Paedyn to accompany him to the ball, which I don't doubt he will, she doesn't want me.

I like a challenge.

But she's made it abundantly clear on what she wishes us to be: competition.

Enemies.

And more importantly, why isn't that what I want as well?

I wake the next morning, drenched in sweat.

This isn't uncommon, not with the nightmares that tend to haunt my sleep. But today is different. Today it is bloody boiling outside. It's only dawn, and my room is already sticky with humidity.

I roll out of bed and make my way to the bathroom where I splash cool water over my already damp face. It doesn't take me long to get ready, begrudgingly pulling on a white cotton shirt before slipping out the door and—

And there she is.

She steps out of her room with her head down, quietly shutting the door before looking up and practically jumping at the sight of me.

'Plagues, Kai, don't scare me like that!' I blink.

It's the first time she's called me by my name, and I realize then that I could get used to the sound of it rolling off her tongue. She seems to notice what she's said and clears her throat before beginning to walk down the hallway.

'Aren't you up early for a prince?' she calls over her shoulder. 'What, no breakfast in bed?' I catch up to her easily, taking about three strides before I'm walking beside her.

'If you're not getting breakfast in bed, neither am I. I'm just a regular contestant, remember? No longer a charming prince for the time being.'

'You were never that to begin with.'

I chuckle as we turn the corner, spotting the kitchen looming just ahead. The smell of biscuits and eggs wafting from within is enough to make me change course.

'So—' Paedyn begins, probably the start of some snide comment that I'll never get the pleasure of hearing because I grab her wrist and tug her towards the kitchen doors. I'm sure she is just as hungry as I am, and breakfast won't be served for nearly another hour.

I'm doing us both a favor.

Apparently, Paedyn doesn't share my sentiment. Her feet dig into the floor at the threshold of the kitchen doors, eyes darting between mine. 'What are you—' she starts, giving me that murderous look I've already grown so familiar with.

'Shh.' I press my finger to her lips lightly and the words die in her throat. 'I suppose my job will forever be feeding you now, hmm, Gray?' Her flustered expression has me laughing quietly before I hear the scuff of shoes, reluctantly drawing my gaze from her wide-eyed one. We've drawn quite the crowd. Several servants stand staring at us, taking in the scene before them. But they scuttle away swiftly, snickering as they try to make themselves look busy.

'Hello, ladies,' I call, looking around the room at the blushing servants. 'I've brought a far more interesting guest today than Kitt.' I place a gentle hand on the small of Paedyn's back, prodding her forward.

It's a question, a tentative test, an innocent inquiry.

Is this okay?

I briefly wonder if she's considering breaking my wrist, maybe contemplating placing a dagger to my throat—

And then she relaxes, easing into my touch.

An answer to my question without uttering a word.

Yes.

I guide her towards the center of the kitchen where I've spotted Gail, currently hunched over the stove. 'Morning Gail.' She spins around, her face lighting up when she sees me. 'You look lovely as always.' My mouth quirks as I hop up onto the counter and sit beside where she flips crispy pieces of bacon over the stove.

'You're such a kiss-ass, Kai,' she teases, lightly whipping a towel in my direction. Her eyes land on Paedyn and she straightens, nodding curtly. 'Ah, Miss Paedyn. A pleasure.'

'Please,' Paedyn sighs with a small smile, 'No *miss*. Just Paedyn.'

I can practically see Gail relax, probably thanking the Plague that formalities aren't needed. 'Now, what is a sweet girl like you doing hanging around riffraff like him?' Gail jabs a thumb in my direction while I snatch a strip of bacon from the pan behind her turned back.

I let out a low laugh. 'Oh, *sweet* isn't the word I would use to describe her, Gail. She held a knife to my throat only a few days ago.'

'He deserved it,' Paedyn says simply, shrugging slightly.

'Oh, I'm sure he did,' Gail replies, grinning at her. 'I probably would have done the same.' She glances at me, nodding towards Paedyn. 'I like this one.'

Paedyn tips her head back and laughs. My body goes still as I listen to the sound of it fill the kitchen. So warm, so bright. Then, too quickly, she collects herself, clears her throat, and turns towards me. 'So, you and Kitt are close with Gail?'

My head tilts to the side as I peer down at her, my eyes never straying from hers as I say, 'Inseparable, aren't we Gail?'

A loud snort escapes the cook. 'Inseparable indeed. The princes won't leave me alone.' Her eyes sparkle with pride when they meet mine. 'I'm the only reason the two of them aren't stick-thin.'

'Ah, yes,' I sigh, 'we have Gail's sticky buns to thank for fattening us up.'

After Gail gladly informed Paedyn of some rather embarrassing stories from my childhood, we talk casually, a regular routine for the cook and me. I ask about her son, stationed as a guard near the Scorches, all while sneaking bits of food as she swats at my hands. My gaze snags on Paedyn from where she watches me curiously, as though trying to puzzle me out.

Funny, normally I'm the one giving her that look.

I jump off the counter and give Gail a peck on the cheek. 'Don't miss me too much.'

Then I turn towards Paedyn who's leaning casually against the counter, a small smile tugging at her lips. I take a slow step towards her. Her head tips up to look me in the eyes as I close the distance between us, so close I can smell the lingering scent of lavender on her skin. I reach around her back, fingers brushing her tank.

Her breath hitches and I feel my lips tug upward. When she opens her mouth to tell me off, I pull my hand back slowly, holding an apple in front of her face. 'Always feeding you, remember?'

She stares at the fruit before snatching it from my hand, huffing in annoyance. And then she smiles, the dazzling action lighting up her face as she rubs the apple on my shirt, right above my heart.

She takes a bite, her eyes locked with mine. 'And you said you weren't a gentleman.'

By the time we make it to the training grounds, I'm slicked with sweat once again.

Almost in unison, several of us peel off our shirts, unable to bear the heat any longer. Kitt and I set off jogging around the grounds at an easy pace. I watch as the contestants pair off to spar or go their separate ways to train. Andy is currently in the form of a red leopard, circling several Sadies in one of the dirt training rings. Unsurprisingly, Braxton is on the ground doing push-ups while Jax occupies himself by throwing rocks as far as he can only to Blink and catch them before they hit the ground.

Finally, my traitorous eyes slide towards a flash of silver hair. She's beating on that padded tree, per usual. She always does this. Her movements are quick, controlled, channeling an emotion I can't place. She spins suddenly, her arm raised before I see her wrist flick. I blink and a knife sinks deep into a tree ten yards away.

Practiced. Purposeful. Precise.

But I'm not the only one watching. Kitt's gaze is locked on her, almost curiously. I clear my throat and pick up our pace. 'So, how are you feeling?'

Kitt's head whips towards me. 'At the moment? Tired.'

I laugh at that, hitting him lightly in the stomach. 'Yeah, you're getting out of shape, Kitty.'

He shoves me at the mention of his childhood nickname. 'Well, I don't exactly have a reason I need to be in shape, do I?'

Though he says this jokingly, I don't miss the bitter edge in his voice.

I sigh, already knowing what this is about. 'You know why you can't.'

'I have no idea what you're talking about.'

'Like hell you don't,' I mutter. 'Kitt, you're the next king of Ilya.

We need you alive. The Trials are no place for you.'

Shit.

As soon as the words left my mouth, I knew they'd struck him like a physical blow.

'Is my own kingdom no place for me either?' His laugh holds no humor. 'Hell, is anywhere outside of the castle not safe enough for the heir?'

'Kitt—'

'I know,' he cuts me off, taking a deep breath. 'I know our duties are different. They always will be. I just wish mine weren't so damn boring.' With that, he shoots me a weak smile in an effort to lighten the mood.

I watch him, waiting to see if he'll say what we both know he wants to. Waiting to see if he'll tell me that he feels trapped, that he feels like he's constantly trying to prove himself, that he wishes he were in the Trials so he could do just that.

But he says nothing of the sort, his smile a silent plea to return to just being brothers and not the future king and his Enforcer.

So, for him, I force a grin onto my face. 'Well, at least I can count on your vote in the Trials.'

The tension seems to melt from Kitt's body, his smile displaying his emotions like it always has. He sighs in relief at the change in topic before saying, 'Oh, I don't know that you can count on my vote after you all but called me fat a few minutes ago, *Kai Pie*.'

I hate that nickname, and the asshole knows it. So, I stick out my foot, sending Ilya's next king sprawling to the ground before he drags me with him.

We finish off our laps, dripping in sweat as the sun beats down on us. I stretch quickly before heading into the ring with Kitt. We dance around each other, using both our powers and bodies to fight. Falling into a familiar rhythm, I let myself mull over what Kitt had said, losing myself in my thoughts.

The world flips. No. I flip.

And then I'm sprawled on my back, trying to suck air into my screaming lungs.

Dammit. Lost my focus.

'Got you on the ground, Kai.' Kitt smiles down at me. 'Been a few years since that last happened, huh?' I can tell he's about to continue gloating, so I don't give him the chance.

My leg sweeps out, catching his ankles and sending him sprawling to the ground beside me.

'Don't get used to it,' I say, resting my head on the ground and smiling up at the sky.

Once he catches his breath, he's barking out a laugh. 'I should have seen that coming . . .' he trails off as I reluctantly stand to my feet and lazily brush the dirt from my clothes before offering a hand to him.

We go our separate ways, Kitt to spar with an insisting Blair, while I head to the targets. I grab the thin knives from the rack beside me and flip one in my hand before flipping it through the air.

Weapons. Fighting. *Killing.*

This was what I was raised to do. This is why I'll be the Enforcer and the one fighting in the Trials, not Kitt.

I hear the pounding of fists and quiet panting a few yards to my left, where the padded trees border the training grounds.

She's back at it.

Once again, she's hammering blows into the tree. Or maybe she simply never stopped in the first place. She looks frustrated, angry – sloppy. Her punches are weaker, her form far less controlled. She's tired and her stance is suffering because of it.

I mindlessly flip a knife in my hand, shaking my head at the sky for what I'm about to do. I send my blade cutting through the air towards the target before strolling over to her, coming from behind while she continues to strike the pads. I'm standing at her back now and—

She pivots in one swift move, sending an elbow flying towards my face. I barely have enough time to dodge before gripping her arm, halting it in the air. Her head whips around, strands of silver hair sticking to her face, now slick with sweat.

My lips twitch into a smile. 'You should keep practicing before you try to hit me.'

She snorts. 'In case you've forgotten how I *saved* you, I know how to fight. I don't need to *try* to hit you, Prince.' She tugs her arm out of my grip and turns back towards the tree, intently ignoring me.

Well that just won't do.

'With that form, you *will* need to try, Gray.'

'Oh, really?' I can't tell if she's amused or contemplating trying to hit me at this very moment. Maybe both.

'Yes, really. You're sloppy. It's not like you,' I state, making her scoff. Once again, she turns back to the tree and begins throwing more punches, decidedly done with our conversation. Her knuckles are red, raw, and nearly bleeding.

Why does she do this to herself?

I shake my head, already knowing the answer. Because I've done it before. I've hit pads, walls, *anything* until blood dripped from my fists. All to find a release for the anger, the frustration, that was pent up inside of me.

And that is exactly what Paedyn is doing.

She's still swinging too much with her arms, rather than using her whole body as momentum. She's typically very technical when it comes to fighting, making this especially unlike her. But she's tired and frustrated.

And despite me knowing all this, I can't fight the urge to toy with her. I step even closer to her back and place my hands on her hips, twisting her body as she throws another punch. She jumps and stumbles into me, her head tipping back against my bare chest. 'Stop swinging with your arms and swing with your whole body,' I say, bending my head so I'm close to her ear. She sucks in a breath when my hand sweeps over her abdomen, the whisper of my fingers dancing along her thin tank.

'Engage your core, Gray.'

Her chest heaves. Then she takes a step forward, the heat of her body leaving mine. My hands are still planted on her hips when she turns her head to shoot me an irritated look.

She knows I'm right. And she hates it.

She got lazy and didn't realize until now, too focused and frustrated to notice. The thought has me smiling down at her as she huffs, blowing a strand of hair out of her eyes before turning back towards the tree.

'Now, throw a punch,' I murmur, leaning in to add, '*Correctly.*'

Shockingly, she doesn't argue, likely realizing it won't do her any good. She squares her shoulders and bounces on the balls of her feet. Then she jabs, her fist flying towards the mat as I twist her hips in time with the punch. There's far more momentum behind it, and I can see how much stronger she's gotten in her short time here with consistent meals and training. When her knuckles sink into the pad, the lean muscles in her back and arms are evident.

'Much better,' I say dully, despite being impressed. After a moment that was most definitely too long, I finally drop my hands from her hips. 'Now, do it on your own. Just to make sure you were paying attention.'

She stills, facing the tree.

And then there's a flash of silver hair as she swivels around, throwing a beautiful jab at my face.

CHAPTER 17

Rai

I almost don't dodge in time. Only years of fighting allow my reflexes to react so quickly.

'How was that?' she says sweetly, flashing that startling smile at me.

I huff out a laugh. 'What if I didn't duck, Gray?'

'I knew you'd duck, Azer.' She's close to my face now, a wicked smile curving her lips when she repeats the exact phrase I told her after throwing a knife in her direction.

'Looks like someone is itching for a fight.' My eyes flick up her body, taking my time. Taking in her stance on the balls of her feet, her slightly raised hands, and every stitch of clothing clinging to her body in between.

'I've just been waiting for an excuse to punch that smirk off your face.' She swings at me again, knowing I'll duck under it. She's toying with *me*.

'Wouldn't be the first time someone said that to me,' I say as we circle each other. We've backed into a small opening between the targets and the weapons rack opposite them. I show her my palms, surrendering before the fight has even begun. 'You don't really want to do this and neither do I. Especially because I wouldn't want to mess up that pretty face of yours, darling.'

She all but rolls her eyes at me. 'That's funny because I won't hesitate to mess up *your* pretty face.'

I smirk. 'I knew you thought I was pretty.'

At that, she throws another punch at my face that I easily evade. We continue circling each other, slowly. Damp hair clings to my forehead and I comb my fingers through it, pushing it off my sticky skin.

'You do know that I have eight powers at my disposal right now, and any one of them could drop you.' I grin as I say it, watching as her eyes narrow.

'I don't want to fight your power – I want to fight *you*. Just you.' Her piercing gaze never leaves mine as she says it, even as the other Elites turn their attention towards us, finding this fight far more interesting than their training.

'So, you just want me? No powers?'

'Yes. I just want you,' she breathes, annoyed with me.

My mouth twists into a crooked grin. 'I knew you wanted me, Gray.'

And with that little comment, a high kick comes flying towards my face.

I block it with my hands and push her leg down, once again surprised by her strength. Before I can take another breath, a beautiful jab heads for my face, this one intended to meet its mark, hard.

I duck under it before grabbing her outstretched wrist and pulling her back against my chest as I twist her arm under her shoulder blade. 'You're going to have to do better than that, Gray,' I whisper against her ear, smiling.

She grunts and drives the elbow of her free arm into my stomach. The air whooshes out of my lungs, and she takes advantage of it. Pivoting, she swings her elbow high at my face, making my head snap to the side when it connects with my jaw. My grip on her arm loosens, and she spins out of my hold before throwing a right cross at the exact same spot on my jaw.

Damn.

I keep my head turned to the side, my tongue roaming over the inside of my cheek as my mouth begins to fill with blood. And then my gaze slowly slides to her. She's on the balls of her feet, hands still

146

raised in a fighting stance as she stares at me. And then she smiles, momentarily distracting me.

I laugh, deep and quiet before spitting blood onto the ground. 'Much better, Gray.' I smile as I circle her, my fists instinctively raised. 'I might actually need to fight back.'

Her smile slips before she's suddenly dropping to the ground and sweeping her leg in a wide arc, intending to knock me to the dirt. I jump over it swiftly but she's back on her feet in a split second, throwing a combination of punches. She peppers me with a series of uppercuts, jabs, and hooks, but I stay on defense, blocking her fists. With her quick movements, she finally gets in a sharp blow to my stomach, stealing my breath away.

Fine. If she wants me to fight, I'll fight.

I won't hurt her. Badly. In fact, she's quite skilled, and despite my mocking, she is a fine fighter. But with my now bruising jaw and stomach, I'm done playing games.

She ducks before my fist meets the air where her head was. Then she kicks out a leg, swinging it towards my ribs. I grab her ankle right before it connects with my side and yank her forward. She stumbles towards me, and I grip her thigh against my side with one hand, while the other lands a blow to her cheekbone. It was a softer hit, but still hard enough to make her head snap to the side.

I let go of her leg at the same moment I wrap my foot behind her ankle still planted on the ground, giving it a good tug. She falls, hard. Violent coughs shake her body as soon as her back hits the dirt as she tries to suck air back into her lungs.

I hover over her with a smile, assuming the match is over. Wrong. She kicks me in the groin. Hard.

I double over, huffing out a pained laugh. 'Cheap shot, darling.'

'Yes, but an effective one.' She jumps to her feet, panting even with a sly smile. Her hands are up, covering her face, while the rest of her body is covered in dirt. And then we are trading off blows and blocks as we toy with one another. It's like a dance, and she is a fierce partner.

But for whatever reason, I refuse to throw my whole weight behind the punches. I rein myself in. Not enough to stop me from fighting back, but enough to keep her *mostly* unbroken. Though she is clearly not doing the same. She's hitting hard, striking relentlessly, *wanting* to hurt me.

One minute we're flirting and the next we're fighting – possibly even both at the same time. I can't seem to figure this vicious girl out.

After minutes of blocking and landing blows, we are both panting in the unbearable heat. Sweat rolls down my brow and stings my eyes as the group surrounding us cheers and grunts each time one of us takes a hit. I strike her with a combination of punches, my uppercut finding its mark under her jaw and jerking her head up. I follow it with a lazy jab which she dodges, grabbing my outstretched arm in one hand, and my opposite shoulder in the other. Then she steps close to me, driving a knee into my stomach.

But she's left the arm that is holding my shoulder open and exposed, so I take advantage of it. I use both hands to grab hold of her forearm and wrist before pivoting so my back is against her chest. Then I use my momentum to raise her off the ground, throwing her over my shoulder and onto the dirt with a thud.

She's on her back, wheezing from the impact of the hard ground as I stare down at her, hoping she's finally given up. Wrong again. With surprising speed, she grips the back of my ankles with her hands and yanks with that strength of hers. Caught off guard, she manages to pull my feet from under me, sending the ground flying towards my back.

She's up and on me in a second, practically jumping on top of my chest, placing her knees on either side of me. And then she cocks a bloody fist back, her smile triumphant.

I take her in, bloody and straddling me. 'If it weren't for my current situation,' I glance at her fist still posed to strike, 'this could be a lot more fun,' I say quietly, looking her up and down before staring into those blue eyes as they widen.

Her focus slips for a moment.

Perfect.

I grab her waist and flip us over. Now I'm on top of her, pinning her wrists into the dirt beside her head. She pants beneath me, glaring up into my face. She's covered in dirt, and I'm certain I look no different. A dark bruise is already beginning to blossom across her cheekbone, and blood leaks from her nose and mouth.

'Nicely done, Gray,' I say, close to her face. She squirms in my hold, but it does nothing to loosen my grip. 'I have a few critiques.'

She stills, and I watch as a slow smile spreads across her lips. 'Seeing that you're the future Enforcer, I wasn't sure if you were capable of showing mercy. Clearly, you are.' I stare down at her, my face morphing into its cold mask at her words. Then she lifts her head off the ground so only mere inches separate us as she breathes, 'I know you went easy on me.'

Was it that obvious or did her Psychic abilities tell her that?

My gaze roams over her face, snagging on the dirt and blood splattering her skin, concealing the faint dusting of freckles I know covers her nose. 'And what makes you think that?'

Her face inches impossibly closer, lashes fluttering, lips quirked into a smile and dangerously close to my own. Her voice is breathy, barely audible as she whispers, 'Because if you weren't going easy on me, I wouldn't be able to do this.'

I barely have enough time to be confused before she headbutts me.

When the crown of her head meets my nose, I see stars. She breaks my hold on her wrists and uses both legs to push me off her. A cloud of dust surrounds me as I lie in the dirt, blinking away the throbbing pain. The hit was hard but not hard enough to stop me from staggering to my feet and facing her, blood streaming from my broken nose.

She doesn't waste a moment.

Her arms are around my neck, her knee driving into my stomach again and again. Before I have time to react, she uses my bent leg as a step stool, throwing her own legs over my shoulders in one swift movement. Using her momentum and the limbs wrapped around me, she throws us both to the ground. I sprawl into the dirt while she rolls, wasting no time before pouncing on me. And then my arms are pinned under her knees once again.

'How was my form, Prince?' she pants, lips bloody. 'Any critiques now?'

Her weight presses down on me and I huff out a laugh. 'I have a few notes.'

'Likewise.' Her hand flashes to her boot, sliding a thin blade from the worn leather. 'For starters, I don't appreciate my opponents going easy on me.' She gently drags the knife's tip across my cheekbone, tickling my skin.

I smirk despite the blade she trails across my face, my gaze burning into hers. And then my eyes flick to the blood dribbling down her face, leaking from the several cuts and gashes I'd given her. 'Looks like I messed up your pretty face after all, despite my best efforts.'

'Oh, this is nothing.' She laughs breathlessly. 'You should see the damage I did to *your* pretty face.'

My lips quirk into a smile as I lift my head towards hers. 'Oh, darling, as long as you still think I'm pretty, I don't give a damn what I look like.' Those blue eyes blink at me in shock before rolling at me in annoyance. With a huff, she shifts and stands to her feet. I follow, dusting the dirt from my body as she does the same.

Before she can turn and leave, I say, 'You're far more fun to spar with than Kitt. We should do that again sometime.'

Her head tilts slightly to the side, her smile sly. 'I'll never pass up the chance to kick your ass, Prince.'

And with that, she's striding away as I watch her retreating form. 'Oh, and Kai?' she calls, her voice casual.

And then I'm ducking.

She spun, throwing the knife so suddenly that I barely had time to dodge before it sank into the wooden target a few feet behind me.

'I don't want your mercy. Next time we fight,' I can see her blue eyes smoldering from where I stand, '*impress me.*'

A low whistle sounds from the crowd – Kitt, of course. Ignoring him, I shake my head, grinning at her as she turns away from me.

Vicious little thing, indeed.

CHAPTER 18

Paedyn

I'm almost certain I'm not an Ordinary. My power may actually be the ability to lie effortlessly. Lie about what I am, who I trust, and how happy I am to be here.

Yes, the Trials are a series of physical games, but they are just as deadly when it comes to the mental ones. I need to win over the people, convince them that I love these Trials as much as they do. I want their votes to stay alive, but I *need* their votes if I want to win this bloody thing. I glance around the dinner table, taking in the stiff shoulders and clipped conversation. The tension in the room is nearly suffocating, choking us into an awkward silence filled mostly with chewing. It's safe to say that we've become antsy as of late. So much so that a fight broke out between Ace and Braxton in the training yard, one that the former unsurprisingly initiated. I can't imagine what Ace must have done to crack Braxton's patient composure, but the brawl took four Imperials to break up, all but piling on top of the two contestants.

My eyes slide over my opponents slowly, stopping on the green gaze already staring at me. I suck in a breath, steeling myself against the rush of rage I feel every time I look at the king—

No, not the king.

Kitt stares back at me with eyes so like his father's that I have to blink the image of the king away, forcing myself to focus on the boy in front of me instead. His smile is warm, his eyes wandering over my face. I return the action before quickly looking away, desperate to avoid his gaze as my eyes crash into a familiar pair.

I'm suddenly swallowed in the storm that is his steely gray gaze framed by dark lashes. Kai tilts his head slightly, smiling at me in a way that has me spinning the ring on my thumb nervously.

I hope he's losing his mind trying to puzzle me out like I am him. Kai's gaze flicks to my thumb and the ring I'm now spinning on it.

There's a glint in his eyes when he leans across the table towards me. 'Something making you nervous, Gray?'

Plagues, how can one person be so equally infuriating and infatuating? 'And what would give you the impression that I'm nervous?'

'Hmm,' he hums, running a hand over his rough jaw. 'Should I start with the fact that you're spinning that ring or the more obvious one being that you're clutching a knife?'

I blink at him before looking down. There is, in fact, a steak knife gripped in my fist, though I'm not sure when it found its way there. I stare at it, huffing out a laugh before uncurling my fingers from the handle. When my gaze finally meets his, it's searching, softer than before.

And annoyingly enough, I'm mirroring that same look he's giving me, though we are seeing very different things.

I see a boy who is confusing and captivating, cocky and calculating. But with every new detail I discover about him, the less I think I know. He has a soft spot only for those he loves dearly, that much is clear. But he's built walls, guarded himself, slipped on masks, making him annoyingly difficult to decipher.

My mind wanders to our fight, to the feel of his hands on me, steady and strong. Watching him fight is like watching a dancer, one who feels the music in their soul, their very bones. He was born for battle. Raised to kill.

And I need to remember that.

I'm jolted from my thoughts when a servant reaches to grab my plate. Out of pure instinct, my fingers itch to snatch a roll or two before they are whisked away. I'm still not used to having regular, let alone nourishing, meals every day, and I find myself constantly fighting my thieving instincts when they scream at me to grab whatever food I can get my hands on.

Chairs scrape against the marble floor as those around me stand to leave. An airy, delicate voice calls out over the commotion, and we all stop to turn towards the sound. The queen has her hands folded neatly in front of her, clasped over her pristine navy gown, shimmering in the setting sunlight.

She smiles at us and the twinkle in her eyes reminds me vaguely of Kai. 'Only a few more days until the first ball! Ladies, I trust you all have selected a gown, or you've spoken to your maids about having one prepared.'

I have most definitely done neither of those things yet.

'Oh, and don't forget to be practicing your dancing,' the queen adds with a smile. 'I trust you'll want to make a good impression on the people.'

Oh, I'll definitely make an impression.

She dismisses us with a nod, and I head swiftly for the door, intending to slip back to my room and seek Ellie's counsel on my gown.

'Paedyn.'

My feet falter, slowing me to a stop. The warmth in that voice and the use of my name tell me it's not Kai behind me.

No, it's his brother.

I turn on my heel and watch Kitt stroll towards me, his blond hair messy and his smile charming. I swallow when he steps close to me, when he looks at me with those emerald eyes he shares with a murderer.

'Hey,' he says warmly. 'Mind if I walk you to your room?'

Yes.

'Not at all,' I hear myself say through the teeth I'm flashing at him.

We start walking down the hall, heading for the contestants' wing of the castle. 'I have yet to congratulate you on your interview,' he says with a pinch of pride in his voice. 'Didn't I say you'd do just fine?'

I think back to the interviews when I'd managed to make a mess of the one thing I was expected to say.

'Survival. I expect to survive this.'

I almost laugh at the thought. 'Well, it's good to know that the future king won't have my head for screwing up his kingdom's motto.'

I bite my tongue, but it's too late to stop the words that have already tumbled from my mouth.

He laughs.

The sound is rich, flooding me with relief. He rubs a hand behind his neck, still chuckling as he says, 'Actually, that was my favorite part.'

I throw him a bemused look. 'Was it now?'

'Yes.' The laughter leaves his voice when he stops to look at me, halting us in the middle of the hallway. 'It was the most real thing anyone's ever said in those interviews.'

I search his face, trying to ignore the flash of his father I see. 'You mean it was the stupidest thing anyone's ever said in those interviews.'

His warm chuckle is echoing off the walls once again. 'Perhaps.' He pauses, peering down at me. 'But, if it makes you feel any better, I don't think you were wrong when you said you expected to survive this, and I admire you for voicing how you truly feel.'

I'm so shocked by the sincerity in his words that I huff out a laugh. 'Then you must admire me often because I tend to speak my mind far more than I should.'

I do admire you often.

His eyes seem to speak those five words as they search mine, voicing something he never intended to. And it's the first time that I can meet his gaze and not see the king gazing back at me.

Clearing my throat, I turn and continue heading down the hallway again. Kitt is by my side when we come to a halt in front of my room, and I'm already pushing open the door as I say, 'Thank you for walking with me.' I pause to give him a small smile over my shoulder. 'Now I can say I've been escorted by the future king.'

I'm stepping through the door frame when words leave him in a rush. 'Yes, and if you'll let me, I'll do it again.'

I spin around, finding him suddenly right behind me. 'What?'

His face splits into a smile that seems almost too shy to be worn by a royal. 'Miss Gray, will you be my partner to the balls?'

I nearly choke on the next breath I suck in. And yet, instead of answering his question, a pointless one of my own falls from my lips with a breathy laugh. 'Since when have I been Miss Gray?'

A sly smile replaces his shy one, reminding me briefly of his brother. 'Since you started referring to me as "the future king".'

'And you don't like that? Me calling you the future king, that is.' My curiosity forces the question from my mouth since I assumed he was quite attached to the title and the power accompanying it.

'I'd rather not be called by a title I haven't earned or lived up to yet,' he says simply.

'That's why I called you the *future* king.'

He smiles, content to let the silence stretch between us before he finally says, 'You never answered my question, Miss Gray.'

I hear the offer in his voice, see the silent question in those eyes I keep avoiding. Say yes to being his partner, and we will simply be Kitt and Paedyn. Say no, and the titles remain.

Say yes, and I play the part.

Say no, and I pass up the opportunity to please the people.

The thought of hanging off the future king's arm and looking up at the similar face of my father's killer isn't personally pleasant, but it would be for the people of Ilya. I would undeniably have their attention – a terrifying yet tempting thought.

A smile lifts my lips at the image of a former Slummer and future ruler hand in hand, the perfect picture of polar opposites.

The most powerful man paired with the most powerless woman.

'It would be an honor to be your partner, Kitt,' I say softly, smiling slightly.

Play the part.

Kitt chuckles, sounding relieved. 'I was hoping you would say that, Paedyn.'

'Ellie. Help. Please.'

I'm staring at my wardrobe, driving myself mad looking at all the colors and styles of gowns hanging inside. 'Which one should I wear for the ball? I need to make a good impression—'

'Yes, you do, and you won't with one of those dresses,' Ellie cuts me off, laughing softly.

I tip my head back and groan. 'What's wrong with one of these?' I gesture to the multiple dazzling dresses at my disposal.

'Those,' she points at the wardrobe, 'are no ball gowns. Though, you'd certainly make an impression if you wore one of them. Just not a good one.'

'So, what now?' I can't keep the irritation from bubbling out of me.

Clearly, Ellie noticed because she says softly, 'We'll need to have a dress made for you. Immediately. I know several excellent seamstresses who could fix you up a beautiful gown in no time, you'll just need to pick out the style and shade of green.'

Apparently, it is common knowledge that the women tend to wear green gowns to these balls, seeing that emerald is Ilya's kingdom color. It isn't a set rule, but something everyone simply *does*. Typical. Tradition.

Tiresome.

Ellie carries on about the seamstresses she knows, how wonderful their work is.

And then it hits me. I know a seamstress, *lived* with one.

I'm suddenly crushed by the weight of what I've done. No, what I *haven't* done.

Adena.

The promise I made to her rings in my head, a reminder of how I'd *forgotten* about her. I vowed to visit her, and yet, only remembered to do so as soon as it was convenient for me.

I'm gripped by guilt, nearly choking from its tight grasp around my throat. I swallow, silently cursing myself for my selfishness.

But this wouldn't be the first time I've been selfish when it comes to Adena.

I was selfish the night she found me on the roof of a shop two years ago, hurt and hysterical and hoping for someone to just *understand*. The rain rolled down my face as I studied the stars, mingling with my tears and stinging the fresh cuts I'd received from an Imperial that morning. Adena pulled herself over the edge of the roof before breathlessly telling me how she was certain she'd find me up there, just as she'd been certain to never again be scaling a shop.

But her smile slipped when her eyes slid to me shaking in the streaming rain, hugging my knees. I was tired. Tired of trying to be something I wasn't while no one knew what I was.

So I decided to study the sky that night, spotting similarities between us. I was lonely in a way that I imagine the stars to be, observed by everyone yet too far to truly be *seen*.

And for once, I wanted to be seen by someone.

It was selfish of me to tell Adena about my past, present, and everything in between. Just knowing about what I am puts her in danger, and yet, we've only grown closer despite that.

She believed me. She listened as the truth spilled from me in a sob, stayed with me even after knowing what I am.

And I've never been more relieved about a moment of weakness. 'Ellie,' I say slowly, deliberately. 'What if I know of a seamstress?'

She thinks for a moment before answering with a shrug. 'That would be fine. Did you meet someone here? In the palace?'

'No, she's from Loot.' Ellie gives me a skeptical look, but I barrel on. 'She's incredible. I can guarantee she would make me the finest dress Ilya's ever seen.'

'Well, I suppose I could talk to Lenny about escorting you there to get her.' She quickly adds, 'As long as he is allowed to.'

My brows knit together. 'Get her?'

'Oh yes. If you get clearance to go, she'll come back with you and be hired here as your personal seamstress until the Trials are over. Or until . . .' she trails off.

The rest of her words are drowned out by the blood pounding in my ears, and my heart is racing so quickly I feel as though I'm in the middle of a fight.

Adena is going to live here. With me.

She'll be fed and *paid*. I'll get to see her. She'll be safe. Relief washes over me, feebly attempting to replace the guilt I still feel.

Ellie promises she'll speak to Lenny about taking me to Loot before saying goodnight and slipping out the door.

I flop onto my bed, staring up at the intricate molding on the ceiling.

I'm not sure how long I lay there, letting the hope and happiness wash over me at the thought of seeing Adena safe and sound.

And then a light knock at the door has my thoughts shattering.

CHAPTER 19

Paedyn

It must be nearly midnight, so who the Plagues is that?

I grip the handle of my dagger and slide it out from beneath my pillow, holding it loosely at my side as I pad across the floor. When I swing open the door, my eyes meet the pair of gray ones on the other side.

Kai's gaze drops to the dagger in my hand before returning to my face, lingering on my bruised cheekbone and split lip that he so generously gave me in our fight this morning. My pride wouldn't allow the Healers to tend to my injuries, and unsurprisingly, the prince seemed to have the same problem. Faint bruises have bloomed across his jaw, a reminder of each blow I landed.

'Do you plan on pressing that to my throat again?' Kai's lips twitch upwards as he inclines his head towards the dagger clutched in my fist.

'Don't tempt me,' I say, running my fingers across the smooth, flat edge of the blade. 'Here for a rematch?'

He shoves his hands into the pockets of his slim, dark pants before crossing his ankles and leaning against the door frame. 'Don't tempt me.' Ebony hair falls over his forehead, making his gray eyes pop against the inky waves. It's clear he hasn't shaved, leaving a shadow of stubble covering his sharp jaw, only emphasized by the darkening bruises I left there.

'What do you want, Azer?'

'Missed you too, Gray,' Kai says, casually picking something from his distractingly thin shirt. Then his gaze snaps to mine, his long lashes in total contrast with his light eyes. 'I'm here for your lesson.'

I scoff. 'I'm sorry, my *what*?'

'Your lesson.' He cocks his head to the side, amusingly puzzled. 'You're Psychic. Did you not sense this was coming?'

'That's not how it works, and you know it,' I say, my tone a combination of irritation and confusion. 'What are you talking—'

'So, you were really going to go to the ball and step all over my brother's toes, then?' He huffs out a laugh. 'You are just full of surprises, aren't you?'

'No, I wouldn't step all over his toes. Maybe trip over my own but . . .' I trail off, watching his grin grow. His dimple mocks me, tempting me to use the dagger waiting patiently in my palm.

And then his words finally sink in.

'*Dance* lessons? That is why you're here?' I let out a breathy laugh, thinking he must be joking.

'Took you long enough.' He pushes off the door frame, taking a step closer. 'Come on, we don't have all night.' Then he smirks. 'Unless you want us to be out all night.'

I don't budge. 'Nope. No way. I don't want or need your help.' I give him a mocking smile. 'But it's good to know that you are always so eager to offer it.'

I grab the edge of my door and begin shutting it on him when he wedges a shiny shoe into my room. He easily pries the door open, his strong arms pushing it back despite my best efforts. With his hand still flat on the wood, he leans in close enough to murmur, 'Just like always, you're too stubborn to admit that you need my help.'

'What I *need* is for you to get out of my room.' I'm smiling at him but it's all teeth.

And yet, with every word that says otherwise, I know he's right. I know I should take him up on his offer and practice to prevent making a fool out of myself beside the future king. But I don't like that he can hold this over my head, don't like that he would be helping me. Again.

'What you need and what you want are two very different things.' The scent of pine washes over me when he ducks his head close to mine, forcing me to meet his gaze. 'Come on, Gray, you're smarter than this. You know that you need to make a good impression at this ball. And next to my brother, there will be a lot more eyes on you than there already normally are.'

It's like he read my thoughts, summed them up, and spit them back at me. I glare at him. I know he's right, and he knows it too.

He must see the fight leave my eyes because a smile twists his lips. 'Good to see you've come to your senses. Let's go then.'

I brush past his shoulder with my head held high. *I* chose to do this, not him, and he needs to remember that. 'Where are we going?' I ask as he begins leading me down the hallway. At the end of it, we climb a wide spiral staircase draped in emerald velvet carpet.

The shadow of a smile settles on his face. 'Somewhere with enough room for you to fall all over the place.'

When we reach the top of the stairs, I'm led down a wide hallway lined with paintings and pearly molding clinging to the walls and ceiling. My eyes sweep over the thin layer of dust covering the frames littering the wall.

It has been a while since anyone's been up here.

This floor happens to be one of the few that I haven't yet explored, seeing that I've crept out of my room multiple times in the dead of night to learn the layout of the castle and its possible exits. Call it my personality or paranoia, but being unaware of my surroundings scares me nearly as much as the Trials.

Since Lenny doesn't guard my door, I can't resist the urge to snoop. In fact, I don't see my Imperial much at all, and surprisingly, the thought sends a sudden jolt of sadness through me. I'm shocked by how much I genuinely enjoy his company and even more shocked by the fact that I would think such things about an *Imperial*.

An uneven rug catches my foot, sending the floor flying towards my face. I'm about to sprawl onto the spiral-patterned rug when an arm slides around my middle, firm and feeling annoyingly familiar.

'There's that clumsy footwork we're trying to rid you of,' Kai says, the smirk evident in his voice. He sets me on my feet, steadying me with a hand that I push away, flustered and feeling the need to put some space between us.

He holds his hands up and takes a mocking step back before turning to head down the hall once again. As we continue walking, the question I've been waiting to ask finally slips past my lips. 'Why are you doing this?'

Kai halts in front of me. He turns slowly, looking almost amused by the question. 'It's simple, really. You're attending this ball with my brother, and he needs to look the best he is able.'

I study his face, stare as a sliver of his mask cracks, displaying all the love and devotion for his brother, all the lengths he is willing to go for him. It's as if he has a duty to fulfill, as if he is already the Enforcer and this is far bigger than just stopping me from stepping on his brother's toes.

And then his mask is suddenly back up, and I'm staring at that cool face once again, void of the emotion once there. When I can't think of a retort, I begin walking instead. We make a right down a smaller corridor and head to the very last door on the left. He grips the handle and swings it open, revealing a bedroom beyond, lit only by the moonlight streaming through the window.

If I thought my room was magnificent, it pales in comparison to *this*. It's easily twice the size of my own, making it seem more like a house than a single bedroom. Though it's filled with a four-poster bed, dresser, and a desk – just as mine is – this room seems lived in. The shelf is overflowing, books stacked at odd angles to make them fit. Several of their worn covers tell me they consist of strategy, combat, and . . . *poetry.*

Interesting.

Everything filling the room is nicer than my own, yet used and worn.

This is his room – his real room.

The desk is covered in dark ink stains, and suits of armor are piled in the corner. My eyes scan over the large slices covering the posts of the bed where chunks of dark wood are missing.

Sword slashes.

He's taken a blunt sword to the bedposts. Multiple times.

I suppose that is better than taking a sword to a human, though I'm sure he does that as well. My eyes finally flick back to Kai. He's leaning against the door frame, watching me curiously as I stand in the middle of his room, though I don't remember walking so far into it.

I nod my head towards the chipped wooden posts of his massive bed, not knowing what to say under his stare. 'Interesting way to relieve stress.'

'So is punching a pad till your fists bleed.' He gives me a faint smile as he strolls across the room to his desk, hands in pockets, before he begins fiddling with the contraption on top of it – one that I recognize.

Father had a record player, one with a wide golden horn I used to stick my head into as a child. He made decent money as the respected Healer in the slums, but the record player was still the nicest thing we owned. Years ago, he used to plop my feet on top of his so we could dance around the kitchen. Well, *he* would dance. I was just along for the ride. But he never got the chance to truly teach me how to dance without literally stepping on anyone's feet.

The crackling of the needle hitting a record is familiar, though the sound of the smooth waltz that follows is not. Kai turns around, casually unbuttoning half his shirt and sending my eyes searching for anything to stare at other than his tanned chest and swirling tattoo.

And then he's suddenly before me, surveying me from head to toe with a slight smile that displays the deeper dimple on his right cheek. His stare is like a caress, and he takes his time. I refuse to squirm under that piercing gaze, knowing how he would love to watch me fidget.

Not wanting to be outdone, I drag my eyes over his strong facial features and even stronger body beneath. Everything about him is lethal. That smile. Those eyes. That cunning mind of his.

'Are you sure you'll be able to focus on dancing, or will I be too much of a distraction, darling?'

His words startle me, and my eyes shoot back to his. I huff. 'I think I'll manage, thanks.'

He gives me a doubtful look. 'I guess we will find out, won't we?' I expect him to reach out and pull me into a dance, and the thought has my heart pounding, has me preparing to feel his hands on my body.

But he doesn't move, doesn't try to close the distance between us.

Good.

'For now, you will start by just learning the steps to the average waltz,' he says. 'Mostly because I don't want you stomping on my toes.'

With his hands still in his pockets, Kai steps in and out, side to side, showing me the basics. He's so graceful, so elegant, so *natural*.

Fighting. Fighting is also a dance to him.

I feel stiff and suddenly so unsure of myself. Even with his hands still in his pockets, Kai easily steps in time with me, though he doesn't dare get close enough to be trampled by my clumsy footing.

I sigh, irritated with myself and the smirking prince in front of me.

'Relax,' Kai murmurs across from me with more than a hint of humor in his voice. 'You're thinking too much. Don't calculate, just move with the music.' I look up to see him already staring at me with a grin. 'Also, you do know this is a dance, correct? So, no fighting stance is necessary.'

Only then do I notice how tight and poised my body is, hands slightly raised as though readying to strike. I straighten and run a hand through the strands of hair falling out of my loose braid. I'm oddly . . . *nervous*. And it's maddeningly annoying.

This would be a lot easier if he weren't staring at me.

Another waltz ends, replaced by a slow, mellow tune. My head is lowered, pieces of hair falling into my face as I watch my feet step in time with the music.

A pressure at my waist makes me jump.

Like a reflex, my hand twitches towards the knife now sheathed under the folds of my dress, but a calloused hand catches my wrist. 'Knives are also not necessary for dancing,' Kai says with a low laugh. Holding my gaze, his rough fingers slide slowly from my wrist to my palm before he folds his hand into mine, raising it into the air.

But it's his other hand that holds my attention, the one that has settled comfortably against the small of my back. The one that is pulling me towards him. Through the thin fabric of the dress I threw on for dinner, I can feel the warmth of his palm seeping into my lower back.

I stare at him as he pulls me close. It's not as if I didn't know this was bound to happen, I just wasn't expecting it so suddenly. He looks at me with an expectant expression before chuckling softly and sliding his hand from my back, making me feel suddenly cold in its absence. He grabs my other hand and lifts it to his shoulder, dropping my palm atop his thin shirt. I can feel every muscle shift beneath it as he returns his hand to my back, firmly flattening it against my dress.

'Let's see what you learned,' he says softly as his feet begin moving in time with the music. I fumble to follow, managing to mirror my steps with his. He leads easily, confidently guiding me through the dance.

My eyes sweep across the room and down at my feet, counting with each step. The pressure on my back is suddenly gone when fingers catch my chin, tipping my head up. 'You'll never learn if you keep watching your feet, Gray. Eyes on me.' He smiles, returning his hand to my back. 'That shouldn't be too difficult.'

I roll my eyes at him, opening my mouth to make a remark only to ask a question instead. 'How did you know Kitt asked me to the ball?'

Kai's laugh is humorless, hollow. 'I'm no Psychic, but it wasn't hard to put the pieces together.' When I only stare at him, he sighs and continues. 'I know my brother, and because of that, I knew he would ask you.'

'That was a terrible answer,' I say simply.

'And you're still a terrible dancer, so my work is far from finished.' I snort.

'Oh,' Kai adds casually, 'he may have also mentioned that he asked you.'

Another laugh escapes me before I can stop it, and I press my lips together to smother the sound. My eyes fall to his chest that is far too close, reminding me that *we* are far too close for competitors, for enemies in these Trials.

And yet, here I am, dancing with him in his bedroom. Alone. In the dark.

If it's even possible, I'm suddenly more rigid than I was before.

Kai feels me stiffen in his hold and leans impossibly closer. 'You're as stiff as a board, Gray. Loosen up.'

Not. Helping.

I try and fail to melt into his embrace like a dance partner should. I'm hopeless. Hopelessly in over my head.

But the prince doesn't give up so easily. No, he wraps his arm fully around my waist and tugs me to him. I drag my feet, not wanting to close the little distance left between us.

A maddening dimple peeks out at me, barely visible in the dim light. 'So, what have we learned today?' he asks, annoyingly amused as ever. 'One, daggers are not needed for dancing, and two, you actually have to be close to your partner during the dance. And shockingly, you seem to be struggling more with the latter.'

'Would you rather I struggle with the first and put a dagger to your throat?' I pause. 'Again.'

'So very predictable,' he chuckles, the sound washing over me before he mutters, 'Always so vicious and eager to stab me.'

He is very close to me. Too close to me.

And it's because I'm so distracted by that fact that my foot lands on top of his, and I stumble forward to collide with his solid frame. Both of his hands wrap around my waist, steadying me before I regain my senses and push away from him. A deep laugh rumbles from his chest, paired with a genuine smile, one that I've only ever seen him wear around his brother.

Lethal.

'How can a fighter have such poor footwork?' His eyes dance between mine. 'You are just full of surprises.'

'Well, *surprise*, I'm done with this lesson,' I say flatly, turning out of his grasp. My back is to him when he snatches my wrist and whips me around, pulling me back.

'But you still owe me one more dance.' His wavy hair tumbles over his brow, the look in his eyes practically begging me to play with him.

'Fine,' I say, playing along. 'Another dance for the answer to a question.'

His eyebrows rise. 'Is that a bribe, Gray?'

'Those are my terms. Take it or leave it, Prince.' His only response is a low chuckle. He turns his head away from me, thinking before he finally meets my gaze.

Slowly, he raises my hand back into the air and rests his other hand comfortably onto the small of my back once again. 'Deal.'

Another slow waltz begins, occupying me with the music and

steps, drowning me in the dance. When I can't seem to ignore the feel of his eyes watching me so intently, I finally meet his gaze.

'Alright, what is it you're dying to know?' Kai asks, leading me through the dance.

I have no idea.

He looks at me, through me, waiting for an answer. His gray eyes are like chips of ice, shards of glass. Like both, his gaze is pointed and piercing. Cold yet captivating. Beautiful in the way only deadly things can be.

And just like that, I suddenly can't think of a single thing I want to ask him. I rack my brain for a question only to blurt out the first thing that comes to mind.

'Do you wish it was you?' He blinks, dark lashes fluttering. 'Do you wish you were the future king of Ilya? The heir?'

It's not at all the question I thought I would be asking, but here we are. 'No,' he says simply, holding my gaze.

I raise my brows in a silent question. When he doesn't continue, I say, 'That's it? "No"?'

'You got your answer, and I got my dance. That was the deal, darling.'

I can barely breathe.

Adena's thin arms are wrapped so tightly around my neck that I'm beginning to see spots. She screamed and squealed when she spotted me waiting by the Fort.

My best friend. My literal partner in crime. Safe and sound. Beautiful and bubbly as ever.

Lenny arrived at my room early this morning, ready to take me into Loot and retrieve my new seamstress. Apparently, he had gotten approval to do so, though I was too excited to bother asking for details. I may have even squealed myself.

'I'm going to be your *what*?!' Adena squeaks.

I sigh, though it comes out sounding more like a laugh. 'My personal seamstress.' I've filled her in on the details about three times now. 'I mean, unless you don't want the job . . .'

'Are you crazy?! Of course I want the job, Pae!' She's practically skipping as we make our way to the coach waiting at the far end of Loot. I survey the market and wide alley before me. My home looks just as dull and dreary as it did when I left it. I let the sound of curses and haggling, the scent of fish and spices wash over me. All familiar. All the same.

Lenny opens the door of the coach and both Adena and I settle in before we are rumbling up the uneven cobblestone street, heading for the palace.

'I can't believe this is happening,' Adena says, in awe as she looks out the tiny window. She turns back to me, taking in the casual dress Ellie forced me into with wide eyes. 'I can't believe *this*.' She looks from my face to the dress before snatching up the hem of the skirt and inspecting it.

'Don't get used to . . . *this*.' I gesture to the dress. 'I typically wear pants during the day, but Ellie insisted I wear a dress to make a good impression on the people who saw me at Loot.'

And there certainly were a lot of people. Despite how early it was, the marketplace was teeming with men, women, and children, all gawking at me as I passed.

I'm not sure what impression I made on them, but I certainly made one, nonetheless.

'It sounds like Ellie and I will get along perfectly,' Adena says, her smile bright.

'Oh, I'm sure you will.' I laugh before continuing, 'And you will be paid, fed, and have a real bed to sleep in at night. I'm told there is a sewing room where you will spend most of your time, filled with every type of fabric you could ever dream of.'

Adena's eyes go glossy at the thought. 'Heaven. I'll be in heaven.'

I fill her in on everything – the training, the interviews, the contestants. She does the same, telling me of her time in Loot while I've been gone.

'I was beginning to think you forgot about me!' Adena says with a laugh, dismissing the idea. 'And now, here you are, taking me back with you!'

A wave of guilt slams into me, threatening to drown.

I swallow before opening my mouth to plead for forgiveness, to tell her I'm sorry, to—

'I could never forget about you, A.'

Never again.

She beams while my heart beats wildly against my chest. She's so very good, and I am so very guilty. I'm weak for withholding the truth from her, but with each beat of my heart, I vow to never do it again.

'Oh, wait! Who are you going to the ball with?' Adena's high-pitched question cuts through my confused thoughts.

Of course Adena would know that detail of the Trials, how we all have to pair up for the balls. She loves this sort of stuff. I run a hand through my hair, combing it out of my face. 'Well . . . I'm going with Kitt.'

Adena blinks. And then she shrieks.

'Kitt? You mean, the *heir*?' She's practically hyperventilating, fanning herself with her hands.

'It's not a big deal, A. Except that I do need to look good,' I say, trying to calm her down.

'Well then you came to the right girl,' she says confidently. 'Wow, okay, you have to look *really* good then.' She swipes at the curly bangs falling into her eyes. 'Well, there are several beautiful shades of green we could choose from. We could put you in an emerald, or a sage—'

I hold a hand up, a smile curving my lips. 'Actually, I have a different color in mind.'

CHAPTER 20

Kai

I'm standing in a sea of black. Black suit coats, black ties, black shoes. Like ink, the men filling the ballroom swirl around on the white marble floors, words hastily scribbled on a piece of glossy parchment.

Servants dance around the room, though they have no music to accompany them as they weave through the crowd. They make their laps, bringing wine, champagne, and extravagant finger foods on even more extravagant plates.

Seeing that the Trials are *different* this year – thanks to me and the testing of the future Enforcer – it's no surprise that the balls would be out of the ordinary as well. Typically, the Trial's balls are just that: balls. They consist of far too many hours of dancing and tedious small talk, both of which require excessive amounts of alcohol to get through.

But this Trial's first ball begins with a banquet.

Black-clad bodies dot the room, men of all ages milling about. That is, men of all ages who are either nobility, of royal blood, or have somehow managed to get an invite to the Purging Trials first ball.

After an hour of hopping between throngs of men, making idle conversation with both young and old, friend and foe, I'm restless

and bored at best. Kitt and I have retired to reside by one of the many beautiful tables bordering the ballroom, brimming with drinks.

I've passed the time by admiring my favorite room of the castle, taking it in for the hundredth time. Its marble columns and large, floor-to-ceiling windows line the room, giving it an ethereal look. Chandeliers droop from the ceiling, dripping with diamonds and elegance. Two sets of emerald-padded staircases mirror each other as they descend to the marble floor from the balcony high above. Golden, detailed doors open onto the half-circle platform overlooking the ballroom floor, which is so shiny I can see my own bored reflection in it.

I sip at my second glass of wine, wishing I had something stronger. *Any minute now.*

The small orchestra seated in the far corner of the elegant ballroom strums to life just as the glistening doors at the top of the balcony swing open. A beautiful woman cocooned in silky emerald steps up to the railing and looks down at the floor beneath her.

Mother.

She beams, practically glowing. Then she begins gracefully descending the staircase to her right with measured, light steps. Sometimes I forget that even she is a fighter with her Volt ability to manipulate electricity that can easily be used in deadly ways if she wished.

The click of her heels sounds against the marble floor as she makes her way across the ballroom. The men part, creating a path for her as she heads for my father seated at the far end of the room.

He smiles – *really* smiles at her. It's a rare expression for him, one that he only seems to wear when she is around. He stands, meeting her in the middle of the room before taking her arm.

The king looks around, eying the men eying him. 'Let the first ball of the Purging Trials begin!' The men cheer as the king and queen walk together, talking and welcoming those they pass.

And so it begins.

Women, both young and old begin filing through those golden doors, one at a time. As is tradition, the men always enter the ballroom first and wait for the women to arrive, in honor of the queen who appeared fashionably late to the ball where she first met Father, every eye on her as she made her entrance. Since then, every woman has been given the opportunity to make their arrival for all to watch and admire.

Dozens of them descend the staircases, all varying in different shades of green. As soon as they reach the floor, their dates whisk them away and take a seat at one of the many tables that litter the far side of the ballroom.

Kitt and I watch the parade of women as we sip our wine, admiring from a distance. They come in no particular order, no ranking or status involved in who gets to walk through the door next. I watch as my cousin sweeps in, wearing a mint green dress that contrasts her wine-red hair. Andy smiles at Jax from where he waits for her at the bottom of the stairs, a goofy grin on his face. She pulls him towards the large table meant for the contestants, centered among the others to allow the guests a perfect view of us. A dinner and show.

I watch them take a seat before turning my attention back to the balcony, finding the steady stream of women beginning to slow. I spot Hera and Ace making their way through the crowd, neither of them looking particularly happy to be paired with one another. My eyes dart back up to the doors when Sadie enters, her brown skin glistening against her light green dress as she walks down the steps to an awaiting Braxton. A shade of lilac catches my eye, revealing Blair standing at the top of the stairs, peering down from the railing. Forest green fabric hugs her waist, her figure, before billowing out at her feet. Her hair is pinned and twisted out of her face, a sly grin already spreading across it when she spots me.

'Good luck, Brother,' Kitt mutters, and I don't miss the amusement in his tone.

After being cornered before dinner a few nights ago, Blair insisted we go to the ball together. And seeing that I didn't have a choice in the matter, a reluctant yes was the only answer I could give.

I shove my wine glass into Kitt's hand with an annoyed sigh. 'Take care of that.' I nod down to the cup he now clutches. 'I'll definitely be needing it.'

Kitt's deep laugh follows me as I make my way to the bottom of the stairs, meeting Blair there just in time. I hold out an arm to her, which she clutches greedily. 'You look stunning, Blair,' I say softly, because she does, in a cold and sharp sort of way.

'Why, thank you, Kai,' she muses, her darkened lashes lowering as she takes in my attire, my hair, my face. 'As do you.'

I lead us to the table, now mostly filled with the contestants sitting stiffly around it. When I take the seat beside Jax, he shoots me that bright smile of his that never fails to make me return it.

'Look at you, J. You cleaned up nice,' I say, surveying his crisp suit and dark pants that are actually long enough to cover his ankles for once. 'You can't even tell I whooped your ass in the ring this morning.'

I hear Andy snort on the other side of Jax before she leans in to add, 'You're not the only one.'

Jax rolls his eyes at our teasing, but the grin never leaves his face. 'Where's Kitt? He's the only one of you who's nice to me.'

Andy presses a hand to her chest, feigning offense while I don't even bother trying to deny that he's right. Instead, I simply say, 'True, but you know I'm far more fun.'

Jax opens his mouth to respond, but it's a cold female voice I hear instead. 'Are you? Because I'm bored.'

I slowly turn to face Blair, having forgotten she was even there. I'm a terrible date, though I suppose she signed up for this when she asked me to be her partner, so I don't waste my time feeling bad about it. 'So sorry I'm not entertaining you, Blair.' I hear Andy snort before I add, 'How are you this evening?'

She smiles, seemingly pleased that I'm providing her my undivided attention. And that is all she needs to begin complaining about the uncomfortable pins in her hair before going on to discuss the material of her gown, insisting I should feel how soft it is.

Jax snickers beside me through it all, unable to stifle his laugh each time I hum in agreement or nod my head at words I'm not entirely listening to. But I'm snapped out of my bored daze when a goblet is set before me.

'Thought you might want that back, Brother.'

I turn my head to find Kitt standing behind my chair before my eyes slide to *her* shimmering beside him.

She is every bit the Silver Savior.

Shining, silver fabric clings to her body. Thin straps wrap over her shoulders, holding up the dress with its plunging neckline, revealing her tanned skin and sharp collarbones. It melds to her waist and hips like melted coins, reminding me of the ones she stole when we first met.

Paedyn's coal-lined lashes sweep over me as I take her in. Her hair is like a curtain covering her dress, making it difficult to tell where the silver strands end and the shiny dress begins. Fabric fans out around her ankles, displaying a large slit sliding up the length of her leg, mirroring the one I tore in her dress that day of the interviews. And there, strapped to her thigh, is a silver dagger for all to see. I fight my smile at the sight of her deadly weapon paired with her dazzling attire – so lovely, yet so lethal.

Every bit of her is draped in silver. Not green. Not expected.

Beautiful, bold, not blending in.

A statement. A reminder of who she is and what she did.

The women aren't necessarily required to wear green to these balls, and it seems Paedyn took advantage of that little detail.

Her eyes briefly meet mine before Kitt leads her to the other side of the table. And that's all it takes to have me downing my own drink and desperately wishing this night was over. My eyes flick up, meeting Paedyn's across the table where she's now sitting. She holds my gaze, only breaking it when Kitt says something softly beside her, turning her attention from me and pinning those ocean eyes on him.

I shamelessly watch them interact, not caring who sees me staring. Paedyn seems tense as they talk quietly, her eyes continually straying to the collar of his shirt rather than meeting his gaze. I watch as she slowly spins that ring on her thumb, almost smiling at the sight of it paired with her gown. But she nods while Kitt does the same, no doubt very aware of the dozens of eyes watching them from the surrounding tables.

Servants begin pouring into the ballroom, carrying trays piled with steaming plates of food. It's not long before we are eating seasoned salmon and buttered asparagus in silence, the only sound the scraping of forks and the chattering of guests surrounding us.

And I would have loved to keep it that way, might have even enjoyed a ball for once if we could have sat there and let the silence swallow us. But instead, my *date* decides to open her mouth.

'That's a lovely gown you're wearing, Paedyn.' Blair's tone is mocking, her mouth curving into a smirk.

I sigh, looking up from my plate to see Paedyn smiling slightly. 'Why, thank you.' Her eyes skim over Blair and her green attire. 'And your dress is so very . . . *unique*,' she says with a pointed look at the rest of the ballroom and the women wearing similar shades.

Blair's eyes narrow. 'I don't know if you were taught this in the *slums*, so let me enlighten you. Ilya's kingdom color is green. Not silver.'

I stiffen at the way she spat out the word *slums*, drawing even Sadie and Braxton from their quiet conversation to cast wary glances around the table. We all seem to be holding our breath, awaiting Paedyn's response.

And she never seems to disappoint.

After taking a slow sip from her glass, she meets Blair's burning gaze. 'Hmm. And did living in the *palace* teach you how to be a bitch?'

Blair snaps.

Before I can blink, the knife placed beside Paedyn's plate is now raised in front of her chest, its point aimed at her heart.

The sight sends a shock of anger through me, but my voice is far cooler than my sudden rage as I say, 'Easy, ladies.' Borrowing the Tele ability, I push the knife back down onto the table with a clatter while ignoring the glare Blair shoots me. 'I'm not normally the one breaking up fights, but let's not try to kill each other before the Trials even start.'

Guests murmur around us, watching their contestants with eager expressions. I can't even begin to imagine how entertaining this must be for them, watching our feeble attempts to be civil with one another when we will be anything but tomorrow.

Ace laughs, the sound haughty and humorless. 'Is that what you intend to do, Kai? Kill us?' When I finally deign to look at him, I don't miss the gleam in his eyes accompanying the challenge in his voice.

I level him with a stare. 'I intend to win.'

'As do the rest of us,' Ace replies before running a hand over his oiled hair, chuckling. 'Well, all of us except for Paedyn, who simply intends to *survive*.'

He's mocking her answer from the interviews.

Hera squirms in her seat beside Ace, clearly as uncomfortable as the rest of the table. And what I'm about to say is going to make things a hell of a lot worse.

'Enough.'

Kitt's voice cuts through the tension, turning all eyes on him. But he only has eyes for one person, one girl wearing the glittering dress beside him as he says, 'Dance with me, will you? Please?'

Paedyn hesitates for only a moment before nodding. And then I'm staring after them as they stride onto the dance floor where several other couples have begun spinning in time to the music.

Blair is suddenly saying something to me, dragging me to my feet before dragging me onto the dance floor. I don't remember when we started dancing. Suddenly, she's in my arms, and we are spinning across the marble floor. The feel of her is foreign to me after the nights spent with Paedyn in my arms. Nights that I still haven't told Kitt about.

I was doing him a favor.

My eyes wander across the dance floor, landing on my brother and the girl in his arms. I'm not wearing green, but I feel it, nonetheless. Envy claws at me as I watch them step in time to the very waltz I led Paedyn through only last night. She looks elegant, enticing, entrancing.

What the hell is wrong with me?

I turn away from their spinning forms, angry with myself for feeling. Feeling jealousy and possessiveness over the one girl who's made it clear that I shouldn't.

So, I distract myself. I dance with Blair and other beautiful women who sweep me onto the dance floor. I flirt and toy with them, focusing on the girls in front of me rather than the one dancing close by with my brother.

I catch her watching me and our eyes lock, sparks dancing between us.

She is the embodiment of a bad decision. The twin of danger and desire. The fine line between deadly and divine.

And I can feel myself drowning.

CHAPTER 21

Paedyn

The world spins around me, green and black blurring together. I gasp, caught off guard by the spin before I'm suddenly pulled back into strong arms, the faint smell of spices and deep laughter washing over me.

'Sorry, I thought you were ready for it,' Kitt chuckles, green eyes daring me to look into them.

'A better dancer would have been,' I say with a small smile, my eyes roaming around the room instead of meeting his. The ballroom is like nothing I've ever seen before with its windows, pillars, and beautiful molding. I'm stunned by the sheer size and elegance surrounding me.

The people filling the space fit in perfectly with the surroundings, all of them groomed and graceful. The men garbed in deep black while the women are draped in every shade of green.

Well, every woman but me.

Adena was stunned into the silence for the very first time when I told her I wanted a silver dress. I needed to stand out. Needed to remind the people of their *Silver Savior*. And since there is no rule declaring that women *must* wear green, the only risk in showing up in silver was drawing more attention to myself if I trip all over the dance floor.

So many eyes, so many people watching as I descended the stairs. So many gazes sweeping over my body, skimming over the slitted dress and dagger beneath. Even now, I'm being watched. They all look at me with varying levels of intrigue, some with curiosity and others with scrutiny. I'm not sure I'll be winning these people's votes tonight, but I am certainly making myself hard to forget.

I look up at Kitt, his blond hair appearing even lighter against the dark suit cut close to his figure. He looks . . . handsome. Charming.

Like his father. He looks like his father.

'Are you ready for tomorrow?' he asks softly, still spinning me slowly. My eyes snap to his of their own accord. 'Am I supposed to be?'

He almost laughs, but instead says, 'No. You're not.'

'And does that seem fair to you?' I blurt before I can stop myself. 'These Trials?'

The song comes to an end, our dancing doing the same. I feel his gaze wandering over my face even after I look away, as if he is searching for the answer there. Then he sighs. 'Why don't I get us something to drink?' I blink. Despite him evading my question, I nod in answer to his. He looks around at the men crowding the dance floor, several suddenly staring in our direction. 'And I suppose I'll share you with everyone else, if only for a few dances.' He smiles before giving me a slight bow of his head and striding away.

As soon as the future king turns his back, a tall young man meets me on the dance floor and sweeps into a bow. I politely accept his offer to dance and don't have time to be nervous before his arms are encircling me. I can't help but feel a pinch of pride at how well I keep up with his long strides, and we talk idly while spinning across the floor.

When a new waltz strums to life, a new partner steals me away. I'm suddenly folded between the arms of a young man, seemingly my age, with pale blue hair meticulously styled atop his head.

'I would have never guessed you were a Mundane from the slums by the looks of you,' he says, his gaze roaming greedily up and down my body. I shift uncomfortably in his tight grasp clamped around my waist, feeling the reassuring weight of my dagger strapped to my thigh. If it weren't for the favor of the people I'm trying to earn, that little comment would have earned him a fist to the face. His voice is lower than before when he says, 'You're a vision.'

'She is, isn't she?'

My heart skips a beat. The voice coming from over my shoulder is so cold I nearly shiver. Kai brushes my arm as he steps around me, facing the stunned boy still clutching me to him.

'I'll be stealing her now,' Kai says simply, completely aware of how inappropriate it is to cut in during the middle of a dance. But, then again, he is the prince, the next Enforcer, *a cocky bastard*.

The man's hand drops slowly from my waist, his eyes flicking over me one last time before he offers Kai a quick bow and steps away. The prince doesn't miss a beat. I'm in his arms before the musicians' finish drawing out their note.

He feels too familiar.

We fit together perfectly, pieces of a puzzle snapping into place. I shouldn't let myself relax into his touch. Shouldn't let the tension ease from my body when he holds me. But I can do nothing to stop it. Utterly and completely powerless.

His palm is flat and firm against my exposed back, calluses brushing my flushed skin. 'You looked like you needed saving,' Kai says, and I catch a glimpse of his smirk before he spins me.

'For once,' I sigh, 'I'm going to have to agree with you.'

'I'm sure I could think of other things we agree on.'

'Oh really? And what would those things be?'

'That he was right,' Kai says softly. 'You are a vision. I'm sure we can both agree on that.'

I swallow, my heart beginning to pound a rapid beat I choose to ignore. Unsure of what to say to him, I instead ask, 'And what other things do we agree on?'

'Hmm,' he hums distractedly as his eyes sweep over my face. 'Are you having a good time tonight?'

I blink at him. 'Well . . .'

'Spit it out, Gray.'

'Fine,' I huff. 'Not particularly, no.'

He cracks a smile. 'Then we both agree that these balls are incredibly boring.'

I can't help but laugh. 'And what if *you're* the reason I'm not having a good time?'

'If that were the case,' he says with a grin, 'you likely would have stomped on my toes or pulled a dagger on me to get away by now.'

'Don't give me any ideas, Prince.'

He chuckles softly. 'You're right. I'd hate to bloody my suit.'

We continue spinning around the dance floor while I ignore how close his body is to mine and look around the crowded room filled with chatter, laughter, and music. I spot Andy laughing with Jax as they stumble around the dance floor, and it doesn't take long to find the other contestants in the crowd.

When my gaze lands on Kitt, I'm surprised to find him already watching me. He's surrounded by a group of fawning girls, but his eyes are trained on Kai and me as we dance, doing nothing to interrupt his brother and steal back his date. And there, clasped in his hands are two drinks, one full while the other is nearly empty.

I'm about to look back at my partner when my eyes snag on a servant. The boy's dark, curly hair bounces atop his head with each stride as he carries a tray of bubbling beverages through the crowd. His brown eyes sweep across the room as if searching for something or someone.

The boy from Loot. The boy with the leather. The boy I stole from. The boy with the note addressed to my house.

A tidal wave of questions floods my mind. Why is he here? I thought he was an apprentice, not a servant. Is he looking for me, looking for the paper I stole from him?

I'm swept from my thoughts when Kai spins me and my eyes dart to his without my permission.

Mistake.

His midnight hair falls over his forehead in messy, silky waves. Smoky gray eyes meet mine, captivating, chilling. His set jaw loosens, pulling his lips into a cocky grin as he watches me take him in.

Dimples. Both of them mocking me.

'Like what you see, Gray?' he croons, knowing that will get a rise out of me. I huff, looking away from him to fight the flush that's finding its way to my cheeks. Rough fingers glide from my back to

181

catch my chin, gently guiding my face back to his as he mutters, 'By all means, carry on. I'll never deny myself the chance of watching you watch me.'

'And why is that?' I ask with a nonchalance I don't feel.

His smile is wicked. 'Because it is far more fun to admire you when the action is mutual.'

I nearly choke on my laugh. 'Don't flatter yourself, Prince. I am not admiring you or your stupid dimples,' I sputter, trying to act as though I wasn't, in fact, doing just that. His smile only grows, causing those dimples in his cheeks to deepen distractingly.

'*Liar.*'

A frustrated sound escapes me as I glare up at him, refusing to give him the satisfaction of avoiding his piercing gaze. We continue dancing to the slow tune, our movements slowing in turn as Kai asks, 'So, what's the score now?'

'What?' My brows scrunch in question at the sudden change of topics, though I'm relieved, nonetheless.

'I've helped you, what, three times? Possibly four, now?' His eyes study my face intently. 'So that makes it four to one, then.'

I huff out a laugh. 'First of all, I didn't *help* you. I *saved* you, remember?' I raise my eyebrows at him. 'Surely that has to count for more than just one point. Besides, I didn't realize we were keeping track.'

'Fair enough.' He shrugs slightly. 'How about we say the score is two to four then? That's generous.'

My eyes light up. 'Look at that. The prince finally admitted I saved him.'

He laughs, the sound rumbling through his chest, crinkling the corners of his eyes. 'I never said—'

Splitting screams drown out his words.

I'm momentarily stunned, only snapped out of my daze when pain tears through my left forearm. The shooting jolt has my eyes falling to the torn, bloody flesh there.

Throwing knife.

Suddenly, I'm crashing to the floor with a strong, solid body landing on top of me. No, a strong, solid body *covering* me. Explosives erupt around the room, and my ears ring from the impact. I feel a wave of heat accompanied by smoke and hunks of stone sailing towards us.

Kai's large frame hovers over me, his hand cradling the back of my head so my skull didn't crack on the hard marble when he threw us to the ground. He's shielding my body from the debris and knives flying around the room. I regain my hearing slowly, each scream amplifying as my ears pop and ring back to life. I hear terror and the trampling of feet all around us, men and women rushing towards the exits, trying to escape the madness.

Kai wrenches me to my feet, ducking low as he half drags me towards the wall, trying to get us out of the open. 'What is going on?!' I shout over the sound of explosions and echoes of screams. But Kai is busy barking orders at the guards and people around us, telling them what to do and how to do it. Every bit the future Enforcer.

The ballroom is utter chaos. Debris from the explosions litter the once pristine floors. Throwing knives glint as they whiz through the air, thrown by the few fleeing figures wearing black strips of leather that cover only the top half of their faces.

Mimicking the Imperials' masks.

Who are these people?

A few bodies scatter the floor, some soaked in blood, others crushed under the large chunks of stone thrown from the explosions and struggling to free themselves. But the element of surprise has passed, and the Elites that were dancing cheerfully only minutes ago now fight back against the masked figures. Guards pour into the room, some Flashes, others Blazers or Brawnies.

A few Shields scatter purple forcefields around the room, protecting those around them from the attack as weapons bounce harmlessly off the glowing domes. Without a second thought, Kai adapts the Shields' ability to throw up his own forcefield around us.

'There's no time to explain.' His eyes are wide, the only sign of his worry. 'How badly are you hurt?' He reaches for me, but I step away, my back colliding with the hard wall behind me. Pain shocks up my arm, but I grit my teeth and ignore it.

'I'm fine, but what is—'

'I need you to get to one of the safe rooms. The guards will take you—'

'Kai, I'm not leaving.'

He flattens me fully against the wall, boxing me in with his arms on either side of my head. His eyes are wild, like smoke smoldering from a blazing fire. 'Then don't think I won't throw you over my damn shoulder and carry you out of here myself. Is that what you want?'

I know he'll do it too. Kai is not one for empty threats. I look over his shoulder at the few masked figures trying to flee and fight their way out. They look unprepared, using weapons rather than powers, doing little damage against the abilities being used against them.

I watch the chaos ensue, confusion clouding my thoughts. Where are the Ignites who caused the explosions? My eyes scan the room, snagging on a round, glass object sloshing with dark liquid, clutched in the hand of a masked figure.

Homemade bombs.

It hits me then.

They aren't using powers because they have none.

Because they are Ordinaries.

'Let me help,' I breathe, my eyes pleading with Kai. I need to get closer. Need to see who these people are and where they came from.

'No.'

'I can take care of myself.'

His laugh is dry. 'Then prove it. Go quietly to the safe room. Now.'

'Make me.' I practically growl the words in his face through gritted teeth.

Wrong thing to say.

He looks away and exhales, shaking his head. 'You're too stubborn for your own good, Gray.'

And then the world flips upside down.

His hand is cupping the back of my knees, and my upper body is slung over his shoulder, hanging down his back. I thrash in his hold, but his grip is firm. I feel like a toddler throwing a tantrum, and I don't care in the slightest.

'Put. Me. *Down*.' My tone promises a slow and painful death, but he ignores me, nonetheless.

'If you knew how to follow orders, I wouldn't have to throw you

184

around like a rag doll,' Kai says coolly.

I grapple for my dagger, dangerously furious. 'Kai, I am *literally* going to stab you in the back if you don't—'

'If you think a stab wound will stop me then you seriously underestimate my abilities, darling.'

Through the silver curtain of hair falling limply over my head, I stop struggling long enough to watch the remaining masked figures blur past us on the outside of our bubble forcefield. And then my eyes snag on one with floppy, dark curls.

Him.

His mask clings to his face like a second skin, and when his gaze meets mine, I take a slow breath. He halts, watching me as I watch him.

He's one of them. And he recognizes me.

The note. The meeting place.

The leather.

Sure enough, each of them is engulfed in leather vests and masks.

Armor. He was making armor for them.

Suddenly, we are standing near a circle of Imperials surrounding something, trying to contain it. Kai pushes through the throng, and I catch Kitt out of the corner of my eye, fighting and thrashing against the guards restraining him.

'I thought I told you to get him out of here.' Kai's voice is deep, deadly.

'Sir, he wouldn't—' an Imperial starts before Kitt cuts him off, more aggressive than I've ever seen him.

'I'm not hiding from this, Kai. This is my kingdom too.' His voice is stern, on the verge of yelling into his brother's face.

'Well, there won't be a kingdom for you to rule if you *die*, Kitt,' Kai fires back, his tone cool. 'You need to lie low until this is cleaned up. This could be an attempt on your life.'

'I'm not leaving this fight!' Kitt roars.

'Then you risk damning us all!' Kai's cool facade finally cracks, sending shards of white-hot anger rippling through the air. He sighs and steadies his breathing. 'We need you alive, Kitt. *I* need you alive. Just . . .' He pauses, collecting himself as he pieces his mask back together. 'Sit this one out. For the kingdom. For me.'

They eye each other, silently communicating in the way that only brothers as close as they are can. I get the sudden sense that this is a frequent fight between them, a reoccurring battle of wills.

I watch as Kitt's face crumples, his walls crumble. I watch him give in. 'Fine. It seems it's my fate to always sit these fights out, right?'

Kai doesn't respond and instead sets me gently on the ground before him. Without a single glance in my direction, he says, 'Get them to a safe room with the others.'

And then he's running back into the thick of the fight, dozens of powers flicking over his skin before he settles on one.

Fire.

CHAPTER 22

Paedyn

itt hasn't stopped pacing since the moment we were shoved into this stuffy safe room. I fight the urge to yank him to the floor, make him explain to me what is going on. Instead, I've watched him mumble and circle the room for the past hour. Watched his fingers ignite like flickering candles when his burning fury seeped out of him, displaying that Dual ability of his.

A thin layer of sweat has slicked my body, likely giving me the appearance of a glazed sticky bun. I'm slumped on the floor of the stone-encased safe room, the cold wall against my exposed back the only slight relief from the heat of the room caused by the dozens of bodies crowded together, all wearing heavy gowns and starchy suits.

The safe room is sealed shut by a hefty metal door, guarded on either side, and trapping the suffocating humidity in here with us. Kitt and I were stuffed into the same room that the king and queen occupy, as well as most of the other contestants and whatever other guests made it in here. It's fairly large, plain, and packed with people.

Out of the large throng, only two Healers are among the crowded room. They buzz about, tending to the wounded and injured after ensuring that the king, queen, and Kitt were taken care of. After a while, a stout lady in a deep green gown finally waddles over to me,

saying nothing as she mends the knife wound on my arm. Her brows knit together in concentration as I feel a wave of warmth seeping into the gash and look down to see the wound nearly gone, leaving only a thin, pink scar remaining.

But it's my heart that aches more than the wound did, feeling more cut and sliced than my body has ever been. I'd watched my father do that very same thing to so many people. Watched him save lives. Fix wounds. Fix *my* wounds. I wish he was here to fix the broken, mangled object that is now my heart. The heart that broke when he left me.

When he was murdered by the man sitting in this very room.

My eyes flick to the king and queen, talking in hushed, urgent tones with each other and the few trusted advisers around them. No doubt discussing what the Plague just happened out there and what to do about it. Kitt has been summoned to his father's side countless times to speak silently with the advisers, but afterward, he always finds his way back to pacing around the room.

I unwedge myself from Jax and Andy who are sticky with sweat on either side of me and step into Kitt's path.

'Hi,' I say stupidly, unable to think of a better introduction.

He almost smiles before sighing, 'Hi.'

If I want him to talk to me, I need to play the part.

I take a deep breath before putting a hand on his exposed arm, his suit coat long forgotten, and the white sleeves of his shirt now rolled up to his elbows. His skin is scalding, and I snatch away my hand with a small hiss as my eyes drop to the faint flames licking over his knuckles.

I blink and the fire is gone, leaving only rough skin behind.

'Did I burn you?' Kitt blurts out, looking alarmed. He reaches for me but thinks better of it, raking his hands through his messy hair instead. 'I can't even keep my damn power in check,' he mutters, turning away from me.

'No . . . no, I'm fine.' He won't look at me. His hands are running through his hair, down his face. 'Hey,' I say, but my words fall on deaf ears. He's about to start pacing again.

I need him to focus.

On an impulse, I reach up and cup his face in my hands, feeling only the natural warmth of his skin beneath my palms. I prepare myself to meet those eyes, knowing I need to do this in exchange for an answer. His gaze snaps to mine, green and crisp like dew clinging to freshly cut grass. Like a lucky four-leaf clover, an emerald sparkling in the sunlight.

Like the eyes of a murderer. The eyes of the king.

'Talk to me.' The words tumble out of my mouth, sounding more like an order than I intended. So I quickly add, 'Please.'

He sighs and ducks his head before gently grabbing my wrists and lowering them from his face. Then, he guides me towards the least crowded corner in the room, his warm hands pulling me to the floor beside him before resting his arms on his raised knees. 'I'm sorry that I'm so . . . flustered,' Kitt finally says. I've never seen him so serious, so stern, so *kingly*. 'I don't like people fighting my battles.' He bites out the words like he hates the taste of them in his mouth.

'I guess that is something you will have to get used to when you're king,' I say softly.

He scoffs. 'You mean, get used to my brother constantly risking his life while I sit back and watch?' Heat seems to ripple off him, and I suddenly wonder if he is partially to blame for this stifling room.

I see it then, the green of his eyes that matches the jealousy, the envy. I can see the part of him that wishes he could run into battle and save the day like his brother. Wishes he could earn his father's favor through brawn and not brains. Wishes he could be the hero, rather than the one the hero is protecting.

And yet, I feel no pity for the boy before me. To envy Kai is to envy a murderer.

Play the part. Play him.

'What I mean,' I say, slowly, 'is that you have your duties, and Kai has his. You're both fighting for your kingdom, just in different ways.'

I can see he's not convinced, but he offers me a smile anyway, one that almost reaches his eyes. 'You would make quite the adviser, you know that?'

'Well, maybe if I survive these Trials, you can hire me.' He chuckles softly at that, and I give him a small smile in return. 'Although,' I say with a sigh, 'advisers are supposed to know what is going on, and I sure as hell don't.'

Come on. Tell me. Trust me.

Kitt sighs. 'Fine, you deserve to know what's going on, seeing that one of them nearly sliced your arm off.' He brushes a thumb over the thin scar on my exposed arm, his eyes tracing it. I shrink away from the touch, and the action doesn't go unnoticed.

Kitt clears his throat and leans away from me. 'They call themselves the Resistance.' His voice is low and steady, intended for only me to hear. 'They are a group of Ordinaries that have been banding together for years. Fighting against the king and the kingdom because of what was done to their kind.'

Their kind. My kind.

I force myself to swallow my disgust and listen as he continues. 'At first, they were barely a threat, a joke of a revolution. We've kept this little group a secret, kept it hidden from the people for a few years now. It hasn't been hard to do till recently. But clearly, they are bigger and stronger than before.'

I think I stopped breathing. All I hear is the blood pounding in my ears as I take in the weight of his words.

A group of Ordinaries fighting against the king and the kingdom.

'How?' The word is raspy, almost drowned out in the chatter of the room. 'How is there such a large group of Ordinaries? How are they such a threat now?'

'Apparently, there were a lot more Ordinaries hiding in Ilya than suspected after they were banished, and as long as they repopulate here in the kingdom, their numbers will continue to grow.' He heaves a heavy sigh. 'But the Resistance seems to be more of a cause than a group. They are spread out all over the city, hiding in plain sight. Which makes things far more difficult since they aren't all gathered in one place. And what's worse, we don't think they are working alone.'

I raise my eyebrows in question, and he continues. 'They have Elites working with them. Powerful ones. Ones that are also pissed off at my father, at the kingdom.'

My forehead crinkles in confusion, trying to figure out what he

190

means. And then it clicks, right as Kitt voices what I've just pieced together.

'The Fatals. The Silencers, the Mind Readers, and the Controllers. Father banished them alongside the Ordinaries during the Purging because of how dangerous they were, even to other Elites, and he only keeps one of each in his court who are loyal to him. But there are still some out there, and we currently have one in the dungeons beneath us.' He nods at me with a small smile. 'We have you to thank for that.'

The Silencer.

'Wait,' I say slowly, trying to puzzle everything out, 'if the Fatals are truly working with the Resistance, then why wouldn't they fight in the attack? They would have done a lot more damage if they had.'

Kitt runs a hand through his hair. 'We aren't sure. Maybe they weren't intending on attacking. They were unprepared and incredibly outnumbered, which makes me wonder why they came here in the first place.'

Words fall out of my mouth, and I can do nothing to stop them. 'And what do you think about this Resistance?'

'What do I think about these criminals?' He sighs through his nose, shaking his head. 'I . . . I understand. I think it's wrong, but I understand why they are doing it.' He looks me dead in the eyes. 'But if they are allowed to live, then the Elite race will slowly die. Who knows how many Elites have already been infected by the Ordinaries hiding among them? I'm sure people have already begun to feel the effects, the weakening of their power.' He pauses, sighing. 'The Ordinaries' sacrifice is necessary for the greater good of the kingdom.'

Right. I forgot that I'm diseased.

I study him, taking in the strong features of his face now etched with tension and stress. 'And that is what you believe?'

I know I should shut my mouth, should nod my agreement instead of risking speaking treason. But something about this boy brings out a recklessness in me, a need to show him how wrong he is, how twisted his kingdom is.

'That is what I know,' he says softly, looking me in the eyes until I tear mine away, unable to unsee my father's murderer in them.

'And yet, you can know something and not believe it.' My voice

191

sounds shaky, and I hope he believes it to be from fear and not anger. 'You have a choice, Kitt. You always have a choice.'

He chuckles, but it's void of humor. 'If I always had a choice, then I wouldn't be in this safe room. I'd be out there, fighting alongside my brother.'

My eyes fall to the flames flickering over his fingers, betraying his frustration. I lift my head and take a breath before looking him in the eyes. 'Do you not want to be king?'

He doesn't hesitate. 'I do not want to be a coward.' I force myself to hold his gaze, seeing all the confusion and consideration reflected in it. 'No one has ever asked me that before.'

'Yes, well, you'll find that I often ask questions that I shouldn't,' I say, looking away from him.

'Don't stop,' he says quickly, quietly. My gaze slides back towards him to rest on the top button of his shirt. 'Your questions, your thoughts, your contradictions – I want to hear them all.'

I open my mouth to reply when a gust of cool air breezes over my face, and the thick metal door swings open with a clang. My head snaps to the handful of Imperials pouring into the room, heading for the king and queen.

'The ballroom is secured, Your Majesty.' The guard's voice is gravelly, his head bowed towards the king who nods curtly.

If I wanted to look into his eyes, I'm sure I would see all the questions swimming in them. Questions about how many dead, how many Ordinaries captured, how much damage. But he doesn't dare voice his thoughts, not in front of an audience and especially not when he's still trying to conceal what is truly happening.

The king stands from his large, wooden chair and clears his throat, further quieting the already hushed room. 'What happened today was unfortunate, and I can assure you it will not happen again.' I nearly snort at the empty promise. 'But we will not let this incident scare us, cripple us, control us. And for that reason, the Trials will continue as scheduled.'

At that, shocked murmurs ripple through the crowd, though I can't say I'm surprised. He needs to keep up his strong facade, show no fear. 'We are Elites. We are power.' The king pauses, scanning the crowded room with that green gaze I avoid. 'Honor to your kingdom. Honor to your family. Honor to yourself.'

The cluster of people around me echo his words, reciting Ilya's motto. My lips move with them, playing the part of the contestant, the one who is honored to be here. The one who is an Elite just like them.

The guards begin ushering guests and nobility out of the sticky room, and I'm nearly trampled by pointy heels and polished shoes from where I still sit on the floor before I scramble to my feet.

'I wish I could walk you to your room, but unfortunately, I'll be trading this stuffy room for another one. Father will likely have Kai and I in meetings right up until the first Trial begins, discussing the *events* that occurred tonight.' Kitt's voice is strained, tired. 'But the guards will make sure you arrive safely to your room, not that there is any real threat now.' His eyes slide down to the dagger hugging my thigh, on display for all to see. 'And if there was a threat, I'm sure you could handle yourself just fine.' He offers me a smile that I barely manage to return.

His eyes drift from me to land on something else near the back of the room. I follow his gaze only to find that the king and queen are staring right back at me. The king is watching through narrowed eyes, and it takes all my strength and training not to throw the same look his way.

'I'll see you after the Trial.' Kitt's voice cuts through my thoughts. 'I *will* see you after the Trial. You expect to survive this, remember?' I duck my head and smile despite myself.

If I make it out of this first Trial alive, I know exactly what I'm going to do.

I'm going to find the Resistance.

And thanks to the curly-haired boy and the note I nicked off him, I know exactly where they will be.

'See you then,' I say to that top button of his shirt before briefly meeting his eyes. They hold a certain warmth and worry, looking less and less like his father's with every blink.

I'm shoved towards the door in a current of human bodies and swept out into the hallway. The corridors are teeming with guards and guests, all scurrying from one place to another. I'm herded down the hallway, swallowed by the sea of people around me. We pass the cracked doors of the ballroom, and through them, I can see rubble and red painting the floors.

My curiosity refuses to release me from its clutches.

It's not hard to slip away from the Imperials, the group. I've mastered the art of going unnoticed and overlooked. Soon I'm pushing open the ballroom doors, the guards completely oblivious in the mayhem.

I'm greeted with gore. Well, the remains of it. Dark blood still splotches parts of the floor, most of it already scrubbed clean with jets of water by the Hydros milling about, leaving nothing but pearly stone in their wake.

Teles are clearing the ballroom of the heavy chunks of rubble, and Gusts wield the air around them to blow all the debris and dust from the floor. In no time at all, the room will be fixed, restored to its pristine state. As if nothing happened.

I'm about to slip back out the door when a mass of messy black hair catches my eye. He's sitting – no, *slumping* on a large slab of stone near the far end of the ballroom, dirty and drenched with blood.

My heart hammers against my ribcage.

He's hurt. And more importantly, why do I care?

I stumble down the steps, taking them two at a time. I nearly twist my ankle in the deadly contraption that are my heels before ungracefully flinging them off my feet, letting them tumble down the stairs before I nearly do the same.

I'm suddenly in front of him, having cleared the ballroom in a matter of seconds. I drop to my knees, looking up into his bloody, dirt-streaked face. His gray eyes only look startled for a moment before they begin roaming over me, searching my body for injuries as I do the same to him. Words spew from my mouth. 'What happened? Where are you hurt?'

I look around, scanning the room. 'And where are those damn Healers?'

'Ah, Gray. Just the person I wanted to see.' He grinds out the words through gritted teeth, though he's still acting like his cool, collected self.

'What happened?' I demand, taking in his ripped clothes and the exposed chest beneath, now covered in gashes. His hands and most of his body are coated in blood, though I'm sure most of it doesn't even belong to him.

'Before we get to that,' he fights to keep the grimace from gracing his features, 'did a Healer get to you?' He's suddenly serious, pain forgotten as his eyes sweep over me yet again.

I'm both confused and annoyed with him – a common occurrence, it seems. 'What? Yes. I'm fine.' I dismiss his question and scoot closer, hands slightly outstretched. 'But clearly, you're not.'

'And here I was thinking you hated me and my stupid dimples. I'm touched you care so much about my well-being, Gray.' Even while in obvious pain he still finds a way to smirk. Along with being a total ass.

'Oh, don't mistake my motives, Prince. I only want to keep you alive long enough so I can punch that smirk off your face. Again.' There's little bite in the words, and he huffs out a laugh as he shifts on the stone, exposing more of his back to me.

I gasp. 'What the *hell* is wrong with you?!'

'Darling, that is a very loaded question.'

I ignore his comment, unable to tear my eyes from the throwing knife buried deep into the flesh of his right shoulder blade. 'You've had a knife in your back this whole time and you just let me talk?' I'm sputtering.

A dimple accompanies his crooked grin. 'Oh, but the sound of your voice was such a welcome distraction from the pain.'

Once again, I ignore him before standing to my feet to inspect the knife slicing deep into his back. Sighing, I mumble, 'Yeah, well, now you get to hear me telling you that you're a complete idiot.'

'That's still one of the nicer things you've said to me, so, I'll take it,' he says smoothly, seemingly undisturbed by the piece of metal impaling his body.

I can't even imagine what pain he's been through to make this wound seem so bearable.

'Okay,' I say slowly, 'tell me what to do.'

His laugh is strained. 'You say that like you'll actually listen to me for once.'

'Kai, I'm about to add another knife to your back if you don't—'

'I just need you to pull it out.'

I blink. He says this so casually that I almost think he's joking. 'Then we need to have a Healer here, ready to mend it as soon as the knife is out.'

He breathes out a strained laugh, the muscles beneath his torn shirt shifting. 'I'm offended you doubt my abilities so much. There's a Healer not too far from me. I can feel their power. I'll heal myself.'

'Right. Okay.' I take a deep breath and grip the handle of the knife. 'This is going to hurt.'

'You know, it's a shame we never got to finish our dance,' he says. 'It was the first time I could actually focus on you rather than dodging your stomping feet—'

I yank the knife out in one fluid motion. He grunts and doubles over on the stone. I smile slightly, having gotten revenge on him for what he said about my dancing, however true it may be.

I step around the rubble and crouch in front of him, my face close to his as I watch the pain crowd his handsome features. I flip the knife in my hand, still slick with his blood. 'Tell me, did that hurt as much as my stomping feet?'

His laugh is gruff, pained. I stand to my feet and watch as he reaches a hand around his shoulder, pressing it atop the wound now steadily gushing blood. I stare as the shredded skin stitches itself back together. Stare as flesh and muscle reform before my very eyes, leaving nothing but a jagged scar to join the others across his back.

The tension eases from his stiffened shoulders and he sighs in relief. 'Much better. Thank you.' I'm wondering how rarely those last two words leave his mouth when the corner of it lifts, and he uncoils to his feet. 'Who knew that you'd be the one to pull a knife from my back and not the one to bury it there.'

'There's still plenty of time for that, don't worry.'

He grins, white teeth flashing against his filthy features. Then he rolls his neck and stretches, acting as though he wasn't just impaled a few moments ago.

His palm is suddenly extended towards me expectantly, and I stare at the calluses blankly. When I make no move, he slowly drops his hand to the one at my side, his rough fingers closing around my wrist.

My heartbeat quickens and I curse the stupid organ. He pulls my arm, my hand, towards him – the one still clutching the throwing knife. Then his other hand brushes against my palm, gently prying the handle from my fingers.

'You have enough of these to bury in my back, don't you think?' he says softly, his hand still wrapped around my wrist where he can likely feel my stupid, stammering pulse beneath his fingers. 'So, I think I'll hold on to this one.'

I step out of his grasp, needing to put some space between us. 'Don't you have an important meeting you're supposed to be in right now?' I ask because I simply can't think of anything else to say.

'Probably.' He sighs, running a hand through his hair. 'I'm assuming Kitt filled you in.' I nod before he says, 'Father will go through with the Trials. A power move, of course. And he'll need to finally inform the people of what is going on. He can't hide who and what the Resistance is after tonight.'

'What happened?' I breathe before I'm suddenly annoyed with him, remembering what he did. 'What happened after you bodily removed me from this room like an ass, even though I could have helped?'

Now he's laughing at me. 'You seem to keep forgetting who I am, Gray.'

'My apologies, Your Highness. What happened after you bodily removed me from this room like a *royal* ass?'

'Well, that's progress, I suppose.' He smiles, looking me over again with that piercing gaze of his. 'And to answer your question, that wasn't your fight. Not to mention that I couldn't risk a contestant dying before the first Trial even began.'

My laugh is bitter. 'You know damn well that I can take care of myself—'

'And you know damn well that I could take care of *it*, myself.'

'You got stabbed, remember?'

'Occupational hazard.'

We stare at each other, faces close. I can smell the sweat, blood, and dirt on him, along with the underlying scent of pine still lingering on his skin. I'm breathing heavily, and after a moment too long, I finally take a step away from him.

'How many casualties?' I ask slowly.

He looks away from me, sucking in a breath before saying, 'Only two Elites dead, multiple injured. Four Ordinaries dead, and only two prisoners.' His eyes trail back to mine as he says, 'There were less than a dozen Ordinaries to begin with, which makes me wonder what their real mission was since I don't believe it was to attack a ballroom full of Elites.' I nod absentmindedly, taking in the information. 'So, some escaped?'

A muscle feathers in his jaw. 'Unfortunately.' With that, he begins to back away from me, his eyes never leaving mine. 'I'll see you tomorrow, Gray.'

'See you tomorrow, Azer.'

He finally turns, making his way across the ballroom as I watch his retreating form.

Then he calls over his shoulder. 'Do me a favor, darling?'

'And what's that?'

'Promise me you'll stay alive long enough to stab me in the back?'

I laugh loudly. 'That's been my goal all along, Prince.'

CHAPTER 23

Kai

I nearly swallow a mouthful of damp dirt. My eyes flutter open and I cough into the wet soil beneath me, soaking my clothes and causing them to cling uncomfortably to my body. I roll onto my back, crunching on moss, twigs, and rocks as I blink against the sunlight streaming through looming, tall trees.

Plagues, where am I?

The melody of chirping birds awoke me from my heavy, deep sleep.

Drugged sleep.

Trees crowd the vibrant blue sky above, most of them tall, ominous pines that extend fingers of foliage high into the clouds – and I'd know them anywhere. One becomes familiar with the trees they're forced to scale countless times to overcome a fear of heights.

The Whispers.

I'm in the bloody forest.

I stand to my feet, feeling dizzy, drained, and drugged. An odd pressure at my right forearm has me looking down to see a thin leather band wrapping around it, the ends fused together tightly. It would be cutting off blood circulation completely if it were any tighter, leaving my arm utterly useless.

The sun beats down on me as I spin slowly in place, scanning my surroundings. There is nothing and no one but trees, rocks, and uneven forest ground beneath me, caging me in with foliage.

Why the hell am I in the Whispers?

Obviously, I knew the Trials were still on. That, and the Resistance were all we talked about for hours last night. The throne room is where I spent my evening and early morning, along with Kitt, the king, and his advisers.

My throat is hoarse and scratchy from the long hours of arguing and debating the best course of action with this Resistance, this threat. And now, more than ever, my men and myself are tasked with finding these Resistance members and putting an end to them.

I attempt to brush off the clumps of dirt still clinging to my clothes as I take in this familiar, yet frightening, place. The Whispers is no whimsical forest. Deadly beasts lurk on its huge terrain, and even deadlier plants sprout from it. I would know, seeing that I spent many nights training here with my father barking orders like I was his soldier and not his son.

But why am I here now?

I expected to at least be able to wake up in my own bed, maybe *interrogate* some prisoners before I had to make my way to the Bowl for the first Trial. But I sure as hell wasn't expecting to be drugged and dragged to the forest.

Different.

That's what Tealah had said. There's never been a Trial that has taken place outside of the Bowl where an audience couldn't be present to jeer and cheer at us.

A twig snaps and I whirl, sinking into a fighting position. I stare at the thin man a few dozen feet away, garbed in plain white clothes that contrast against his dark skin. He stares back, his eyes glazed and unmovable.

A Sight.

I feel it then. The tingle of his power beneath my skin. I was too occupied with my thoughts to feel his ability, the power to record as well as project what he sees with nothing but his own two eyes. And that is exactly what he is doing now.

I've always found them unsettling with the way they stare, unblinking, when recording what they are seeing, but I've grown used to them since dozens are always present at the Trials. They run around the Bowl, documenting the events and contestants while using their abilities to project what they are seeing onto large screens high above the Pit floor.

And it seems that they are doing the same for this version of the Trials. Except, he's not projecting what he is seeing and is instead storing the images away for a later time. There must be dozens of them, all running around the forest, following contestants and documenting the first Trial to play back for the audience when this is all over.

I don't take a single step towards him. It's forbidden to interact with the Sights, touch them in any way during the Trials. They are simply the eyes and ears for the audience that can't be here to witness themselves.

The man finally blinks, his eyes clearing slightly after apparently getting all the footage he wanted of me. He moves to step away, no doubt to go collect other images or stalk other contestants. But he pauses mid-step and slowly pats his long, dark fingers against the pocket of his pants, holding my gaze before scurrying back into the forest.

I stare after him before tearing my gaze away and looking down at my own pocket. They threw me in here with only what I had on when I staggered into bed, apart from the shoes they so generously slipped onto my feet. Other than that, only one accessory was added to my body – the strange leather band around my arm. I silently thank the Plague that I kept my thin shirt on last night, too exhausted to pull it off.

I reach into the pocket of my thin pants, fingers closing around a rough scrap of paper. I unfold it carefully, revealing precise, looping penmanship:

Welcome to the first Trial,
In the Whispers you will be.
We hope you stay a while,
In this game of honor and dignity.

The goal of this game is quite clear,
And for the winner we will cheer.
Become victorious by collecting the bands,
The ones that rest high above your opponents' hands.

Collect from those who have been banded,
And be warned if you return empty-handed.
If you wish to win you must have the most,
Then of your glory, we'll brag and boast.

But the end is drawing near,
With only six moons to play.
Welcome to the Trials' sixth year,
And pray to the Plague that you will stay.

The task of stealing as many bands as possible seems fairly simple; that is, if you can survive in the forest for a week. But I read between the lines of the poem.

They are forcing us to fight one another.

No one will give up their band easily. Blood has been spilled over much less than a leather strap in these Trials. I crumple the paper in my fist, shoving it deep into my pocket before glancing at my own strap of leather encircling my bicep. Tight. So tight that the only way to get these Plague forsaken things off is to cut them from the skin, which will inevitably draw blood despite delicacy.

It's intentional, clever.

Father has outdone himself this year.

Sweat trickles into my brow, stinging my eyes. The heat could rival that of the Scorches, and I peel off my shirt to wipe at my slick face. My throat is already dry, parched from baking in the morning sun.

Find water first. Opponents second.

I stop, my feet crunching on the vegetation and rough dirt beneath me. Sighing, I look up at one of the menacing pine trees standing in my path. I shake my head, my shoulders, trying to shake away my nerves. Then, I grab hold of the lowest branch and swing my legs up.

Yes, I've scaled these trees multiple times, and yes, I've conquered my fear of heights. But just because a fear has been conquered, doesn't mean it's enjoyable to be confronted with again and again. And yet, here I am, climbing up the tree, taking each branch at a time.

The wind blows and the sun blinds as I continue up the pine in search of water. Minutes, maybe hours later, with limbs aching and heart racing, I finally reach the top. Well, the last branch that will hold my weight. I'm a couple hundred feet in the air now, suspended there by nothing but a large twig beneath my feet. I look down only to instantly regret it.

Keep it together, Kai.

Falling to my death during a Trial would be a pathetic way to die and would completely ruin my reputation, even in death. With that in mind, I clutch the now thin trunk of the tree beside me as I peer through the leaves and over the top of the canopy of trees.

I feel like I'm back in the ballroom, looking out into a sea of several shades of green. Branches full of leaves swaying in the wind like the finely dressed women swaying on the dance floor only yesterday.

There.

My eyes sweep over a break between the line of trees, a pause in the dance of their leaves. A sliver for a river, a brook, a source of water. At the moment, I don't care if it's a damn puddle.

I painstakingly make my way back to solid ground, my breath coming in quick pants. By the time my feet meet the soil, the sun has inched its way across the sky, informing me that it is already late afternoon.

And then I'm off. Off in the direction of the water every contestant craves after being drugged and having to trudge through the forest for hours. Father has woven a trap for us, one we are all willingly walking into.

Hours. Long, tiresome hours of trekking through foliage is what my life has come to. I've encountered several venomous snakes and plants, daring me to draw close.

I'm so bloody bored.

My eyes and body are alert as I trudge forward, though my mind wanders as much as I do. I think on the Trials, the contestants—

And then my thoughts are on *her. Stop.*

If Paedyn is so determined to hate me, I could make it very, very easy for her. It wouldn't take much. But I'm selfish, weak, and unwilling to make it anything but difficult for her to push me away.

She's bewildering as much as she is beguiling. That pretty mouth of hers says one thing, but those ocean eyes say another. She pulls a knife from my back only to say she'll bury another one there. She's confusing, captivating, and we're completely wrong for each other in all the right ways. She's a flame, and I'm going to get burned. An ocean and I'm going to drown.

I run a hand over my face, wanting to blame my dehydration for whatever the hell is wrong with me.

I've never been so affected by a single girl, and it's absurd, absolutely annoying. But then I grin, remembering her heartbeat hammering beneath my fingers, her breath catching every time I touch her, her eyes drinking in every smile and dimple she supposedly hates.

The feeling of absolute annoyance for being so affected by someone is most definitely mutual, though I'm sure she'd deny it with a dagger to my throat.

So very vicious, that one.

Something glints in the light of the sinking sun, catching my eye.

There, hanging from a branch to my right is a sheathed sword, its silver handle winking in the light as I step towards it. It only takes me a moment to climb up and untie the belt from the branch before hopping down from the tree.

There's likely weapons and other items hidden all over the Whispers for us to use.

Easier to draw blood that way. Easier to make things interesting.

I sling the belt and sheath low on my waist before drawing the sword to chop through the thick foliage.

Almost there.

The ground is covered in shadows, and I now have a rabbit that needs to be cooked along with a stomach that needs to be fed. I'd come across a single throwing star lodged deep into the bark of a tree and used it on the unsuspecting rabbit now tied to my belt.

I pause, hearing it before seeing it.

Gurgling, glorious water. Then a small, shallow creek emerges from the trees, running water skipping over the rocks that occupy it. I hesitate, eyes scanning the seemingly peaceful place.

All is clear – for the time being.

I creep to the edge of the creek, sinking to my knees before it and darting a look over my shoulder every few seconds, not wanting to leave my back exposed. I splash the cool water on my face, letting it drip down my skin and bare chest.

The bubbling brook flows from a small pool a few dozen feet away, the water clean, crisp, and cool.

Man-made.

And fresh. The work of Hydros, no doubt, allowing us this small favor of fresh water. I thank the Plague that the water is so clean, so purified, that it saves me the trouble of having to boil it somehow.

I'm scouring the area for kindling and firewood when I nearly smack my head on something hanging from the tree above, hidden in shadows. Canteens. Two of them, swinging in the evening breeze.

I find myself thanking the Plague once again.

Whittling two sticks together is about as fun as it sounds, but with years of practice and patience, I soon have a fire crackling before me. And though skinning a rabbit with a longsword is as difficult as it is damn annoying, it's soon roasting over the flames.

And then—

A trickle of power tingles through my body, igniting my nerves and sending a familiar chill down my spine. The hair on the back of my neck stands up, feeling that power, that strength, flood my body.

Someone's coming. And I know who.

A twig snaps to my left. Then another.

I don't remember when I stood up, but I'm now dancing on the balls of my feet, unable to help that familiar itch for a fight and looking forward to that dance of dominance and destruction. Fighting is my favorite waltz, and I know the steps by heart.

Braxton barrels through the line of trees, eyes wild when they land on mine. He saw the smoke from my fire and figured he'd ambush whoever had lit it. But unlucky for him, I felt him coming before I even heard him sprinting through the forest.

I see him hesitate as if he's debating turning back around rather than risking a fight with me. But the uncertainty flickers from his face as he begins slowly striding closer. He steps into the ring of firelight, his silhouette large and lumbering.

'Hello, Brax. Nice of you to stop by.'

He tips his head towards me in that same way he always has. 'Evening, Kai.'

The Brawny has never been one for talking, instead choosing to patiently observe before uttering a word, making him and Sadie oddly similar. We slowly begin to circle each other in silence, sizing one another up.

'So, I'm assuming you're here for my band and not a friendly chat,' I sigh, taking a step towards him.

'Your assumption would be correct.' He tosses a glance at my cooking rabbit. 'If you offer it to me, I'll leave and let you get back to your meal. There's no need for this to get messy.'

I don't see any weapons on him, so I refrain from reaching for mine. We've known each other since we were boys, and I'd like to keep knowing him if I can help it. 'You and I both know I can't let you have my band, Brax.'

Because it's my mission to win these Trials.

I think I see him nod in the growing darkness before he is suddenly charging at me. I drop low and use his momentum to throw him over my shoulder, hearing him hit the ground with a heavy thud.

I've trained with Braxton for years. He's predictable, but that doesn't make him any less powerful. He's back on his feet in a flash, fists raised and ready to knock my teeth out.

And then calculated chaos ensues.

Fists fly, heads bob, feet weave. A dance. A brutal, bloody, beautiful dance. We are currently equals in ability, seeing that I've let his power escape from my veins and flood to the surface. My blows are brutal and swift in the flickering firelight.

His fist connects with my jaw, nearly breaking it, causing hot blood to pool in my mouth. I stagger back as he steps behind me and he wraps his massive arm around my throat in a chokehold. I can feel his hesitance before my head snaps back, skull meeting his nose with a sickening crunch. Now he's staggering, blood streaming from his nose and into his mouth.

I use the split second to pepper him with swift blows that he can barely block. He recovers quickly, jabbing at my ribs with a powerful fist. I duck under his next swing and land a blow to his jaw.

It's a vicious circle. I hit him. He hits me back. To his credit, I'm impressed. I've never seen him so focused, so determined. This is the best fight I've had with him to date. It's a shame I'll have to put an end to it.

A dark hand comes flying straight at my face. I easily take a step back, my heels connecting with something, as heat warms everything from the back of my legs to the nape of my neck.

The fire.

He's cornered me against the fire.

Clever.

I bob under a fist intended for my nose and bury my own deep into his stomach. He grunts, doubling over, but grabs my arm in one swift movement. Then he twists, pulling both my arm behind my back and my chest towards the fire. Pain laces up to my shoulder as the flames glow in front of me.

Maybe I should have tried harder.

He kicks in the back of my knees, hard, before the even harder ground sends a jolt up my legs when I collide with it. The flames are close to me now, nearly licking my bare chest.

'Just let me cut off the band, Kai,' Braxton says from above me, sounding like a plea. It's good to know that he doesn't exactly like the idea of burning me alive. 'This can all be over.' His voice is deep, but I catch the slight quiver in it. He's caught off guard, shocked that he has me hovering over the flames like the now burnt rabbit beside me.

I was sloppy and tired, a fool who underestimated him, but now he has the future Enforcer at his mercy. 'This is the best fight we've ever had, Brax. I'm impressed, truly,' I pant, the heat of the fire drawing beads of sweat down my face. 'But you're going to have to burn me before I let you have my band.'

He heaves a sigh. 'I had a feeling you'd say that.' A pause. 'And I wish it didn't have to be this way.'

Flesh meets fire.

Skin meets searing, hot flame.

I expect a scream to tear from my throat, but nothing but a strangled cry slips past my lips. Braxton's knee drives into my back, angling my body and forcing the left side of my chest into the flames.

I'm burning, boiling, blistering as he holds me there before finally pulling me back, allowing cool air to wash over me. I'm gasping as he reaches with his other hand towards the sword at my side, ready to draw it from its sheath and cut the band from my arm now that I'm dazed with pain.

Oh, but I've known pain far worse.

His arm reaches beside me, and I grab it, standing to my feet in the same motion, adrenaline drowning out the ache of my burned flesh. I pull his arm over my shoulder and tip my body forward, using my momentum and Brawny strength to lift him off the ground and send him flipping over my back and straight into the flames.

He lets out a cry but doesn't linger for long before rolling out of the flames, yelping as he wriggles in the dirt to smother the fire eating away at his clothes, his skin. Smoke is curling from his burned clothing when I crouch over him.

'I wish it didn't have to be this way either,' I say softly as he pants heavily beneath me. 'But you have something I need.'

I slice the band from his forearm, unable to stop from nicking him and drawing more blood. His breathing is raspy as I search his pockets for any other bands he may have stolen on the way, finding none. I stand, staring down at him and uttering one word. 'Go.'

He stares up at me for a moment before grunting in pain as he scrambles to his feet, limping into the woods as quickly as his charred body is able. I watch him leave, hearing him struggle to navigate through the dark woods, knowing he won't dare to come back. Then I turn, looking directly at the Sight I knew had been documenting the entire fight.

'Hope you enjoyed the show,' I say with a mock bow of my head. As soon as the words leave my mouth, the woman in white blinks and vanishes into the forest.

I tuck Braxton's band into my pocket as pain racks my body.

Blinding, blistering pain. I look down at the red, inflamed patch of skin right above my tattoo.

The adrenaline is gone, and I'm left with nothing but pain coursing through my body. I stagger over to my canteens, unscrewing one and pouring the cold contents over the burn. I hiss through my teeth when water meets burned flesh, but it's a relief, however small it may be.

I grab my crumpled shirt from my pocket and tear a large strip of cloth from it with my teeth before beginning to gingerly wrap the fabric under my arm and over the burn. The result is a makeshift bandage to try and lessen the chance of infection. But it won't do for long. I need to find some herbs, something, *anything*, to clean the wound.

Because dying is not an option.

And losing these Trials certainly isn't either.

CHAPTER 24

Paedyn

'I am going to wring your neck if you don't shut up.'

The bird completely ignores my very real threat of death and continues to squabble on the branch above my head. It's been squawking for nearly half an hour, resulting in me throwing at least a dozen rocks in its direction.

I'm annoyed, angry, anxious, and above all, absolutely starving. Of course, these are all side effects of waking up in the middle of the wilderness with nothing but the clothes I slept in. I look down at my tight, cloth pants and even more revealing tank. A skimpy, silky thing that I regret ever putting on, considering it will now be my only shirt for the next week.

A week.

That's how long I must survive in this forest. In the Whispers. In this place crawling with enemies of all shapes and sizes, though it's already midday and the only opponent I've faced so far is the snake that nearly bit my foot off. I've been trekking through the thick foliage since the moment I woke up, facedown in the dirt, after blinking awake to a staring woman clad in blinding white.

A Sight. Here to spy on the opponents. Here to record this bloody Trial. Here to document what the audience is not able

to witness for themselves.

I'm sure the rest of Ilya is just as confused as I am about this year's Trials. Though, I can't say we weren't warned.

Different. That's all the warning we got.

Except that *different* does not even begin to describe how drastically these Trials have changed. In the past three decades, there has never been a Trial outside of the Bowl walls, outside of the prying eyes of the audience. But only the best, the most brutal and bloody Trials, are fit to test the future Enforcer, I suppose. I just wish I wasn't a part of it.

We've all been unwittingly thrown into the deadly Whispers, left to die by the elements or by the hand of our enemies. It's brilliant. It's dastardly. And I don't know whether to clap or cry.

I should expect nothing less from the king.

My eyes dart to my right forearm where the leather strap is wrapped tightly.

'Collect from those who have been banded and be warned if you return empty-handed.'

I laugh bitterly to the emptiness surrounding me. They want us to fight, truly fight one another for these strips of leather. So, in an effort to stay alive long enough to find another opponent, I set out to find water. The trees here are tremendous and terrifying, towering high in the air and scraping the low clouds. It took me ages to scale one to find the closest water source, and the past several seriously boring hours have consisted of trudging towards what I'm hoping is a creek.

Except now I'm sitting under a tree and arguing with a bird. I chuck another rock at it for good measure before turning my attention back to the bundle of sticks at my side. I pick up another arrowhead that I've collected along the way, one of the generous gifts left to aid us, and fasten it onto one of the sticks. I've been making arrows for far too long now to accompany the bow and quiver I found conveniently resting against the trunk of a tree.

As if the Elites need weapons.

The feathers supplied by the annoying, yet useful bird above complete the arrow. I stare at my handiwork with a small smile, studying all seven wobbly arrows now filling the quiver. Thanks to my father, this was not my first time having to craft an arrow from scratch, and my smile grows at the distant memory.

I throw the quiver over my shoulder and cross the bowstring along my chest, saying my goodbyes to the bird still perched in the tree. I heave a sigh and begin, once again, heading towards the water I so desperately need. My feet are light and quiet as I tread across the terrain, my eyes peeled for any animal I can devour.

There.

A fat rabbit hops out of the bushes a few dozen feet away, completely unaware of my ill intentions for it. I pull the bow over my head and slip an arrow from the quiver. I nock it, aim, and breathe deeply just as my father taught me to. And then I send the arrow flying towards its mark.

Straight through the rabbit's eye.

It's dead before it even crumples to the ground. I snatch up the animal, wipe the arrowhead on a nearby plant I hope wasn't poisonous, and return the arrow to my quiver.

Find water. Start a fire. Eat food.

And then I'm back to walking, tripping over tree roots and stumbling over stones.

Riveting.

I let my thoughts run wild as I keep a steady pace through the foliage, thinking of my opponents, the ball, the calloused hands on my back and gray eyes studying my face.

I huff in annoyance and kick a rock harder than I should. A string of curse words spills from my mouth – directed at the rock, myself, and the cocky bastard I hate for not completely hating.

The sun is making its descent across the sky as I continue to trample through the greenery, swearing at the multiple spiderwebs I walk through and the giant spiders that accompany them.

A Sight catches up to me and I try my hardest to ignore his presence. Once he's satisfied with the footage he's collected of me stomping and huffing through the forest, he turns and disappears.

Warm, late afternoon sunlight streams through the trees, casting the forest in golden shadows. For a moment, I allow myself to take in the ominous beauty of this eerie place.

And then something hits me in the face.

Well, I hit something. I nearly trip backwards, sputtering, only to find that I walked right into a large, cotton shirt hanging from a low branch. I grab it, grumbling about how I don't need the king's *kindnesses* even as I slip on the garment.

I walk and walk.

I'm bored. I'm bored during a bloody *Trial*.

And then something catches the light, glittering out of the corner of my eye. I pivot towards it, leaves crunching beneath my feet. My mouth nearly falls open at what lies no more than thirty yards away from me.

A deep pool of crystal water sparkles in the sunlight, rippling slightly in the warm breeze. Welcoming and wonderful. I blink. I didn't see this pool when I was high in the tree, scouting. Then again, the shimmering water is surrounded by trees, nearly swallowed by the foliage around it.

I practically trip in my haste to reach it.

Water. Water. Water.

I'm so thirsty, so greedy to gulp as much as I can. Then build a fire, cook my rabbit, and—

There's something *in* the water, bobbing on top of it.

I'm much closer now, the sun not so blinding as it glints off the clear surface, and I can make out an outline on top. A *human* outline. I creep forward, pulling my bow from across my chest, clutching it in my fist.

The figure isn't moving.

The figure with dirty blond hair plastered to his tanned forehead.

The figure with the same glassy green eyes as the king, staring unseeingly up at the blue sky.

A strangled scream rips from my throat, sending birds scattering out from the trees around me.

Kitt.

He's *dead*.

I'm gasping, stumbling to the edge of the pool. I may hate his father and the kingdom he will one day rule, but that doesn't mean I wish to see him dead. The thought startles me, considering how very much I crave that fate for the king that looks so much like him. But what if their familiar features are where the similarities between them end? What if there is hope for the prince to step out of his father's shadow, out of his footsteps, and create change in his kingdom?

I force myself to meet his glossy gaze where I now only see the potential of the prince rather than the presence of his father. Those once amused green eyes will never crinkle with laughter again. Instead, they stare up at nothing, wide, dull, and leached of life. That crooked grin will never again grace his lips. Instead, his mouth is pressed in a thin line – blue, kissed by the chill of death.

I jump into the pool, wanting to pull him from this watery death. Instead, my feet are met with solid ground.

My bones sing with the impact, feeling as though they will crack with the force.

I blink away the pain, though it does nothing to clear my confusion. There is suddenly no pool under my feet, no Kitt floating dead on its surface. I look at the dirt beneath me in disbelief, trying to puzzle out what is going on.

'Help me.'

I nock an arrow and draw my bow before I've even turned to face the owner of that broken little voice.

I choke on my gasp.

It's me.

Deep blue eyes bore into mine – sad, starved eyes. Long silver hair, tangled and matted, hangs from the little girl's head. She is – I am – small, so small. Weak and weary and wide-eyed as she stares up at me.

She stretches a bony finger towards me. 'Please,' she whispers, whimpers. I stumble back at the sound of that – *my* – broken voice, nearly losing my footing when she takes a shaky step closer.

This isn't real.

I turn, ready to run from this nightmare, only to nearly run into another little Paedyn, her cheeks sunken and eyes hollow.

I'm delusional. Dehydrated.

I bite my tongue to keep from screaming as I turn to my right, finding another starved version of myself staring back at me.

I'm surrounded. Completely surrounded by pleading Paedyns. They step forward, begging me to help them as they reach out, trying to grab hold of me.

This time, I don't bother biting back my scream.

They are closing in, crowding me. I'm crying out, confused and—

No, not delusional.

They stagger towards me, seeking help I can't give them.

This is Ace.

Even knowing that, I still can't stand to look at them, to look at myself. Can't stand to hear them begging for help as I do nothing. This was me. I was this starved and sad girl once. Because when my father died, so did a piece of myself.

This isn't real. This isn't real. This isn't real.

I cry out, dropping to my knees and clutching my head in frustration. 'I know it's you, Ace,' I shout through clenched teeth. I hear haughty laughter grow louder as he makes his way towards me. Taking a deep breath, I stand to my feet, shaking with disgust and rage as I prepare myself to be surrounded by sickly Paedyns.

But the pleading stops and the Paedyns vanish, leaving only Ace standing before me. His gaze drops to the arrow pointed at his chest before traveling back to mine. He has the audacity to smirk.

'Hello, Paedyn.' His voice is smug as he quirks an eyebrow. 'Did you enjoy catching up with your younger self?'

'You're sick,' I spit, pulling my bowstring taut.

He sighs, already bored with our conversation. Sticking his nose in the air, he says, 'Just let me take your band and I'll be on my way.' A pause. 'In fact, I'll even let you take it off yourself, so I don't cut you.'

'How generous.' I'm practically growling at him. 'But I'll pass on the offer.' My teeth are bared, and I'm a flinch away from sending an arrow flying towards that black heart of his.

He blinks at me, slicking his brown hair back from his face with an irritated huff. 'Fine.' His eyes darken. 'Have it your way. I don't mind having to get messy.'

And then he's striding towards me, reaching for my arm. I don't hesitate before firing my arrow into his thigh, aiming to injure and not to kill. I refuse to give the king and the people what they desire: death.

Except, the arrow never meets skin, never sinks into flesh. It flies right through him. The illusion blows away like smoke on the wind, tempting me to scream in frustration.

Another Ace steps out from behind a tree a few feet away, leaves crunching under his feet as he claps slowly. 'Wow. Good try.' He grips a sharp spear in his hand, smiling like a cat.

'Quit hiding behind your illusions, you coward!' I'm fuming, adrenaline pumping through my veins.

This one is the real Ace, I'm certain of it. The leaves gave him away, crunching when he stepped on them, unlike the first time he walked over to me. He seems to sense that I figured it out, and right as I'm about to bury an arrow in him, he surrounds himself with a dozen duplicates, hiding within them.

They all speak in unison as they begin to surround me, masking the sound of any crunching leaves. 'If you give me the band now, I won't hurt you. Badly.' They laugh and it's a sickening sound, seeming to bounce around in my skull.

I spin in a circle, not knowing who to aim for. I only have six arrows now, and I can't afford to waste a single one. They are closing in on me, closing in for the kill.

Find the real Ace.

Easier said than done. They all look and move exactly the same, all holding spears and ready to stab me, though only the real one can do any damage.

'I'm going to enjoy this, Paedyn,' they say, smiling.

My eyes flick over each of their bodies. I take in their identical stances, their identical facial expressions, their identical *everything*.

I will not die. I will not die. I will not die.

And then my eyes snag on a particular Ace, identical to the others.

Found you.

The tiny bead of sweat trickling down the side of his temple is all it takes to give him away, the only sign of his struggle to cast the illusions.

I raise my bow towards him at the exact moment he lunges towards me. I jump to the side, but not before pain erupts across my stomach. Searing, stinging pain that I ignore as I release my arrow, letting it fly straight into the flesh of his leg.

He screams, dropping to his knees in the dirt, hands trembling as they wrap around the arrow protruding from his thigh. But I don't give him, or the Sight now watching, a second glance before I spin and sprint.

I don't know how far I've made it. Don't know how much distance I've put between us before the adrenaline bleeds from my body, reminding me that *I'm* bleeding. The searing pain is back, punching me so hard in the gut that I'm panting.

I lift my loose shirt to reveal the silky tank beneath it, now sopping with blood. I take a deep breath and pull up the layer of cloth separating me from the wound before shuddering at the sight of it. A long, bloody gash slices open the skin right beneath my rib.

A spear wound.

My breaths come in shaky, shallow pants.

At least I'm alive.

But I sure as hell don't *feel* alive. It's excruciating. The pain is biting and blazing, setting my nerves on fire. I gingerly pull off the large shirt, wincing and choking back cries of pain with every lift of my right arm. The movement pulls at the skin, the gash, causing it to gush even more blood.

I rip the bottom hem of the shirt, creating a wide strip of white fabric. I work as swiftly as the injury will allow me, gingerly wrapping the cloth around my waist and over the wound. I gasp for air at the throbbing pain this causes, blinking away tears as I pull on what is left of the shirt, so large it still covers my stomach.

I need to find water.

I heave a shaky sigh, that action alone jolting a sharp pain through me as I begin walking again through the forest.

No, *stumbling* is more like it.

CHAPTER 25

Paedyn

tay awake. Stay awake. Stay awake. My traitorous eyelids feel like
lead. With each blink, I'm afraid they won't open again. I've
been slowly stumbling through the shadowy forest towards the creek
for what feels like hours, blindly hoping I'm still headed in the right
direction.

I'm tired. So very tired. I want nothing more than to slump against
a tree and close my eyes for a minute. Just one blissful moment of
peace—

No.

I pinch my arm, hard, causing my drooping eyelids to fly open.

If I fall asleep, I likely won't wake back up.

I'm in bad shape, and I don't need to be the daughter of a Healer to
realize it. I've lost so much blood, making my head swim as I try to
keep my footing. I shake my head, trying to ignore my fevered skin
and shivering body. Just like I ignore that the strip of cloth I used as
a bandage is already soaked with blood, staining the cotton scarlet.

I need to clean the wound and soon. If I don't, I'm as good as dead.

What I need is water.

Every part of me burns. Burns with pain and thirst and hunger. If I
can just get to some water, I can wash out the wound at the very least,

cure my dehydration, and come to my senses long enough to create a concoction of herbs to clean the injury.

I hope.

Then I'd worry about eating, seeing that I can barely pull back my bowstring, and the rabbit I shot is long forgotten at the site where Ace ambushed me.

Leaving me defenseless *and* starving.

Get to the creek. Get to the creek. Get to the creek.

A faint, orange glow peeks through the trees ahead of me, blurry from my drooping eyes. I squint at it, unsure if I'm hallucinating or not. I tighten my sweaty grip on the bow, already nocked with an arrow, though it's practically useless if I can't pull back the damn string to fire it. I continue to creep closer to the fire flickering a few dozen yards away, completely unattended.

The light it casts reflects off something shimmering beside it.

The creek.

A relieved, breathy laugh escapes me as I cautiously continue forward. I'm being reckless, of course, but I don't particularly care in this state. Someone started this fire, and I may be walking straight towards them. But I'll die if I don't get to that water, though I might be killed if I do.

Both options will likely lead to my imminent death. Great.

I'm only a few feet away from the fire now, my eyes searching the shadows for any sign of the human who lit it.

Get to the water. Get to the—

'You just can't seem to stay away from me, can you, Gray?' I halt, heart hammering.

I can hear the amusement in his voice, practically picture the dimples peeking out on either side of his smirk. I take a deep breath, mentally preparing myself for the excruciating pain I'm about to endure.

Whipping around, I raise my bow and pull the string taut. I swallow my cry of pain as I feel my wound tearing, stretching with the movement.

I can't let him see I'm injured. Put on a show. Get to the water.

The tip of my arrow is pointed at his heart, and I just make out his exposed chest in the flickering light. It looks as though I'm not the first opponent he's encountered, nor am I the first one to aim something at his heart. He's wrapped a strip of cloth under his arm and around a wound just above his swirling tattoo.

My eyes flick back to his, willing the agony from my features. Willing him to see me as a threat. His gaze sweeps over me with an expression I can't decipher, but I'm not in the mood or headspace to puzzle him out. 'Leave or I shoot.' My arm is beginning to tremble with the effort and pain of keeping the bow trained on him.

He only chuckles and takes a step towards me. 'Good to see you too, Gray.'

'You think I'm kidding. How cute.' I bite out the words, my chest heaving.

'What, that's it? You're just going to shoot me?' His lips twitch. 'Where's the fun in that?'

'Oh, it'll be fun for me, I assure you.' My voice is shaky. I'm shaky. Kai takes another step towards me, cocking his head to the side. His hands are casually in his pockets as he looks me over again. 'I'm confused. You do realize that the point of this Trial is to take my band, correct?' His smirk grows. 'Or at least *try*.'

'Well, I'm letting you off easy by allowing you to *leave*.' The words don't sound threatening in the slightest. I'm swaying on my feet now, head spinning.

I can't do this for much longer.

I can feel the hot blood running down my stomach from my torn wound, and black dots are swimming in front of my eyes, threatening to swallow me whole.

I'm going to pass out. What if I don't wake up? What if die because I wasn't strong enough? Because I'm a weak Ordinary—

'Gray . . . ?'

Between my drooping eyelids, I can see Kai take a hesitant step towards me, all amusement wiped from his face. And I must truly be hallucinating because I think I see worry flickering in his gaze.

'Gray, what happened?' He's stepping slowly towards me, but I can't keep my hold on the bow any longer. For a reason I can't explain, I aim at the ground instead of him, releasing my grip on the string and letting the arrow fly into the dirt at his feet before the bow slips from my sweaty hand.

I can barely hear Kai's shout through the ringing in my ears. 'Gray!' I don't remember hitting the ground.

My face connects with the packed earth, but I barely feel it. My whole body is on fire, hardly breathing as I burn from the inside out.

'Paedyn! Hey, Pae, look at me.'

Rough hands are gripping the sides of my face, forcing my eyes to flutter open. They feel cold against my fevered skin, now slick with sweat, and concern is written all over the beautiful face hovering over me. I've never seen him so worried, so full of emotion. His cool mask has cracked, shattered, splintered into a million pieces as he lifts my head off the ground, pulling me towards him to search my face with wide, gray eyes.

And then he's gone. Darkness.

'Hey, hey, hey.' Calloused hands are pushing the damp hair off my forehead while words are muttered close to my face. 'Pae, stay with me.' His voice is stern despite the panic lacing each word.

Slowly, I force my eyes to crack open while I croak out quiet words through cracked lips, words that suddenly seem so important. 'You've never called me that before.'

I've only ever heard him say my real name once when he had me pinned against an alley wall while he tested the word out for the first time. But I haven't heard my name slip past his lips since. Haven't heard the way the two syllables sound rolling off his tongue.

And I've certainly never heard him call me *Pae*.

I'm smiling up at him now, grinning like an idiot. I can't stop.

Delusional. I'm completely and undeniably delusional.

But in this moment, I don't want to die – if only so I could hear him say my name one more time.

Delirious. I'm so very delirious.

He's suddenly still. His eyes roam over my face, lips slightly parted as he takes me in. Then he blinks. Once. Twice. His dark lashes flutter, gray eyes flicking between mine as he says, 'Remind me to make you smile like that again, when you aren't dying, and I have all the time in the world to memorize it.'

Now it's my turn to blink at him. Once. Twice.

That comment was all it took to wake me up because now my eyes don't seem to want to stray from his. I must have heard him wrong. I'm so delirious that my mind is playing tricks on me, playing with my emotions, my feelings.

But I'm certainly *not* imagining the hands that are running up my body. I nearly choke on my ragged breath when his fingers brush my ankles, slowly running up each of my legs.

He's trying to find the wound. I open my mouth to tell him where it is, but my head is spinning and I'm on the verge of passing out from the pain. I breathe heavily, trying to calm my pounding head and heart.

His fingers pass over my legs, gently poking and prodding as he searches for the wound. Once he's satisfied that my legs are functioning just fine, his hands slide up to my hips, lifting me slightly off the ground to run a hand over my lower back. His brows are knit in concentration as his fingers feel over my lower stomach, his movements swift, steady, sure. This isn't the first time he's done this.

His hands slide up my abdomen, around my waist—

Pain like I've never experienced before erupts from the wound when his fingers dance over it, followed by a strangled sob tearing from my throat. The pain is so blinding that I think I'm about to black out. And I find myself wanting to, if only so I don't have to feel like this anymore.

I watch through blurry vision as he lifts the hem of the tattered shirt to reveal the silky one beneath soaked with blood. He sighs through his nose before lifting the hem of the tank, exposing my fevered skin to the cool night. There's a flash of something small and sharp in his hands as he begins to carefully cut the bloodied cloth from around my middle.

His jaw tightens at the sight of the jagged wound stretching below my ribcage, a muscle ticking in his cheek. His eyes, full of an emotion I've never seen from him before, trace the bloody mess on my stomach.

And then my own eyes slam shut, sealing the image of him out.

Leaving him in the world that is beginning to fade.

'Paedyn.' Kai's voice is so far away, so distant from where I'm slipping into oblivion. 'Paedyn, open your eyes.' It's an order, strong and stern. And I ignore it. How very typical of me. Even in death my body refuses to listen to the commands of the future Enforcer. 'Open your eyes, dammit!'

Tired. I'm so very tired.

Far, far away, I hear a male voice muttering panicked words. 'If you die, I'm going to kill you.'

CHAPTER 26

Kai

She's too stubborn to die, and I'm too stubborn to let her. I brush a hand over her forehead, her fevered skin hot to the touch, her breaths coming in shallow pants. She's dehydrated, delusional, dying of hunger . . .

Just dying.

My eyes flick back to the bloody gash slicing under her rib, inflamed and no doubt infected. I pull out the remains of my crumpled shirt and begin dabbing at the wound, trying to sop up some of the blood so I can see exactly what I'm dealing with. The skin is torn, jagged, and likely looks much worse when it's not concealed by shadows.

But what's even more concerning, is that I have no idea how to help her. I have no supplies and no healing ability around me to draw from, making me utterly useless.

I'm holding her life in my useless, unequipped hands.

I stand to my feet, searching for my canteens in the dim light. She needs water.

That's what she came here for after all, why she risked walking straight into someone's camp. She needed water. Needed it to drink, to wash out her wound. But that won't save her.

I can't save her.

I sigh in frustration, threatening to lose my temper as I run my hands through my hair, still searching for those damn canteens. But my mind won't stop replaying the scene, won't stop reeling over what just happened.

I knew something was wrong when I saw her arm trembling. Saw it shake with the strain of keeping the bow aimed at me, ready to make good on her threat to shoot. Then I saw her knees shake, saw the fire extinguish from her burning blue eyes. But above all, she wasn't playing with me, wasn't teasing me or twisting her mouth into that sly smile of hers that I enjoy so much. And that's what worried me the most.

And now I'm suddenly furious with her.

She wanted me to leave. She was going to try and deal with this alone. She would have died alone. She's so damn stubborn that she would choose to fight me until she collapsed rather than let me see her injured. The image of her crumpling to the ground sends a chill through me, icing over my burning rage. You would think I'd be numb to witnessing hurt by now, watching Death claim another victim. But when she crumpled, something inside of me cracked. The sight of her so weak, so vulnerable, so unlike herself, was enough to shatter a piece of the soul I'd forgotten I had.

My feet stumble over something in the darkness. Finally.

I bend down to snatch up the canteen only for my fingers to fold around a small, tin box. I step closer to the firelight, casting a glance over my shoulder at the wheezing Paedyn.

I don't have time for this.

I'm about to chuck the box as far as I can out of fury and frustration when the symbol painted onto the lid catches in the light, catching my attention. A faded, green diamond stains the top, and I don't hesitate before ripping open the lid to reveal a small vial of inky liquid.

I stare at it. Stare at the miracle in the form of a healing salve crafted by the Healers themselves, strong enough to mend even the most menacing wounds.

And then I'm laughing dryly, unable to stop. The absurdity, the sheer impossibility of this all has me hysterical. Braxton must have picked it up in the forest somewhere and dropped it during our fight.

Paedyn's salvation has been hiding in the shadows this whole time. 'Thank the Plague,' I mutter, shaking my head in disbelief as my foot finally meets one of my canteens on the ground.

I'm on my knees beside her in a matter of moments, her chest barely rising with shallow breaths. I yank the salve from the box, revealing a needle and thick thread for stitching wounds lying beneath. I find myself laughing again.

Unbelievable. Bloody unbelievable.

I carefully pour some of the dark liquid onto a clean corner of my remaining shirt. This is going to sting, so it's convenient that she's unconscious when I press the cloth against her wound, letting the salve seep into the gash. Slowly, I make my way across the cut, watching as the steady flow of blood already begins to slow. I dab the fabric against a particularly deep part of the gash and her eyes fly open before her hand flies towards my face.

Damn.

Her slap is shockingly hard for someone who was just dangerously close to meeting Death. My head is still turned to the side from the shock and impact of her hit, but a slow smile pulls up my lips.

'Ouch.' I finally look at her, finding wild blue eyes staring up at me. She's panting, clearly confused. 'Is that how you thank me for saving your life?' I scan her face, relieved to already see some color blooming on her cheeks, see her eyes gleaming again with that familiar fire.

'I'm the one who should be saying ouch. What the hell is that? It stings.' She's breathless and shaking all over. Her eyes dart from her clean wound to the salve still clutched in my hand. And then she's trying to sit up. It's a good effort, despite her grunting in pain.

'Easy, darling.' I place a hand on her uninjured side, fitting right into the curve of her waist as I slowly press her back down to the forest floor. 'You can slap me all you want once you're healed, but until then, try to keep your hands to yourself.'

'How am I alive?' Her voice is so quiet that her question is nearly drowned out by the chirping crickets surrounding us. Her eyes are trained on the sky, not daring to look at me.

'We have Braxton to thank for that.' I grab the water canteen and push it to her lips. 'Drink. You're dehydrated. Though you are quite fun when you're delusional.' She glares at me as I tip the canteen back, letting her gulp down the water greedily. She eyes me expectantly, and I sigh, elaborating, 'Braxton paid me a little visit earlier, and he must have dropped the salve he'd found during our fight.' I sigh. 'And I doubt he's too happy about that, seeing that he could have used it for himself.'

She pushes my hand away, refusing to drink any more until she gets some answers.

Stubborn, little thing.

'So you didn't—' Her eyes glance between my bandaged injury to my face, trying to read me.

'No, I didn't kill him,' I say dully, answering the question in her gaze. She gives me a strange look, one I've only seen her offer me a few times before. I clear my throat and look away, leaning back on my palms as she continues to study me. 'Killing isn't a hobby of mine, I'll have you know.' I felt like I needed to say it. Felt like I needed to admit that to her, to myself. What I do — what I've done — has had a purpose, a reason. I'm still a monster, just not the kind that loves the hateful things they do.

There's that look again. It's like she's seeing straight through my many masks, tearing down my walls, stripping me bare with nothing but her gaze. I hate it — I love it. I feel free — I feel trapped. The thought that a single pair of blue eyes can leave me so vulnerable, so exposed, is alarming.

So, I do what it is I do best — deflect.

I clear my throat before leaning forward and grabbing my ragged shirt. After dumping the rest of the salve onto the fabric, I gently press it to her wound. She hisses and her eyes fly to mine, full of a fire that makes me chuckle. 'Oh, this isn't even the worst part, darling. I still have to stitch you up.'

She steadies her shaky breaths, long lashes fluttering shut as she says, 'Why are you doing this?'

A very valid question, though I don't intend on answering it until I get some answers of my own. I grab the brutally blunt needle and begin the painstaking process of threading it through with the thick medical string. 'Why don't I ask the questions?' My stare is leveled at her, unyielding and unfeeling. But it's simply another mask, seeing that I'm currently simmering with rage.

'Which one of them did this to you?' Her eyes fly open, looking more confused and unsure of herself than I've ever seen before. But she recovers quickly, huffing out a shaky laugh.

She turns her head to the side to look at me from where she lies on a bed of moss, dirt, and leaves. 'It doesn't matter.' And that is the only answer she deigns to give me before rolling her head back towards the starry sky hanging above us, avoiding my gaze.

My fingers find her chin and then I'm tugging her face back in my direction so I can look her in the eyes as I say, 'I'm going to ask again. Who did this to you?'

My hand is still gripping her chin, her strong jaw, as she holds my gaze and says, 'Why do you care?' Then she's laughing bitterly, the sound vibrating under my fingers.

'Because I don't tolerate my toys being played with.' She is going to hate that.

'Your what—?' She stops, her eyes smoldering, her temper rising. 'Is that what you think I am? Some toy you can play with?'

'Yes. And clearly quite a fragile one at that.' Plagues, if I wasn't already going to hell, I am now.

She sputters. Actually sputters. I've never seen her at such a loss for words before, and I must say, it's very entertaining. 'What the hell is wrong with you? Oh, so you think I'm fragile? I'll show you just how fragile I—'

'There,' I say calmly, cutting her off mid-threat. 'The first stitch is always the worst, especially with how blunt this needle is.'

She blinks, snapping her mouth shut when she looks down to see the needle I've pushed through the gash without her even realizing, too angry to feel the pain. Which was exactly what I was hoping for.

'You . . . you are—'

She's sputtering again, so I kindly finish for her. 'Intelligent? Irresistible?'

'Calculating, cocky, and a completely arrogant bastard,' she pants. 'That is what I was going to say.'

A smile tugs at my lips. 'Good to see you're feeling well enough to insult me.' I grab the needle again and pinch the skin around her wound closer together, preparing to make another stitch by the light of the fire.

'You distracted me,' she murmurs, as though she's still taking in the information. Then she huffs out a laugh as she adds, 'You distracted me by being an ass, but it worked nonetheless.'

I look up at her briefly before saying, 'Yes, I was an ass. And I need you to know that I didn't mean what I said.' I push the needle through her skin as I speak, using my words as another distraction, though she still lets out a small hiss of pain. 'You're no toy, let alone a delicate one.' She watches me work, and I will myself not to melt under her burning gaze. 'Tell me about home. About Loot,' I say, trying to take her mind off the needle piercing her skin.

'Loot wasn't exactly a home to me.' She's quiet, and I catch her chewing the inside of her cheek before she continues. 'I had a home once. It was just me and my father, but . . . but we were happy.' She winces when I make another stitch, but her next words are as blunt as the needle. 'And then he died, and my home became Adena. We made a living in Loot together. She made Loot worth living in.'

'How long have you lived on the streets?'

'Five years. I was thirteen when my father died, and ever since then, I've lived in a pile of garbage Adena generously called the Fort.' She laughs bitterly at that. 'From ages thirteen to fifteen, the two of us were barely surviving. But then we grew up. We figured things out and fell into a routine that kept us fed and clothed. We each had our own skills that kept us alive.'

I let her words, her story, sink in. I wonder silently what had happened to her father, or her mother for that matter. 'So, your father taught you to fight, then?' I ask curiously.

'Ever since I was a child. He knew my ability wasn't one I could use physically, so he made sure I was never truly defenseless.' Her voice is shaky as I thread the needle through the deepest part of the wound. Her hand shoots up and grips my forearm, nails biting into my skin as she bites her tongue to keep from crying out in pain.

'And the dagger you like to wear on your thigh so much,' I clear my throat, 'was that your father's?'

'Yes, it is – it was.' Her laugh is strained. 'I suppose you have him to thank for my violent tendencies.'

I glace up and grin before saying warily, 'And your mother . . . ? Do I have her to thank for any of your wonderful qualities?'

'Dead.' Her tone is flat. 'She died of sickness shortly after I was born. I never knew her.' I'm reminded of Kitt and how his mother died in a similar manner, a tragedy the two of them share.

Her grip on my arm only tightens as I keep pushing the needle through her skin, slowly making my way to the end of the gash. Her eyes are squeezed shut against the pain, refusing to cry or even cry out.

So stubborn. So strong.

'Just a little more, Pae,' I breathe. She shudders and I don't miss the movement. Whether because of the pain or because I finally said her name, I'm not sure. I'm reminded of when she hit the ground. When I was feral, frantic, and I was suddenly aware that I hadn't said her name to her since we met.

And in that moment, I realized that I'd wanted to say it – wanted her to hear it from my lips. Realized that if she died, I would never again get to look into those blue eyes and utter those two syllables that have been a constant in my mind.

So I said her name, again and again. I finally let myself do it. Let that last piece of attachment to her lock into place. Just saying her name felt intimate, personal, somehow.

And now I forever want her name on my lips and rolling off my tongue until I'm drunk on the taste and sound of it.

What the hell is wrong with me?

Her eyes find mine, sparkling like a body of water in the firelight. 'Why are you doing this?'

Her gaze tells me that there's no escaping the question this time, though I'm not even sure I have an answer for her or myself. All I know is that I have this urge to protect her, be with her, tease her, touch her.

It's terrifying.

'What's the fun in winning by default?' I say instead. 'What kind of gentleman would I be if I took your leather and left you to die?'

230

She lifts her head off the ground, eyes searching mine as she scoffs, 'So you're telling me that you did all of this to be *gentlemanly*?'

'Why does that come as such a surprise to you?'

'Maybe because you have to be a gentleman to be gentlemanly.'

'And who says I'm not?'

'I'd like to find someone who says you are.'

I smile at her, taking in every detail of her face beneath mine. I open my mouth to say something witty and wildly inappropriate when a twig snaps to my left. A Sight watches us with glazed eyes, documenting the scene before him. And I'm embarrassed that I have no idea how long he has been standing there, not with how distracted I was with the girl before me.

I can only imagine what Father will make of this – of us. Of me helping, saving, enjoying being with the girl from the slums.

Wouldn't be the first time I've disappointed him, and it certainly won't be the last.

The Sight blinks, clearing his blurry eyes before disappearing into the night. I turn back towards Paedyn, her attention still fixed on the spot where the man once was. Then I look down at her exposed stomach, and the wound now completely stitched there.

I begin wrapping the remains of her large shirt over the wound and around her waist. Paedyn's eyes follow my movements, tracking my hands and tracing my face.

'You never did answer my question,' I say far more casually than I currently feel.

'You'll have to be more specific than that, Azer.'

'I asked who the hell did this to you.'

She laughs dismissively, turning her head from mine. 'Oh, that question. It doesn't matter.'

'If it doesn't matter, then tell me.'

She shoots me an annoyed look before she sighs, giving in. 'Ace. Happy now? He used his illusions to draw me in.' She's suddenly pale again. 'He made me see . . . things.'

I've never seen her look so haunted, and I'm shocked by how much I hate it. 'Did you kill him?'

'No,' she says softly. 'No, I didn't kill him.'

We fall silent, and I run my hand over her crude bandage, making sure it's secure as she stares at me. Then I hand her the water canteen before forcing her to choke down some burnt rabbit.

I busy myself around the small camp, and when I look back at Paedyn from where I stoke the flames of the dying fire, her lids are drooping, eyelashes fluttering with the promise of sleep. Then I catch her shiver slightly in the brisk, night breeze.

Well that just won't do.

I kneel beside her, scooping her into my arms before pulling her off the ground and carrying her closer to the fire. She grunts groggily against my chest before I lay her down on the packed dirt, watching her chest rise and fall with steady breaths, so unlike the ragged, shallow ones she choked on earlier.

And then I sit there. I can't seem to tear my eyes away as she drifts to sleep beside the fire, alive and breathing deeply. She shakes again, making me wish I had a blanket to offer her, had something to offer her. The truth of that thought hits me like a blow to the gut.

I have nothing to offer her.

I am wrong, so wrong for her. She is too brave, too bold, too bloody good for me. Maybe I could be a better man. Maybe I could be more like Kitt with his heart on his sleeve and happiness on display. Maybe the future Enforcer could break down a few walls, become a man who is more than the masks he wears around his people.

But ever since she discovered I was the prince and declared us enemies, I've played along, not wanting to be outdone. And it's fun. It's a distraction for the both of us, the toying and teasing with one another.

But now?

If I am to be her enemy, I want it to be because she loathes herself for wanting me.

CHAPTER 27

Paedyn

I wake to the unfortunately familiar sound of birds squawking above me.

I woke up.

Squinting in the blinding sun, I gently run my hands over where my healing wound hides beneath the folds of battered cloth.

I'm alive. I'm breathing. I'm healing.

Then my fingers find their way to the strap of leather tight around my arm. I'm shocked to find it's still there. Shocked that Kai didn't cut it from my dying body in the first place. Shocked that he saved my life, nursed me back to health, and let me keep my stupid strap of leather through it all.

Apparently, he went through all this trouble to be a good sport, a *gentleman*.

My ass.

'Good morning. Well, it's almost afternoon, actually.'

My head whips towards the deep voice coming from behind. And there he is, hands in pockets, ankles crossed, and leaning against a low hanging branch. Now that I'm not a breath away from death, his appearance and lack of shirt is suddenly extremely distracting. I avert my gaze quickly, though I don't miss the smirk sliding to his

lips when he catches me staring.

Annoying, arrogant ass.

'I'm surprised you're still here. Along with my band,' I say, casually dusting the dirt from my clothes.

He huffs out a soft laugh behind me. 'Eager to be rid of me, darling?' I clear my throat and turn to face him, leaning back on my palms as I eye him curiously. His hair is messy, strands of it clinging to his forehead with sweat, right above where his eyes shine like bits of silver. There's a shadow of stubble clinging to his sharp jaw, and I can just make out the faint divot of his right dimple, equally distracting and devastating.

I can't stand it.

'So, what's the plan?' I ask, gesturing between the two of us.

'The plan for . . . ?' He tilts his head slightly to the side, peering at me, playing with me. He knows exactly what I mean.

'For us.'

'*Us.* I like the sound of that, don't you?'

I roll my eyes, ignoring him. 'What do we do now?'

'That is a very loaded question, Gray.'

I blink. He didn't say my first name. And for some maddening reason, I wish he had.

I'm annoyed with both myself and him, so naturally, I take it out on the latter. 'Why didn't you take my band? And why not try to take it now that I'm healed?'

Amusement tilts up the corner of his mouth as he pushes off the tree branch and strides towards me. 'That's another loaded question.' That right dimple deepens. 'First of all, you're not completely healed. Second, why would I pass up the opportunity to work together? You know we make a great team. And third,' he crouches down in front of me so we are eye to eye as he continues, 'it's cute that you said I could *try* to take your band from you.'

Now both dimples are taunting me.

'Well, if you're so confident, go ahead and *try*.' My face is close to his, my voice full of challenge. 'I'm sure you remember how our last fight ended.'

'You're still injured, remember?'

234

'And you don't look much better,' I say, frowning at his wrapped shoulder, though no blood dots the white fabric.

'Concerned for your new partner?' A wicked grin spreads across his face as his eyes flick between mine. He's close. Too close. He smells of pine and rain and sweat and, Plagues, I need to distract myself.

I tear my gaze away from his and pull on my bow and quiver as I stand to my feet. *Struggle* to my feet is more like it. Kai stands with me, bracing one hand on my shoulder and the other on my uninjured side. I move to take a step away, annoyed that he thinks I need his help. But my legs feel like jelly, like stone, all at once, proving that I do need his help when I stumble into his solid frame. His chest shakes with rough laughter which only annoys me further.

'Yeah, I don't think I would have much trouble *trying* to get this band from you.' He traces a finger across the leather strap, brushing my skin as he does so.

I catch his wrist and look up at him. 'Well, if we are going to be partners, you won't need to hurt yourself by *trying* to take my band at all.'

He looks me up and down, brows slightly raised. 'So, you agree, then? Partners?'

I contemplate it, considering how I would much rather be fighting alongside the future Enforcer than against him.

I narrow my eyes at him. 'How do I know I can trust you?'

He scoffs. 'Did me saving your life mean nothing to you?'

'And I've saved yours. That doesn't mean you trust me.'

'And how do you know I don't?'

We stare at each other.

Plagues, what am I getting myself into?

Maybe it's because I'm too weak to fight him, or worse, maybe it's the part of me that doesn't want him to leave that makes me say, 'Fine. Partners.'

I glance from his injured shoulder to the tall stump behind him before placing my palms on his chest, his skin hot beneath mine. I push him back until his legs collide with the stump before pushing his shoulders down until he's sitting before me.

Mischief dances in those smoky eyes of his as he looks up at me. 'What are you doing, Gray?'

'Fixing up my partner,' I say simply, beginning to unwrap his makeshift bandage. I smile before adding, 'You won't be of any use to me if you're injured.'

'Your concern for my wellbeing is truly heartwarming,' he says dryly. I ignore him and pull at the stubborn cloth that's sticking to the skin beneath. I swear under my breath when I finally glimpse the patch of burned, blistered skin beneath his collarbone. It's inflamed and sticky and I didn't need to observe the tight set of his jaw to know that it's extremely painful.

I look at him, finding his eyes already trained on me so intensely that I swallow before asking, 'Where is the healing salve?'

His expression is blank. 'Gone.'

I try to blink away my confusion to no avail. 'You used all of it on me?'

'Without hesitation.' Cool, calm, collected. That's Kai.

'Well, that was . . .' I sputter, trying to find the right word.

'Selfless?'

'Stupid,' I finish instead.

I heave a sigh before muttering, 'You're always making things more difficult for me, aren't you?'

I spin on my heel and walk to the edge of the creek. I can feel Kai's eyes on me as I kneel, looking for specific plants to make my own makeshift salve with. It won't miraculously heal him like the Healer's salve would have, but it will help significantly with pain and inflammation.

Thankfully, most of the plants I need tend to grow near water, so I'm able to find them easily. I grab some more cooked rabbit to nibble on as I search for my ingredients. After a good while of walking up and down the creek while being feasted on by mosquitoes, I finally grind the leaves and stalks I've found with a rock. Adding water to the crushed plants, I'm left with a thick, green paste.

I turn to find Kai still watching me when I walk back to him nearly half an hour later. I stand over him, ignoring the feel of his eyes on me as I hold the rock with the salve atop it and take in his wound once again.

'You are full of all sorts of surprises.' He nods at the green goop now on my fingers. 'Talented little thing, aren't you?'

I dab the salve onto his wound, and he hisses when it stings. 'Daughter of a Healer, remember?'

'It's getting hard to keep track of your many skills.' Another grunt of pain before he adds, annoyed, 'Plagues, Paedyn, what the hell is this stuff?'

A snort escapes me. 'Who knew the future Enforcer was such a baby?'

I lather more salve onto his skin, and he grits his teeth. 'And who knew the girl from the slums was capable of *torture*.'

'Oh, please. Don't be so dramatic.'

'You know, I'm not entirely convinced that you're not trying to kill me.'

I quirk an eyebrow at him. 'So, you don't trust me after all?'

'I don't trust *that*,' he says, throwing a skeptical glance at the green paste I'm rubbing onto his wound.

I laugh loudly, shaking my head at him.

He suddenly goes still at my touch, his eyes dancing between mine with a small smile pulling at his lips.

I clear my throat. 'So.' I'm grasping for anything to say before finally deciding to let him do the talking. 'You heard about my home so tell me about yours. What was it like growing up in the palace?'

He watches me, his expression blank. 'Living in a castle is not as appealing as it may seem. It can be cold, crowded. Not to mention that you're constantly watched by prying eyes.' His lips twitch into the hint of a smile. 'But Kitt and I, we made it a home. Plagues, we ruled the place. We made—' He hisses through his teeth, cutting off his words. '*Shit*, Paedyn, now I'm convinced you're trying to kill me.'

'Oh, come on,' I laugh, adding more salve to his wound. 'It only stings.'

He pokes me in the stomach, carefully avoiding the gash there. 'You got to slap me when your wound stung, so I think I'm allowed to complain a little.'

I give him a look. 'This is a *little* complaining?' He narrows his eyes at me, but I can see the amusement in them. 'I'm sorry,' I sigh. 'Continue with your story and your *little bit* of complaining.'

'As I was saying,' he continues with a huff, 'Kitt and I made the palace a home. We made friends with the servants, raced through the halls, ditched balls to sneak into the cellar and get drunk so we could forget about everything and simply laugh until the sun came up. We've probably fought in nearly every room in the palace. Twice.'

He grits his teeth when I pack more salve onto the wound and shoots me an annoyed look before continuing. 'We needed it though. The constant sparring or stupid pranks we'd pull on poor Gail and the rest of the unsuspecting servants. Because when we weren't laughing and distracting ourselves, we were both training and studying. Though that looked very different for the both of us.'

He looks past me to the blue sky painted above, his gray eyes scanning the clouds as he says flatly, 'I don't remember my life before I became the future Enforcer. I don't remember a day when all the tests and trials and training began. It feels as though it's always been that way.' He lets out a humorless laugh, sighing as he says, 'Fate is a funny, fickle thing, offering you no choice in how you live.'

I've stopped rubbing in the salve and am instead staring intently at him. 'And your training? What was that like?'

He sighs a heavy sort of sigh, one that makes me wonder exactly what he's endured in his short lifetime. 'My upbringing looked very different from Kitt's. Where the future king's training consisted of tutoring and education on how to lead his kingdom one day, mine was more . . . hands-on. As the future Enforcer, I didn't just strategize battles, I fought in them. I didn't just learn the art of torture, I endured it.'

My hands hover above his chest. 'You . . . endured it?'

He studies me for a moment, seeming to decide what he wants to say before settling with a simple, 'Yes. Often.'

'Who,' I swallow, 'who did that to you?'

'It doesn't matter,' he says with a slight smile, spitting my own words back at me from last night.

So I do the same to him. 'If it doesn't matter, then tell me.'

His smile widens. 'Good to hear that you listen to me when I speak, Gray.'

'That wasn't an answer,' I say softly.

He blows out a breath, his smile vanishing. 'My . . . the king took it upon himself to train me regularly. I had other tutors and generals of course, but when I wasn't with them, I was with my father. Let's just say that his methods were . . . severe.'

I didn't want to know. I didn't want to know what it was that the king did to his son, what horrors he put him through. It makes me sick. And yet, I shouldn't be surprised. He killed my father after all, and it's my hatred for the king that has me needing to know what other twisted crimes he's committed. So, I slowly ask, 'What did he do?'

He's quiet for a long moment. 'Gray, I don't think—'

'Please,' I cut in quietly. 'You don't have to tell me if you don't want to, but I'm asking you to if you are willing.'

There is something about the quietness of the forest, the cover of the trees, that makes you feel safe enough to spill secrets. Something about knowing you might not see tomorrow that has you doing things you'll only regret if you survive. The Trials aren't meant to build trust, and yet, here we are, divulging the deepest parts of ourselves to one another. Offering our opponents ways to cut us deeper than any weapon ever could.

He meets my gaze then, holding it as he says, 'I'll spare you the details, but he showed me what it was to torture. What it was to *be* tortured. He taught me everything I know. Trained me both mentally and physically until he was satisfied with what he created.' He takes a breath. 'Kitt's relationship with our father is far different from mine. They spend time poring over paperwork and bonding over their positions while Father instructs my brother on how to follow in his footsteps. And Kitt will do just that. He will do anything to make the king proud, and he always has. Me, on the other hand . . .' Kai laughs but it holds no humor. 'I'm not the heir. I'm the expendable son. The future Enforcer that my father has molded and sent on missions for years.'

He sighs, almost smiling. 'My brother and I have very different roles, very different relationships with our father. But because of it, Kitt will make a great king. And I will be his killer.'

I pause, watching him closely as he says those last few words.

And I will be his killer.

Nothing. No emotion, no expression crosses his face. I peer at him for a moment, wondering if perhaps the masks he has crafted for himself are a result of having to suppress his emotions from his own father. And perhaps that's exactly what the king wanted, for his future Enforcer to be seemingly unfeeling.

'You asked me once if I wished it was me who would be king,' Kai says. 'And I stand by what I said. I don't want Kitt's role in life because I refuse to give him mine. My brother is no killer, and it's better me than him.'

I let his words sink in before clearing my throat to ask, 'And these Trials that are different this year? Is this all just another mission for you to complete?'

'Not just complete. Win,' he says simply. 'The Trials are just another way for me to prove myself to my people, prove myself valuable to the king.'

I watch him, wanting to know what he's thinking. He's never told me so much about his life, about what he went through as a child – what he still goes through today. He is the reason this year's Purging Trials look so different, and the rest of us are simply pawns in a game that isn't even meant for us.

I lather more salve onto his wound and wait until he finishes muttering about how he's certain I'm plotting to kill him before asking the question that's been nagging at me. 'Your role in life as the future Enforcer. What do you think of it?'

'I think that it is my duty.'

I frown. 'And I think that you have more thoughts on your own life than that. I'm asking *you*, Kai. Not the prince and not the future Enforcer. Just you.' I pause, and he studies me as I repeat, 'What do *you* think of it? Your role? Your life?'

He's quiet for a moment before the flicker of a smile crosses his face. 'If I answer as Kai, will you quit with the goop?' He shoots a pointed look at the paste in my hand.

I crack a smile. 'Yes, I'll quit with the goop.'

His faint smile fades, leaving a set jaw in its place. 'The truth then?'

'The truth always,' I breathe.

When he finally answers, his tone is dry. 'I never wanted this. Never wanted to be what I am today. But monsters are made, not born. And I had no choice in the matter. I *have* no choice in the matter. But I won't deny what I am, and I'll do what I must for my kingdom. For my king.'

His words hit me hard, their meanings hitting harder. He knows exactly what he is, what he does. He's a pawn to be played in a game he is forever trapped in, and each horrible act he commits is in the name of duty, the name of Ilya.

But this boy before me looked into my eyes and admitted he was a monster, acknowledged what he has been created into without so much as a hint of horror. Instead, acceptance is written across his features, acknowledging what he is and always will be.

Distracted by my thoughts, I reach to rub more salve onto his wound only for him to catch my wrist. 'We had a deal, Gray. I may be accustomed to torture, but this salve of yours is unbearable.'

He offers me a small smirk, clearly wanting to lighten the mood now. Wanting to do what we do best – play with one another. So I do just that. 'You're right. A deal is a deal.' I quickly wipe my hands in the grass before adding, 'Thank you for telling me about . . . you.' At that, he huffs out a laugh that I quickly cut off. 'And remind me to take a page out of your book and ditch the next ball to go get drunk with Kitt.'

I could have sworn he stiffened slightly at my words. 'And why would you do that when I'm so much more fun?'

I laugh lightly. 'If by *fun* do you mean flirty? Because you certainly are more of that.'

He flashes me a wicked, wide grin and my heart trips over itself stupidly. 'I can't seem to help it when I'm with certain company.'

I scoff. 'Yes, if *certain company* extends to the entire kingdom because you seem to be flirty with every female in Ilya.' I think back to the many women he danced with at the ball, the way I watched him slip on that charming smile of his.

His eyes search mine. 'What, wanting me all to yourself—'

My palm connects with his face, stunning him into silence. He blinks. Confusion and the smallest hint of amusement flicker over the face I just slapped. When he finally turns his head back to me, I raise my hand in front of him to reveal the squashed bug in the center of it.

I smile at him innocently. 'Mosquito. You're welcome.'

'How kind of you,' he says dryly.

My smile is full of mock sweetness as I wrap the fabric back around his wound and shoulder, covering the salve with the battered bandage. 'Just looking out for my new partner.'

'Is that so?'

'Mhmm,' I hum distractedly, biting the inside of my cheek as I examine my handiwork.

'Well in that case . . .' Kai stands to his feet, steps close, and hits me lightly across the face.

I let out a humorless laugh, touching my fingers to my cheek. Then my gaze locks with his amused one. He shrugs casually. 'Mosquito.'

'Prove it,' I challenge.

The corner of his mouth twists upwards as he raises his hand to cup my face. 'My proof happens to still be splattered on your cheek.' I hold my breath as he swipes his thumb gently over my skin before holding it up to display the smudged bug. 'Just looking out for my partner.'

His tone is mocking, and yet, laughter begins bubbling out of me.

I can't seem to stop, can't seem to control my cackling. The thought of us hitting each other like children in the middle of a deadly Trial is extremely comical. And for once, I hope there is a Sight watching this unfold.

The glimpse of confusion and concern on Kai's face only make me laugh more, and I clamp a hand over my now throbbing wound as I shake with laughter.

Maybe I am still delusional after all.

I snort loudly, and that's all it took to get Kai laughing with me – well, at me. The sound is rich and deep, and irritatingly enough, I find myself quieting so I can hear it better. And then, all too quickly, the sound stops.

He's looking at me, and I'm looking at him. I don't know what to say or think or do as his eyes trail over my face, taking in my dirty and disheveled appearance.

He, on the other hand, looks just as annoyingly attractive as always.

I shake the thought from my head, running a hand through my tangled hair as I struggle to form words. Meanwhile, Kai is content to watch me squirm as I try to come up with something to break the heavy silence that has fallen between us.

My eyes drop to his bandaged wound and words tumble out of my mouth. 'So, I'm assuming Braxton did this to you?'

Kai chuckles as he runs a hand through his own hair, only causing the messy, black waves to tumble over his brow again. 'You should see what I did to him.' He says the words so casually that I would think he was kidding if I didn't know what he was capable of.

'Yeah, well.' I look away, about to say something that will likely piss the prince off, when he holds up a hand, quieting me.

'Don't. Move.'

I scoff. 'What, is there another mosquito on my—'

His hand clamps over my mouth before he whirls me around by the waist, pinning me against his solid frame. I'm stunned for a heartbeat before I contemplate biting the fingers covering my lips. But something about the way his breathing quickens makes me pause my plotting to escape his hold. And with his chest pressed against my back, I can feel his heart hammering quickly. Too quickly.

I spot movement in my peripheral, my eyes snapping to the large, looming shape now stalking towards us through the wall of trees. Silver fur gleams in the sunlight, shifting with every move of the powerful body beneath. Glowing yellow eyes lock with mine as the beast halts, eying us from afar.

Wolf.

No. Wolves.

My eyes scan the trees, finding four more massive bodies covered in fur, all ranging in color. The five of them watch us, half covered by the surrounding pine trees as they size up their next meal with hungry eyes. My heart is thumping against my ribcage, my breathing shallow and quick. It's a good thing Kai's hand is still covering my mouth, because I nearly yelp at the sudden feel of his lips brushing against the shell of my ear. 'You never seem to listen, do you?'

I reach up slowly, keeping my eyes trained on the wolves as I grab his wrist and pull his hand away from my mouth. 'Technically, I did listen. I talked, not moved,' I whisper back, my voice sharp.

I can feel his mouth smiling against my ear. 'Smartass.'

'So, what's the plan? What are we doing?' My voice is urgent as I eye the wolves.

'There is no *we,*' he says softly, releasing his hold to step slowly around until he's standing in front of me. 'You are still injured,' he murmurs, 'and I'm not risking you tearing my stitches open.'

Absolutely not.

I step to his side, irritated. 'What happened to us being *partners?*'

'Well, we won't be partners for much longer if you insist on getting yourself killed,' he mutters, silently drawing the sword from its sheath at his side.

'And you're just going to take on five wolves by yourself? I don't think so,' I whisper harshly. There is no way in hell I'm letting him fight on his own. My pride and paranoia won't allow that.

'Then you clearly underestimate me, Gray.'

Slowly, so slowly, I pull the bow from my back, watching the wolves as I do. They don't make a move, though they've sunk closer to the ground, ready to pounce and bound towards us.

I nock an arrow.

'Your wound is going to open back up, and I'll have saved your life for nothing,' Kai hisses, his voice urgent and agitated.

I draw back the bowstring, pulling it taut as my stitches do the same, threatening to tear. Pain sears through my abdomen and along my ribs but I bite my tongue, ignoring it.

I smile slightly as I say, 'Sorry to ruin your handiwork, *partner.*'

'Pae, don't you dare—' I fire.

The arrow finds its mark in the chest of the closest wolf, burying deep into that shiny, silver fur. The other wolves are charging towards us before their friend even hits the ground. I already have another arrow ready, nocked and aimed at a brown blur bounding closer. A shooting pain skitters along my abdomen as I fire the arrow, hitting the wolf in its hind leg.

Two of the beasts have separated from the others to circle around us, and I feel Kai's back press against mine as he faces them. I ignore the limping wolf I shot and turn my attention towards the one that is now bounding towards me. I try to slow my panicked breathing before loosing an arrow at the creature. I curse when it misses, sailing past the beast's ear and sinking into the ground behind it.

Kai's back is no longer pressed against my own, leaving me clueless as to what is going on behind me. All I hear are snarls and the swipe of a sword against skin and bone. But I don't have time to turn towards the scene at my back because I now have a snarling beast of my own before me. Its red-tinted fur shimmers almost as brightly as its bared, white teeth. It comes to a halt no more than two yards away from me and crouches, creeping closer. It's massive and menacing and looking at me like I'm its next meal.

I can feel my wound bleeding, and the pain is brutal. If I pull back my bowstring one more time, I'll likely rip my stitches if I haven't done so already. But I have no other weapon, no power, no strength to fight.

The wolf slinks forward, growling as it plays with its food.

What do I do. What do I do. What do I do.

I pull back my bowstring – the wolf pounces.

It's a large, strong leap that sends it flying towards me with its jaw open and razor-sharp teeth displayed, ready to rip me to shreds.

Impulsively, instinctively, I rip the arrow from my bow and grip the shaft in my fist before thrusting the metal tip upwards to meet the wolf in the air. The arrow sinks deep into its heart, spraying me with hot blood before it falls to the ground with a thud.

I'm panting, still trying to process what just happened when I hear a grunt coming from behind me. I spin just in time to see Kai drag the blade of his sword down a wolf's side, splitting it open with one easy motion. He turns swiftly to the other beast crawling towards him, already suffering from a brutal stab wound, though it still advances with a growl. When the wolf launches towards him in one final attempt sink its teeth into his flesh, Kai sweeps his blade upwards in a high arc. The sword slices the creature across the chest with ease, and when it hits the ground, Kai grips the hilt with both hands and drives the tip of the blade down into the wolf's side.

He stands there for a moment, looking every bit the killer he was raised to be. Then he yanks the sword out, wiping the bloody blade on the fur of the dead animal beneath him. He begins turning around as he says, 'You still alive back there?'

I inhale sharply when he turns, displaying the deep bite on his shoulder. Blood oozes from the imprint of jagged teeth, trailing down his arm and over his fingers in rivulets. His eyes find mine before widening when they find something over my shoulder.

'Duck,' he orders, and I don't hesitate before dropping into a crouch. In a flash, he pulls a throwing star from his pocket and sends it sailing through the air where my head was only a moment before. I hear something heavy hit the ground with a thud and turn to see the wolf I had shot in the leg only a few feet behind me, creeping in for the kill. Only now, it's lying dead on the ground with a throwing star protruding from its eye.

I stand slowly to my feet as I breathe, 'You're right. We do make a great team.'

He looks away from me, shaking his head with a dry laugh. 'Yeah, except for the fact that you don't listen to orders.'

'Orders?' I scoff. 'I'm not one of your soldiers, Kai.'

'You're right, you aren't.' He strides towards me, and the sight of him so bloody is suddenly intimidating. But I force myself to stand my ground when he halts before me, close enough now for me to see his smoky eyes turn to ice. 'My soldiers don't mean anything to me. They are expendable and easy to replace.' His chest heaves, his eyes locked with mine. 'So, yes, Gray. You *aren't* one of my soldiers.'

I open my mouth, but no words come out of it. He closes his eyes and sighs deeply, only opening them again when he is back to his cool and collected self. All traces of the frantic, ruffled male are gone. I can sense him shifting back into his cocky, casual self as he attempts to lighten the mood.

Spinning slowly, he takes in the carnage around us and simply says, 'Well, looks like we won't be going hungry tonight.'

I play along, but my voice is weak. 'Good to know that we didn't survive a wolf attack only to die of hunger.'

His eyes darken as they snap to where my wound lies bleeding beneath my clothes. 'Your stitches. Did they—'

I lift my tank and peek under the folds of the bloody bandage.

Relief floods me when I see the thread still pulling my skin together. The exertion of the fight only stretched the stitches, causing the wound to bleed, but thankfully they didn't tear. I suppose I would be in a much worse state if they had.

'No,' I breathe, 'they didn't tear.'

He runs a hand through his hair before sheathing his sword, but I don't miss the slight wince the action causes due to his torn shoulder. I point to the stump behind him and say, 'Sit.'

Now I'm the one giving orders.

He humors me, smirking as he sits down before I come to stand over him yet again. 'You're covered in blood,' he remarks far too casually.

'And you're dripping blood. But, lucky for you,' I smile sweetly, 'I can make just the right salve for this.'

He blows out a breath, shaking his head at the sky. 'Of course you can. You and your *salves* will be the death of me.'

'You know,' I mutter, examining the bite closely, 'I'm beginning to think that you enjoy getting hurt, if only so you can have my hands all over you.'

He lets out a low laugh. I can practically feel his gaze gliding over me as he says, 'Oh, I'm not making you do anything, darling. You can leave me to bleed out if you must. Because I only want your hands all over me if you *want* them to be.'

My eyes snap to his gray ones already pinned on me. I am playing a very dangerous game.

Walking on a sharp blade and hoping I don't get cut. Playing with fire and hoping I don't get burned. Swimming in a dangerous current and hoping I don't drown.

He is dangerous.

And even with that one thought echoing in my mind, I hold his gaze and put my hands on him.

CHAPTER 28

Kai

It's been three days since a wolf took a bite out of me. Three days since Paedyn put her hands on me after I told her to only do so if she *wanted* to. And I don't think I've been able to catch my breath since. Every time she looks at me, I feel like I'm gasping for air. I hate it.

Liar.

It's been three long and boring days. The most profitable thing we've managed to do is find a shirt for me to wear — another gift left for the contestants. The creek and small clearing around it has become our base, though we don't spend much time there during the day. Our riveting routine consists of splitting up into the forest and scouting for any other opponents. And yet, our efforts to collect more bands have not only been futile but also unbearably boring. I'd rather not split up, simply because I'm far more entertained when Paedyn is with me, but she insisted that we'd cover more ground separately.

A lot of good it's done us so far.

The sun is sinking rapidly, and stars splatter the sky as it begins to disappear for the night. I trudge back towards the camp, taking out my frustration on the plants littering my path by slicing them with my sword as I walk.

Nothing. Neither of us has come across another opponent yet. The only things we've managed to find are snakes and lots of them. Those, along with coyotes, have been the only visitors we've had to fight off as of late.

I hear the bubbling creek before I even see it. The small clearing comes into view and so does Paedyn. She sits on a stump, twisting that thick, silver ring on her thumb as she stares blankly at the fire, her hair blowing in the soft breeze.

I grab some kindling and make my way over, throwing it on the fire before sitting down on a stump across from her. 'Well, I don't see any fresh wounds, so no luck, I'm assuming?'

'I'm offended that you think I couldn't come out of a fight unscathed.' After I give her a skeptical look, she finally grumbles, 'No. No luck today.'

I watch her closely, assessing how she bites the inside of her cheek, spins the steel on her thumb, bounces her leg.

She's a mess of pent-up energy, anxiety eating away at her. But I let her think, giving her time before I pry for answers on what it is that has her so tense. So we sit in silence, me gnawing on stringy rabbit while Paedyn gnaws on the inside of her cheek.

The sun has dipped to the horizon, painting the sky with deep oranges and soft pinks when I finally break the silence with a sigh. 'All right, what's wrong? Out with it.'

'Hmm?' She looks up from the fire, meeting my gaze before deciding that the flames are more interesting to look at. 'Nothing. I'm fine.'

I almost laugh. I've learned the hard way that those are words you never want to hear a woman say to you, and it's obvious that she is anything but fine. I stoke the fire as I sigh, 'You're a horrible liar, Gray.' She finally dares to look in my direction. And then she's laughing loudly. I hold my breath, watching the way her head tips towards the sky, her silver hair cascades down her back, her eyes crinkle with amusement.

She looks back at me too quickly, and I hope I've wiped the look of wanting from my face fast enough.

She's so stunning, yet so stubbornly oblivious to how the sunset behind dulls in comparison to the vibrance that is *her*.

What the hell is wrong with me.

'I'll have you know that I am a *great* liar.' She can barely say the words without snorting like she's told a joke, and I've missed the punchline.

'Hmm.' I pop a piece of meat into my mouth. 'I'm going to have to disagree.'

'Oh, really?'

'Really.'

She leans forward, resting her elbows on her knees. 'Enlighten me, Prince.'

Good. Let me distract you.

My lips twitch into a smile. 'You have a tell, darling.'

'Do not.' She's not laughing anymore and I almost regret saying anything at all.

'You tap your left foot when you lie, ever so slightly.' She gapes and I grin. 'I started noticing it when you said you hated my dimples. And obviously, we both know that is a lie.'

I duck before the rock she throws at me can connect with my skull. Now I'm the one laughing. She turns her attention back towards the fire, fighting her smile. 'I didn't realize you had watched me so closely.'

'Watched? Darling, I've never stopped.' She meets my gaze as an emotion I can't place ripples in those ocean eyes of hers.

And there she goes again, spinning that silver ring on her thumb.

Interesting.

'Why are you really doing this?' Her words cut through my thoughts, and I look at her, though her own gaze is now fixed on the flames in front of us. 'Why didn't you just take my leather and leave me?'

I hear her unspoken words echoing in my head.

Leave me to die.

She looks at me then, her eyes flooded with emotions. She wants an answer, *needs* an answer as to why I didn't act like the monster I've been molded into.

I open my mouth, expecting a good answer to fall out. Wishful thinking, I suppose, because I sigh and say, 'You know, we never got to finish our dance.'

She blinks at me. 'That wasn't an answer.'

'That's because we haven't danced yet. You should know how this works by now, Gray. We dance, you get your answer. Or we don't and, well, you'll be left to ponder all your burning questions about me.'

She huffs out a laugh. 'You're kidding. Not this again.'

'Yes, this again.' I stand to my feet and walk over to where she sits on her stump. 'So,' I hold out my hand to her with a lazy bow, 'are we dancing or not, Gray?'

She rolls her eyes, trying to fight the smile that's tugging at her lips. 'Fine.' She lays her palm on my own and the mere contact has my pulse quickening.

What has this girl done to me?

We take a few steps away from the fire, the pale moonlight beaming and the stars twinkling. I guide her hand onto my shoulder and take the other to hold, careful not to strain her stitches. My other hand finds her waist, wrapping my arm around her back to pull her close. She feels so familiar in my arms, and I drink in every detail, memorize every movement.

We begin stepping in time to nothing but the sound of our own heartbeats and the crickets chirping around us. We're swallowed in darkness, mere shadows in the flickering firelight.

'There's no music,' she says flatly, her voice laced with amusement.

'Well then I guess we won't know when to stop dancing. How unfortunate.' My chin brushes the top of her head before I dip her towards the ground, making her gasp in surprise.

'Don't tempt me to stomp on your toes,' she threatens breathlessly.

I raise her back up slowly as I say, 'Oh, we can't have that. I'm still recovering from the last time we danced.'

We're quiet for a moment, listening to the crunch of twigs beneath our feet and the crackling of the fire. Through her thin and battered tank, I can feel the heat of her body, feel her skin beneath my hand.

Distracting.

Her voice is quiet when she breaks the silence, as if almost reluctant to interrupt the moment. 'So, the answer to my question?'

Right. That.

'Is it really so shocking that I don't want you to die?' I lean back slightly so I can meet her eyes. 'So shocking that I would help someone?'

She doesn't hesitate. 'Yes.'

I almost laugh. 'I can't say I'm surprised.'

'It's just that,' she pauses, her eyes flitting between mine as if searching for the answer in them, 'I thought you were more like your father.'

Her words slam into me. Father is . . . well, he is a king. He's cold and strict and very rarely impressed, even with his own sons. I suppose in some ways he's made me to be like him, schooled me on how to act, what to feel, and more importantly, what not to feel. Thanks to him, I've crafted a jumble of different masks that I can slip on and off at will.

I'm a mess. A mess of muffled emotions and well-built walls.

But because I don't quite know the answer to her question myself, I ask her one of my own. 'Is that why you hate me so much? Because you thought I was like my father who you clearly don't care for?'

'I don't hate you,' she answers too quickly, pausing to wonder if she's said the right thing while I wonder why she hasn't said it sooner.

My smile is crooked. 'Oh, you don't hate me? So, what, every threat on my life is a declaration of love, then?'

'I said I don't *hate* you, Prince. That doesn't mean I don't despise you.'

I duck my head, eyes searching hers. 'I think you despise that you *don't* despise me.'

Her mouth falls open before she snaps it shut and fixes me with a glare. I seem to have rendered her speechless.

Well, that's a first.

'Use your words, Gray.' I smile, spinning her before pulling her back to me. 'Tell me, am I wrong?'

'I thought I was the one asking *you* the questions?' she says, distracting and diverting my attention with that devastating smile and deliberate words.

And she thinks I'm the calculating one.

She looks away from me, biting the inside of her cheek before meeting my gaze again. 'Would you have helped one of the others?' A pause. 'Someone other than Jax or Andy?'

Someone other than the few people I truly care about.

A slow smile spreads across my face. 'Darling, I doubt that the sight of someone dying would affect me as much as you do alive and well.'

She swallows. 'You're a shameless flirt, Azer.'

'Only for you.'

'Hmm. Now it seems you're also a shameless liar.'

I huff out a quiet laugh before saying, 'My turn to ask a question.' She opens her mouth, most likely to argue, but I cut her off. 'So, out of all the people roaming around Loot that day, why was I fortunate enough to be robbed blind?'

Her mouth snaps shut before splitting into a smile. 'You fit a description.'

'A description?'

Her smile is anything but sweet. 'Yes. You looked cocky and chock-full of coins. Those are my favorite targets.'

I lean closer towards her. 'Well, *this* target knew you stole from him.'

'You knew I stole from you *too late*.'

'Funny, I seem to remember that I caught you not shortly after.'

Her smile is smug. 'Only because I came back and *saved* you.' Then she laughs. 'So, what, you don't think I could steal from you again without you noticing?'

'I think that I notice everything you do. So, no.'

She pauses, her face close to mine, momentarily stunned by my words. I smile, enjoying the sight of her flustered. Her next words are soft, slow. 'Is that a challenge, Azer?'

'It's a fact, Gray.'

'Is it?' she says, suddenly dangling something between our faces. 'That's interesting, because I nicked this off you almost immediately after we started dancing.'

I squint in the dim light, swearing under my breath when I realize what it is that she's holding. Braxton's leather strap, once safe in my pocket, is now pinched between her fingers and swinging in front of my face.

'I'm impressed, Gray.' I shrug casually before adding, 'I'm mostly shocked I didn't notice with how closely I pay attention to you.'

She rolls her eyes at me. 'Distraction.'

253

My gaze sweeps over her quickly before returning to that smile. 'You are quite good at that, aren't you?'

She's quiet as she watches me closely before looking away. I avert my gaze too, preparing myself for another one of her prying questions.

'What's your favorite color?'

My eyes snap to hers. 'What?' I nearly choke on my laughter.

'Your favorite color. What is it?'

For once, *I* almost step on her toes out of shock and sheer wonder. 'Of all the things you could ask me, you ask what my favorite color is?' I can't keep the smile from spreading across my face.

She blows a strand of hair from her eyes in annoyance. 'I feel like I don't know many *things* about you, so I figured I'd start with the basics.' An amused sigh. 'I'm letting you off the hook with an easy question, so don't disappoint. What is your favorite color?'

I spin her if only to give myself some time to think. I'd never thought about what my favorite color was before. It never seemed important.

Not until I looked into a pair of ocean blue eyes and realized that perhaps drowning was a beautiful thing.

Not until I looked into a pair of fiery blue eyes and realized that perhaps burning was a painless thing.

Not until I looked into a pair of sky blue eyes and realized that perhaps falling was a peaceful thing.

I'd never thought about what my favorite color was before because I hadn't seen one that was worthy of the title. Until now, that is.

'Blue,' I say, my voice low.

'Hmm.' She's looking at me thoughtfully, studying me sincerely. 'I would have never guessed.'

Neither would I.

'And yours?' I ask, watching her as she thinks.

She opens her mouth and then shuts it, considering something. Her jaw sets. 'I don't have one.' With a small shrug, she asks, 'Favorite food or dessert?'

'We're in the middle of a Trial, and you're asking me about my favorite food?'

She ignores me. 'Well, I know it's not rabbit. I see the way your mouth twists when you eat it—'

'I do not twist—' I pause, grinning. 'Have you been looking at my mouth, Gray?'

She opens her own mouth to argue only to huff instead. 'Just answer the damn question, Azer.'

I chuckle and spin her slowly. 'Easy. Lemon tarts.'

She snorts. 'You're kidding. Lemon tarts? You're a rich prince who could have any food he wants, and you would choose *lemon tarts*?'

'Yes, *lemon tarts*,' I mimic. 'And now I'm making you eat some with me when we finally get out of here.'

'Over my dead body.'

My smile is wicked. 'That can be arranged.'

And there she goes, making good on her threat to stomp on my toes, seeing that her feet are her only weapon at the moment. 'Oops.'

'Vicious little thing,' I murmur under my breath.

'You don't know the half of it, Prince.'

'Oh, but I hope one day I will.'

We are silent for a moment, studying each other before I finally say, 'Tell me, what's your favorite food then, since you seem to think it's so much better than lemon tarts?'

'Oh, trust me when I say that it is *far* better than lemon tarts.'

'Well don't keep me guessing, Gray.'

She tilts her head up towards mine as she confidently says, 'Butterscotch.'

'Butterscotch,' I repeat, committing the information to memory.

'Yes.' She smiles, but I see the sadness in it. 'My father used to give out the candy to his patients. And every time he would fix up one of my wounds, or I would help fix up someone else's, we would eat butterscotch after as a sort of reward.'

We are quiet for a moment. 'You two were very close.'

'We were,' she states. 'But you and your father aren't, are you? Not after what he's put you through.'

I'm thankful for the lack of pity in her voice, though her disgust is clear. A quiet, bitter laugh escapes me. 'No. I'm more soldier than son, and he's more king than father. It's hard to be close when our only time spent together was training, and I didn't exactly look forward to those encounters.'

'And your mother?' she asks quietly.

'She's everything I could have asked for,' I state simply. 'Everything I needed as a boy. She's been one of the only constants in my life, a source of kindness and caring.'

'And yet,' Paedyn says hesitantly, 'she let your father do what he did?'

I pause, speaking to her even as I remind myself. 'She didn't exactly have a choice in the matter. And becoming the future Enforcer is my duty, no matter the methods it takes to get there.'

She eyes me with that expression I can never quite seem to place. Is it wonder? Confusion? One moment she's an open book, and then the next, I can barely crack the spine.

And then she's peppering me with questions. Most of them random, though all are deemed equally important to her. She tells me stories of growing up, and I do the same, listening to her laugh at Kitt's and my stupidity.

'So, tell me about the split lip you had when we met?' I ask, brows raised.

She laughs and the sound snakes up my spine. 'I wasn't lying when I told you that it was a gift from one of your Imperials.'

'Right. You informed me of that when you had your dagger to my throat, I believe?'

'Sounds about right.'

'Well, I'm still unaware of the details behind how you earned it.' My eyes darken at the thought. 'I don't react kindly to my Imperials hitting women.'

'Oh? Then you should probably know that this wasn't the first time.' Her words are casual, blunt. 'Long story short, he didn't believe I was a Psychic, so I proved it to him. And clearly, he didn't like what I had to say.'

I stare at her in disbelief. 'And, what, you just took the hit?'

'Yes, but not before I took some of his pride.'

'Why am I not surprised by that?'

She gives me a sly smile. 'Probably because you've gotten so used to me humbling you, Prince.'

'That I have.' I pause, taking her in. 'You never cease to amaze me,

Gray.' I smirk as I release her hand to flick the tip of her nose lightly.

She bats my fingers away with a huff. 'And you never cease to annoy me.'

I grab her hand again and guide it up my arm until both of her palms rest on my shoulders. Then I slip my hands around her waist and behind her back, careful of her injured side as I pull her closer.

And then we just sway.

No fancy footwork, no waltz to step in time to. Just us, in the middle of a forest, surrounded by thousands of winking stars. Her lashes flutter, and then her fingers are laced behind my neck.

The tension between us pulls taut, like an invisible tether connecting the two of us. My pulse quickens and so does her breathing, her chest rising and falling rapidly.

'I never cease to annoy you, huh?' I watch her face while pulling her impossibly closer. 'What about now. Is this the exception?'

She swallows and dips her head, not offering me an answer. I smile slightly as I try to get her to speak, a problem I've never had to deal with before. 'Pae?'

Still no answer.

My fingers catch her chin, gently guiding her gaze to meet mine. There is confusion etched all over her face as she lets out a shaky laugh. 'I'm annoyed that I'm *not* finding this annoying.'

My hand tightens around her waist like it might catch fire from the feel of her. I'm embarrassed by how much this one girl engrosses me, afraid of how affected I am. It makes me feel equally weak and wonderful. Alarmed yet *alive*.

'Why didn't you shoot me, Paedyn?'

The question tumbles out of my mouth, curious and quiet. She tilts her head, studying me. 'You're going to have to be more specific than that, Azer.'

Deflecting.

I crack a smile, knowing that she is aware of what I'm referring to. 'You could have shot me a few days ago but you fired at the ground. I want to know why.'

She pauses, pondering her answer. Then her eyes are pinned on mine. 'Just because I was doomed for death doesn't mean I wanted to damn you as well.' Her eyes roam over me, and I relish the feel of her gaze.

And then she pulls away.

Her hands are back on my shoulders, stiff and stubbornly unmoving. Then her eyes are on the sky, choosing to stare at the stars rather than me. She sighs through her nose, silently collecting herself.

And I'm doing the same, trying to pull myself together after she pulled away.

Yes, we are opponents. Yes, I am the future Enforcer. Yes, I'm a killer that has no right to want to keep her. But there is something else, something that has her refusing to admit this confusing connection we share.

Plagues, I'm pissed that I admitted it to myself.

My masks are still at the ready, my walls still in place, but she is slowly breaking down both my facades and fortresses. And I'm suddenly angry at myself for allowing it. For allowing myself to *care.* For allowing myself to think of her in any way other than my competition.

Because she's made it clear that that is all I am to her.

'Kai,' she says quietly, the sound of my name on her lips ripping me from my thoughts. 'I—'

A soft, female voice cuts through her words. 'Sorry to interrupt, but you both have something I need.'

CHAPTER 29

Paedyn

The voice echoes from all around us. Kai and I jump apart, instinctively swiveling around to press our backs against each other. I squint in the dim light where the outlines of tall, dark figures begin to take shape. A reluctant sigh rings out into the darkness, amplified by the numerous bodies surrounding us.

We're trapped.

They all take a measured step forward, enclosing us in a human cage of bodies. Dozens of hazel eyes shimmer in the firelight, dark hair and skin gleaming.

Sadie.

'All I want is your bands, and I'll be on my way.' And then she almost smiles as she looks around at her copies. 'Well, *we'll* be on our way.'

Kai sighs, seemingly annoyed by all of this. 'You knew we wouldn't give you our bands and yet you interrupted us anyways.'

'Fine,' Sadie says curtly. 'Then give me one band and no one has to get hurt.'

My eyes dart to my bow lying a few feet away from me – a few feet away *and* behind the wall of Sadies. I don't have a single weapon to use to defend myself and I've never felt so exposed. It's like I've

been stripped bare. I can almost feel the ghost of my father's dagger against my thigh, making me wish more than anything that I had it here with me.

Several sets of hazel eyes flick between the two of us, still back-to-back, before locking with mine. 'I don't want to hurt you, but I will if it comes to that.' She pauses, and her voice is even, unfeeling as she says, 'I will if it means I'll win.'

I'm about to open my mouth and respond when calluses brush my own, gripping my hand behind my back. I nearly jerk at the contact, but Kai pries my fist open, pressing something cool and hard into my palm before curling my fingers around it. Then, just as quickly, his hand is gone.

The thing bites into my skin, pointed edges piercing. I fight to keep the smile from my face when I realize what he's given me.

A weapon. He's given me a fighting chance.

It's a small one, but a weapon, nonetheless. I clutch the throwing star in my fist, not caring if the sharp edges pierce my skin. This tiny object could be the difference between life and death.

The only weapon Kai has is the sword belted at his side, but then again, he is a weapon himself. I'm shocked he didn't feel Sadie's power creeping up on us, but I suppose I can't blame him, considering how distracted *I* was with his hands on me, his words with underlying meanings, my hammering heartbeat when he gets too close.

I take a deep breath.

Let's deal with one problem at a time.

'Then I guess you're going to have to hurt me if you have any hope of getting my band,' I breathe, eying the Sadies as they take a slow step forward.

She shakes her head at me, as though disappointed in my decision. 'Fine. But don't say I didn't warn you.'

And then she's suddenly in front of me, holding the tip of a short dagger to my throat. Before the next thud of my heart, she's yanked my arm and pulled my back against her chest. The blade she still holds against my throat sinks deeper into my flesh with every shallow breath.

'I'll only ask once more.' Sadie's voice is sharp, so unlike the soft tone I'm used to from her. 'Give me your leather, Kai, or I'll slit her throat.'

The prince blinks at the scene before him, looking completely unfazed.

He knows I can take care of myself, and though I'm flattered by that fact, I could use his help at the current moment. Hot blood begins to trickle down my neck, and I will myself to remain calm.

Kai simply shrugs at the threat. 'Go ahead then.' He nods towards the blade pressed to my throat. 'See if I care. We are only opponents, after all. Less competition.'

I can practically hear Sadie blink behind me. She's clearly stunned by his lack of concern, especially after seeing the two of us dancing together only minutes ago. I would be stunned myself if I wasn't so used to seeing his masks – if I didn't recognize the cold one he's just slipped on.

She stiffens behind me. 'I'm calling your bluff, Prince.'

I feel her hand begin to jerk, begin to slice deeper into my skin. And then I strike.

I slam the razor-sharp throwing star into the soft tissue of her stomach, pushing it deep as I push her hand still clutching the knife away from my neck. She screams and jerks away, sending me stumbling into Kai. Well, one of them. There are now several muscled forms, all mirroring his messy black waves and stormy eyes. He's taken on her ability.

I ram into his chest before strong hands grip the sides of my arms. When I look up into his face, he has the nerve to *wink* before saying, 'Good work, Gray. I can always count on you and your violent tendencies.' With that, he spins around and drives his sword through one of Sadie's duplicates.

A throng of Sadies surround Kai and his own copies, keeping him occupied and unable to get to the real one and end this fight quickly. I'm reminded of a day spent training at the castle, when I watched Sadie sparring with Braxton. They would fight and dance around each other until Braxton made his way to the real Sadie, finally taking her down and ending the fight.

And that is exactly what I am going to do. Except, unlike Ace's illusions which I've already had the pleasure of facing, Sadie and her copies can touch and hurt me. With this unsettling thought in mind, I dance on the balls of my feet, prepared to strike. I turn away from the copies swarming Kai, knowing that he can handle himself while he trusts I can do the same. There are only three Sadies left, two of which guard the real one currently clutching a bloodied hand to the wound on her stomach. Their heads snap towards me, and I barely have enough time to sink into my fighting stance before one of them charges at me.

Unfortunately for me, Sadie knows how to fight. Since her power is simply duplicating her own body, she automatically has strength in numbers. But she's trained so that those numbers have strength of their own.

A right hook flies at my face and I duck under it, landing a quick blow to her stomach. The Sadie stumbles back with a grunt, and I use the opportunity to send a kick connecting with her side. She catches my leg and pulls me forward. Exactly what I was hoping for. I grip her shoulders and jump, driving my other knee deep into her stomach. She drops my leg with a cry of pain, and I slide my ring onto my middle finger before throwing a fist at her temple. I mutter a curse as I shake out my stinging hand, but she's out cold before she even hits the ground.

A hand pulls at my hair, hard, and my head yanks back. I let out a strangled gasp as an elbow hooks around my throat, crushing my windpipe. I can't breathe, dizzy with pain as spots swim before my vision. But I stomp on her foot before elbowing her hard in the stomach. She loosens her hold, and I whirl around, grabbing the back of her neck and slamming her nose into the knee I drive upwards. She sputters and flings her fist out, managing to connect it with my jaw. I ignore the aching pain and drop, sweeping my leg out before she's swept off her feet. She slams into the ground with a thud, but I've already turned my attention away from her sprawled form.

My eyes find the smoldering hazel ones belonging to the real Sadie. She steps towards me, blood oozing from between her fingers as she covers her wound. 'Just know that I don't want to do this,' she says, her voice strained. 'But I have to.'

And then her fists are flying at me in a combination of hooks, jabs, and uppercuts. I'm impressed by how much speed and strength she still has after being stabbed, forcing me on defense. I dodge her blows until I land one of my own, square in her jaw.

She grunts in pain before sending a roundhouse kick at my temple. I barely block it, her heel still clipping the side of my head. We dance around each other, throwing various combinations of punches and kicks. Her fist crashes into my lip and my head snaps to the side before I spit blood. I send a hard kick into her already wounded side and she screams in pain. Then I land a blow under her jaw, another to her wound, a kick to her temple.

She cries out, trying to hit me with a lazy punch but I catch her wrist easily, twisting it at an odd angle before kneeing her in the stomach. I grab her shirt in one hand while the other is balled into a fist currently cocked back and ready to strike. I send it flying towards her face, ready to end this fight with one final blow.

Except my fist doesn't move.

Cold hands clamp around both of my wrists, pulling at my arms until they are tucked tightly behind my back. I'm so shocked, so strained and tired that I can't fight the strong grip, can't do anything to break my hands free.

My head whips around and I'm face-to-face with a bloody-nosed Sadie, the one I fought immediately before.

'Look at me, Paedyn.' My head snaps back to the original Sadie now clutching a knife in her bloody hands before me. I kick at the legs of the Sadie behind me, only causing her to kick in the back of my knees, sending me crashing into the ground.

Helpless. Powerless.

Sadie stands over me, seeming to contemplate something as I kneel before her. 'You are never going to stop fighting me, are you?' In response, I writhe in the Sadie's grip, desperately trying to break free. She shakes her head at me, offering an apologetic look. 'Maybe Kai was right. The less competition, the better.'

She grabs the handle of the dagger in both hands, raising it above her head.

So this is how I die.

I've survived my whole life as an Ordinary, and yet, this is how it ends.

By a measly dagger. I can't tell if I want to laugh or cry.

Sadie holds the knife above her head, ready to plunge it into my rapidly beating heart as she whispers, 'I told you I didn't want to do this. But I have to.'

Kai will be furious that he saved my life for nothing.

'I'm sorry,' Sadie chokes out as the tip of the blade comes racing towards my heart. And impossibly, unbelievably, I'm suddenly ready for it.

I'll see you soon, Father.

Nothing.

The blade stops mere inches away from my heart.

I'm shaking, my eyes trailing from the halted knife to my almost-killer. Blood pours out of Sadie's mouth, followed by a gurgled gasp slipping between her lips. She looks down, wide-eyed, and I follow her gaze to the sword now protruding from her chest.

The dagger slips from her fingers as tears slip down her cheeks. She stumbles back, gasping, into a broad chest. Kai wraps his arms around her and gently guides her to the ground, a sickening gargling sound slipping past her lips.

And then she's suddenly silent, her hazel eyes staring up at the black sky – wide, unseeing, and glossy.

The Sadies around us flicker out of existence, leaving my hands free to cover my mouth as I choke on a gasp. I'm trying to take in what just happened, trying to take in air as I wheeze weakly.

Kai drops to his knees beside me, worry crinkling his brow. 'Are you hurt?' His eyes roam over me like the fingers now lightly roaming up my body, checking for injuries just as they had a few nights before. 'Paedyn, look at me.' Rough hands are cupping my face now, guiding my gaze towards him. 'Tell me, did she hurt you?'

'I–I'm fine.' I'm not fine.

I hate these Trials because they kill people, and now I've just witnessed it firsthand. I've been a part of it. I didn't ask for any of this, didn't want anyone to die. And now, another victim of the Trials lies motionless mere feet away.

'I told you I don't want to do this. But I have to.'

Sadie didn't want to kill me, and yet, I almost wish she had. Almost wish I had a reason to hate her, a reason to wish this fate upon her. But it's these twisted Trials that forced her shaking hand to raise that dagger above her head, forced her into nearly taking a life.

I glance at her bloody body lying limp and so close. An image of my father flashes before my eyes, replacing the girl who tried to kill me with the father who would have killed for me. I witnessed him die similarly, and I try to blink the image away. But his bloody body doesn't budge—

'Hey, look at me, alright? Don't look at her, look right at me.' Kai's hands are still gently holding my face when I slide my gaze back to his, trying to focus on something other than the death in front of me. Except, the prince himself seems to be death incarnate, a wielded weapon.

'Focus on my eyes. I know how much you like to stare into them.' His gray gaze sparkles with amusement, and the corner of his lips kick up while my own mouth falls open. He knows me well enough to know that I'm about to start telling him off in response to that little comment, so he presses a finger to my lips before I get the chance.

'Focus on the dimples you try to convince yourself you hate, even though I know you look for them every time I smile.' Sure enough, his grin spreads, and my traitorous eyes flick to the dimples framing it.

The thumb he runs over my bottom lip has my eyes dragging from his dimples to meet his gaze. 'Focus on my lips.' His voice is a murmur, a caress like the fingers brushing my face and mouth. 'Don't be shy, I know this wouldn't be the first time.'

My eyes drift to his lips, trailing over the sensuous curve of them. He's so very easy to look at, to admire. Everything about him is annoyingly alluring, distracting so easily—

Distracting.

When my eyes light up with the realization of what he is doing, his slight smirk tells me I'm correct. This calculating boy just distracted me from a dead body using nothing but himself to do so.

'Are you sure that was to distract me and not to boost your ego?' I ask, my voice deceptively calm.

'Why can't it be both?'

'Ass,' I mumble.

He hasn't stopped smiling at me. 'I may be an ass, but I just saved yours.' And then, without warning, his smile vanishes and is replaced by serious scrutiny as he looks me over. 'How are you? Have you calmed down?'

I breathe and shut my eyes for a moment. An image of Sadie's bloody body flashes in my mind before shifting into my father's.

'I'm fine now,' I lie, hating how strained my voice sounds.

He shakes his head at me, muttering, 'I told you. You're a horrible liar, Gray.'

A shaky laugh escapes me. The sound is so wrong with a lifeless body so close, but I can't seem to control myself. At this point, my only options are laughing or crying, and I refuse to do the latter.

Kai studies my face, seeming to see the battle raging within me. Without a word, he wraps an arm around my middle and helps me to my feet. I know I should push him away, should tell him I don't need his help. But I'm weak in far more ways than one, and his closeness is my only comfort right now.

He guides me to a stump and sits me down, crouching to look up into my face. 'Pae,' he speaks the syllable so softly, 'stay here and calm down. Just breathe, all right? You're still in shock.'

I nod numbly as he assesses me again. His gaze never strays from my own as he slowly raises a hand to slide his fingers over mine, seeming to search for something. They halt on the cold steel around my finger before spinning the ring idly, mirroring a movement I'm all too familiar with. 'Distract yourself. Spin this like you always do to keep busy, to keep your mind off things.'

I blink at him, shocked that he knows my habits, knows how to help me. I'm stunned at how calm and collected he is after killing someone, though I shouldn't be. He was raised for this, molded into a murderer who's numb to the death he doles out. I suppress a shudder at the thought of the horrors this haunted boy has committed. The horrors he's *endured*. Kai stands to leave. 'I'm going to go . . . clean this up. I'll be back soon. And for once,' he sighs, 'listen to me and stay put.'

And then he's gone, leaving me to spin my ring restlessly.

CHAPTER 30

Paedyn

Unsurprisingly, I didn't listen to him. As soon as my ass got numb from sitting on that bloody stump, I stood and paced circles around our camp before splashing cold water from the creek on my face and body. Then my ass got cold, and I moved next to the fire to lie down on the hard ground I'm so familiar with.

I refused to watch as Kai lifted Sadie's body over his shoulder and stalked off with her. Where he dumped her, I have no idea. And I don't want to know, I realized. But I let my thoughts wander while he wanders around the woods with a dead body slung over his shoulder.

I watch the dying fire from where I lie on my side, the crook of my arm tucked under my head making for an uncomfortable pillow. My breathing is now under control, the shaking from leftover adrenaline and shock now faded. I might have been lying here for hours if I cared to try and keep track of time.

A shadow suddenly sweeps over me, belonging to the someone now crouching behind.

I grip the handle of Sadie's knife and flip around in one swift movement, bringing the tip of the blade to the throat of whoever decided it was a smart idea to creep up on me. My eyes crash into stormy ones, looking amused rather than afraid.

'Easy,' Kai murmurs, gently wrapping a rough hand around my wrist and pulling the dagger away from him. 'It's just me.' The corner of his mouth twists up as he says, 'Although, I doubt that knowledge would stop you from keeping this blade to my throat.'

I manage a slight smile at the thought, running a hand through my tangled hair as I look up at him crouching beside me. 'Since we're partners now, you don't have to worry about me stabbing you for the time being.'

He lets out a deep chuckle, and I hope the dim light hides most of my smile at the sound. 'And when we aren't partners anymore? Should I fear for my life?'

'That would be wise, yes.'

I just barely hear him mutter, 'Vicious little thing.'

We are quiet for a moment, and my smile begins to slowly fade. I'm tired and surprisingly comfy on the packed earth, so I don't bother moving as I say, 'Did you—'

'Yes,' he cuts me off, sparing me from having to speak about Sadie's body.

My gaze snags on his hands and the thin layer of dirt covering them. It's under his nails, splattered up his arms. A dusting of yellow on his fingertips catches my eye, a fine powder staining his skin. *Dirt. Pollen.*

My voice is little more than a whisper. 'You buried her.' Kai stills beside me.

'Not only that,' my eyes slowly slide up to meet his, 'you laid flowers on her grave.'

His smile is almost sad, filled with fatigue. 'Nothing gets past you, Little Psychic.' He reaches out a hand then, flicking the very tip of my nose like he'd done when we danced. Somehow, the simple action feels far more intimate than I care to admit, as though he is sharing something precious with me, saying something without uttering a single word.

I catch his hand before he pulls away, trying to ignore the feel of his calluses against my own. 'Thank you, Kai. That was good of you to do that for her.'

His lips twitch, and his eyes drop to our joined hands before trailing back to mine. 'Oh, I didn't do it for her.'

The intensity in his gaze makes me swallow, but I don't look away. I don't *want* to look away. He runs his thumb over my knuckles, the action so soothing, so gentle.

He cocks his head to the side, inspecting me. 'How are you feeling?' I open my mouth, but Kai beats me to my rehearsed response. 'And don't bother saying that you're fine, because we both know that's a lie.'

Another stroke of his thumb across my knuckles.

'I . . .' My eyes flutter closed, and I take a deep breath. 'I'm feeling like I almost died today. I'm feeling overwhelmed and in over my head. I'm feeling furious and frustrated because I don't know *how* to feel about all of this.' I pause while Kai waits patiently for me to continue. 'And I'm feeling like I owe you a thank you. I would have died today if it weren't for you saving me.'

He leans closer, eyes brimming with barely bottled-up emotions. 'And I'll save your life again and again, aimlessly hoping you will allow me to stay in it.'

We stare at each other.

Those pretty words of his have my heart pounding, brain puzzling over possible meanings. The tension between us is tangible, taking my breath away as he takes me in. I'm grasping for something, *anything*, to say, but I'm too busy staring to think straight.

And then a quiet question slips past my lips, snapping the tension between us. 'How are you so calm after all this?'

I know the answer, and yet, I find myself wanting to hear it from his own lips. 'I didn't always used to be like this,' he says softly. 'But practice makes perfect, and I've had a lot of it.'

We stare silently at one another, and once again, I'm struggling for something to say. Then I remember the leather strap I had stolen from him and slip my hand out of his to pull it from my pocket. 'Well, I suppose this is the only way I can repay you. Though, it's yours to begin with.'

He gives me a lazy shrug. 'Keep it.'

I huff. 'I don't want your pity.'

'It's not pity, Paedyn.' He sighs out the words, my *name*. 'Besides, I have another one of my own now, and taking down Sadie was a joint effort.' I level him with a look, prepared to argue since we both know he didn't necessarily *need* my help with Sadie. He doesn't miss the fight in my eyes. 'Just take the damn leather, Gray.'

If he wants to offer me the one thing I need to help me win these Trials, then fine.

I'll take the damn leather. But not before I've had some fun. A smile twists my lips. 'Say please.'

He looks away from me, shaking his head at the starry sky. 'You have just been waiting to make me say this, haven't you?'

'Dying to, actually.'

His forearms rest on his bent knees as he leans even closer, face hovering close above mine. The smile he gives me is equally as lazy as his gaze traveling over my face. 'Please, Pae.'

A shiver runs down my spine at the caress that is his voice. 'That seems to be a foreign word to you, Prince.'

'Thanks to you, I have a feeling I'm going to grow very familiar with it. Few have the power to make me plead.'

I swallow, choosing to ignore his words as I shove the leather into my pocket and roll to face the fire once more, suddenly cold and content to be quiet. The temperature has dropped significantly tonight, and my thin tank does little to keep me warm.

'I do have one condition, though.' I roll my eyes.

Of course he does.

'And what would that be?' I ask through my teeth, not bothering to look at him.

An arm wraps around my middle, carefully avoiding my wound while tugging me against a broad chest. I startle at the sudden contact, and a soft laugh sounds close to my ear. 'I get to use you to keep me warm.'

There's a certain hesitancy to him, the type of timidness he only lets me see in moments like these. He holds me loosely, delicately, like whatever shared fragile feelings between us could shatter if handled with a lack of care.

A question laces every lingering touch, every look too long, every layer of ourselves we choose to divulge to one another. The arm

270

around me is no different, speaking volumes in the form of hovering fingers and hesitant hold.

Is this okay?

I swallow hard. My throat has gone dry.

My answer is agonizingly slow as I slide closer to him.

It's more than okay.

Eagerness is an emotion I've always been able to blame on circumstance, and I wish desperately it wasn't desire driving my decisions.

I hear him take a breath, only realizing then that he had been holding it.

And then all remanence of hesitation is gone.

His hand settles on the far side of my waist where my tank is slowly beginning to slide up. He's wasted no time pulling me against him, allowing me to feel the rise and fall of his chest, feel the steady beat of his heart pounding against my back.

'Tell me, does *this* annoy you?' he asks quietly, breathing the question close to my ear. He's throwing my words back at me, and I can almost feel him smirking. He *wants* this to annoy me. Wants this to get under my skin and make me flustered with every finger he has on my body.

Bastard.

I simply can't allow that. So, I say with a confidence I don't currently feel, 'Not at all. I can't be bothered, Azer.'

'Good,' he says coolly. Then he lays his head on my arm and shoulder, his soft, inky hair tickling my skin. 'Who needs a pillow when I have you?'

I huff with what I hope sounds like annoyance. Thanks to him, I'm now suddenly wide awake and unable to focus on anything else but the heat of his body against mine. He finally drops his head from my shoulder and lays it close to the back of mine, practically buried in my hair.

'Sweet dreams, Pae.'

'Sweet dreams, Kai.'

His hand tightens ever so slightly on my waist in response to the sound of his name rolling off my tongue. And then his thumb is brushing lazy, light strokes over the fabric of my thin tank. I suppress a shiver, swallow, and shut my eyes.

Just go to sleep.

Easier said than done.

I'm far too focused on his sweeping thumb, his arm wrapped tightly around me, his chest rising and falling against my back.

I hate that I *don't* hate it. And that's when it hits me. *Distraction*.

He's doing it again. He's taking my mind off the death I just witnessed, off the fact that I watched him kill someone because they were going to kill me. He's the only thing keeping my thoughts from Sadie's dead body, the only thing that will chase the nightmares away for tonight because I'm too occupied with the thought of *him*.

And this is a distraction that benefits the both of us.

I find myself smiling as I think about the calculating boy behind me.

The calculating boy, who for some reason, *cares*.

CHAPTER 31

Kai

We spend our final day in the Whispers trying to get out. It was late afternoon when a Sight interrupted our routine of eating stringy rabbit together. The girl was young and timid, only managing to drop a folded piece of parchment onto a nearby stump before she vanished into the forest.

The note, to no surprise, was incredibly cryptic. It offered no details, only informing us that we are to meet at the edge of the Whispers at sunrise.

So, after climbing another Plague-forsaken pine tree to see which direction to head in, we set off trudging through the forest. And after several long hours of this, we've grown restless, to say the least.

I hear Paedyn swear, stumbling behind me. 'These damn snakes!' I turn around in time to see her flip the dagger in her hand, holding it by its blade before effortlessly sending it flying into the head of a snake slithering by her feet. The hissing dies along with the rest of the creature before Paedyn casually tugs the blade out of its skull.

I turn back to the path of thick foliage in front of me, a smile tugging at my lips thanks to the girl behind me. Then I hear a muttered sentence followed by a string of curse words that only manages to make my grin grow. 'I'm sorry, what was that, Gray?'

I ask, not bothering to look over my shoulder.

'We are all only being forced into one area for a bloodbath,' she huffs, brushing past me.

'That sounds about right,' I say with a sigh.

The sky above us is quickly darkening, and under the cover of the trees, the light is even dimmer. She turns, and I see her open her mouth to likely make some smartass comment before clamping it shut when the sound of a twig snapping echoes around us.

We halt, eyes scanning the endless trees and plants surrounding us. Whatever it is sounded heavy and heading our way. Then, I hear a muffled voice grow louder as the owner of it grows closer.

'Please, there is no way you can Blink from here to the edge of the Whispers.'

'I most certainly could. It's just dark now, so I can't. Oh, and there are too many trees blocking my view. But if it weren't for that, I totally could.'

'Sure. Use that as your excuse.'

'I think you're just jealous.'

'Keep telling yourself that.'

I hear the echo of laughter, and the sound of scuffling feet no doubt the result of playful shoving. The power of the two opponents nearby seeps into my bones, but I don't need to know their abilities to know who they are.

Paedyn hesitantly follows behind when I head in their direction. I push through the trees and plants, my pulse quickening in anticipation. Shoving aside a branch, I spot the two figures walking towards us.

Andy sticks out her foot and catches Jax's ankle, nearly sending him sprawling to the ground. Their quiet laughter is abruptly cut off when they see me and halt in their tracks.

'Well don't look too excited to see me,' I say dryly, taking a step towards them.

'Kai?' Jax is squinting through the growing darkness, but his eyes light up with recognition. He's before me in a few of his long strides, and I catch his head in the crook of my arm to scruff up his short hair despite his protests.

Andy walks up with a smile. 'Good to see you're alive.'

'Yeah, that's great,' Jax agrees, rubbing his head. 'But I could do without your usual greeting.'

'So, how was your stay in the Whispers—' Andy stops short, her eyes sliding to something over my shoulder.

Paedyn steps beside me, offering a hesitant smile. She doesn't trust them, and I don't blame her. But it's clear that she trusts me, or else she would've run rather than follow me out here. I suppress a smile at the thought as I say, '*We* have had quite the eventful stay in the Whispers.'

Andy offers Paedyn a smile and a nod of her head while Jax grins sheepishly. My gaze flicks to the darkening sky, and I sigh. 'We better keep walking if we want to make it to the edge by dawn.' We turn and begin heading through the thick foliage, fumbling slightly in the dark. 'So, tell us what happened to you two.'

Andy laughs bitterly. 'A better question would be what *didn't* happen to us.'

'We found each other on the third day,' Jax cuts in, 'but before that, I was lying pretty low since my ability doesn't do so well in crowded terrain like this. I saw Blair once but Blinked high into a tree before she could spot me and rip my arm off to get my leather.'

'And Plague knows she would, too,' Andy mutters under her breath while Paedyn hums in agreement.

Jax continues with a shrug. 'But other than her, I didn't see anyone else when I was on my own. My biggest competition was just surviving in the forest alone.'

'And what about you, Andy?' Paedyn asks curiously.

'Well, unlike Jax here, I was lucky enough to encounter two opponents on my own.' She almost rolls her eyes in annoyance. 'I came across Blair, and the fight was . . . intense. But unfortunately, the bitch got my band. And then,' she draws out the words, 'the day before I found Jax, Hera paid me a visit. I woke up in the middle of the night to an invisible knife trying to saw the leather from my arm. I eventually got her band, but it wasn't easy considering that I couldn't see her half the time.'

'Then Andy found me, and we've been together since.' I hear the easy smile in Jax's voice. 'Braxton found us, but after we – well, mostly Andy – took him down, we found that he didn't have a leather on him.' Jax's eyes widen, and he blurts, 'Oh, and he was covered in all these nasty burns. It was gross.'

I clear my throat. 'Yeah, that's thanks to me.'

Andy laughs. 'That's not surprising at all.'

'Oh! We also fell into a pit of snakes,' Jax cuts in with a shudder. 'Those things were worse than the Trial itself.'

A snort escapes Andy. 'Yeah, I'm surprised every contestant in the Whispers didn't hear Jax screaming like a little girl.'

At that, Jax simply shrugs, not bothering to deny it. 'And then we found Ace. With the both of us, it wasn't too difficult to take him down and steal his leather.' Jax scratches his head, considering something. 'Especially because he was limping so badly.'

I can see the flash of Paedyn's grin even in the darkness beginning to swallow us. 'And *that* is thanks to me.'

Paedyn and I quickly fill the two of them in on what we endured this past week, though she carefully avoids the more intimate details of our time together.

'So, Sadie is dead?' Andy asks, the question sounding more like a statement.

'Yes,' I say simply. 'She is.'

We talk for a long while as we continue heading towards the edge of the forest. Inevitably, we eventually fall silent, the only sound coming from the birds above us and the crunch of leaves and twigs beneath us.

I see the opening just as the sky begins to lighten. Freedom yawns hundreds of yards away as the trees start to thin, and the edge of the Whispers draws nearer. Our pace quickens, all of us itching to be rid of this place while the sun races us, heading for the horizon as we head towards freedom.

A mass of bodies comes into view between the trees. Less than a mile past the edge of the forest, hundreds of people are gathered within the wide field, waiting patiently to watch the show.

An audience.

We are all silent as we finally step to the edge of the tree line. The sun has slowed its pace, too lazy to rise. So the Trial isn't over just yet.

276

I look towards the sea of people, all pointing in our direction. Though their powers are just out of my reach, I do feel the weight of Sights all around us, preparing to document the finale.

Movement flickers in my peripheral. We all swivel towards it, Paedyn's bow already drawn and aimed at the figure stepping out of the trees and into the open field on the other side.

Tangled, lilac hair blows across Blair's face as her lips twist into a sneer, taking us in. Her cold gaze is pinned on Paedyn as she says, 'Don't you know that alliances ruin all the fun?'

Paedyn sighs. 'I would say I'm happy to see you're still alive, but apparently I'm a horrible liar, so why try.'

My mouth twitches into a smile at her words when Braxton steps out through the trees. His eyes flick between us, looking determined and desperate to get a band before the Trial ends.

So his solution is to start charging at Blair.

I tear my eyes away from him when I hear a branch crunch behind us. I turn, staring at nothing but the crisp air. And then Jax doubles over from the impact of an unexpected and unseen punch. '*Ouch*,' he wheezes.

Hera has arrived.

Andy transforms into her wolf form, sniffing the air to find Hera before suddenly charging in what can only be her direction.

I whip my head around, searching.

There's only one Elite left.

And then I see him. He's the farthest from us, standing with his arms crossed over his chest, observing the chaos that is unfolding before him with a smug smirk. Ace's eyes lock with mine. His grin grows.

Found my target.

The scene around me is a blur of blood and bodies. Paedyn and Andy are fighting off Braxton and Blair while Jax and Hera disappear and dance around each other, landing solid blows before vanishing.

That leaves Ace entirely to me.

I barely bat an eye at the violence surrounding me as I take on Hera's power and disappear into the chaos. I only shed the Veil ability when I'm right before him so he can see my face when I send a fist into his nose with a sickening crunch. He staggers back, clutching the broken bone as his eyes fly to mine.

And then I suddenly see nothing at all. A thick, stone wall encases me, and yet, something pierces my side. The sharp pain only sharpens my senses, reminding me that this is only an illusion, though the pain in my side is anything but. I step through the wall, and it vanishes in a wisp of smoke, revealing Ace clutching a spear in his bloody hand.

The same spear that nearly killed Paedyn.

I Blink behind him, having taken on Jax's ability, and drive my knee into his back. Then I'm Blinking around him, hitting him hard without hesitation. I'm playing with him. I could easily finish this fight quickly, but I won't deny that I'm a monster who wants to have a little fun with him first.

After I send a blow to his jaw, he suddenly multiplies before my very eyes. Dozens of Aces surround me, all moving and mixing up with one another, leaving me to guess where the real one ran off to.

I filter through the powers at my disposal, the ones dancing beneath my skin from those surrounding me. Blair's Tele power surges in my veins, begging to be used.

That could be fun.

Now I just need to find the real—

Pain laces up my leg when the tip of his spear dives into it. I grit my teeth and turn towards him. 'There you are.' I smile as I lift him off the ground with nothing more than my mind.

He gasps, choking as I crush his windpipe, his feet dangling a good two feet off the ground. His mouth is moving, making odd noises as he tries to get air into his screaming lungs.

I'm still smiling. 'What was that? I can't quite hear you.' His duplicates vanish into smoke beside me, and the cries of fighting around us fade as I focus on him. Focus on his life that I hold in my hands, my mind.

But the cry of pain I hear next doesn't belong to him.

I know that voice. I've heard that sound and silently hoped I never would again. My head whips to the crumpled body lying so close to me, silver hair sticking to her fevered face and the tears rolling over her faint freckles. Blood gushes from a jagged tear beneath her ribs, and a strangled sob escapes her.

'Kai . . . help me.' Paedyn's whisper is so quiet, a single breath away from death. Blood covers her hands, her hair, her body – staining her a revolting red. 'Kai, it hurts!' She screams the words in agony, her body racking with sobs and spasms of pain.

I hadn't realized my hold on Ace had slipped, hadn't realized I'd let him drop to the ground until he was on top of me, knocking the breath from my lungs. The tip of his spear is digging into my throat, his legs pinning down my arms. And then that smug smile is back, as though he wasn't just gasping for air a moment ago.

'And here I was, thinking you were the strong one. The prince who didn't let his emotions get in the way.' He smiles as the pointed tip of the spear pierces my skin, drawing hot blood. 'But look at you,' a condescending laugh, 'caring for her has made you *weak*.'

He's about to drag the blade across my throat— 'Kai!'

Jax's voice startles the both of us, and I turn my head to the side just in time to see him toss a single arrow towards me. It's all I need. I catch it by the shaft, and in one swift motion, plunge it deep into the closest, open spot of Ace's flesh while pushing the spear's rod away from me.

He screams when the arrow sinks into the soft flesh of his shoulder. His hold on me loosens, and I throw him off before staggering to my feet, the slice on my neck leaking blood. I spin to find Ace suddenly behind me, to my right, my left. I'm surrounded once again.

'Over here,' one of the Aces calls, and I spin, grabbing my forgotten throwing star from my pocket. Ace's duplicates are vanishing and reappearing as I aimlessly search for the real one. 'Behind you,' he mocks, and I whip around, anger boiling my blood. 'You know what I'm going to do after I kill you?' one of them asks as another whispers loudly, 'I'm going to do the same to Paedyn.' Then another Ace chimes in, 'Such a shame, too. I'm going to miss looking at her.'

I'm going to kill him. Now. No more games. No more toying. I'm ending this.

Suddenly, the multiple Aces vanish, leaving only one remaining.

And I don't hesitate before raising my throwing star to send it sailing through the air at his heart.

I see his eyes widen when the blade sinks into the center of his chest, embedding deep into his flesh. He stumbles back, gasping as he stares down at the fatal wound. A twisted smile finds its way to my lips.

I'm going to enjoy watching him die.

I take my time walking over, watching as he drops to his knees. I'm standing over him now, staring down into his shiny eyes, glistening with tears.

My smile falters.

Those aren't his eyes.

No, the eyes looking up at me are warm and large, the deep brown of melted chocolate. Sweet, like the boy those eyes belong to.

I drop to my knees.

For the first time in years, I feel true, terrible terror.

The illusion blows away in the soft breeze, sending tendrils of smoke into the morning sky.

Leaving behind a bloody boy. My bloody brother.

Jax.

CHAPTER 32

Kai

'No!' The word tears from my throat as disbelief and disgust claw at me, threatening to rip me to shreds.

Jax doesn't make a sound, his eyes wide and locked with mine. Silent tears slip down his cheeks, clinging to the thick lashes that surround those big, brown eyes. He looks at me, horrified as he begins to tip backwards on his knees, unable to stop himself from falling in his final moments.

Not him. It wasn't supposed to be him. Never him.

I grip his shoulder and the back of his head, carefully lowering him to the ground through my blurry vision. I swipe at my eyes, trying to compose myself as I inspect the wound. The throwing star is embedded deep into his chest, blood oozing out from around it. Dark, heavy blood that isn't stopping, isn't slowing. The type of blood that accompanies a goodbye.

I did this to him. He's going to die because of me. Because I'm a monster.

I physically shake my head, trying to clear it of the horrific thought and instead focus on the horrific scene before me. 'Hey, look at me Jax, okay, buddy?' My voice is soft, shaky, but his eyes find mine, nonetheless. I can see the wound already leaching the life from him, his eyes unfocused, his breathing shallow.

'You're going to be fine, alright?'

His eyes flutter closed, and I pat his cheek, forcing him to look at me, to stay with me.

'Do you hear me? You're going to be okay.'

My eyes well with tears, the feeling foreign as I blink furiously. 'I'm going to fix this.'

My voice breaks just like I am about to.

My little brother.

The sound of the Elites fighting around us suddenly comes into focus again, and I can hear the clink of weapons and the cries of pain. Everything floods back. I remember why I'm here, what is going on around me, and who *really* did this to Jax.

A cold, chilling laugh echoes close by. *His* laugh. I whip my head around, scanning the field for any sign of the bastard that I will make bleed and brutally die for this. But he's nowhere to be found. I hear his laugh again, coming from only a few paces away.

Nothing. No one is there. And then it hits me.

He cast an illusion on himself.

The bastard molded himself to our surroundings, wrapping his body in an illusion that makes me see nothing at all while letting Jax play his role. If it weren't for my dying brother beneath me, I would scour every inch of this field until I found Ace. And then I'd rip him to shreds. Slowly. Jax grunts weakly, his eyes drifting shut. My gaze darts to his wound.

If he doesn't get to a Healer, he *will* die. And it will be all my fault. My heart hammers against my chest, my head spinning. There are no Healers among us for me to draw power from.

Jax's head rolls to the side with a soft moan.

My little brother. My little brother. My little brother.

I look up at the sky and find the sun peeking back at me. It has almost fully risen above the horizon, and when it does, we'll be free of this Trial. My eyes land on the crowd of people less than a mile from the chaos all around me.

There will be a Healer in that crowd.

I wipe away tears that I don't remember shedding and pull Jax into my arms. And within the next heartbeat, I'm standing up and running towards the throng of people. Jax is barely breathing now. He might be unconscious, I'm not sure, but I sprint as fast as I can towards his salvation.

I push Braxton's Brawny ability into my muscles, making Jax significantly lighter in my arms and allowing me to run faster. I don't need to make it all the way to the crowd, only close enough so I can latch onto a Healer's power and use it to save him.

'Jax!' I shout at him. He barely stirs. 'Jax, just hold on a little longer!' I'm panting, petrified that I'm too late. But the crowd of people is getting closer, and I can see them pointing and shouting as they watch me sprinting straight for them.

And then I begin to feel it – a tingle spreading through me, my bones, my very veins. It grows into a buzz before it becomes a roar and a rush of power. There are so many abilities at my disposal provided by the crowd still dozens of yards away from me. I feel overwhelmed as I search for the Healer's ability within the wave of power crashing into me.

There it is.

I focus on it, hone it, and shut out all other abilities fighting to come to the surface. Lying Jax on the ground, I drop to my knees at his side. I ignore the fact that I don't see his chest rising and grip the part of the throwing star still peeking out of his chest, needing to pull it out before I can heal him.

'If you can hear me, Jax, this is going to hurt like hell. Sorry.' And then I yank. It rips from his skin with a sickening sound. He doesn't so much as stir.

I ignore the dread pooling in my gut and place my hands over the now exposed, opened wound. I let the Healer's power seep into his body, the gash, and begin mending and molding the skin back together. I recall learning to mend each wound my father inflicted on me as a boy and push that power into the boy beneath me.

The blood stops. The skin knits back together. Leaving nothing but a large, pink scar decorating the center of his chest.

But he isn't moving. 'Jax?'

I pat his cheek lightly. Nothing. Then shake him vigorously. Nothing. Now I'm shouting shakily. 'Jax!' My voice cracks as he lies there, lifeless. My fingers frantically search for a pulse. 'No, no, no, no, no . . .'

Little brother. Little brother. My little—

His eyes fly open, and then he's gulping down air.

I half-laugh, half-sob as I watch him blink, his hand flying to feel the smooth skin where my throwing star once was. He looks around, his brown eyes landing on me. His grin is weak, his voice hoarse but humming with humor. 'Are you going to try to kill me again?'

I croak out a laugh and run a hand over my face, wiping away the tears on it. 'I'm not planning on it, bud.' And then I'm pulling him against my chest and crushing him into a hug, my hand ruffling his hair.

The sound of beating drums startles us both, and we turn towards the crowd not too far from us. They are cheering, applauding, stomping their feet in celebration.

The sun has risen just above the horizon. The first Trial is complete.

CHAPTER 33

Paedyn

Thousands of eyes pin me to the uncomfortable seat I've been forced into. The Bowl is packed to the brim with buzzing Ilyans, all bubbling over with excitement. The last of the audience has filed into their seats high up in the benches of the stadium encircling us, now staring down into the Pit beneath them expectantly.

It's been three days.

Three days since the final fight at the edge of the Whispers.

And there are only seven of us left.

I hear the stomping of impatient feet coming from the crowd around us, and my heart trips at the sound. Suddenly, I'm back in that clearing, the sound of thundering feet morphing into the pounding of drums, signaling the end of the Trial.

But no one stopped.

The drums meant nothing to us. We were all still at each other's throats. If it weren't for Andy's help, Blair would have torn me limb from limb and scattered whatever remained of me across the field for the birds to feast on. But just because she didn't kill me doesn't mean she didn't leave her mark on me. Several, actually. Marks and mangled flesh that the Healers had a hell of a time mending back together.

It was as if none of us saw the risen sun or heard the drums sound.

We were ravenous, refusing to simply lay down our weapons and surrender to each other. The Flashes made it to us first, weaving around and between us. Then the Brawnies arrived, using force to pull us away from one another. I was rudely ripped off Blair after finally managing to pin her down and was thrown over the shoulder of a burly man before being carried through the gawking crowd. But I wasn't the only one. The opponents around me were all being hauled away and shoved into separate coaches to *cool down*.

It wasn't hard to figure out why the king wanted to break up the fight and cut us off before we could do any more damage. Since it is forbidden to fight another contestant outside of a Trial, keeping our anger stifled will only ensure that the rest of the Trials will be even more interesting. Even more bloody.

I'm suddenly sucked back to reality, remembering the stiff chair I'm sitting in, the stiff dress clinging to my body, and the equally stiff contestants beside me. I shift in my seat, my arm brushing against the hard one that belongs to the prince I haven't spoken to in days.

I run a hand under my rib where I can almost feel the jagged scar given to me by the same boy who was almost the cause of Jax's death. I sneak a glance at Kai beside me, cool and collected as ever, despite what happened. Or so he seems. I've gotten quite good at pinpointing the cracks in his masks, picking apart his facade.

I suddenly realize that Tealah is speaking to the crowd, gesturing at us with excited movements. I don't care enough to listen to what she is saying, but the crowd is eating it up. They love this, these Trials. It makes me sick.

'—now for what you have all been waiting for!' I finally decide to pay attention to Tealah's words as she amplifies them across the arena. 'As you all know, this year's Purging Trials will be . . . unique.' She gestures to Kai, clearly indicating that he is the reason for this. Another test for their future Enforcer.

She continues with a flash of her blindingly white teeth. 'And because of that, the first Trial was outside of the Bowl with no audience to witness it.' The crowd murmurs at that, clearly unhappy that they couldn't witness the violence. 'But do not fret, citizens of Ilya!' Tealah exclaims enthusiastically. 'You will still get to watch the highlights, but without all of the boring bits.' She laughs and the crowd joins her, rumbling the stadium.

'So, here is the first Trial in the sixth ever Purging Trials!' The audience roars with excitement before falling silent as we all shift in our seats to get a view of the enormous screen at the far end of the oval arena. Recordings flicker to life, snippets of each of us provided by the line of Sights standing below it.

I watch myself, and every other opponent, wake up in the forest, confusion and concern written on each of our faces as we read the note left for us. I witness Blair's fight with Andy before the scene cuts to Hera, sinking in quicksand she stumbled into deep in the forest. She's screaming, eyes pleading with us – no, with the Sight standing idly by.

She vanishes from the screen, and I'm suddenly staring at Kai. But he's not alone. He's brawling with Braxton by a fire, trading punches in the dim light before burning each other with the flames.

The crowd cheers and quiets, claps and stomps while watching the Trial as though they were there. I'm silent, still, stiff-backed like my opponents beside me. We are watching ourselves fight to survive.

Suddenly, my own face flashes before my eyes. And then I'm watching the horrors of those illusions all over again. Kitt's dead body floating lifelessly in the pool. The starved little girls begging for help – *myself* begging for help. I see the terror on my face, see myself crumple to the ground.

The body sitting beside me shifts, and my eyes drift slowly towards him. My gaze crashes into Kai's, ignoring his clenched jaw and taut brows. It's his cold eyes I focus on. I've never seen a stare so icy, yet so full of fire. The look in his eyes is chilling, and I shiver. It's like icicles, his gaze. Pretty but sharp. Cool but deadly. Captivating but cutting.

He doesn't break my gaze, and I swallow. Then he's saying something, though his mouth doesn't open. My head whips to the screen, and I'm watching myself strain to hold my bow up with the pain of my wound. I watch Kai rush over to me as I crumple to the ground. Watch something like *worry* cross his face as he tries to keep me awake. Tries to keep me *alive*.

I glance at him again, but he's focused on the screen, not bothering to return my gaze. I hadn't realized he could look at me like that. Look at me like he *cared*. It frustrates and flusters me all at once, but I can't seem to tear my eyes away from the scene playing out before me, playing out before the entire crowd.

I hadn't realized just how often the Sights were watching us, and my face feels hot as most of my conversation with Kai while he stitched me up is blasted for all to hear. And the crowd is loving it. I swear I hear a collective sigh each time Kai touches me or says my name, accompanied by murmurs of jealousy for that very reason.

I watch Jax Blink from tree to tree, and then Andy and him together, screaming as dozens of snakes surround them. I watch Hera stumble across Blair before a sloppy fight ensues, one where the latter is mostly yelling in frustration because she can't find her invisible opponent.

Kai and I are back again, and this time, I'm nursing his wounds. The crowd buzzes as they lean in to hear our teasing. I throw a glance at Kai beside me who doesn't bother to look my way, though the corner of his lips twitch, telling me he finds this *amusing*.

Flashes of each opponent over the days flit across the screen, fighting one another while fighting against the dangers that inhabit the Whispers. Kai and I are back too soon, and—

Oh, Plagues, no.

Thankfully, the Sight only caught the very end of our dance before Sadie interrupted, but it's enough to get the crowd hollering with delight. I can't say I blame them. Too much bloodshed can get boring, and this is quite the unexpected twist. Their future Enforcer is giving them quite the show.

I stare down Kai who is, to my annoyance, smirking now. My voice is hushed and highly agitated as I say, 'Why didn't you tell me there were Sights around?'

His eyes finally flick to mine, causing my heart to hammer against my ribcage.

Stupid, stupid organ.

He leans in so close that his lips brush the shell of my ear. 'I was a little distracted.'

I will my pounding pulse to slow and force my eyes away from his, turning my attention back to the screen where I watch myself fight Sadie.

And then I watch her die all over again.

It seems that a Sight failed to catch Kai burying her, though part of me wonders if that was intentional. The king would have likely found a decency such as that to be a weakness, a flaw in the Enforcer he's created. So, the kingdom will never see that shred of kindness Kai showed. It seems that secret solely belongs to the two of us.

There's movement flickering across the crowd as the audience around us presses their pointer and middle fingers together, the symbol hovering over their hearts. A diamond. Ilya's image of strength, power, and honor.

They are paying their respects to the fallen.

The contestants beside me do the same, and the crowd is silent, utterly still until the final fight at the edge of the Whispers lights up the screen.

Blood. So much blood. The scene is utter chaos, and I have no idea where to look or who to focus on. The angle switches back and forth between different Sights documenting the fight, focusing on different Elites. I watch each of us battle against one another, out for blood and those bloody bands.

Then I finally get to see how Hera died.

I knew she didn't make it out of the Trial alive, I just didn't know why. The Sight focuses on Braxton, blood leaking from a stab wound as an invisible knife pierces his skin repeatedly while he roars in anger and anguish.

Hera stabs him in the side, and he screams, reaching blindly to grab the invisible knife. His fingers wrap around the hilt, and he pulls it out, flipping it around before stabbing wildly in front of him.

I hear the sickening sound of steel sinking into skin and bone before Hera is flickering into view in front of him, the blade buried in her small chest. She blinks up at him with tears slipping down her face before buckling to the ground.

Triangles are being pressed against hearts for the dead girl as the rest of the final fight flits across the screen. I barely watch Kai running towards the crowd with Jax dying in his arms before the scene cuts to one last shot of the Elites, covered in blood and bloodthirsty. And then the screen goes dark, and the crowd is only silent for a breath before erupting into applause.

I barely hear Tealah as she begins speaking to the cheering audience, thanking them for joining us in watching the first Trial. 'Oh, and don't forget!' she practically squeals. 'Your vote is more important than you know. Honor to your kingdom, honor to your family, and honor to yourself.'

The crowd recites the motto with her, and then they are free to leave. I watch hundreds of people shuffle between the rows of benches and through the wide tunnels leading out of the Bowl. They toss their votes into giant glass bowls beside the exits as they pass, not realizing the power they hold with the name they scribble down.

I hate the lack of control I have or the fear constantly following me. I hate feeling so helpless. So powerless. So Ordinary. I am competing in games meant to flaunt the powers and strength of the Elites – the powers I don't possess.

Yet here I am. Alive.

And I intend to keep it that way.

Someone is following me.

I was heading back to my room after dinner when I suddenly felt someone close behind. I whirl, my hand flying to the hilt of my dagger on instinct. My eyes meet wide, startled green ones before I quickly avert my gaze. 'Easy, Paedyn!' Kitt laughs, raising both hands in surrender. 'You're jumpy today.'

I turn on my heel and begin walking down the hallway again. 'Well, don't sneak up on me and you don't have to worry about getting stabbed.'

'I have a feeling you'll stab someone for less than just sneaking up on you.' I can hear the amusement in his voice, coating his words.

The hint of a smile has me ducking my head to hide it when he falls into step beside me. We are heading down the hallway towards my room when a firm hand grips my wrist, and I'm pulled into one of the many hallways branching off to my left.

I open my mouth to object, but even with his back turned, Kitt senses it. 'Don't stab me yet. I want to show you something.' He tosses a grin over his shoulder as he leads me through the maze of hallways.

I've finally learned my way around the main corridors, but when it comes to the dozens of small hallways scattered throughout the castle, I'm completely lost. Kitt easily navigates them, winding in and out of different corridors, passing other sections and rooms of the enormous castle I've never even seen. I'm sure he could find his way through the palace blind, a skill that only comes with growing up in this maze he calls home.

Golden sunlight warms my face when Kitt pushes open a large wooden door at the end of a hallway, nodding to the Imperials guarding it before we step out into the balmy evening. My breath hitches. I'm surrounded by color, by *life*. A wide stony path lies before us where several others branch off, all surrounded by hundreds of flowers.

The gardens.

It's beautiful, breathtaking. Living in the slums, surrounded by dreary alleys and dull colors, I'd nearly forgotten how bright the world can be. Every place the cobblestone isn't touching is teeming with flowers and plants of every kind and color. Pops of fuchsia and royal blue stand out among the pale yellows and lavender. Statues litter the garden, dark vines clinging to several of them.

It's the neatest kind of chaos I've ever seen, with rows of flowers crowding around the paths, creating a railing of blossoms and foliage. Each of the stone walkways loops in a large circle, creating several rings around the massive fountain at the heart of the garden.

I've never seen anything so bright, so vibrant, and I have to blink rapidly, nearly blinded by the colors bombarding me. Between my blinks, I can see Kitt watching me curiously, intently.

He clears his throat and takes a step onto the path, guiding me beside him. 'I promised I'd show you the gardens one day.'

My eyes sweep across the flowers as we slowly walk along a path. Kitt is content to fill the silence by telling me of Kai and his adventures in this very garden, pointing to the statues they've toppled over or the fountain they couldn't resist taking a dip in. I snort at his stories despite my best efforts and clamp a hand over my mouth to stifle the sound.

I stop abruptly, throwing caution to the wind when my curiosity gets the better of me. 'Why? Why do this?'

'Why do what, exactly?' He's trying not to laugh at me while I'm trying not to hit him for that exact reason.

'Take me out here. Tell me personal things and . . .' I stumble over my words in frustration.

I dare a glance into those green eyes that match the foliage around us when he slowly says, 'With the . . . future that I have, it's hard to meet people. *Really* meet people. Get to know them. Most of the people in there,' he points towards the stone wall of the castle, 'they want something. And they'll say whatever they think I want to hear to get it. But you . . .'

My dry laugh cuts him off. 'But I tend to say things I likely shouldn't.'

'And I tend to enjoy hearing those things,' he says softly.

My eyes wander over the flowers rather than meeting his gaze. 'Then I will keep that in mind the next time I wish to tell you off.'

I bite my tongue as soon as the words tumble out of my mouth. I may say whatever I please to Kai, but this is the future king. If I wish to keep my head, I'll have to learn to hold my tongue.

But the boy beside me only laughs, seeming less kingly by the second. 'Good,' he chuckles, 'because I have something to ask, and I expect nothing but brutal honesty from you.'

I swallow.

There is nothing honest about me.

'The Trial . . .' he says slowly. 'Your thoughts?'

I choke on my scoff. That was certainly not the question I was expecting. 'My thoughts? You mean, other than the obvious?'

He stops walking to take a step closer to me, dwindling the little distance between us. 'And what would the obvious be?'

My eyes are pinned to the top button of his shirt, so I don't have to look into his father's eyes. 'That these Trials are a twisted way to celebrate a tragedy.'

And there I go again, biting my tongue too late. But there's something about this prince that makes me reckless, makes me want to tell him exactly what is wrong with everything he thinks he believes.

'Tragedy,' he echoes, his voice even. 'You mean the Purging.'

'Yes, the Purging,' I breathe. 'The banishment of thousands of people and the continuous killing of them that follows.' I'm practically spewing treason, but I can't seem to stop now that I've started. 'Those are *your* people, Kitt. Innocent people who are still being killed today because of something they have no control over.'

He stares at me while I stare at his collar, avoiding his gaze. 'The Purging needed to be done, Paedyn. You know that.'

His voice is gentle while mine is anything but. 'Why? Because the Ordinaries are *diseased*? Supposedly weakening the Elites' powers? Even though they lived alongside the Elites for decades?'

He blinks. 'You think they're not diseased?'

I am playing a very dangerous game.

I clamp my mouth shut, knowing I've said too much. To answer that question truthfully is a risk even I'm not willing to take, so I take a breath before hurrying to change the topic. 'I just think that as the future king, there are a lot of things you need to think about.'

I don't look at him, but I can feel his eyes on me. 'And you're going to enlighten me about those things? Enlighten me about my own kingdom?'

Play the part. Play the part. Play the—

I bark out a bitter laugh. 'Don't be an ass and don't pretend you know your kingdom! Have you seen the slums? Seen the segregation, the starving citizens? *Your* starving citizens.'

So much for playing the part.

I throw my hands up, shaking my head at the flowerbeds. 'Would you even listen to me if I tried to enlighten you, tried to tell you to make a change?' He stands there, silent and still. So I ask again, voice urgent. 'Well? Will you listen to me?'

His hands are suddenly cupping my face and guiding it towards him as I fight the urge to flinch. 'If I listen to you, will you *look* at me?'

My breath catches in my throat. 'Look at me, Paedyn. Please.'

And it's the softness, the pleading in his voice that has me taking a breath and shutting my eyes for a moment. When I finally open them again, I see so much compassion and concern filling his green gaze. And for the first time, I allow myself to study those eyes. Because they have never looked less like the king's. The warmth in them washes over me, overwhelms me.

'All this time,' he says quietly, 'I've been searching for a gaze you wouldn't give me, waiting for you to want to look me in the eyes.' He pauses to take a breath. 'Why do you avoid my gaze, avoid *me*?'

So, clearly, I've done a terrible job at playing the part.

'You . . .' I swallow. 'You reminded me of someone from my . . . past. But the more I get to know you, the more different the two of you seem.' I study him for a moment, surprised by my honesty. The king and his heir may look similar, but in this moment, they've never seemed less alike.

He smiles softly at me. 'Does that mean you'll start looking me in the eyes?'

'Only if you start listening to me,' I reply with a small smile of my own.

'Deal,' he says simply before we slowly begin to head down the path once again. 'I have another question for you.'

I almost laugh. 'And I likely have an answer for you.'

He smiles before his face is suddenly serious, and he tucks his hands behind his back as we walk. 'In the Trial, Ace made you . . . see me. And at the sight of me dead, you seemed . . .' He shakes his head, searching for the right word. I'm reminded of how he watched that scene play out on the screen in the Bowl, saw the look on my face upon seeing him, heard the scream that tore from my throat.

'Upset?' I say weakly. 'Terrified, even?' For once, I look at him until he meets my gaze. 'When I saw you dead, I guess I suddenly saw all the potential you have die with you. All the potential to be a better king for Ilya, to make changes, to rule how you *should* and not how you are *told*.'

We've finally made it to the center of the garden where we stop beside the fountain. Now that I'm finally willing to look at him, Kitt's eyes don't seem to want to leave mine. 'Thank you,' he says with a smile. 'I know I can always count on that brutal honesty of

294

yours. You're the first *real* person I've had the pleasure of knowing in a while.' I almost laugh at that.

If only he knew. I'm a liar and a deceiver who used him as my partner so I could get the people's attention. I stand before him as an Ordinary, one he would have killed if only he knew the truth, and I would die by the hand of his future Enforcer I'm too stubborn to admit my attraction to. And in the end, it wouldn't matter how *real* he thought I was.

But I offer him what I hope is a sweet smile before turning to face the beautiful fountain that is so large, I now understand why the princes couldn't fight the urge to swim in it. I lean over the edge, peering into the crystal water reflecting my face back up at me.

Shillings.

There had to be hundreds of them, just casually lying at the bottom of the pool. I recall how I felt on my first night here after seeing all the wasted food. I feel sick. So much money lying idly. And for what? So the rich could make their petty wishes?

I gulp down my disgust.

Play the part.

'Alright, what is it?' Kitt asks with more than a hint of humor.

'Hmm? Nothing.' I pause and peer up at him. 'What do you mean?'

He laughs deeply. 'You are fighting the urge to tell me off, aren't you?'

I blink at him before sputtering, 'How do you—?'

'You do this thing where you scrunch up your nose before you start arguing. It's a dead giveaway.'

I open my mouth, and for once, no words seem willing to fall out. He smiles as he watches me struggle before I finally clear my throat and say, 'Fine. The reason for me scrunching my nose,' I throw him an annoyed glance I likely shouldn't have, 'is because of all the shillings.'

When I don't say anything more, Kitt urges, 'Go on.'

'Well, money like this could feed dozens of Ilyans in the slums for weeks, months even,' I say evenly. 'And yet, here it sits, wasting away for people's *wishes*.'

Kitt's eyes flick to the fountain, and he frowns. 'You're right. I'll see about having it removed and distributed.'

My heart leaps against my chest. 'Really?'

His frown flips into a wide grin. 'We made a deal, remember? You keep looking at me, and I'll keep listening to you.'

I almost snort before turning back to the fountain. I remind myself that this small victory with the shillings could mean nothing. In fact, removing and distributing them in the slums may never happen. But he's listening, and that is progress. It's potential.

I bring my face close to the surface, trying to see through the ripples to the shillings beneath.

'How much money do you think is down th—'

My words are cut off by the cold water that rises from the pool to meet my face, splashing me lightly. I straighten and whirl to find Kitt laughing, his hand slightly raised at his side.

That damn Dual ability of his.

'You were right,' I say with a deceptively sweet smile. 'I will stab someone for less than just sneaking up on me. Perhaps for even splashing me in the face.'

He raises his hands innocently and chuckles, a wide grin lighting up his tanned face. 'Hey, you're the one who called me an ass earlier.'

My mouth falls open at the realization that I had, in fact, said just that to the future king of Ilya. The look on my face has him laughing even harder, and I don't think before dipping my hand in the water and thoroughly splashing him.

That was a mistake. I should know better than to start a water fight with a Duel who could drown me if he liked. After Kitt has finished thoroughly splashing me, water is dripping from my hair and clinging to my lashes. And then I'm laughing at the sight of us, sopping wet in the middle of the castle garden.

I'm still wiping sticky strands of hair off my face when I say, 'This was not a very fair fight.'

CHAPTER 34

Paedyn

The familiar stench of Loot fills my nose, and I suppress the urge to gag.

Home sweet home.

The long, wide street is cast in shadows, cleared of merchant carts and beggars for the night. I pass clumps of homeless huddling together in the adjacent alleys jutting off Loot, gambling or using their powers to entertain themselves.

It's nearly a quarter past midnight already, and with a huff, I pick up my pace. Because tonight I have somewhere to be, and questions to be answered.

Tonight I'm finding the Resistance.

It wasn't hard to slip out of the palace, especially since Lenny doesn't guard my door at night. The Imperials that litter the palace weren't a problem either, seeing that I'm used to sneaking around unseen. I crept out through the garden and followed the road by the Bowl all the way back to Loot since I haven't the slightest idea how to ride a horse and figured tonight wasn't the best time to figure it out.

I pass by the alley where I first met Kai, and smile at the fond memory of robbing him blind.

Good times.

I push thoughts of him away, not allowing myself to get distracted as I turn down a familiar street. My street. The one where the small, white shack of a house resides. I swallow the lump in my throat at the sight of it. I haven't been back here since I fled from it five years ago. When it was covered in my father's blood, and I was smothered by grief.

But this is where that boy's note led me, the one I now know is a part of the Resistance. I'm suddenly standing at the door, breathing hard as I stare at the familiar cracks and dents in the wood.

Here goes nothing.

I take a deep breath and pull at the door. Locked.

But bolted doors are child's play to a thief. I pull out my father's dagger and pick the lock with ease, seeing that he taught me that skill with this exact door and this exact blade so many years ago.

The door swings open, creaking on its rusty hinges as I step through it. I clutch my dagger tightly while I cautiously peer around my old home. It looks completely ordinary, completely the same. The old furniture resides in the exact same spot I left it in, the cracks in the walls still climbing up to the ceiling. Cobwebs cling to almost every surface in the house, looking as if someone hasn't been here in years.

Maybe I was wrong.

'Well, well, well. Look who the Plague dragged in.'

I have my knife raised, aimed, and ready to throw at the figure standing in the shadows behind me.

In the darkness, I see the shadowy outline of hands raised in surrender. My eyes adjust to the dim light, catching a flash of red, tousled hair falling over a freckled forehead.

'Lenny?' I whisper, my mouth falling open. He takes a slow step forward and his familiar brown eyes and grin come into focus.

'The one and only.' His voice sounds as light and kind as it always is in the palace. But that doesn't mean I drop the blade still raised in my hand. I'm confused, disoriented, and in need of answers *now*.

'What is going on?' I demand, staring at him suspiciously. 'Why are you here?'

Is he a part of the Resistance? He must be, but—

'Yeah,' he rubs the back of his neck sheepishly, 'we have a lot to fill you in on.'

I blink. 'We?'

'Yes.' He points a finger to the creaky floorboards beneath our feet. 'We.'

I just stare at him, waiting for an explanation on what the hell is going on, why the hell he is here, and who the hell he is with.

His gaze flicks between my face and the knife still ready to fly into his heart. 'And once you put the knife down, I'll show you what I'm talking about.' He speaks slowly as if trying to calm a crazed animal, and I'm sure I look like just that.

I lower the knife slowly and nod, once. He puffs out a relieved breath, his shoulders losing some of their tension. 'Plagues, you really are terrifying sometimes, you know that? I mean, sure, I'm the Imperial here but, man, you could probably whoop my ass—'

'Oh, and I just might if you don't tell me what is going on,' I say, teeth clenched.

'So demanding,' Lenny sighs, gesturing for me to follow him. 'On second thought, you might be better suited as a royal than an Imperial, aye Princess?'

He tosses a smile over his shoulder as he turns towards the study. My father's study. The room where he was murdered. I feel like my lungs are being crushed, my heart being squeezed, as we step into the room.

Ordinary. Completely ordinary, just like me. There's no blood soaking the floor or the chair—

The chair he was murdered in.

It's gone. A pang of sadness hits me as my eyes sweep the room, trying to find the chair he loved to read in so much. I'd sit at his feet or on his lap as he told me stories about better worlds, ones with magic and heroes and girls who didn't have to hide who they truly were.

Lenny walks up to the leaning bookcase in the corner of the room, littered with books covered in dust and cobwebs. I'm about to ask what exactly he's doing when he suddenly grips the edge of the bookcase and pulls. I watch, awestruck, as the wooden shelf slides easily to the left on some sort of track beneath it. And behind lie descending stone steps.

I have never seen that before.

Lenny flashes me another grin, gesturing towards the darkness that lies behind the bookcase. 'Ladies first.'

What I should have done was laugh in his face before making him go down the staircase first, but I've thrown caution to the wind and hastily replaced it with curiosity. The sound of my footsteps against the stone echoes as I brace a hand on the grimy wall and continue down into the darkness. When I'm standing on smooth, solid stone at the bottom of the steps, I stop.

Lenny runs right into me, nearly running me over. 'Ow, *shit* – I mean, sorry – uh, I didn't see you stop.'

'Yeah, well, that's because we can't see *anything*,' I snap, assuming I'm glaring at his face in the darkness.

'Now that, I can help with.' A female voice coming from the darkness makes me jump, and I collide with Lenny all over again. I hear the flip of a switch and the hum of dim lights turning on. Then I'm blinking, trying to understand what I'm seeing.

I'm standing in a large, damp room, filled with tables overflowing with charts, maps, and supplies. Notes and papers are plastered to the walls, making for an odd sort of wallpaper. On the other side of the room, there are mismatched chairs scattered in a circle with papers thrown on top of them, and messy cots are lining the far wall.

And, arguably the most important detail, there are people standing in this room. One of which I immediately recognize as the boy I stole from, the same one from the ball. The male to his right is older, around the age my father would be, with straw-colored hair and pale blue eyes that watch me closely. The girl beside him looks only a few years older than I am, a mere copy of the man beside her.

His daughter.

Then my eyes land on the smiling girl next to the light switch. Her olive skin seems to glow against the rich black of her waist-length hair, and her deep brown eyes watch me curiously.

'Sorry to keep you in the dark,' she sighs, 'literally.' The girl crosses her arms over her orange tunic, taking me in. 'Lenny's bat ears heard the door open, so we plunged ourselves into darkness, just in case.'

Lenny gives her a sarcastic grin before he casually answers my unspoken question. 'I'm a Hyper. I have enhanced senses, which *some people* like to make fun of. Even though it's saved their life a few times.'

I give him a confused look. 'You're a Mundane? But Imperials—'

'Are normally Offensive or Defensive Elites,' he cuts in with a sigh. 'Trust me, I know. It took forever to climb up the ranks to get to the position I have.'

Well, that only slightly cleared up one of the dozens of questions whirling around my brain. 'Okay, can someone please tell me what the *hell* is going on?'

Lenny shakes his head beside me, murmuring, 'So demanding . . .'

'I wondered when you would find your way here.' It's the boy from the ball who cuts in before I can kick Lenny's ass like I promised. 'I mean, after you stole half my silvers and the note in my pocket, I figured you would show up eventually.' He's amused. 'Took you long enough.'

I open my mouth only to find that I'm speechless.

Plagues, what is going on?

The blond man clears his throat before saying, 'Finn, would you grab Paedyn a chair, please? We have a lot to catch her up on.'

Finn nods and does just that, adding another chair to the circle of seats awaiting us. The four strangers walk over and plop down without another word.

There's a hand on my shoulder one moment, and the next, I've twisted it at an odd angle out of pure instinct. '*Shit*, Paedyn! Easy!' Lenny gasps. I blink, look at what I've done, and drop his hand.

'Sorry,' I mutter. 'I'm a bit on edge.'

He's rubbing his sore arm, looking at me cautiously. 'So, note to self, the princess doesn't like to be touched—'

'Don't call me princess, Lenny.'

'Okay, so, the princess also doesn't like to be called princess.' I fix him with a glare, but he rushes on. 'Alright, look. You are going to hear a lot of information tonight. Information that will shock you. So just . . .' His eyes search mine. 'Listen, okay?'

'Of course. I'm a great listener.'

He snorts. 'We'll see about that.'

'Why are you here?' I ask abruptly, my voice calmer than I currently feel.

301

'Patience, Princess. I'll tell you that soon.' He slowly puts a light hand on my shoulder, eying me to make sure I don't snap his wrist. When he deems himself safe, he gently guides us to the circle of chairs and sits beside me.

The blond man is seated across from me, sighing as he looks me over. 'You must have taken after your mother because you don't look much like your father.' My heart stops, my eyes widening at his words. 'But you have his spirit, his will. That much is evident in how you showed up tonight.' I open my mouth to let the questions loose, but he cuts me off. 'And I see you still have your father's dagger. Good.' He nods to the knife still clenched in my fist, the handle now slick with sweat.

'My dear, you have . . .' His eyes bore into mine so intensely that I fight the urge to look away. 'So many questions. For starters, I'm Calum. Welcome to the Resistance. Well, a small part of it. We've been patiently awaiting your arrival.'

'You've been awaiting—?' I start.

'Good listener, my ass,' Lenny mutters beside me. I cut him a look that makes Calum chuckle and Lenny squirm, eying the dagger still clenched in my fist.

'I promise I'll answer all of your questions, Paedyn. But first, let us make our introductions. This is my daughter Mira,' he gestures to the blond girl beside him who barely offers me a smile, 'and this is Leena.' He nods towards the girl with the raven hair falling elegantly down her back.

'You are smaller than I thought you would be,' Leena says with her head tipped to the side. 'Now I'm even more impressed you survived the first Trial.' Her tone isn't mocking, but rather, curious.

'I'm tougher than I look, I assure you. The strongest weapon a woman has at her disposal is that she is often underestimated,' I answer with a small smile. 'And I wield that all the time.'

Leena's face splits into a beautiful smile that lights up her features as she says to no one in particular, 'I like this one. We're keeping her right?'

'She's not a dog,' Mira mumbles with a roll of her eyes.

'And you've already met Finn,' Calum cuts in. Finn gives me a quick wink and I almost scoff. 'Now, I have a lot to explain in only a short matter of time, so I'll get right into it.' He takes a deep breath. 'Your father and I were very close.'

And yet I've never seen this man in my life.

'And I know you don't know who I am.' His words cut into my thoughts. 'And that is because your father kept me a . . . well, a secret. Just like he kept the Resistance a secret from you.'

My head is spinning and I'm suddenly thankful that I'm sitting down. 'But your father didn't just *know* about the Resistance. You see, the Resistance has been around for nearly a decade now, and Adam was one of its original leaders. That is the very reason we are still in this house, using it as a headquarters like we did when he was alive.'

'Why did he keep this all a secret from me then?' I ignore the look Lenny shoots me at my interruption.

Calum heaves a sigh. 'It wasn't just you he kept the Resistance secret from. In those beginning years, we lay low, silently spreading word of our cause through those we could trust. It was dangerous for you to be a part of the Resistance, so he wanted to wait until you were older to join.' He pauses before quietly adding, 'But he never got the chance to tell you. And when we found your father . . . you were gone.'

I manage a slight nod, swallowing the lump in my throat before I ask, 'Is that why the king killed him? Because he learned of his role in the Resistance?'

A look of confusion crosses Calum's face as he continues to stare at me. The intensity in his gaze is almost unsettling before he looks away and nods slowly. 'That is what I assume, yes.'

I swallow, hoping I would feel lighter after finally discovering the reason for my father's death after years of guilt and guessing. And yet, I don't.

'You, and most of Ilya, are only just now beginning to hear of us because we have grown,' Calum continues. 'Grown in size and strength. We have kept the Resistance quiet for many years now while we gained more members and found more Ordinaries. But the king is having difficulty containing us now. Difficulty keeping us under wraps and under control.'

'So where are the rest of you?' I quickly add, '*Who* are the rest of you?'

'We are *everywhere*,' Mira says, but her piercing gaze speaks volumes. It's clear she doesn't trust me any farther than she can throw me.

Calum calmly continues, 'During the Purging three decades ago, more Ordinaries remained in Ilya after the banishment than originally believed. They hid in secret, right under the king's nose. There are Resistance members spread all over Ilya since it is obviously both unsafe and unpractical for us to all reside in one area. Even I do not know where or who they all are. We have leaders assigned to different areas of the kingdom, allowing us to spread information to Resistance members smoothly and without suspicion. Word travels fast when the leaders converse and pass on information to the members in their section.'

'And that is why we met here tonight,' Leena says brightly. 'To discuss plans and then make our sections aware of them.'

I blink at them all. 'You are all leaders? I mean, you're so . . . young.'

'And handsome,' Finn sighs. 'But yes, we are some of the leaders that were able to make it tonight. Honestly, we are just glorified carrier pigeons who pass along information secretively so the Resistance can stay united despite not being able to gather all together.'

'I am no carrier pigeon,' Mira huffs.

'I'm not sure why we are talking about *birds*,' Lenny sighs, 'but, yes, they oversee informing Resistance members in certain sections of the kingdom. And it's no simple task. Ordinaries are still killed constantly, and if information of who is a part of the Resistance gets out, even more will die.'

'So,' I glance between them, 'are you Ordinaries?'

Finn grins. 'I sure am.'

'Same here,' Leena says proudly.

I stare at the two of them, these people who are just like me, just as Ordinary.

My eyes snap to Mira as she says, 'And I'm a Silencer.'

Calum cuts in before I can spew any more questions. 'The Ordinaries in Ilya tend to adapt the ability of the Hypers since it is a fairly easy power to pose with.' At that, Leena shoots Lenny a smug look. 'When Ordinaries find us and join the Resistance, we help them build a life, teach them how to survive.' He offers me a sad smile. 'Not everyone had a father like yours who taught them to actually *become* powerful. Your Psychic ability has been trained into you since you were a child, and it's the most convincing cover I've ever seen.'

He pauses for a moment, collecting his thoughts. 'As for *who* we are, well, obviously most of us our Ordinaries. But we also have Elites on our side.'

'The Fatals,' I breathe.

'Yes.' He seems to stiffen at the title. 'And it seems you have already encountered one.'

The Silencer I fought in the alley comes to mind as I say slowly, 'Was he . . . ?'

'Yes, he was a Resistance member.' Calum holds up a hand, silencing the apology I was about to utter for taking one of their members down. 'There is no need to apologize, Paedyn. It was Micah's own foolishness that got him caught.'

'He always was a hothead,' Lenny mutters. 'And a dumbass. A reckless dumbass. To think he could take down the prince, the future *Enforcer*, without consequences . . .'

My eyes dance between the five of them. 'Do I get to know exactly why this Micah is a reckless dumbass?'

'Because he saw the prince already weakened and his anger got the best of him,' Mira says, her expression void of sympathy. 'Long story short, Prince Kai killed someone very close to Micah, consuming the Silencer with rage and a need for revenge. When he saw the prince in that alley, worn out and preoccupied, he took the opportunity to try and take him down.' She pins me with a stare. 'But you took him down instead.'

'At the time, we didn't know who you were,' Lenny adds. 'We put the pieces together when we saw your name on the banner in Loot and saw you at the interviews.'

'I thought you were dead, Paedyn,' Calum says gravely. 'And then you suddenly showed up in the Trials, and we had found Adam's daughter. Well, you found us.'

'Who would have thought that Adam Gray's daughter, the kid of a Resistance leader, would be the one to rob me blind and find that note,' Finn says with a sigh. 'The note that led you right to us and right back to your own home.' He looks up at the ceiling and smiles to himself. 'When I saw you at the ball, saw you recognize who I was, I knew it wouldn't be long before you came and found us.'

I swallow, unable to move on from the prior topic. 'I'm sorry about the Silencer . . . about Micah.' I can't help but feel guilty, seeing that I'm the reason he was caught. 'Do you know if he is still alive?'

Calum's expression grows grim. 'We aren't sure. But if he is, it likely won't be for much longer.' He continues before I can try to apologize again. 'And there is no need to feel guilty, Paedyn. Micah was his own undoing.'

He takes a deep breath before casually carrying on the conversation. 'Now, as I was saying, the Resistance is made up of both Ordinaries and Elites, including the Silencers, Mind Readers, and Controllers. Since the king also tried to kill the Fatals off and has continued to do so, they want justice as well. Other Elites have joined the cause for their own reasons. Those who care enough to think about it don't buy in to the idea that the Ordinaries were suddenly banished because of a disease.'

'So, the Resistance members don't believe the Ordinaries are weakening the Elites,' I say, watching as Calum nods. 'Does anyone have proof to use against the king and his Healers?'

Calum's eyes search mine before he sighs. 'No, we don't have proof.'

Lenny adds, 'We are just the Ilyans who care enough to realize that it doesn't add up. Ordinaries lived with the Elites for decades before the Purging, and even now, they hide under the king's nose and live right alongside the Elites with no complaints of any abilities dwindling.' He sighs. 'But just because the king and his Healers said the Ordinaries were diseased, most of the Elites won't think twice if it means their powers and lives are at stake.'

I nod slowly as my brain is suddenly flooded with questions once again.

What exactly is the Resistance's goal, and what could I possibly offer them?

I open my mouth to ask this, but Calum beats me to it. 'The Resistance is finally ready to take action. And unlike what the king has said about us, we are not radicals who kill for the sheer fun of it. We want justice. We want the truth to be told. We want Ordinaries and the Fatals to live in peace with the rest of the Elites once more. To not be hunted and killed for things they cannot control simply because the king wants an Elite society and is willing to lie about Ordinaries to get it. So that is our goal. That is our cause.'

And that's exactly what I want, exactly what I've hoped for all my life.

To be accepted and *free*.

I realize it then, how badly I want to be a part of this. How badly I want to help and make a difference. I think I've been waiting all my life to find such a purpose.

'What about the ball?' I blurt out. 'Why attack at the ball?'

Lenny and Calum exchange a look before the latter sighs and says, 'Our attack was as much of a surprise to us as it was to the guests.' I'm reminded of how unprepared the few Resistance members looked, how they were trying to fight their way *out* of the ballroom.

'It was never part of the plan,' Lenny interprets as I raise an eyebrow, urging him to explain further. 'So, basically, the ball was the perfect cover to sneak in a small group to search the castle, using the festivity as a distraction. And, well, let's just say they got caught.'

My gaze slides to Finn. 'You were there and escaped. What happened?'

Finn clears his throat. 'I won't bore you with the details, but a guard found me in a back hallway during my search, and thought it was rather suspicious that a serving boy was so far from the festivities. So, when he asked prying questions, naturally, I lied my ass off.' He ducks his head, shaking it at the floor. 'Only after he dragged me back into the ballroom did I discover he was a Bluff who could sense each of my lies.'

'But Finn wasn't the only one caught,' Mira cuts in, looking grim. 'Turns out, there were a lot more Imperials crawling around the castle than anticipated.'

Finn heaves a heavy sigh. 'We were all equipped with low-damage bombs, knives, and suicide capsules, though we weren't planning on having to use any of it. But we discreetly wore our leather armor and had our masks as a precaution in case we needed to fight our way out. And that's exactly what it came to. An Imperial was the first to set off one of our bombs, not knowing what it was, and that's when the ballroom broke out into chaos. We tried to escape, but Elites started fighting us, and all we could do was try to fight our way out.' He pauses, swallowing his sorrow. 'In the end, we all used the bombs while those who were caught used the suicide capsules.'

Leena's pretty face is pinched with grief, her next words hollow. 'Our secrets are too valuable to lose, and they were too loyal to divulge them. They knew they would lose their lives anyway.'

The room goes silent as if taking a moment to honor the lives of those they lost.

'We weren't intending for the kingdom to learn of the Resistance that night, or in that way, but it seems fate had other arrangements,' Calum says softly. 'Sadly, sometimes it takes martyrs to show people that there is something worth fighting for.'

I let the information sink in, sitting silently before voicing the question that has slithered its way to the forefront of my mind. 'What was it that you were searching for?'

It's Lenny who offers me an answer. 'As an Imperial, I've been informed that the final Trial will be held in the Bowl, and that is where we are going to show ourselves to Ilya. Now, the castle is riddled with secret passageways and tunnels that lead in and out to various places. We need to find the one that leads right under the box in the arena. Securing the king is the trickiest part of this, so we need to use the element of surprise against him while the rest of the Resistance can come through the many tunnels leading into the Bowl.'

My brows knit together in confusion. 'How do you know there is even a tunnel leading into the waiting room beneath the box?' I don't remember seeing a door down there before the interviews, but then again, I suppose I was rather distracted.

'Because I've seen it,' Lenny says simply. I open my mouth, but he quickly cuts me off. 'And that's all good and dandy, except that the tunnel doors only open from the *inside*, and I have no idea where the other end of that passage is.'

'Oh,' I say softly.

Lenny's laugh is dry. 'Yeah. *Oh.*'

I look between all of them expectantly. 'So, what, you need me to find the tunnel that leads there?'

Their response is practically in unison. 'Yes.'

I choke on a laugh. 'If Lenny hasn't been able to find it yet, I'm not sure I—'

'Yeah, well, it would be a hell of a lot easier if I had the future king wrapped around my finger,' Lenny murmurs under his breath.

I shoot him a look as Calum slowly says, 'Your relationships with the princes are . . . valuable. Specifically, your *connection* with Prince Kitt.' He leans forward, urging me to understand. 'Paedyn, I believe you hold far more sway over that boy than you give yourself credit for.'

I'm not sure he's right about that, but I nod slowly, taking in his words. 'You want me to use Kitt to find the tunnel.'

'Bingo,' Finn says.

'He has already begun to trust you,' Calum insists. 'So, use it. What was it you said earlier? "The strongest weapon a woman has at her disposal is that she is often underestimated." So let him underestimate you. He is a means to an end. Make this boy bow if he must.' His eyes are locked on mine. 'Just get us into the Bowl. We've been planning this for a long while now, and it will be the first time that most of the Resistance will be in one spot. So, this needs to go *right.*'

I nod again. 'I can do it. I *will* do it.' There is a beat of silence before I ask, 'What exactly *is* the plan?'

'It's really quite simple,' Calum says. 'The majority of us will finally all gather together, and we'll show the people of Ilya who we are and what we have to say. Show them that we are not a threat while also reminding them of who they have been killing for decades. The king is going to have to either admit his lies about the Ordinaries or simply give us our freedom. And you are going to help us do it.'

'We need you to find the tunnel,' Lenny urges. 'I'll be there to help with anything you need, of course, and we will check back in soon with Calum.'

So, Calum is the head leader?

'Yes, I suppose you could call me the that, though none of us really have titles,' Calum says coolly, running a hand through his tawny hair.

Plagues. He's a—

'Yes, I am a Mind Reader, Paedyn.' My breathing quickens.

He's been reading my thoughts the entire time. He's probably reading them right now—

'Yes, I have been reading your thoughts the entire time, and yes, I did just read them again.' I don't try to hide the look of betrayal on my face, which only softens his expression. 'I'm sorry for invading your thoughts, but I had to make sure you were truly on our side. Truly willing to help us.'

Get. Out. Of. My. Head.

He almost smiles. 'So very headstrong, just like your father. But now that I see you are trustworthy, I will leave you to your thoughts.'

Lenny clears his throat and stands, offering me a hand. 'We should get going. We have a lot of work to do. And you need to spend as much time with the future king as possible, so you can find us our passage.'

'Yeah, I still need to figure out exactly how I'm going to get that information out of him,' I admit.

'Flirt,' Finn chimes in at the same moment Lenny says, 'Bat your eyelashes or something.'

I snort before Lenny waves me over to the stairs. 'Come on. We need to get you back to your room.'

I nod to the small group before me. 'Thank you. You gave me something to fight for.' And with that, I turn away, heading for the stone steps behind Lenny.

'Paedyn?' I spin on my heel to see Calum watching me. 'Your father would be proud.'

CHAPTER 35

Rai

Training and torturing have kept me sane over the past couple of days, though I'm well aware that only an insane person would admit that.

It's almost been a week since the first Trial ended.

Almost a week since I buried a blade in Jax's chest.

Almost a week of restraining myself from doing the same to Ace.

So I keep busy, pounding my fists into mats so they don't find their way to somebody's face, seeing that I don't have the Silencer to beat down on anymore.

It's a shame that I killed him.

I'm sure he had information, yes, but I'm not one for empty threats. I promised Micah I would kill him if he didn't prove his life worthy of saving. And when he failed to offer me the information I wanted, I followed through on that promise.

He was a liability, too dangerous to keep alive as my human punching bag. I knew he had no intention of telling me what I wanted to hear, and I had no intention of wasting my time.

Though I do miss taking my anger and frustration out on him.

Despite that, I still spend most of my days with Father's Silencer. His ability is one of the few I've never trained with, never even

encountered until a month ago. So I train with Damion for hours, trying to understand and develop this new power as best I can. I never want to feel powerless like I did when Micah ambushed me in Loot. No, I *want* his power. Want to be able to use it and deflect it so I can never be crippled like that again.

Easier said than done.

The training is tedious and tiring. Learning to use the Silencer's ability is far easier than defending yourself against it. I'm smothered daily by his power while trying to tap into it, trying to use it against him. I'm struggling, to say the least, despite being determined, and despising feeling so helpless.

But I'm restless. I keep myself busy all day in the hopes that the nightmares are too exhausted to chase me from my sleep at night.

The blade of my sword sinks deep into the wood of the practice dummy I'm currently hacking into.

I sigh in annoyance and grip the heavy hilt with both hands, yanking the sharp steel out of the splintered wood. I mindlessly flip the weapon at my side before raining down blows on the hunk of wood once more, letting my mind focus on the power and precision of each swing – focus on what it feels like to wield death, hold it in my palm, bend it to my will.

And yet, all it takes is a familiar laugh to shatter that focus.

She's leaning against that padded tree she likes to pummel so much, Kitt standing close. Something begins burning inside of me, but I ignore it, not bothering to acknowledge the jealousy painting me Ilya's kingdom color.

My eyes are glued to the two of them as they talk casually. Paedyn seems to be far more comfortable with Kitt as of late, spending time with him outside of training and meals. I will the jealousy to seep from my bones, to simply evaporate, but it gnaws and nags with every thought of the two of them together.

Paedyn nods to Kitt with a smile before he turns and heads back towards the castle while I force myself to focus once again on training. I cut and slice at the wood with my sword, the tension in my shoulders easing with every swipe.

'How about a rematch?'

I hit the wood hard, slicing the sword deep across the dummy's chest. Paedyn waits patiently as I slowly turn around, swinging the sword in slow circles at my side. I don't bother smiling as I casually say, 'Someone's in the mood to lose.'

The shadow of a frown shades her face as she crosses her arms. 'And someone's just in a bad mood.'

I chuckle humorlessly. 'Darling, this is not me in a bad mood. There would be a lot more blood if that were the case.'

She gives me a small smirk. 'Well, I won't have to take your word for it, because after I beat you, I'm sure I'll get to witness one of your bad moods firsthand.'

I sigh, giving in. 'Fine. Hand-to-hand again?'

'No,' she says slowly, 'I was thinking we could do something different.'

'And why's that?' I take a step closer to her, leaning in as I say, 'Is hand-to-hand too distracting, having to be so close to me?'

She somehow manages to take a step even closer. 'Not at all. I don't get distracted, Azer.'

'That sounds like a challenge.'

'Only if you're in the mood to lose.'

Plagues, this girl.

She smiles up at me. 'So, how about archery? Unless, of course, your pride can't handle losing to me. Again.'

'Oh, that won't be a problem. Because I won't be losing.' I pull my face away from hers and brush her shoulder as I pass. I know what she is doing, and I welcome the distraction. Welcome *her* being the distraction. I pull a bow off one of the weapon racks and throw a handful of arrows onto the ground between us. Paedyn already has her weapon in hand, already facing the battered target over fifteen yards away.

'Three rounds,' she says, not taking her eyes off the target. 'We each get three shots per round. Highest score wins.'

'Fair enough.' I extend my hand towards her to shake on the rules, as is customary. She slowly grasps my hand, holding it firmly as her calluses brush my own. Then I tug her towards me, pulling her against my chest where I murmur close to her ear, 'Good luck, Gray.'

She rolls her eyes at me but mine are locked on her. 'I don't need luck when it's you I'm competing against,' she says coolly, her growing smile smug. I can't help but huff out a laugh. After a moment too long, I let her go, and she turns to face the target with a smile. When I don't move to nock an arrow, she throws an expectant glance at me to which I respond with a gesture towards the target. 'Ladies first.'

'Oh right. I forgot you were a *gentleman*.' She snorts before nocking an arrow. I cock my head, watching her as she holds the bow as if she is left-handed, though I know she isn't.

Interesting.

I blink, and an arrow is sailing through the air, landing just shy of the bullseye. She places another arrow on the bow and pulls back, taking a deep breath. She shuts her eyes for a moment, only firing when she opens them. Bullseye. I watch her follow the same routine with her final arrow. Watch her arm strain as she pulls the bowstring back. Watch her eyes flutter shut in concentration. Watch her breathe deeply before sending another arrow sinking into the bullseye.

Damn.

Archery has never been my favorite, and clearly, Paedyn doesn't feel the same. She's a natural. So confident, so controlled, as if the bow is nearly an extension of her arm. The arrow obeys her as she wills it to land exactly where she wants.

And I'm suddenly thinking she's right. I might lose this.

'You're up.' She steps back beside me, and with a mocking whisper, says, 'Good luck, Azer.'

Plague knows I'll need it.

I step up and settle an arrow onto my bow. I can feel her eyes on me, tracking every move I make and it's annoyingly *distracting.* I pull the bowstring back, aim, and fire. Then I'm cursing under my breath for just barely missing the bullseye before I nock another arrow. This one follows the same pattern, and I'm now frustrated and feeling the overwhelming need to punch something. I fire my last arrow and it finally lands where I want it to. Barely. Its silver tip sinks into the farthest edge of the bullseye, guided by sheer luck to get it there.

Paedyn doesn't say a word as she steps up and fires her next three arrows. And just as before, two hit the bullseye, one just shy of it. She's mesmerizing to watch, to witness her work with this weapon.

I am going to lose. I don't like losing.

And Paedyn knows it too. She walks past, smiling at me as if she's already won. And she probably has. I take my time firing my next three shots, trying to concentrate and calm my breathing before letting them fly towards the target. Not helping. Two on the rings, one on the bullseye. I glare at the target while Paedyn grins. She nocks an arrow as she says, 'Now I see why you wanted to stick with hand-to-hand. You knew you had a better chance of winning that.'

She's not wrong. She's still smiling as she focuses her attention on the target, calming her breathing before she even draws the bowstring back.

There is no way I'm winning this.

I fight a small smile at my sudden idea.

If I'm going to lose, I might as well have some fun.

I take a step towards her. Then I slowly step behind her – close behind her. My chest presses against her back at the same moment I let my hand lazily find her waist. She jumps at the sudden contact, and I laugh softly, close to her ear.

'What are you doing?' Her words are breathless, but she doesn't move, frozen against me.

My lips are close to her ear as I murmur, 'Distracting you.'

She lets out a forced laugh, feigning confidence. 'I told—' Words fail her when my hand begins exploring farther along her waist, her abdomen, atop her thin tank. She swallows. 'I told you I don't get distracted.'

'Yes,' my fingers begin tracing lazy circles up and down her side, 'and I could have sworn you tapped your left foot as you said it.' I lean in even closer, whispering against her ear, 'And we both know that means you're lying.'

The truth is, I'm the one lying. Her foot is the last thing I'm paying attention to. But I know she's lying nonetheless, and I'm going to prove it.

'Well,' she clears her throat, trying to concentrate on forming words and not my fingers, 'you're wrong.' And with that unsure remark, she lifts her bow and draws the string.

I wrap an arm around her waist, slowly, and let my other hand brush from her knuckles curved around the bowstring all the way to her straining shoulder. With her body still pressed against mine, I feel a shiver snake up her spine as my fingers dance slowly up and down her arm. I smile against her ear, and I know she feels that too since she huffs in annoyance.

I feel her take a deep, shaky breath as she tries to calm down, tries to pull herself together. And then she fires. I chuckle against her ear when the arrow lands the farthest away from the bullseye yet. She whips her head around so our faces are mere inches apart and scowls at me. I'm amused, smiling as I let my eyes wander over her face, catching on every faint freckle and dark lash framing her blue eyes.

Then those ocean eyes tear from mine when she turns back to the target, grabbing another arrow. But she never tries to step out of my grasp. She's too stubborn. If she moves now, she knows it will only prove just how much I truly distract her.

So, she nocks the next arrow and breathes as the breeze blows a strand of silver hair into her face. I reach around and gently, slowly, tuck it behind her ear as I whisper into it, 'Why is it that you're shooting with your left hand?' It's a random question, used to distract as well as satisfy my curiosity.

She takes a deep breath before answering, 'Would you believe me if I said it's because I wanted to go easy on you?'

I laugh, shaking my head before resting my chin on her shoulder. 'Liar. You would never go easy on me.'

'You're right about that.' She exhales a shaky laugh. 'My father taught me to shoot with both hands and after my injury in the Trial, I figured I should practice more with my left.'

And with that, she doesn't hesitate before pulling back and firing the arrow, hitting far outside the bullseye with a soft thud. 'Don't. Say. A. Word,' she mutters through clenched teeth, not bothering to look at me as she grabs another arrow angrily.

'I wasn't going to say a thing,' I say with mock innocence.

'Liar. I can practically *feel* you smirking.'

My lips are against the shell of her ear, and I am, in fact, smirking. 'I can't help it when I'm right.'

She's still fiddling angrily with the arrow, her voice deceptively sweet as she says, 'Well if you keep smirking like that, I'm going to turn around and point this arrow at your heart.'

I smile at her sentiment, my fingers continuing to draw circles across her stomach. She takes another shallow breath, about to pull back and fire when I mumble, 'Yeah, well at least you might be able to hit my heart, unlike the bullseye—'

I'm not surprised when I feel the hard jab of an elbow sink into my stomach. The air whooshes out of me, but as soon as I catch my breath I'm laughing. Paedyn huffs and I tug her closer to me, using this game as an excuse to hold her, touch her.

Her head rests on my chest as she examines the target, breathing deeply. And I'm doing the same. My chest heaves, the feel of her against me almost too much to breathe properly. We fit together so perfectly, so *right*. I can hardly think, or breathe, or move when my fingers glide across her skin, her waist, her body.

Then, she lifts her head, lifts her bow, and lets the arrow fly. Bullseye. But barely. I lean down and rest my chin on her shoulder once again, admiring the arrow that finally made it to its mark. 'It's about time, Gray.'

'Let's see you do any better,' she scoffs, pulling away as I reluctantly let her. I sigh and grab an arrow, settling it onto my bow. I fire quickly, hitting the ring closest to the bullseye, swearing under my breath. Then I grab another, determined to make the arrow land where I want it to.

Something brushes my arm, a whisper against my skin.

My head whips to the side, eyes crashing into blue ones below. She looks up at me through her lashes, eyes burning into mine, full of fire. Her hand hovers just above the exposed skin on my arm, teasing without touching.

'What are you doing, Gray?' I ask, turning my attention back towards the target.

'Distracting,' she says slowly, drawing out the syllables. Her hand brushes my arm again, lightly. So lightly.

I smile. 'Darling, you're going to have to do better than that.'

'No,' she says coolly, 'I don't think I do.'

The tips of her fingers meet my skin. She lets them trail down my arm, stopping at my wrist before making their way back up, painfully slow. Her fingers find their way under the sleeve of my cotton shirt, climbing up and up and—

Gone.

Her touch vanishes, leaving me aching for her to lay her hands on me—

That's when it hits me.

She's right. She doesn't need to do anything more to distract me.

The mere thought of her being so close and barely touching me has my head spinning. I'm melted by the promise that her fingers gave me, promise of more, promise of *something*. Nothing. She won't lay her hands on me. Instead, she'll drive me mad by teasing me with her touch, only to pull it away, leaving me wanting more. Leaving me cold without the fire her fingers trail along my skin.

I exhale, noticing how shaky the action sounds, how shaky my body has become. I pull back the bowstring as another finger traces under my forearm, grazing my skin.

My arrow lands two whole rings away from the center but my mind is elsewhere, on the phantom touches making their way up and down my arm. I don't remember grabbing another arrow, but it's nocked onto my bow when I look down.

Slowly, so damn slowly, she lets her fingers slide over my skin, heavier than before. A single touch has never made me feel so on fire. And she knows *exactly* what she is doing. She knows that barely feeling her at all will drive me mad in a way I can't explain, in a way I've never felt before. 'You're a cruel little thing, you know that?' My voice is deep, desperate.

'But I've barely laid a finger on you,' she says softly, emphasizing her words with a single finger tracing up my forearm.

'Exactly.'

Maybe I did it on purpose. Maybe I chose to *distract* her because I knew she was too stubborn to not do the same to me. Maybe I did it all just because I wanted her hands on me too. Because it was an excuse for me to hold her, for her to hold me. And now that she isn't, I'm craving her touch. Craving her.

I fire the arrow, not bothering to wait and see where it lands before I've thrown my bow to the ground, spun around, and gripped her wrists instead. I pull her towards me, staring into her startled eyes. Her lips part, either in surprise or because she's about to tell me off, I'm not sure.

'Don't,' I pause, swallow, exhale slowly, 'play with me like that.'

She stares at me. Her mouth opens and closes again, clearly hoping words will fall out. I hold her gaze as I guide one of her hands to my arm, dropping her other wrist to pull her closer by the waist. Her palm meets my skin and it's almost like I remembered how to breathe again. I press my hand on top of hers, holding her skin firmly against mine. I smile now that she's finally, fully touching me, rather than taunting me with the tips of teasing fingers.

A single touch from her, or the lack of it, is enough to drive me mad.

What has she done to me?

I take my hand off hers, fingers trailing down her arm before dropping it to my side. But she doesn't drop hers, instead leaving her palm in place. She stares at where her skin meets mine before her gaze finally trails up to my face. She smirks, but it's as weak as her voice. 'I didn't realize a single touch could affect you so much.'

'Neither did I.'

Her eyes dart away from mine, almost looking timid as she lets her hand trace down my arm before dropping it completely. Then she cranes her neck, looking around me at the target behind.

She smiles at what she sees. 'You lost, Azer.'

CHAPTER 36

Paedyn

'Focus, Paedyn. Just calm down and focus. You can do this.'

I nod in response to Kitt's reassuring words, shutting my eyes before taking a deep breath. After a moment, I peek at him and nod again. 'Okay. I'm ready.'

Kitt heaves a dramatic sigh, his eyes filled with amusement. Then he says, slowly, 'Three . . .' I smile knowingly back at him. 'Two . . .' I tilt my head up. 'One.'

In a flash, he throws something into the air. I open my mouth expectantly, ready to savor the sweetness of the chocolate, only for it to land on my nose before bouncing off onto the floor.

Kitt's laughter echoes off the walls of the busy kitchen, and I catch the servants smiling at the familiar sound. He holds a hand up to me when I start to speak, clearly needing a moment to collect himself before he looks at me. But when he finally straightens and meets my gaze, he's laughing again.

'Okay, so my coordination when it comes to catching food in my mouth isn't . . . great,' I mumble, unable to stop my smile from spreading.

'Isn't *great*?' Kitt runs a hand through his messy hair, still choking on laughter. 'Tell that to Gail who has wasted half her chocolates on you.'

I cross my arms defiantly. 'Well, you didn't catch every chocolate either, *Your Majesty*.'

Kitt leans closer and flashes me a smile. 'True. But I at least ate the evidence. You, on the other hand,' his gaze slides to the floor now littered with sweets, 'did not.'

I snort, drop to the ground, and begin collecting the tiny chocolates in my cupped hand. Kitt's suddenly crouching in front of me, helping place them in my awaiting palm. I stare at him for a moment, still stunned with every show of kindness or shared smile. But with all the time I've been spending with him lately, the differences between the king and his son seem to surprise me less and less.

A partnership I only accepted to get noticed by the people has now blossomed into an unlikely friendship. It isn't hard to spend most of my days talking and spending time with the future king to find the tunnel for the Resistance. None of it is hard, though the guilt that is eating away at me for doing it is. I selfishly find myself wishing he was more like his father because it would make this betrayal far more bearable.

A small, pretty servant passes by, gasping at the sight of us. 'I know, I know.' Kitt sighs. 'She's horrible at catching things in her mouth.'

'No, no, Your Highness!' The servant rushes over, alarm written all over her face. 'Please, don't trouble yourself! I'll clean this up right away!' Before I can speak, she's already dropped beside me and begun plucking the chocolates from my palm.

'Thank you, Liza,' Kitt says, standing. He holds out his hands for me, and I take them, letting him pull me to my feet.

Liza smiles at her prince. 'It's my pleasure, Your Highness.'

Of course he knows his servants by name.

Dozens of them bustle about around us, bumping into each other in their haste to get where they need to be while a booming voice calls out to us. 'Kitt, I love you, dear, but I don't think my kitchen can hold one more person!' I spot Gail eying us from across the room, smiling at what she sees. Then she gestures with her hands, shooing us out the door. 'But since I'm kicking you out, you will have to come visit me again soon.'

Kitt chuckles and places a gentle hand on my back, and I don't flinch away from his touch. He guides me towards the door while calling out, 'Oh, you couldn't keep me away, Gail.'

The hallway is teeming with servants, all busy and bustling in preparation for the next ball tomorrow night – a reminder of the dwindling time I have left to find the tunnel that leads into the box.

I have spent day after day with Kitt, earning his trust all while crafting a plan to get the information I need.

I almost run into a servant, or rather, he almost runs into me. The gangly boy shouts his apologies before scurrying off to wherever it is he needs to go.

Perfect timing. Here goes nothing.

I turn towards Kitt and force out a laugh. 'Don't you ever just need a break from the chaos of the castle?' Even as I say it, I already know the answer. He practically admitted to feeling trapped in the palace, in his position, when we were stuffed in the saferoom together. And yet, here I am, using that information he trusted me with against him.

He looks at me, eyes seeming to search mine with a certain sadness. 'You have no idea.'

I throw my arms out, exasperated. 'So, why don't you? You could visit Loot for a day. Granted, there's just as much chaos there as in the castle, but . . . it's a different kind of chaos. You blend in. Let the chaos wash over you until it's a familiar feeling. Until you become a part of it, swallowed in it.'

Come on. Say yes.

Kitt's staring at me like he can't believe what he is seeing. A slow smile is spreading across his lips, green eyes sweeping over my face as though he's worried I'll stop looking at him again.

'What?' I ask, slightly concerned.

He blinks and shakes his head slightly, trying to clear it. 'Nothing. It's just . . . the way you talk about Loot.' He looks away, muttering something that sounded like, 'Hell, just the way you talk.'

I don't dwell on it before slowly asking, 'So . . . is that a yes?'

His smile slips. 'I wish I could see Loot. Truly. I haven't been since I was a boy. Since before I was . . .'

'Trapped here?' I supply softly.

I hadn't realized we'd stopped walking until Kitt tugs me from the

322

middle of the hallway, sparing us from being trampled by bustling servants. 'Exactly,' he says with a small smile. 'You're one of the few people who understands that.'

I nod slowly, smiling slightly. 'Kitt, I'm about to tell you off, okay?'

He laughs at that. 'I would expect nothing less from you. Go on.'

'As the future king,' I sigh, 'you should see your people. See how they live in the slums. See how they *survive*.'

'I know,' he says hollowly.

'So what's stopping you?'

He huffs out a humorless laugh, rubbing the back of his neck as he simply states, 'The current king. I never leave the castle unless it's absolutely necessary and seeing my people is not, according to him. I'm the heir to the throne and he won't risk me leaving the palace, let alone helping like I tried to when the Resistance attacked the ball.'

I try not to stiffen at his ignorance, at the idea that the Resistance *attacked* the ball. But it's best to not tell the prince off about matters I should know nothing about.

'And do you agree with him?' I ask carefully.

'I understand him. And I respect him—'

'And you will never stop trying to prove yourself to him, so you'll do as he says. I know.' There's a bitter bite in my voice that I quickly try to conceal. 'Then just one night, Kitt. Go see *your* people. See what it was like for me in the slums. Don't trap yourself here.'

Kitt leans his head back against the wall and laughs. 'I can't exactly leave, Paedyn. There are guards everywhere and I don't have the clearing to just walk right out.'

And that's exactly what I hoped he would say.

Still, I give him a flat look. 'But you're the prince.'

'Yes, well, sometimes I'm only a prince in title, not in privilege. I can't just walk out the front door.'

'So, walk out a different door.' I take a step closer, throwing my hands up only to let them slap against my sides, feigning nonchalance. 'You can't tell me there isn't some way out of here that no one knows about? Some sort of door that isn't guarded?' I sound totally casual, curious even.

Come on. Trust me. Tell me.

If I can get him talking about the tunnels, get him to take me through them, there's a chance of him telling me about the one I need to find. I would act like I'm curious, ask questions about the other tunnels in order to learn about one in particular. It's not my most solid plan, but it's a start. He looks me over in a way that vaguely reminds me of Kai. I push thoughts of the other brother away, instead choosing to focus on the one in front of me. The one who is easy to be around, easy to talk to—

Easy to trick, betray, use—

'Oh, yes. There are plenty of ways for me to get out of the castle unseen,' Kitt says with a smile, cutting through my screaming thoughts.

My heart is pounding, my voice quiet when I say, 'I'll take you. One night. You'll see Loot and your people. What they're like, what their lives are like . . .' He's staring at me so intently that I stop for a moment, swallowed by those emerald eyes I didn't dare look into a few days ago. 'A king who doesn't know his people cannot be a king *for* his people.'

Despite the truth of my words, they taste bitter in my mouth for the reason behind me voicing them.

All it takes is one seed of doubt, one grain of uncertainty to fester and grow.

And I just planted it.

I give him a reassuring smile as though I'm not lying through my teeth.

Trust me.

'Maybe,' he says, studying me. I fight the urge to try to convince him further, careful not to sound desperate or draw suspicion. 'I'll think on your offer.'

'Kitt.'

The hair on the back of my neck stands up at the sound of that voice. That cold, callous voice. I slowly turn on my heel to see the king at the end of the hallway, making his way to us. I give him the smallest curtsy, biting my tongue as I offer a small smile.

'Kitt, I need you in the study to finish our discussion with the advisers.' His eyes sweep over me, finally deeming me worthy to look

324

at. They are the same bright green as Kitt's, and yet, they couldn't be more different, more . . . cold. I nearly shiver, reminded of why I could barely meet his son's eyes. The king's gaze flicks back up to Kitt before saying, 'Now.'

Though he doesn't sound too thrilled, Kitt replies with a curt, 'Of course, Father.' He steps beside the king, ready to walk with him back to the study.

'Go ahead, Son. I'll meet you there.' His stern voice leaves no room for argument, and Kitt nods slowly in response before throwing me a small smile and turning on his heel.

I can barely stand to look at him, but I force my eyes to meet those of my father's murderer. He's looking at me like I'm the scum he scraped from the bottom of his shiny shoes. I can't stand it, but I force myself to be still rather than squirm under his scrutiny. So I offer him a bright smile all while wondering if it looks like I'm baring my teeth. 'Your Majesty,' I say in farewell before moving to go around him, to escape this man and my raging, revengeful thoughts.

His shoes click against the stone floor as he steps in front of my path. I halt, looking up at his large frame. He's in great health for his age, making it easy to see where his sons get their strong build and handsome features from. The similarities between Kitt and his father are astounding, but it's the king's Brawny ability I'm focused on, reminding me of the fact that he could snap my neck with ease.

'Miss Gray, good to see you made it out of the first Trial mostly unscathed.' He doesn't sound happy about my well-being in the slightest. 'Well, thanks to my son, that is.'

I can only imagine the king's reaction upon seeing the footage of Kai with me in the Trial. I know he hated it. Hated that his son helped me – a no one, a Mundane, a Slummer.

An Ordinary.

'Yes, I am grateful I had Kai as my partner,' I say coolly, unsure of where this conversation is heading.

'Hmm.' The king looks down at me, eyes narrowing.

Before he can say anything else, I add, 'And I am very much looking forward to the next Trial. And the one after that.'

Lies.

I just wanted to see the look on his face when I sounded so confident about surviving that long. I follow up my statement with a fake smile, ready to leave him and this conversation behind when he says, 'Let me be frank, Paedyn. You are not winning this.'

I stiffen. 'I'm sorry?'

'I know that is what you want. To win the Purging Trials and have a better life for you and your seamstress friend.' He laughs, bitter and biting. 'That reminds me. I should congratulate you for the little stunt you pulled with your dress at the ball. You certainly got what you wanted. Reminding the people of their *Silver Savior*.'

I look away, unable to stare at him any longer as he continues with a wave of his hand. 'Tell me, have you seen the polls?'

I had. A day after the showing of the first Trial, the contestants' scores and votes from the people were combined and tallied up. The rankings of the remaining seven opponents were everywhere, displayed on banners and fliers throughout the city. Kai was at the top, followed by Ace with Andy close behind in third. That left Blair and I tied for fourth with Braxton and Jax tied in last.

It seems that the kingdom of Ilya doesn't quite know what to do with me. Those from the slums are likely voting for their *Silver Savior*, while those outside of it are likely rooting against me, hoping to watch the Slummer die an entertaining death. And if I'm receiving any votes from those outsides of the slums it's no doubt because they find me amusing.

'Yes. I have seen the polls,' I say through my teeth.

'Good. I doubt your ranking will get any higher, so what I'm most concerned about is your involvement with my sons. They don't need you dragging them down, or worse, *influencing* them.' I stare at the king's chest, watching as he fixes the cuffs of his jacket. 'I doubt I need to remind you of your place, so stay out of their way and we won't have any problems. Understood?'

The dagger tucked into my boot has never tempted me more, tormenting me with the thought of shoving its blade through his chest like he did to my father. But he didn't just kill my only parent that day, he killed a piece of me in the process.

And I have never hated someone so wholeheartedly because of it.

My fists are clenched tightly at my sides, fingernails biting into my palms. But I school my face into a submissive, sweet expression when I say, 'Understood, Your Majesty.'

If I didn't want to win before, I certainly do now.

'Good,' he says curtly. 'Then we should thank the Plague that you are alive and well, isn't that right?'

There is a certain challenge ringing in his tone, flashing in his eyes. I mirror his smile, even as I swallow my pride.

I've never said the filthy phrase, and I swore I never would. And yet, here I am, opening my mouth to let the words fall out as though they aren't foreign on my tongue. As though they aren't leaving a foul taste in my mouth.

'Yes, thank the Plague indeed.'

'Hold still or I'm going to poke your eye out.'

I grumble while Ellie only grins. She's still swiping a wand across my lashes despite coming dangerously close to accidentally blinding me on several occasions. She likes to blame it on my squirming, and I like to blame it on her unsteady hands.

'Alright, time to suck it in!' Adena is bubbling over with excitement behind me, her hands gripping the laces of my dress. She allows me one final breath before pulling the ties tight, squeezing the air out of my squished ribcage. She works the laces, slowly pulling the bodice tighter to cinch the open back together.

Gripping the chair in front of me, I gasp, 'One more pull, A, and I think a rib will puncture my lung.'

I doubt Adena can even hear me over her squeals of delight. 'Pae, it's perfect! You know, I was a bit worried about the hem but look at it! It falls just right and, oh, the cut is incredible . . .' She pauses, huffing out a sigh. 'Ugh, forget it. Just look at you!'

Her hands grip my arms as she spins me towards the mirror, her glowing face peeking over my shoulder. I blink, and the girl in the mirror does the same.

The silver dress I wore to the first ball was stunning, seductive, where this one is simply beautiful, breathtaking. Deep red fabric envelops me, pooling to the floor. It's shimmery and sleeveless, but rather than the bodice being rounded at the top, the edges end in elegantly pointed corners. It's tight, cinching in my waist with the laces at the back, now tied into a neat bow and exposing skin between the fabric holding the dress together. The skirt is full, revealing the wide slit up my right leg where my father's dagger is displayed for all to behold and be baffled at.

'Adena, I love it . . .' I trail off while my eyes trail over the fabric hugging my body. Then my gaze meets the excited hazel one in the mirror, and I turn to face my best friend. 'I love you, Adena.'

She glows, beaming at me brightly. 'And I love you, Pae.' Her smile turns sly. 'And *everyone* is going to love you in this dress. Especially a certain prince . . .'

It's not difficult to figure out that she's referring to Kai. I shoot her a look, not particularly wanting to talk about this topic. 'Adena . . .'

'What?' she asks far too innocently. 'In case you've forgotten, I watched the recap of the Trials. I saw what happened between you two.' She quirks an eyebrow. 'And I've been waiting for you to come and talk to me about it.'

'Well, there's nothing to say.' She gives me a flat look, forcing me to add, 'Alright, I don't know *what* to say. He's confusing and captivating and I'm failing miserably at keeping my distance.'

'Right,' she says quietly. 'Because you're . . . you.'

'And he's . . . him,' I sigh.

Because I'm an Ordinary, and he's the future Enforcer.

Adena huffs dramatically. 'Well, I don't blame you for not being able to stay away. I mean, look at him.'

I roll my eyes, laughing despite myself. In an attempt to avoid this current conversation, I marvel in the mirror at what the girls have turned me into. My hair is pulled into a complicated braid down my back combined with dark makeup that frames my eyes in shadow and my lips in shiny gloss.

Miracle workers. That's what they are.

We're talking and laughing when a sharp knock sounds at the door.

Lenny whistles when he sees me. 'Look at that. You actually look like a princess, Princess.'

CHAPTER 37

Paedyn

'If I get stung, I'm blaming you,' Lenny mumbles. He leads me through the gardens, passing dozens of gawking guests. 'Not only is your dress attracting a lot of attention, but it's also attracting a lot of bees.'

I try to stifle a snort as I look down at my gown that matches the deep roses lining the stone path we are walking. Guests mill about the gardens, making their way to the decorated wide patch of grass beyond the fountain where I splashed their future king in the face only a few days prior.

Since the Trials themselves aren't the only things different this year, the second ball is being held in the gardens where the setting sun glints off goblets of champagne, casting everything in a dull gold. We step off the path and onto the edge of the plush open grass, eying the tables of desserts and grand garlands strung from surrounding sweeping trees. The musicians are tucked under a drooping willow, half-hidden behind the curtain of swaying leaves as they strum a lively tune. At the center of the festivities lie overlapping patterned rugs on the grass, all varying in size and style to create a colorful dance floor where several couples are already spinning.

'Well, unfortunately for you, I'm not your date,' Lenny says with

a dramatic sigh. 'So this is where I must say my goodbyes.'

I huff out a laugh. 'However will I make it through the night without you?'

He sweeps into a mocking bow. 'I know. Be brave, Princess. Now go find your prince.' And then he straightens, winks, and walks off into the gardens.

I shake my head at his retreating form before taking a breath and heading farther into the makeshift ballroom for the night. I scan the swirl of dancing bodies, trying to find Kitt among them.

'It's a good thing you're wearing that dress, or I might have never found you.'

I jump at the sound of Kitt's voice behind me and spin to face him, my skirts swishing around my legs. He smiles and shakes his head, taking me in from head to toe. 'Although, even if you were wearing green, I doubt you'd blend in.'

I swallow, unsure of what to say to that before settling with a soft, 'Thank you.'

He holds out his hand. 'Dance with me?'

I place my palm in his and nod before I'm swept onto the dance floor. I feel as though I'm dancing with an entirely different boy than I did at the previous ball. Except, the only thing that's changed is my perspective of him. We talk casually as we dance, and it's a relief to be able to look into his eyes, to not flinch away from his touch.

'Did my father say something to you yesterday? After I left?' Kitt asks curiously when the song comes to an end.

I open my mouth, ready to spew a lie when a cold voice cuts me off. 'May I cut in?'

I take a deep, annoyed breath before turning my head towards Blair who is waiting to whisk my partner away. She's paired her smirk with a deep green dress decorated by intricate beading that clings to her form.

The look Kitt gives me is comical. I choke back a laugh as his eyes bore into mine, pleading with me not to leave him. I give him a small smile, hoping he sees the apology in my eyes as I say, 'Of course. He's all yours.'

He shakes his head at me, pinning me with a stare as I step out of his arms and am quickly replaced by Blair. 'Have fun,' I add, unable to hide my smile. Kitt gives me a look that promises revenge, and I choke back a laugh at the sight of it. I spin around, still smiling—

And collide with something solid. No, *someone* solid.

Something wet splatters across my cheek as I back away from the body I've so ungracefully rammed into. The scent of wine mixed with pine hits me, and I swallow, knowing exactly who stands in front of me before I raise my face to meet his.

Kai smiles, looking equally rugged and handsome in the final rays of the setting sun. His hair is messier than normal with his ruffled, inky waves falling wherever they please. His eyes are a bright, cloudy sort of gray, alight with amusement. The suit he wears and crisp white shirt beneath are not only slightly rumpled but now partially stained a deep red.

Red wine sloshes in the glass gripped in his hand. Well, there's little left seeing that he's now wearing most of it thanks to me.

My eyes snap to his when he bursts out laughing.

Several of the guests around us cast bewildered glances in our direction, having heard his unusual outburst. And I'm quite certain my expression mirrors theirs. His shoulders are shaking with laughter, and I halt, holding my breath. His grin is wide, wild, displaying a stunning smile accompanied by deep dimples.

I'm suddenly concerned.

Wine is dripping from the edges of his suit, and he can't seem to stop laughing long enough to notice, or even care, that my clumsiness has ruined his clothes. I clear my throat, eying the guests eying us as I say, 'Kai,' another deep rumble of laughter at the sound of his name, 'why don't we go get you cleaned up?'

I grab his hand before he has a chance to argue or laugh some more, and lead us to the bordering trees, aware of the eyes tracking our every move. I snatch a handkerchief from one of the long tables before shoving us under the drooping branches of a shadowy willow tree, shielding us from the gossiping guests.

Kai leans against the rough trunk, grinning wickedly at me. I give him a quick once-over, assessing the damage I did to his clothes along with his strange behavior.

He leans close, too close, studying me thoroughly. 'You know,' he breathes the words in a way that sends a shiver down my spine, 'you didn't have to spill my drink all over me to get me alone. You could have just asked me to dance.'

I meet his gaze before it begins to trail lazily down my body. I hold my breath, practically feeling the path his eyes are burning. Then, slowly, so insufferably, sensually, scandalously slow, his gaze makes its way back to mine. 'Better yet, you would have made me come to you in that dress, sooner or later.'

I swallow. My eyes scan over him, taking in the rumpled clothes, the rumbling laughter, the flirty rambling – though I suppose that's nothing new.

'You're drunk.' I sigh out the words, shaking my head at him.

He's smirking at me again, though it's wilder than the ones I've grown so used to. 'Maybe a little.'

I roll my eyes, wadding up the cloth I grabbed and beginning to undo the button of his suit coat to try to sop up the shirt beneath as best I can. 'Are you undressing me, Gray?' His face is close to mine again, breath tickling my cheek. 'I mean, I can't say I didn't think this day would come.' He adds with an amused whisper, 'Couldn't resist me, darling?'

I look up at him then, flashing a smile of my own with a confidence I don't currently feel. 'Oh please,' I snort, 'the only thing I'm *resisting* when I'm around you is the urge to put a dagger to your throat.'

His eyes are locked on mine. 'I love when you threaten to kill me, do you know that?'

'Oh? And why is that?'

The corner of his mouth twitches up. 'Because every time you don't, it only proves that you don't want to.'

And then he flicks the tip of my nose with a satisfied smile.

I bat his hand away with a huff, flustered and frustrated and hating that he's the reason for my frazzled state. I fix my attention on his stained shirt, the fabric now sticking to the muscled body beneath.

Plagues, well that isn't helping.

I begin dabbing at the red splotch, forcing myself to focus on the task rather than the boy before me. I try to forget that it's him I'm helping all while simultaneously trying to remember why I'm helping him in the first place.

Then fingers catch my chin, and my breath catches in turn.

Kai tilts my head up to meet his gaze, fingers dancing along my jaw. He's looking at me like one would a painting – drinking in every detail, delighting in its originality, deeming it a work of art.

He tilts my head to the side, turning my cheek towards the light.

I should push him away.

His thumb strokes my jaw.

I don't want to push him away.

He chuckles and it's a drunkenly delightful sound. 'I forget how talented you are. Managed to spill my drink on the both of us.' His thumb swipes across my cheek, wiping away the wine I had forgotten splashed onto my face.

'Well maybe if you'd kept your eyes on the dance floor and your nose out of your glass, we wouldn't be in this situation,' I say coolly.

'Oh, darling, my eyes *were* on the dance floor,' he says casually. 'They were on you dancing with my brother.' Then he huffs out a laugh, craning his neck to shake his head at the canopy of leaves above us. 'Why do you think I've been drinking?'

My heart is pounding against my ribcage, against the tight confines of this dress, threatening to burst and tear Adena's careful stitching. He's looking at me again, shrugging sloppily. 'Besides, *this*,' he looks down at his stained shirt, 'was most definitely the doing of your clumsy footwork.'

I fix him with a glare, willing myself not to smile. 'Oh, is that right?'

'Shh.'

His fingers have found their way back under my chin, my jaw, cupping my face. Gray eyes drop to my mouth, gaze heavy. And then he's dragging his thumb along the length of my bottom lip.

Wine.

I can taste it still coating the thumb he's swiping across my mouth. I'm stunned, stone-still as his eyes track where his finger traces, ever so slowly, back and forth.

I should push him away.

But I don't.

Instead, I watch him watch me. Watch his eyes roam over my face. Watch his chest heave with shaky breaths. Watch a muscle tick in his cheek. Watch a smile twitch his lips.

His next words are a murmur, as if he's muttering his innermost thoughts while his thumb continues to wander over my lip. 'Will you forever be the prize I am aimlessly trying to win?'

I inhale sharply, staring him down as I say, 'Is that all I am to you? A trophy?'

A small smile twitches his lips as he shakes his head at me. 'Oh, darling, a trophy implies that I won it, earned it, *deserve* it.' He leans in farther, a certain reverence reflecting in his gaze. 'But if I get to have you, it will be because you let me.'

I swallow, my mouth suddenly feeling far too dry.

It's just the ramblings of a drunk man, that's all.

His thumb is tracing my mouth and I allow myself one more moment to memorize the feeling.

And then I push him away.

One of my palms finds his chest, forcing some space between us while the other catches his wrist. I pull his fingers away from my mouth, my lips still tingling from his touch. I feel dizzy, like I could get drunk off his touch alone.

Dangerous.

'You're not sober.' Tilting my head, I give him a smile. 'So, you're not allowed to touch me.'

He copies me, cocking his head to the side as he looks down at where I'm holding his wrist. 'But you're touching me.'

'Yes, well, I'm sober.'

A smile plays at his lips. 'So, you're saying I'm allowed to touch you when I'm sober?' His tone sounds more like a challenge than a question.

I consider it. Then I laugh. 'I'm only saying yes because I doubt you'll remember much of this conversation in the morning.'

His gaze flicks between my mouth and eyes, a drunken smirk twisting his lips. 'Oh, darling, I doubt I could forget this.'

I shake my head at him, not bothering to suppress my smile before remembering that I'm still holding his wrist. I lower it slowly, letting it drop to his side as I distract myself by assessing the stain again.

I sigh, exasperated. 'Obviously, that stain is not going to come out like this. You'll need to take off your shirt and soak it.'

His grin is wicked. 'You're trying to get me naked? Again?' He says this far too loud and I'm sure far too many people hear it. I pin him against the tree, clamping a hand over his mouth so no more nonsense can come spewing out of it.

I'm trying not to laugh and failing miserably. I snort and clamp a hand over my mouth, shaking with less than silent laughter at my current situation. At that, I feel Kai's lips smiling against my palm and tug my hand back before I can change my mind.

'Don't stop,' he murmurs.

I nearly choke on my laugh. 'Stop what?'

'That. Laughing.'

I still at his words, unable to stop myself from falling silent.

He gives me a look, frowning slightly. 'You never listen to me, do you?'

And with that, I'm being pulled towards the carpeted dance floor. 'What are you—?' I sputter as he stops abruptly at the edge of the dancing couples and spins around. Words fail me when he lifts the back of my hand to his lips, brushing a kiss over my knuckles. Then his mouth finds the pad of my thumb, lips lightly pressing there before they vanish so quickly I wonder if I've imagined it.

I'm stunned into silence. Kai seems pleased by this.

Still holding my hand and grinning widely, he sweeps into a surprisingly steady bow as he says, 'May I have this dance?'

I don't get the chance to answer before he tugs on my arm, pulling me into him and onto the dance floor. I'm wrapped in his arms, pressed tightly against him. His mouth is suddenly at my ear, murmuring, 'I wasn't really asking.'

I pull back so I can look into his face, scoffing. 'I thought you said you were a gentleman?'

'Only when I want to be.'

My eyes wander to his stained shirt, visible to everyone around us. 'Kai, your shirt. Maybe you should change—'

'Darling,' he cuts me off with a humored huff, 'I'm used to being covered in other red, sticky liquids far worse than wine.'

True.

I try to push the gory thought away and let him sweep me across the rugs. The sun has set, casting the guests beside us in shadows and flickering lamplight. It's so familiar – the feel of each other, the footwork, the flirting. *Familiar.* But what amazes me the most is how steady and sure Kai is on his feet. How articulate he manages to be even while intoxicated. I suppose some masks never seem to slip.

And then it finally happens. Kai stumbles, if only for a moment. A slight trip of his feet.

'Look who has the clumsy footwork now?' I smirk, not realizing how badly I've wanted to see him struggle during a dance. During *anything.*

He gives me a dull look. 'Yeah, well, that tends to happen when you're drunk.'

'You said you were only a little drunk, remember?'

'Fine. Then you can cut me a *little* slack.' He's looking me over, shaking his head at what he sees. 'Besides, your dress is *very* distracting. I like it.'

I huff out a laugh. 'That is a terrible excuse.'

'That's because I was giving you a compliment, not an excuse.'

'Well then that was a terrible compliment.'

I see the challenge flash in his eyes before I hear it in his voice. 'Then why don't you give me an example of a good compliment, Gray?'

I should have seen that coming. Of course he is going to use this as an excuse for me to finally flatter him – except that I won't. 'Fine,' I say curtly. 'Your hair looks very . . . soft.'

'Soft?' Kai echoes with a cough that might have been a laugh. 'Oh, come now, you can do better than that.' He leans in closer, his voice taunting as he adds, 'And if you want to run your fingers through my hair, I wouldn't be opposed to—'

'Your smile.' I cut him off before his offer can tempt me. 'I like when you truly smile. When you're not wearing the mask of the future Enforcer or the prince, and you simply allow me to see *you*. It's a smile I wish you would share with me more often.'

I swallow and fall silent. That was not at all what I intended to tell him, and yet, that doesn't make it any less true. At the sight of that smile, it's easy to forget who he is and what he does. At the sight of that smile, I see a boy instead of the king's deadly pawn. At the sight of that smile, I see someone who is more than a friend instead of someone who would kill me if they knew what I am.

And suddenly, that smile is sounding very dangerous.

'Even with my stupid dimples, you still like my smile?' Kai's words are soft, slightly breathless, and my answer is equally so.

'Even with your stupid dimples, Azer.'

His lips twitch into a variation of that smile I shouldn't be seeking out, though it's softer than the ones I've seen before. He opens his mouth and—

'Malakai.'

Our eyes snap to the queen now standing a few feet away, a pleasant smile on her stunning features. 'Do share her with the other gentleman, won't you?'

'She's mine for the night, Mother.' Kai's eyes are back on me. 'A small price to pay for ruining my clothes.'

But the queen is gone, whisked away by chattering guests and dancing figures before the words even left Kai's mouth.

I blink at him, unable to stop the smile spreading across my lips. 'Your name is *Malakai*?'

'Yes, well, I've also been called devilishly handsome, devastatingly powerful, and more recently, a cocky bastard.'

'Whoever called you that must know you quite well.'

'Yes, more than I care to admit,' he says quietly. The drone of violins fills the silence that stretches between us. When he finally speaks, Kai's question is quiet. 'Are you ready for tomorrow?'

I'm reminded of Kitt's same question at the previous ball as I say, 'Are you?'

He exhales slowly. 'I have to be.' There's a long pause.

The smile I give him is sad. 'That's not what I asked.'

'Smartass,' he mutters under his breath, managing to truly make me smile. 'The truth then?'

'The truth always.'

'Then no. I'm not ready,' he sighs, ducking his head close to mine. 'But we'll be fine. We always are.'

I nod numbly, not needing him to explain what he means. Both of our lives have been a series of trials that we've had to survive. Only now, we are going through one together, one we will fight our way out of just as we've done in the past.

As if to emphasize his words, he reaches up and flicks the tip of my nose, sharing that smile of his with me. And rather than pushing him away like I know I should, I find myself smiling back.

We settle into a comfortable silence as we spin. The garden is now bathed in moonlight, and lamps are flickering warm light over the faces swirling beside us.

Kai suddenly dips me, his fingers grazing the bare skin peeking through the slit of my dress before lazily gliding up the cool dagger resting upon my hot skin. I bite back a surprised yelp while he only laughs. 'Didn't I tell you that daggers aren't needed for dancing?'

He places me back on my feet as I breathlessly reply, 'Depends on who your partner is.'

I hate that he makes me feel like I'm always trying to catch my breath. And what I hate even more is that he knows it.

I hate it. I hate it. I hate it.

I drill those words into my head, forcing them through my thick skull.

I refuse to get caught up in *him*.

He must be able to see the battle raging in my brain because he grins at me.

Dimples.

Those *damn* dimples.

I'm practically panting now, trying to breathe, trying to ignore this boy in front of me. Trying to ignore his dazzling smiles and difficult past I now know so much about. His caring and charming side, the little things that make up him, *his hands that are on me—*

I hate it. I hate it. I hate it.

Gray eyes flick between mine, worry reflecting in them. 'Is everything alright?'

I hadn't noticed how quickly I'm breathing, how I'm trying to gulp down air and failing miserably. Kai looks suddenly sober and suddenly serious, which I can only assume means that he can see the panic plastered all over my face. His arm tightens ever so slightly around me, ever so protectively.

I hate it. I hate it. I hate it.

'Pae . . .'

Oh, why can't I hate it?

'What's wrong?' His voice is stern, cutting through my haze of hysteria.

There are so many bodies around me, so close, so pressing. The air feels so thin, so hot in my lungs. I feel so confined, so trapped. Body locking, heart leaping, mind laughing at how weak I am.

My head is spinning and so are we. I stumble to a stop – my partner, my thoughts, my breathing all halting with me. I can't swallow the panic, can't swallow down air, can't swallow my pride to admit to myself that something is *wrong*.

Calm down. You're fine.

Suddenly, I'm that little, helpless girl again. The one with the dead dad and murdered dreams. The one being beaten against a pole for stealing to survive, running to rid herself of haunting memories. The one who would curl up in a ball, crippled by grief and consumed by panic. The one who couldn't be in large crowds or small spaces without gasping for air or grappling to escape. Weak from worry, powerless from panic. No, just *powerless*.

Calm down. You're fi—

I'm having a panic attack.

The dress is abruptly too tight, squeezing my ribs, choking me, forcing the air from my lungs. The crowd around me is suddenly doing the same: squeezing me, choking me, pressing in, oblivious to how the garden packed full of people is suddenly petrifying me.

'I – I can't breathe.' The words are a gasp, and I'm embarrassed that I have to admit to him, to *myself*, a fear that hasn't haunted me in years. 'Claustrophobic.' I barely manage to get the breathless word out, but he doesn't wait for me to struggle through an explanation before I'm pressed to his side, letting him lead me to the edge of trees.

339

'Just a little farther. Hold on,' he murmurs, pushing us through the crowd and back under the dark willow. I feel the rough bark of a trunk against my back and open my eyes, not realizing I had shut them in the first place.

In the shadows, I can barely make out Kai standing in front of me, wearing the same look he had when I was bleeding out on the forest floor before him. 'Breathe, Pae. Breathe.' He seems to be struggling for air himself, his eyes scanning my face as mine dart around frantically.

'Hey, hey, hey. Look at me,' he says softly, more softly than I've ever heard him speak. And for once, I listen to him. I'm blinking rapidly, studying his shadowed face in the darkness, trying to calm myself. Though, technically, he was the reason for this panic attack in the first place. *He* made me panic. He *makes* me panic. I let my mind get out of control and spiral, my deep-rooted fear of claustrophobia only uprooting after the initial panic that was caused over *him*.

Caused by frustrating feelings for him.

I'm still breathing heavily, struggling to get enough air into my lungs. He's kept his distance from me, giving me space. But now he's slipping an arm around my back, gently, slowly.

'What are you—?'

Air floods into my lungs as if I've been underwater this whole time and only just broke through the surface. I gulp it down, greedily, relishing how it feels to fully breathe again. The panic begins to dissolve, my mind finally settling after spinning out of control.

'Much better, I'm sure.' Kai sounds relieved, though the faintest smirk is lifting his lips.

And that's when I feel it. My dress *shifts*.

I look down and nearly gasp at the gaping fabric that was once stretched tight across my chest. The waist is loosened, no longer cinched to fit my figure.

The whole dress is about to fall off me.

I clutch the top of the sleeveless gown and tug it up, gawking at him. 'What were you *thinking*—'

'I was thinking,' Kai shoves his hands in his pockets, the perfect picture of nonchalance, 'that you couldn't breathe. And as much as I like that dress on you, I figured you would look just as good in it with the laces undone.' He dips his head and smiles to himself, apparently humored by this. 'So you could breathe, of course.'

He winks. He *winks*. I'm fuming.

'I am going to—'

'Thank me?' he cuts in, pulling at the cuffs of his jacket. My eyes have adjusted to the dim light, and I'm not surprised to see the amusement reflected in his when he meets my gaze. There is no trace of the worried male only moments ago.

I have one hand holding the top of the dress up while the other grips the two pieces of the back together, since, thanks to Kai, the laces aren't doing that anymore.

'If I had a free hand right now,' I say through clenched teeth, 'I would pull my dagger on you.'

'I'm glad to see you are feeling well enough to threaten me again.' He tilts his head, giving me an assessing look.

He's right. I should thank him. I hadn't realized how tight the dress was until the panic had me panting for air. Hadn't realized that simply being able to take a deep breath again would clear my head more than I ever thought possible. Untying the laces was brilliant. But I'm not willing to tell him that.

Distraction.

The word echoes in my head, and I begin to wonder if that is what Kai is doing. Again. Using the banter as a buffer. Turning my attention from my panic and pinning it on him. Using my anger and annoyance to distract, divert. But it's not his calculating that shocks me anymore, it's his caring. It's that he understands exactly what I need.

'Pae.' He's closer to me now, all amusement wiped from his face. 'Are you alright? Truly?'

'Yes. Thank you.' His lips twitch. 'Not for *undressing* me,' I huff, 'but for . . . helping me.'

He shrugs. 'Same thing.'

I roll my eyes at him while my hand toys with the laces of my dress despite knowing I won't be able to tie them. 'Can you—' I heave a sigh, annoyed that I have to ask this of him. 'Can you tie the laces again for me?'

He studies me for a long moment. 'You should retire for the night. Get some rest.'

'Well then I'm going to have to make it back to my room without this dress falling off of me.'

His lips twitch, and I know him well enough to know that he's likely restraining from saying something wildly inappropriate in response. But when he takes a step towards me, he only says, 'Fair enough.'

'It doesn't need to be tight,' I say, turning slowly towards the tree. 'But I do need the dress to stay on.' I barely hear his soft steps behind me before I feel his fingers brush my bare back as he gathers the laces.

He pulls gently at the ties, as though almost unsure of himself. I almost laugh. The action feels far too timid to belong to the prince behind me. 'I must admit that I'm far better at undoing laces than tying them,' he says distractedly.

I huff. 'Of course you are.'

His quiet laugh stirs my hair, and I still. He tugs on the ties one last time before tying them swiftly, his calluses brushing my skin.

I suppress a shiver and turn towards him, smoothing the skirts of my gown. That gray gaze glides up my body before meeting my eyes, his voice rough when he says, 'You're not suffocating?'

'No,' I laugh, 'I'm breathing just fine. Thank you.' I move to step out from under the cover of the willow's drooping branches when Kai steps beside me.

'I'll walk you to your rooms,' he says simply.

'You don't need to do that.'

'You're right. I don't.' He threads my arm through his as we begin walking through the crowded garden towards the castle. 'But I want to.'

I duck my head and smile. 'I could get used to you being a gentleman, Azer.'

He's quiet for so long that I think he might not respond. But when he does, I hear the smile in his voice. 'And I could get used to being one for you, Gray.'

CHAPTER 38

Kai

'You're terrible at this game.'

Kitt responds with a loud laugh that is only cut off when he brings the flask to his lips and takes a sip. After swallowing, he sputters, 'The game is to drink every time Jax steps on Andy's toes. How can I be terrible at that?'

I take in my brother's flushed cheeks and messy hair, knowing I likely look the same. We've been sitting on the grass and watching guests spin across the colorful carpets under the starry sky for nearly an hour now. The rough bark of the tree I'm leaning against digs into my back now that I've discarded my suit coat, wearing only my stained button-down.

Kitt gives me a look, still patiently waiting for an answer to his question. And I don't hesitate to give him one. 'You're terrible at it because you keep missing your mouth.'

We're both laughing when Kitt wipes at the whiskey dripping down his chin. It seems we haven't outgrown our tradition of drinking during these balls, and I'm happy to see that some things never change.

'Wait for it . . .' Kitt murmurs, his eyes trained on Andy and Jax dancing with the other couples. Jax stumbles with a laugh, his long

legs getting tangled in the steps before his foot lands on top of Andy's. 'And there it is. He never disappoints.'

'Cheers,' I sigh, grabbing the flask from him to take a sip that burns my throat.

Kitt watches me. 'Are you sure you should keep drinking when you have a Trial tomorrow?'

'Have a little faith in your Enforcer, Brother. I've faced worse things than a hangover.'

When he doesn't respond, I follow his gaze, finding it pinned on Father and Mother swaying slowly.

'This is the happiest I've seen him in . . . well, years,' Kitt says quietly, all traces of humor gone from his voice. I nod in agreement, watching the king smile at his queen in the way he's only ever done for her. He never fails to give her the affection he never gave to us. To me.

With that thought in mind, I'm taking another swig from the flask. 'Maybe once the Resistance is taken care of, he'll be a happier man,'

Kitt adds with a sloppy shrug, 'Speaking of which,' he tears his eyes from the dancers to look at me, 'did you get any information out of the Silencer?'

'Killed him,' I say with an equally sloppy shrug.

He isn't the slightest bit fazed by this. 'Is that a no, then?'

I sigh. 'Yes, that's a no.'

'Hmm.' Kitt frowns. 'What about the Ordinary near Loot you were sent to find? Did you get any information then?'

The little girl's face flashes in my mind, her red hair bright like the fire in her eyes. 'The Ordinary was a child. I doubt she knew anything about the Resistance.'

We are silent for a moment before Kitt clears his throat. 'How young?'

'Too young.'

He nods slowly. 'So, you didn't go through with it?'

I stiffen slightly. Kitt and I never talk about this. Never talk about the time he found me in the stables, covered in blood and vomiting after one of my first missions into the city to kill an Ordinary. I was a boy, only fourteen when I took the life of a child not much younger than I was. And I vowed to never do it again.

344

The king has sent me on countless missions since, all a part of my training. Kitt may be the one trapped in the palace, but I have never known freedom from killing. Never known choice. So, I steal back the one stitch of sanity I can by banishing Ordinary children with their families.

Even if I am still condemning them to death.

'No, I didn't go through with it,' I answer slowly, only trusting my brother with the weight of those words. It took him years of putting pieces together before he came to my room to drink one night, confronting me when I could no longer see or think straight.

Destruction is my duty, and the king has made me grow numb to killing. But for the children, I force myself to feel.

Even monsters can have morals.

I heave a sigh, bringing the flask to my lips. 'I'm not drunk enough to talk about this right now.'

'Neither am I.' Kitt snatches the flask from my hand with a grin before his eyes drop to the stain on my shirt as if noticing it for the first time. 'What the hell happened to you?'

'Paedyn.' I sigh again. 'Paedyn happened to me.'

Kitt chuckles, but the sound is strained. 'She certainly is . . . something.'

'You have such a way with words, Kitty.'

He shakes his head and runs a hand over his face. 'I don't even have words to describe her but, Plagues, does she never fail to have words for me.'

My shoulders stiffen, but I force myself to sound relaxed. 'Does she?'

He huffs out a laugh. 'Yeah. She's the only person who doesn't tell me what I want to hear, isn't afraid to speak her mind. And quite often, might I add.'

'Would you like me to call you out on your shit more often, Brother?' I ask casually. 'Is that what I'm hearing?'

He gives me a lazy shove, ignoring my comment. 'She's got this sort of fire. Even called me an ass the other day.'

My lips twitch despite the tension coursing through me. 'Sounds about right.'

'It's strange,' he says quietly, his eyes scanning the crowded garden. 'I haven't known her for long, and yet, I find myself wanting to know her for longer.'

Silence stretches between us, his words hanging in the air.

'Maybe I was wrong,' I say stiffly. 'Perhaps you do have a way with words.'

He turns towards me with a crooked grin. 'And what do you think about her, hmm?'

My eyes drop to the stain on my shirt. I smell of wine and whiskey and the faintest hint of lavender that always clings to Paedyn. And with the way she clung to me tonight, the sweet scent of her has seeped into my clothing to distract me.

What do I think of her?

When do I not think of her?

I grab the flask from Kitt's fingers and repeat the same words I said earlier. 'I'm not drunk enough to talk about this right now.'

Lies.

Even sober she has my head spinning. I don't need to be drunk to admit what she's done to me, how she's made me *feel*.

The swishing of skirts and chatter of excitement has me looking up. I watch as the guests begin to head out of the gardens and towards the training grounds. I throw Kitt a confused glance, to which he responds, 'I have no idea.'

We stand, only slightly unsteady on our feet, and follow the crowd. Before we've even made it to the training yard lit with torches, I spot rising platforms surrounding a large dirt ring where guests begin taking seats.

Tealah steps out into the middle of the ring and spins in a circle, smiling at the guests surrounding her. 'How fun is this! Not only did we get a ball, but we also get a brawl!'

I was certainly not planning on fighting tonight.

The crowd cheers and claps as they look around, likely searching for the contestants. And I'm doing the same. There's no sign of the girls, only Jax, Braxton, and Ace on the opposite side.

I run a hand through my hair, suddenly dizzy from the alcohol and all the powers pressing down on me. The flask grows sweaty in my hand and I'm wishing I hadn't drunk so much of it even as I contemplate downing the rest. When I move to head over to the contestants, a hand grasps my arm.

'Kai.' I turn to find Kitt's eyes pinned on me. 'In case I don't see you before tomorrow . . .'

'I know,' I say, not needing to hear the three words to know that he means them. 'I know.'

'Be careful,' he says with the hint of a smile. 'And don't you dare die.'

'Don't worry. You won't be able to get rid of me that easily, Kitty.'

CHAPTER 39

Paedyn

'What is taking so long? You know, you really are a princess sometimes.' Lenny's grumble is muffled by the door separating him from my room as I tear off my dress.

'Calm down,' I mumble back. 'I'm trying not to rip my gown.'

'Yep. That's something a princess would say.'

I roll my eyes and pull on my thin training pants, pairing them with a loose cotton shirt. 'Well, would a princess be going into a fight to entertain guests at a ball?'

I slip on my boots, and my hands itch to snatch my dagger and slide it into one of them. But when Lenny came banging on my door to inform me that I was needed in the training yard for an impromptu brawl, he also made sure to mention that outside weapons were prohibited. I sigh at the sight of my silver dagger, wishing I could have it on me for comfort alone.

When I swing the door open, Lenny nearly topples over after leaning heavily on it. I snort and he gives me a sarcastic smile before we begin at a quick pace down the hallway.

'Is this normal?' I ask in a hushed whisper, leaning close to him so none of the other Imperials can overhear. 'Making us fight at a ball? And right before a Trial?'

He throws me a look, and even with the white mask obscuring half his face, I see the worry in his eyes. Lenny's emotions are always on display, always written all over his features. 'Nothing about this year's Trials is normal.'

I nod as we round the corner and head out towards the training yard. The rising platforms around the dirt ring are filled with elegantly dressed guests in green and black, looking out of place among the muddy yard. Torches surround the ring, casting eerie shadows across the excited faces in the crowd.

'Did you get any information from your prince yet? Perhaps about a certain tunnel?' Lenny asks quietly.

I sigh and shoot him a look. 'Not in the few hours since you last asked, no.'

He cracks a smile at that, but it quickly vanishes when we step up to the ring and the crowd around it. My eyes sweep over the scene, taking in Tealah at the center and the crowd leaning in to hear her every word despite it being amplified loudly.

'Since you are all unable to witness the Trials firsthand, as is typical, we have a special treat tonight!' The crowd claps as Tealah continues, 'The contestants will be selected at random to fight, and the outcome may aid in your decision of who to cast your vote for!'

My heart skips a beat.

Not only am I going to lose this, but I am also going to lose their votes.

I scan the crowd for my fellow contestants, spotting them across the ring. It seems that only the girls were allowed to change, their gowns gone while the boys still wear their pants and dress shirts.

My eyes roam over a stretching Andy next to a stiff Blair. Beside them, Jax and Braxton talk quietly while the latter begins rolling up his sleeves to reveal his massive arms. Ace stands farther off, content to stick his nose in the air and observe the crowd.

And then my eyes stop on *him*, roaming over his rolled pants and the now see-through shirt sticking to the body beneath. He's dumped water on himself in an effort to sober up, and a faint smile lifts my lips at the sight of him shaking out his wet hair.

When Tealah calls out his name, Kai lifts his head and meets the eyes of his opponent. Braxton stares back at the prince for a moment before offering him a nod and stepping into the ring. Within the next few frantic beats of my heart, the boys break into a brawl.

Unsurprisingly, Kai is sloppier than normal, which is to be expected since he isn't exactly sober. But even with his disadvantage, years of training has him quick on his feet as he falls into a familiar rhythm. The fight is fierce, captivating the crowd with every punch and dodge. Only when Kai barely manages to pin Braxton to the ground for several seconds does the crowd erupt. Imperials quickly rip them apart before they can do any more damage.

Andy and Ace's names are called next, and their fight is a fast one. Upon stepping into the ring, Andy shifts into a wolf with a sleek burgundy coat. She growls when Ace uses his typical trick of surrounding his opponents with identical illusions of himself. But with Andy in her animal form, she sticks her nose in the air and smells the real Ace among them, pouncing before he can even react. She knocks him to the ground and sinks her claws into his chest, looking far more animal than Andy.

'Next up is Blair Archer and . . .' Tealah skims the card before saying, 'Paedyn Gray!'

I let out a shaky breath while my heart slams against my ribcage.

Of course it's her.

I move towards the ring, ready to face my fate when rough fingers wrap around my wrist and whip me around. My braid flies over my shoulder and nearly hits me in the face when I turn to see Kai staring down at me. I barely glimpse the bloody cuts and bruises that are already beginning to bloom on his face before he pulls me against him.

To anyone else, it likely looks as though I stumbled into the prince.

He dips his head so his lips are brushing my ear as he begins speaking in a hushed, hurried tone. 'Stay on your toes and keep moving. You're scrappier than her so use your head and use anything you can. She's weak physically where you are not, so take advantage of it.' Then he leans back enough for me to look up into those smoky eyes as he murmurs, 'Distract her. You're good at that.'

And then his fingers find the bottom of my braid, giving it a gentle tug before giving me a quick wink and walking away.

I blink, trying to clear my head as I turn and step into the ring.

My eyes scan over the crowd, stopping only when they meet the king's from where he is sitting in a carved wooden chair beside his queen. I don't think I imagine the flicker of smug satisfaction that crosses his face, making me wonder just how *random* these pairings truly are. It wouldn't surprise me in the slightest if this were the king's doing, wanting to see Blair tear me apart just as much as the people likely do.

Kitt's smile couldn't look more different than his father's beside him. He gives me a small nod, encouraging me with one slight gesture. A flash of lilac draws my attention back to the ring and the opponent standing before me. Her hair is currently tied up with a strap, swinging back and forth as she strides forward.

The moment her feet meet the dirt, the game begins.

A knife whizzes over my head right as I drop to the ground. I hear a cynical laugh bubble from her throat as an axe flips through the air towards me. She is pelting me with weapons from the racks surrounding the ring, and though I'm not entirely sure that's allowed, I don't exactly have the time to think about it with all the dodging I'm doing.

I lunge to the side as a small, wickedly sharp knife cuts through the air, cutting my skin along the way. Hot, searing pain slices across my cheekbone, bestowed by the blade.

'Did your Psychic abilities not warn you that was coming?' she croons, continuing to hurtle scattered weapons at me. I can vaguely make out shouts coming from the crowd circling us through the blood pounding in my ears.

The only thing I've accomplished in this fight so far is tiring myself out. It's clear she doesn't want the match to end any time soon, or else she would choke me and call it a day. No, she wants to have some fun with me first, wants to show the crowd what she can do.

I can't stay on the defensive much longer, but I also don't want to end up like a pin cushion, needled with knives.

Here goes nothing.

I charge at her. But instead of running at her head-on, I zigzag. Her eyes widen slightly, clearly not expecting this, but she recovers quickly and continues to throw weapons, branches, and rocks at me.

If I can just get my hands on her . . .

She's no fighter, and she knows it. That's why she hides behind her power like most Elites do. This match would already be over if it weren't for her ability.

Despite all my zigzagging, she keeps pushing me back towards the edge of the ring. I can't gain any ground with her hurtling sharp objects and forcing me to dodge them.

A rock hits my shoulder, hard. Think. *Think*.

Blair halts her assault of flying objects only to raise me off the ground with a flick of her wrist. A strangled cry tears from my throat as I hover a meter above the packed dirt.

And then she drops me.

I hit the ground with a thud. The air rushes out of my lungs, leaving me gasping for breath. A cloud of dust drifts up from where I lie sprawled on the ground, choking on the humid air.

Get up.

Everything aches but I scramble to my feet while Blair looks slightly surprised I even bothered.

Distract her.

Kai's words ring in my head, followed by an idea.

I snatch a rock from the ground, the one that's likely the cause of my aching shoulder and clutch it in my fist. She's resumed pelting items at me, and as I dodge, duck, and roll, my fingers find a knife lying in the ring alongside several other weapons.

In one quick movement, I cock my arm back and fling the knife at her face before chucking the rock right after. She stops everything and lazily raises her hands to halt the blade and rock before they meet her, amused that this is the best I can do.

Or so she thinks.

With her full attention on stopping the objects midair, I waste no time. I tackle her around the middle, and we tumble into the dirt. With a huff, the air is knocked from her lungs, giving me seconds before she throws me off her.

But that is all I need.

This was never about winning — it was about making a point.

Proving to myself, and everyone watching, that I am still a threat. Whether I have a power like theirs or not, I will find a way to hurt them.

My fist crashes into her jaw, snapping her head to the side. She's likely unfamiliar with the pain accompanying a punch, unfamiliar with people getting this close to even try. She's stunned. I get in another solid hit to her perfect, little nose, and watch as blood gushes from it. I raise my fist again—

But she's finally come to her senses.

With a shriek, she throws me into the air like a rag doll. I collide with the hard ground and once again find myself staring up into the starry sky, gasping for air.

I hear her shriek in frustration, probably rubbing at her aching jaw and clutching her bloody nose. The sound of boots stalking angrily away tells me she's hurrying off to a Healer, refusing to be seen with injuries to her flawless face. Especially when I'm the one who gave them to her. She wouldn't dare be seen injured by a *Slummer*.

I hear clapping, cheering, and confused chattering ripple through the audience. A smile tugs at my lips and before I know it, I'm shaking with laughter. I can't stop it from bubbling out of me as I lie sprawled in the dirt.

I may have lost the match, but it's Blair who lost her pride.

CHAPTER 40

Kai

I woke up on the edge of a mountain.

Plummet Mountain.

I only know this because I've been here before with Father, casually conquering more fears and such.

But I'm not alone.

Andy groans beside me, her eyes fluttering open before she bolts upright, head swiveling as she scans her surroundings just as I had done a few minutes prior.

My head is pounding. Between all the alcohol, the fights last night, and the drug that knocked me out to be dragged here, I've felt better on the battlefield. But upon arriving at Plummet, the first thing I noticed was the pen scribbled on my hand. My slanted, hasty handwriting is scrolled across my palm, relaying a very important message:

She said I could touch her when I'm sober.

I'm shocked that I have no recollection of writing this, considering how vividly I remember everything else about last night. Paedyn pressed against me, our conversation, her panic before I untied the laces of her dress. My lips twitch at the thought before I'm suppressing a smile when I remember how she pinned Blair during their fight and made her bleed.

'Plagues, what is going on?'

Braxton is up now, blinking in the afternoon sunshine. Blair's lilac hair shimmers behind him as she sits up, looking just as confused and tense. We eye each other, remembering how brutally we fought last night and how we were forced apart before we could finish.

I pull the crumpled note from my pocket and toss it on the dirt before us. 'We were left with this.'

I hear Blair scoff as she snatches the paper up and reads aloud, her tone bored:

Welcome to Trial number two,
We think a little teamwork is due.
You have twelve hours to reach the top,
To beat the other team, you must climb nonstop.

'You've got to be kidding me,' Andy grumbles beside me, running her hands over her dirty face.

'I'm sorry,' Blair huffs, 'we're supposed to work *together*?'

Father is having fun playing with us.

He had us fight each other last night to fuel the tension between contestants and leave us wanting to tear each other apart. We were forced through several rounds of fights against random opponents, lasting well into the evening and only aiding our fatigue. And now, we're forced to work side-by-side while fighting the urge to finish what we started last night.

I stand to my feet, head throbbing as I scan the sky. The sun tells me that it's nearly mid-afternoon, which means we will be climbing through the night.

Riveting.

'We're losing daylight,' I say with a sigh. 'Let's get a move on.'

Then we are climbing, confused by this Trial and how we are expected to work together rather than rip each other apart. Plummet isn't an enormous mountain, but it is intimidating, to say the least. For the time being, we are trudging through the thick barrier of trees and rocky terrain at its base. Once we get higher, the trees will thin, replaced with steeper rocks and slippery slopes. Other than its deadly terrain, Plummet is also home to even deadlier animals. We will be climbing for twelve hours straight with no food, no water, no weapons, and no trust in one another.

I spot Sights out of the corner of my eye, swift and silent beside us as they document our progress. There must be dozens of them stationed all along the mountainside, trading off with one another, waiting for us to come into their range.

Blair and Braxton climb stiffly nearby, eying one another with equal amounts of suspicion while Andy stays close to my side, reassuring me of where her loyalties lie. She has become my only source of entertainment, her rambling taking my mind off the mountain looming above. I listen to her complain about how she would have already transformed into a falcon and left us all in the dust if it weren't for us tying her down with our *teamwork*.

'Okay,' she says, slightly breathless after climbing for nearly two hours already, 'I spy with my little eye—'

'Oh, Plagues, make it stop,' Blair whines, picking up a pinecone with her mind and chucking it at Andy. 'You've been *spying* things for nearly an hour despite being the only one playing. It's tempting me to forget about this *teamwork* thing and *rip your head off*.' She's practically growling while Andy is grinning.

'You know,' Andy says with a smug smile, 'you haven't changed one bit, Blair.' She shrugs. 'Once a bitch, always a bitch, I suppose.'

With that, Blair raises an army of pinecones off the ground in a silent threat. 'I would keep your mouth shut if I were you. Or you might just find a pinecone lodged in your throat—'

'You're only proving my point,' Andy singsongs.

Blair's abandoned the pinecones for one of the many giant rocks littering the ground. She sends it flying towards Andy and inevitably flying towards me in the process. With the flick of a hand and the borrowing of Blair's ability, the boulder changes directions, flying away from us and crashing into a nearby tree.

'That's enough, ladies.' My tone is bored, portraying my current mood. 'I'd rather not be in the middle of this.'

Braxton grunts in agreement, and we fall into a tense silence as we continue to climb. The sun crawls across the sky at a slow pace, beating down on us until sweat is rolling down my face and my throat aches for water.

Then a scream shatters the silence.

I spin to find Andy clutching her calf, her eyes glued to the ground. 'Kai.' Her voice is little more than a whisper. 'Don't. Move.'

I follow her gaze to where dozens of beady, black eyes stare back at me, forked tongues flicking. Snakes. Huge and hungry. I can't even make out how many of them there are with all the underbrush and rocks scattering the ground, but I know that there are enough for me to be worried.

Blair bites back a scream when she spots the slithering creatures surrounding us while Braxton swears under his breath.

'Alright,' I say slowly, never taking my eyes off the ground, 'this is going to have to be you and I, Blair.' She turns her wide gaze on me, her cold demeanor thawing from fear.

'What do we do?' she whispers harshly, trying to hide her horror.

I draw out a breath, not sure if I have an answer for her. The snake nearest to me is drawing closer by the second, and I eye it, mind recling. 'I'll deal with the snakes over here,' I nod to where Andy and I stand, 'and you handle yours over there.'

'*Handle?*' she hisses, sounding like one of the snakes encircling us.

'Yes. *Handle.*' I sigh. 'It's not a great plan but just . . . throw them.'

'*Throw them?*'

'Ready?' I ask, ignoring her question. She grumbles something, and I take that as a yes. 'Good.' I pause. 'Go.'

I reach out blindly with Blair's power towards the snakes slithering at our feet. I lift three of their massive bodies off the ground and send them flying far down the mountain. I hear a chorus of hisses and spot two more before letting them sail through the air after their friends.

There are dozens of them. Blair and I are sending snakes flying left and right, all of us dodging and dancing on our feet when they get too close. I hear a yelp from Andy and spin to see a snake lunging towards her, mouth wide and fangs ready to sink into flesh. I suspend it in the air before it can add another bite to Andy's leg.

After finally scrambling up and away from the nest of snakes, Andy staggers, and I'm at her side in a heartbeat. 'You got bit.' It's not a question. 'Let me see.' Her face is pale as she peels her hand from her leg, revealing two deep fang wounds, blood dribbling down her foot and into her shoes.

I brush a strand of deep, red hair from her sticky forehead, searching her eyes. 'How do you feel?'

'Well,' she chokes on a laugh, 'my pride seems to be hurting more than I am. I didn't even see the snake coming. And then the rest of them showed up and . . . I'm sorry.'

She trails off, focusing on the sun now beginning to sink behind the mountain.

'Hey, none of us saw them, remember? But I need you to tell me how you're feeling.'

Plagues, please don't be venomous.

'I feel alright. It hurts like hell, but I'm alright.'

For now.

The unspoken words hang in the air between us.

I'm hoping that our only problem is the pain she is in and nothing more. Hoping that I don't almost lose another one of the few people I can't afford to.

'Can you walk?' I ask.

She takes a step, her face scrunching in pain. 'Yeah. I'm fine.'

'Bullshit,' I mutter before crouching down in front of her. 'Come on. Get on my back.' I throw her a small smile over my shoulder. 'Just like old times.'

She laughs hoarsely. 'Seriously, I'm fine—'

'Well, clearly you're not,' Blair's agitated voice cuts in. 'So get on his damn back so we can get a move on.' She starts climbing upwards, muttering something that sounds like, 'Plagues, I hate teamwork.'

'I could try to transform into a small animal so I'm easier to carry?' Andy sounds doubtful. 'But I'm not sure I could hold that state for long . . .'

'Save your energy. Come on. Up you go.' I help her onto my back, gripping the back of her knees as she grips my shoulders. She's tall and lanky, her weight barely bothersome.

For now.

And then we are climbing again.

CHAPTER 41

Paedyn

There is a rock in my shoe. The same one that's been there for the past half hour, but my hands are too busy keeping me from falling to my death to do anything about it.

We've been climbing for hours. There are far fewer trees now, giving way to steep slopes covered in slippery plants. My hands are grasping at large boulders as I catch my breath, turning my eyes towards our destination.

The peak.

Despite our constant climbing, it still looms far above us. Jax is beside me, panting just as hard as I am. 'I think we're out of shape,' I say breathlessly.

He flashes a smile before rasping, 'You think?'

I huff out a laugh while forcing my feet to move again. My legs are shaky, strained from climbing nonstop for hours with no food and no water to aid us. I hold out a hand to Jax, helping him over a particularly steep patch of rock, returning a favor he has done for me multiple times.

'How cute.'

Jax and I stiffen at the sound of that voice, considering that the owner of it tried to kill the both of us. I bite my tongue, forcing

myself to stamp down the flare of anger igniting inside of me and ignore him instead.

Ace sighs dramatically as he continues to climb nearby. 'Well, this is awkward. The three of us being paired together to be a *team*.'

It's not awkward – it's intentional.

Everything the king does is deliberate. Twisted. And this Trial is no exception. The fights, the teams, and the tension between contestants are all calculated.

'What? Are you just going to ignore me until we reach the top?' Ace croons from behind.

I'm thankful that Jax happens to be the other Elite I'm paired with, so I don't have to fight the urge to kill both of my teammates. Though, that may be a bad thing considering that I likely trust Jax too much. But I ignore the thought just like the boy behind me and continue carefully climbing.

'At least—' Ace's words die on his tongue before he cries out, 'Paedyn! Look out!'

I turn to face him and instead spot the giant snake slithering around my ankles. A strangled scream tears from my throat before I can stop it, and I stumble. My ankle catches on a rock, and I trip, falling backward— The last thing I see before I'm about to fall down the mountain and likely to my death, is the snake scattering into shadows when my foot connects with it.

Illusion.

But it's too late. My body is falling and I'm going to tumble down the slope with no way to stop myself.

What a pathetic way to die—

Hands are suddenly at my back, pushing and pulling me to my feet before I can collide with the rocks and roll down the mountain.

'I got you,' Jax grits out behind me. 'I think.'

I reach out a hand and claw at the closest jagged rock, helping to get my feet beneath me. When I'm standing mostly upright on unsteady legs, Jax Blinks back in front of me, sweaty and panting. I'm sure I look no different, but I offer him a weak smile and hope he sees the gratitude in my gaze. This boy Blinked behind his opponent to save me from—

The thought vanishes from my head, along with any other rational one that might have been residing there. I whirl on Ace even as I cling to a rock, not trusting my shaking body.

His smile is cold. 'Careful. I wouldn't want my teammate to get hurt.'

'*You*,' I spit. I'm about to slide down the slope and strangle him with my bare hands—

'Don't,' Jax says quietly. 'Not yet.'

I hesitate, slowly returning my eyes to his dark ones. After a long pause and a deep breath, I nod. Jax is not only right for reminding me I can't kill our teammate, but he's clearly far better at reining in his rage than I am. So, I stiffly turn back towards the mountain, focusing all my attention on scaling it.

We climb in silence for a moment before I clear my dry throat and say softly, 'Thank you, Jax. You didn't have to help me, but you did.'

'Of course I helped you,' he says with a shrug. 'Besides, I'm not sure my brothers would forgive me if I hadn't.'

His brothers.

That night Kai and I danced during the first Trial – the night we spoke so openly about our lives – was when I had first learned of just how close the princes truly are with Jax. Kai briefly told me of the advisers' shipwreck on the Shallows, and how they took their son in when he was barely six.

I force out a quiet laugh. 'I don't know, I'm sure Kai wouldn't mind having less competition.'

He gives me an odd look, clearly trying not to laugh. 'Not if that competition is you.' I huff in response, but Jax carries on cheerfully. 'Speaking of Kai, I wonder how he is handling this.'

'Handling what?'

Jax pulls himself over a jagged rock with a grunt before breathlessly saying, 'The mountain.' When my expression remains confused, Jax adds, 'He hates heights.'

'What?' I choke out. 'But I watched him climb up one of the pines in the Whispers during the first Trial. He seemed—'

'Fine?' Jax finishes for me with a laugh. 'Calm even? Yeah, he's pretty good at hiding what he feels.'

'Just another mask he slips on,' I mutter under my breath.

Jax nods, causing a bead of sweat to roll down his face. 'He's gotten a lot better with heights though, but only because of all the training the king put him through.'

I knew enough about the king's twisted *training*, but Kai had never mentioned anything about his fear of heights. 'What did the king do?'

'He . . . he made him climb the highest trees in the Whispers, over and over again until he was convinced Kai had gotten over his fear.'

'What?' My voice is as shaky as the legs carrying me up this mountain. *His own father forced him to relive his worst fear over and over again.*

It seems that the torture Kai spoke of enduring was not all physical. 'I was little when Kai was going through most of his training to be the future Enforcer, but I'll never forget the nights he would come home covered in blood and tears.' Jax looks down at his feet, suddenly more serious than I've ever seen him before. 'I think he was afraid that I'd be scared of him, so he'd sneak back into his room every night. But I still caught glimpses of him, heard him hacking at his bedposts with a sword.' We climb in silence for a moment, and I ignore my screaming thoughts just as I ignore the tightness in my throat and the pressure behind my eyes. Then a weary smile spreads across Jax's lips as he says, 'But I couldn't ask for better brothers.'

'I'd hate to interrupt your cute conversation,' Ace drawls, 'but am I the only one who feels that?'

I'm about to dismiss what is likely another attempt to trick me with an illusion when I start to feel it. A slight tremor runs through me, coming from the mountain. The small rocks are rattling around us, and I bend closer to the ground, clutching at anything to hold on to.

'Rockslide,' I breathe.

Dread floods me, followed quickly by determination.

I will not die today. Least of all, from rocks.

I swallow down my panic at the sound of heavy boulders tumbling towards us, crashing against one another as they race to crush us. 'So,' Jax pants beside me, 'what's the plan?'

'Don't die,' I say simply.

'How incredibly helpful,' Ace mutters, far too casually for our current situation.

The rumble of rocks grows louder as I watch the boulders come tumbling towards us. Dodging them is far easier said than done. The mountainside is steep, making it hard to jump around without fear of falling to our deaths. I'm grasping at plants and divots in the rocks beneath me as I scramble out of the way of the rolling boulders.

Jax is Blinking out of the path of falling rocks, flickering in and out of my vision. Ace is somewhere behind me, and if I'm lucky, a boulder has already sent him tumbling down the mountain.

I scramble to the right, barely saving my arm from being crushed. Then I jump to the left and—

Something collides with the side of my head.

Spots dance in my vision. I'm dizzy, dazed, only vaguely comprehending that my name is being shouted. I look up just in time to see that I'm about to be flattened by a boulder. I dive out of the way, landing hard as I claw at anything to grab hold of. And as quickly as it happened, the mountain seems to still beneath me as the rocks slowly stop their slide.

I struggle to my feet, blinking away the hot, heavy liquid that is threatening to spill into my eyes. I can feel the blood oozing down the side of my face, can feel the pounding pain of the wound there. I'm almost certain I have a concussion, just like I'm almost certain I'm going to puke.

'Jax? Are you alright?' I call, taking a step forward and reaching out to steady myself against the rocks. Yes, I think I'm going to be sick.

'I'm okay,' he calls, Blinking in front of me. We are both covered in scrapes and bruises already beginning to bloom across our skin.

'Thank you for asking, Paedyn. I am quite alright,' Ace says, his voice lacking any tone or tenderness.

I wipe the back of my hand over my eye, clearing it of the blood that is dripping from my wound. 'How unfortunate.'

CHAPTER 42

Kai

Everything aches. My feet. My back. My *body*.

I'm achingly tired, achingly hungry, and achingly aware of how annoyed I am with myself because of it. I've endured torture, faced my worst fears, led armies into battle, and yet, climbing a mountain with a hangover may just be the death of me.

Andy clinging to my back isn't helping either. It's not her weight that's the problem, especially since I'm borrowing Braxton's strength. No, it's the fact that she is so damn lanky that her long limbs are hindering my climbing.

'It's absurd how bony you are,' I mumble, earning a weak punch in the shoulder.

Good. At least she has the strength to hit me.

'When we make it out of here,' I continue casually, 'I'll make sticky buns myself to fatten you up.'

She grunts her approval of that idea, her voice weak. She is fading fast. Her skin is sickly pale, only emphasized by the moonlight, and her breathing is quick and shallow.

I know the difference between pain and venom, and this is certainly the latter.

So, I keep her awake, keep her occupied. My voice is low as I

quietly talk to her, teasing her and reminiscing on old times. She mostly responds with breathy laughs or a nod of her head, but I'll take anything over silence.

The moon is our only guide, casting pale light that does little to illuminate the mountain we have been climbing since the moment we woke up. The terrain is so steep now that Andy is clinging to me with her legs wrapped around my waist, freeing my hands to help me climb.

I feel her head slump against my shoulder, overcome by exhaustion and excruciating pain. 'Hey,' I say softly, gently jostling her to keep her awake. 'We're almost there. Just a little longer.' I feel her nod wearily and try to pick up my pace.

I can see the flat plateau of the peak looming above us.

Nearly there.

I'm climbing, hands scraping at the stone and rocks slipping from beneath me. I've lost my footing, lost my hold more than once and almost sent us falling to an unfortunate death. But we are nearly there. This nightmare is nearly over. We're nearly free.

I see the shadows of figures lined all around us. Awaiting us. The Sights watch as we scramble to the top, breathless and beaded with sweat, starving and exhausted.

Exhilarated.

We've done it.

I drag myself over the edge, Andy clinging to me fiercely. Only my dignity forces me to my feet, though fatigue threatens to cripple me.

'We did it,' Braxton exhales beside me as we all stand, stunned. The plateau is a large slab of uneven rock and dirt, stretching far wider than it appears from below. I look around, scanning my surroundings, spotting dozens of Sights dotting the peak.

Then my eyes sweep over a tall, wooden pole, buried into the ground at the far end of the peak. A green, battered flag hangs at its top, whipping in the wind.

What new game is this?

Movement stirs in the corner of my eye, and I squint in the dim light to focus on the figures climbing up the opposite side of the plateau, joining us. And despite the darkness, I know exactly who they are.

Jax. Ace. Paedyn.

We all stare at each other, each group stunned and still.

A Sight steps forward, his voice clear as he reads a message off the tattered paper in his hand. 'We are glad you learned to work as one, but oh, this Trial is not done. The rules of the game have changed a bit, so the first to capture the flag will win it.' He clears his throat before continuing, 'There can only be one winner among you. The only question is *who*?'

Silence. Stillness.

His words sink in, seeping their way into my brain. I shouldn't be surprised. This will make for great entertainment, watching us work together only to tear each other apart in the end.

Because it was too easy, despite how very difficult it was to reach the top of Plummet. And I should know by now that there is always a catch, always a price. My own father taught me that.

We all stare at each other, eyes shifting between our competition and the ragged flag that has suddenly become so vital to our victory.

And then we turn on one another. Chaos.

CHAPTER 43

Paedyn

Darkness and destruction are all I know. The two groups crash together, powers clashing, shouts cutting through the night. But when my eyes find his in the dim light, I don't hesitate before my fist collides with his jaw.

Ace stumbles back, stunned by the force and fury I packed into the punch. I smile at the sight. I've been itching to do that all day. *Every day.*

The fight around us falls away. All I see is him and the red blurring my vision, the cause of both blood and rage morphing together.

I'm going to kill him.

My foot sinks into his stomach, forcing the air from his lungs before I throw a jab at his nose, feeling it crack with sickening delight. My body is my only weapon. I have no knives, no bow, no swords to hide behind. But I wouldn't have it any other way. I want to do this with my bare hands.

I'm almost impressed by how twisted and talented the king is at putting on a show. He knew that we went into this Trial hoping to get revenge and instead told us to work together. So our enemies became our teammates. But now, the king is giving us and the people what they want.

We are tearing each other apart.

Ace has finally caught his breath, panting as he smirks up at me, hands resting on his knees. 'Oh, you've just been waiting to do that, haven't you?'

'Ever since that coach ride to the castle, actually,' I say, remembering how I disliked him even then, even before he attempted to kill me. Twice. 'Well, I've never really liked you much either,' he spits as blood streams from his nose and drips down to his chin. I move, aiming to send a kick cracking into his temple, but I'm suddenly shrouded in darkness.

It's as though he's thrown a heavy blanket over my head, smothering the light around me.

Now I'm angry *and* annoyed.

But I know how this game works and wave my arms, taking a few steps forward. The illusion pulls apart, and like smoke, the darkness blows away on the wind. I blink, eyes adjusting as I try to find Ace in the commotion.

And then I'm choking.

The air is being cut off from my lungs, my windpipe being crushed. A hard, rough object is pressed against my throat, forcing me to gasp as I try to gulp down air. I claw at the thing pressing against my neck, the thing separating me from life and death.

I kick at Ace behind me, twisting and fighting to slip out of his hold. Rough bark is biting into my nails as I tear at it, trying to rid myself of its choking hold on me. I'm being strangled with a stick.

A stick.

My vision is spotting, the wound on my head throbbing, my lungs screaming for air.

No. Not today. Death can claim me when it finds a less pathetic way to end my existence.

I still my frantic hands and stop struggling, willing myself to slump, to sag, to stop looking like I'm alive and seething with anger. I let my knees buckle, the branch sliding from my neck as I crumble to the ground.

'Never forget that your wit is a weapon to be wielded if only your mind is as sharp as your blade.'

My father's words echo in my head, reminding me that not all battles are won with brawn. So I'll win this one with brains.

My limbs are a tangled mess in the dirt, and my head has landed painfully on a jagged rock. But I can breathe again. Barely. I force myself to take shallow breaths, willing my attacker to step closer and finish the job.

Boots crunch over loose rocks before a body crouches over my limp one. A deep, labored sigh washes over me and the faintest brush of fingers over my brow nearly makes me flinch.

'Such a shame that the pretty ones are always *bitches*.' Ace tucks a strand of hair behind my ear, almost gently. It makes me sick. 'Such a shame. Such a *waste*.'

His hand begins to pull back and I know I need to act. My eyes fly open and his do the same as he looks at me, shocked. He's crouched over my body, one of his hands caught in my own, and the other clutching a rock only slightly smaller than the size of my head.

He was going to bash my skull in.

In one quick movement, I twist his arm at an odd angle, hearing the bone snap and a scream tear from his throat. I lift my legs and push my feet against his chest, throwing him sideways with a powerful push. He's thrown onto his back beside me, the rock tumbling from his hand.

I'm on top of him within the next beat of my hammering heart.

My knees are pressing his arms to the ground, letting my full weight settle on his chest. I bring my hand down on his wrist, pressing on the broken bone now jutting against his skin. I never thought a scream could bring me so much joy.

'Such a shame I don't have my knife to carve out your black heart.' I'm smiling, relishing the pure hatred flaring in his eyes, knowing he must see the same reflected in my own gaze. 'Such a *shame*.'

When did I become this vicious?

Something catches my eye and my attention darts to the wispy figures now encircling us.

It's me.

Dozens of sickly, pale Paedyns. They're stumbling closer, arms outstretched and reaching for me. They're pushing towards me as they plead for help, plead to be put out of their misery.

I stare at them, and they stare at me. And then I smile, sad and slow.

'I'm not afraid of myself anymore,' I whisper.

That girl – that haunted, weak girl begging for help, for love – is *me*. Without her, I wouldn't be who I am today. I'm still haunted, maybe even still hoping for love, but I am no longer weak because of it.

And when my gaze slides back to Ace, I'm no longer smiling. 'You think you can use myself against me? Again?' My laugh is humorless. 'Fool me once, shame on me. Fool me twice – well, you won't get a chance to do that, now will you?' I cock my head, peering down at his face now twisted in pain.

I grab the rock that was intended for my skull and raise it above his instead. 'Goodbye, Ace,' I say breathlessly, wondering if I should be feeling any remorse for this boy.

Something shifts in my peripheral.

The illusions are gone now, drifting away as Ace weakens from pain beneath me, allowing me to dare a glance at the figure close by.

He is covered in blood, most of which likely doesn't even belong to him. Our eyes meet, and the sound of the fight around me that was once so deafening begins to dull. The connection is electric, empowering even, as he watches me but does nothing to stand in my way. Does nothing to try and convince me not to take a life. Does nothing because he knows I can handle myself.

Does nothing because Kai would do no differently.

The boy beneath me tried to kill his brother, tried to get Kai to do it for him. And as I stare into the gray eyes of the prince, the future Enforcer, the deliverer of death, I know that he has been patiently waiting to kill him. Patiently waiting for revenge.

And yet, he is simply standing there, dripping with blood, and doing nothing to stop me from ripping his revenge away from him.

This is not my life to take.

'I would kill you . . .' My voice is stern and strong, loud enough for Kai to hear. I see Ace's eyes light up with the assumption that I'm too weak to go through with ending his life. How very wrong he is. 'But you are not mine to kill,' I finish, watching as his eyes darken, hatred replacing hope. My gaze finds Kai's again, his eyes bright in the moonlight and smoldering like smoke from a fire. A muscle ticks in his jaw, his hands twitch at his sides. I give him a single, slow nod.

And then he is striding towards us, shadows clinging to his silhouette. I barely have time to get off Ace before Kai is hoisting him to his feet with powerful arms. 'You're lucky I don't have the time or patience to rip you limb from limb at the moment.'

Then Kai's eyes flick to me, flick over me. The future Enforcer is resisting his urge for revenge and instead scanning my body for injuries. The thought has me swallowing the lump in my throat as his gaze lingers on the gash still gushing on my head before slowly sliding to my neck which is likely already bruising. Then his eyes dart to something far behind me.

The flag.

No one has made it there yet, too busy fighting and focused on revenge to break away. When I look back at Kai, his eyes are already trained on me. 'Go,' he murmurs the word, nodding towards the flag that will bring me victory. 'Win this damn thing, Gray.'

I blink at him, but his attention is already back on the task in front of him. So I turn towards the flag. My boots scrape against the rocks beneath my feet as I stride towards that seemingly insignificant piece of cloth.

Screams join the shouts and cries of the fight, and I don't need to turn around to know that Kai has begun his work on Ace. I ignore it, my focus solely on the flag.

And then I'm suddenly standing beneath it, looking up at my prize.

Looking up at my victory.

And no one stops me as I rip off the flag.

CHAPTER 44

Funny how killing makes me feel most alive. I feel lighter than I have in days. My mind is clearer, sharper, now that thoughts of Ace are no longer consuming it.

My only regret is that I didn't have more time to play with him, and if I were a better man, that thought might have repulsed me.

The recap of the Trial was tedious, mostly consisting of each team trudging up the mountain in silence. But the final fight atop the peak was enough to have the bored crowd cheering. The chaos was captured by the Sights and replayed for me to relive.

I watched Paedyn meet my eyes and grant me a gift. The gift of a life. The gift to take a life.

She handed Ace over to me despite wanting to dole out his death herself. She let me have my revenge without even knowing that it was partially for her. Because before I wanted to kill Ace for nearly killing Jax, I wanted to kill Ace for nearly killing Paedyn.

Death is no stranger to me. I've killed more than I can count, and the blood clinging to my hands and staining my soul can never be scrubbed clean. And yet, she looked at me as if I was *deserving* of Ace, of kindness, of—

Her. I only want to be deserving of her.

I watched as Death claimed another victim. Blair was the one who brutally took Braxton's life. Well, she can't take all the credit. I may have helped. Her mind sent a blunt branch that was scattered on the ground into his chest. Flesh and bone tore apart, making room for the new addition impaling his body. It slowly leached the life from his surprised eyes before he fell to the ground.

But the surprise in Braxton's gaze reflected in Blair's.

She wasn't aiming for Braxton. No, that blunt, brutal death was heading for the silver-haired girl striding unsuspectingly towards her victory. I may have cheated Death of its intended victim, but I gave it a life, nonetheless. I borrowed Blair's power and nudged fate in another direction. And it found Braxton.

But I wouldn't hesitate to do it again, and again, and again to save that silver-haired girl.

Quite the team, Death and I.

But I've had three days to recover from the Trial. Three long days spent in the training yard, slicked with sweat, or locked within a study with my father's Silencer where I am also likely drenched in sweat. Damion pushes me hard, smothering me with his ability while I fight to use it against him.

Whether it's my body or brain aching from either type of training, I welcome it. Distraction is the best form of passing the time, and I seem to have a lot of things I wish to be distracted from these days.

'Kai, are you listening, boy?'

I give my head a shake, returning to the conversation at hand. 'Intently, Father.'

The king sighs deeply and Kitt cuts me a look. We've been stuffed in his study for hours, discussing everything from guard rotations to the Resistance, which we have no new information on since the few prisoners from the attack at the first ball are now all dead. Although, Father doesn't seem particularly concerned by that fact now and has instead been talking about the Trials for far longer than I have been listening.

He eyes the two of us as he asks slowly, 'It is *interesting* how the Slummer girl won this last one, don't you think?'

I stiffen, and I think Kitt might have done the same.

I all but handed the victory to her, choosing revenge over winning. Torture over triumph. I wonder if Father knows this. Knows that I let her walk over to that flag without another thought. Knows that I smiled at the sight of her, strong and sure, as she raised that flag into the air.

'She won fairly. I don't find that *interesting*.' The words are out of my mouth before I can think better of them.

A humorless chuckle fills the room. 'That's just the thing,' Father says, green eyes piercing through me in a way Kitt's never could. 'Slummers don't win.'

I stiffen at the word he spits but don't dare to break his stare. 'And yet she did.'

Kitt shoots me a look, but my eyes are pinned on the king as he says, 'And you better not let it happen again. Don't forget that it is you who must win these Trials, and if you need me to remind you what will happen if you don't, I will.' He leans forward, his voice lethal. 'I trained you for this, so you will not disappoint me. Understood, Enforcer?'

The threat in his tone is clear, and I hear it ringing in my ears.

Lose and you are nothing.

'Understood, Your Majesty.'

And with that, I stand to my feet and stride out the door. I'm pacing the halls, feeling like I need to hit something, need to drive my sword into my bedpost for the hundredth time. After all my years of training and mastering my masks, it's always been my father who is the only one able to make me lose control. I drag my hand through my hair as I make my way back towards my room, collecting myself with every step.

'Kai.'

I run a hand down my face, sighing as I spin to face a very unhappy Kitt. 'What the hell was that?' he asks harshly.

I almost laugh. 'That was one of the more civil conversations we've had, and you know it.'

Kitt heaves a sigh, sounding tired. 'Look, I know your relationship with Father is . . . difficult. I get it. After all the training he put you through and the expectations he has for you now, believe me, I get

374

why you two have trouble getting along. But everything he does is for the best.'

I scoff and shake my head at the ceiling, wondering if Kitt will ever stop trying to prove himself to the king. 'You know, you might think differently if he had cut you open as a boy and watched you try to stitch the wound.' I take a step towards him. 'Or maybe after being forced to face your worst fears over and over and *over again*, you would realize that not everything he does is for the *best*.'

I laugh bitterly, and Kitt nearly flinches at the sound. 'He made me a murderer, molded me into a monster. But that was for the *best* right?' I jab a finger into his chest as I say, 'That was for your benefit, so you can use me when you're king. Just like he has.'

Wrong thing to say.

The words hit him like a physical blow. I see the shock and hurt settle on his face as I force myself to take a step back, to calm down. I'm losing my temper for reasons I don't even understand, and that is only making me angrier. It's as though every pent-up piece of my past is fighting to free itself, fighting to flood to the surface.

'Kai—'

'I think you will make a great king, Kitt,' I say quietly, cutting through his words. 'And I will proudly serve you. But you need to learn to think on your own because one day, Father won't be there to do it for you. So, I suggest you start figuring out what *you* think is for the best.'

And with that, I turn and head down the hall.

CHAPTER 45

Paedyn

The gardens are quiet at night. Only the chorus of chirping crickets and the soft howl of the wind follow me as I make my way to the familiar willow bordering the open lawn where the last ball took place.

I've come here often since that night, finding comfort in the shelter of the shadowy willow when I can't sleep. I've grown used to sitting under there for hours, simply allowing myself time to think.

Brushing aside the low-hanging branches, I step underneath the canopy of leaves. I sigh, suddenly feeling more settled as I breathe in the warm night air.

But the peace I feel is short-lived when a shadow shifts beside the trunk.

I whirl, my fingers flying towards the dagger at my thigh only to be caught by a rough hand. 'Easy, Gray, it's just me.'

I blink through the darkness as my eyes adjust to the dim light, landing on the amused gray ones before me. 'What are you doing here?' I sputter.

'I could ask you the same question.'

'And I could have stabbed you!'

Kai's brows raise. 'So you're not going to try? I'd say that's progress.'

'Oh, but I should for you scaring me like that.'

He lets go of my hand slowly, studying me all the while. 'I scared *you*? You're the one who crept up on me.'

'Well, I didn't exactly know you would be here,' I whisper harshly.

'Clearly,' he says with a smirk twisting his lips. 'But you're more than welcome to stay.' And then he settles himself onto the ground, looking rather comfortable with his arm tucked behind his head.

I stare at him. 'What are you doing?'

'Waiting for you to get down here and join me.'

I stand there, watching the slow smile spread across his face.

'Is it the dress?' he asks as he sits up and begins shrugging off his suit coat. When it's slid off his shoulders, he lays it on the ground beside him. 'There, now you won't get all dirty.'

I look down at the simple silk dress I slipped on for our dinner with the king and queen. It's rather comfortable, and I was far too lazy to take it off before making my way out here. Kai must have felt similarly since he's still wearing his fine attire.

But my hesitance to join him has nothing to do with dirtying my dress and everything to do with the fact that I shouldn't stay here. What I should do is turn, wish him goodnight, and head back to my room without another word. And yet, my feet make no move to carry me away from him.

He pats the coat expectantly, and the sight has a choked laugh slipping past my lips. 'How very gentlemanly of you, but that coat is not nearly big enough to save my dress from getting dirty.'

'I can take off my shirt and lay that down for you as well if you like,' he says casually.

'On second thought,' I mutter, 'the coat will suffice.' He chuckles and I'm suddenly walking towards him, ignoring my screaming thoughts that tell me to do otherwise. I sit and slowly lie down beside him, our shoulders brushing. We are quiet for a long moment, both of us content to stare up at the drooping canopy of leaves above while listening to the crickets chirping beside us.

I'm almost reluctant to break the comfortable quiet, but I ask softly, 'Why are you here?'

He almost laughs. 'I've been coming here since I was a boy. In fact,

I fell out of this very tree after Kitt dared me to climb it. Broke my arm, too—' A bubble of laughter slips past my lips, cutting him off. 'Are you laughing at me, Gray?' He's trying to fight his own smile as he adds, 'I'm glad you find my pain so amusing.'

I clear my throat, trying to compose myself. 'So, what, you come here to reminisce on the fond memory?'

'Something like that.' He sighs. 'I come here to think, to cool off. I've always liked the quiet out here. The escape from the palace.' He glances over at me before asking, 'So why are you here?'

I smile slightly and echo his words. 'To think. I like the quiet. The escape.'

I see his lips twitch out of the corner of my eye, and we are quiet for a moment before I ask, 'Is there a reason you dragged me down onto the dirt?'

I look over at his shadowy profile as he stares at the branches above us. 'To talk. To lie here in silence.' He shrugs lazily. 'It doesn't really matter.'

I look away from him. 'So, you just want someone to keep you company?'

'Not someone. You.'

I can feel his eyes on me, but I don't turn to look at him. 'Do you want quiet company or talking company?'

He makes a sound that might have been a laugh. 'Only you would ask me my preference on your company.'

I finally turn my head to meet his gaze. 'That wasn't an answer.'

He's quiet for a long moment, seeming to study my face, search my eyes. 'Talk to me.'

I stare at him, my voice suddenly very quiet when I finally ask, 'About what?'

I watch a faint smile curve his lips. 'Anything. Everything. What you're thinking at this very moment, darling.'

I almost laugh. 'Well, I'm currently thinking that this coat I'm lying on is far too itchy for a prince to wear.' He chuckles while I add, 'And I'm also wondering how many bones you and Kitt broke.'

'Too many,' Kai sighs, shaking his head. 'It was mostly me with the broken bones and injuries, though not all of them were due to Kitt's brilliant ideas.' He pauses. 'Most were from my training. Especially when I was learning to use a Healer's ability.'

When his words sink in, I stiffen. 'You don't mean . . .' I trail off before trying again. 'You didn't have to—'

'Yes, I did,' he says simply, looking me right in the eyes. 'I had to break my bones and then heal them. Or sometimes I'd be sliced open with a sword and have to learn how to stitch my own skin back together.'

He says this so casually that I can't even begin to imagine the horrors he has been forced through. 'How do you not hate him?' I whisper.

Silence stretches between us.

The small smile he wears is sad. 'Because he made me strong.'

He says this far too calmly, and I want to shake him of his cool composure. It doesn't matter how *strong* the king made him. The prince before me has been nothing but a pawn created by the man he calls Father. The thought makes me sick, makes me want to scream.

And yet, I understand.

His words strike me, hitting home. Our lives seem to share sad similarities, unfortunate fates. Both our childhoods consisted of training to become what we had to be, neither of us growing up the way we wished. Except, the fathers who raised us couldn't be more different – one doing everything out of love, the other out of greed.

People aren't born strong; they're made that way. And the prince and I know that better than most.

Kai continues casually as though his words didn't just knock the air from my lungs. 'Well, Kitt and I suffered several injuries for our stupidity, but not all of our games were dangerous. In fact, because our favorite activities as boys likely consisted of some sort of violence, my tutor would make us sit and play games she considered *safe*.' He heaves a sigh. 'We considered them boring.'

'Oh really?' I huff out a laugh. 'What games?'

'Well,' he reaches out a hand to take hold of mine, 'Madame Platt's personal favorite to torture us with was thumb wars. Though, we'd still find a way to make even those violent.'

'Thumb wars?' My brows crinkle in confusion. 'That has the word *war* in it, and it's still considered safe?'

I've never seen Kai look so bewildered before, and I nearly laugh again. 'You've never heard of a thumb war?'

His own thumb strokes over my knuckles, forcing me to focus on my next words. 'Well, in the slums, the only game I tended to play was trying to guess how many coins were in someone's pocket before I stole them.'

The corner of his mouth kicks upward. 'And did you play that game before you robbed me?'

'No, but I would have lost if I had,' I huff. 'You had far more silvers than I'd ever seen in one place.'

'Well, only until you stole half of them.'

I smile at that, and he watches me quietly for a moment. When my eyes drop to where he's still holding my hand and distracting me with that thumb still sliding over my knuckles, he clears his throat and finally says, 'Well, the game I'm going to teach you isn't nearly as fun as yours, I'm sure.' Then he shakes his head at me, muttering under his breath, 'I cannot believe you don't know what a thumb war is.'

'Well, from the way you talk about it, it doesn't seem like I'm missing out on much.'

'Very fair point.' His lips twitch into a smirk. 'And that's exactly why I'm going to teach it to you, so we can suffer together.' He twists onto his side and props himself up on an elbow, watching as I do the same. 'The rules of this *very* riveting game are simple.' He curls our fingers together as I watch. Then he chuckles and reaches out with his other hand to pull my thumb into the air. 'Now, you win by pinning the other person's thumb down, but you have to keep your hand and arm still.' He peeks up at me and asks, 'Understand?'

I frown at our joined hands. 'I'm starting to understand why you find this game so boring.'

He laughs before muttering, 'Go.'

I don't even have time to react before his thumb is crushing mine, pinning it to my hand. When he looks up at me, his smile is smug. 'I really thought your reflexes would be quicker than that, Gray.'

'I wasn't ready, Azer.'

'Well, that's kind of the whole point of *reflexes*.'

I halfheartedly roll my eyes at him. 'You're insufferable.'

'And yet, you're still here,' he says softly, his eyes bright even in the dim light as they flick between mine.

We are quiet for a moment as I assess how to beat him at this game. Per usual, distraction seems to be the best option, so I say, 'Tell me something I don't know about you.'

He only seems slightly surprised by my random request, but it only takes him a moment to answer. 'Blueberries. I don't like them.'

I choke back my laugh. 'You don't like blueberries?'

'No, I take it back.' He pauses, seeming to consider something. 'I hate blueberries.'

'Is there a reason for this loathing?'

'Have you tasted them?' he asks, and I nod in answer. 'Then, there. That's my reason. They're disgusting.'

I huff out a laugh, and when he opens his mouth to say something, I cut him off with a quiet, 'Go.'

My thumb lands on his and I'm about to brag my victory when he easily slips it out from beneath mine. And then, once again, he has my thumb pinned. 'Adorable effort to distract me, darling.'

I sigh in frustration. 'I see why you hate this game.'

'No, I hate this game because it's boring. You hate this game because you're bad at it.'

I glare at him, and he grins at me. His thumb sweeps down the length of mine, and I refuse to tear my eyes from his. 'Now,' he says slowly, 'tell me something I don't know about you.'

'Easy.' I give him a bright smile. 'I *love* blueberries.'

Kai groans. 'Of course you do.'

'They are just *delicious*. I mean, talk about the perfect blend of tart and sweet and—'

'I am never going to hear the end of this, am I?'

'—honestly, I think they might be the best fruit out there. I could easily eat them with every meal and—'

Kai leans closer and sighs out an exasperated, 'Paedyn.' I clamp my mouth shut at the sound of my name. 'I am content to listen to you talk for hours, but if you must speak about fruit, then at least pick one we both enjoy.'

I press my lips together to smother my smile. The future Enforcer is willing to listen to me ramble about *fruit*. The thought has me on the verge of both bursting out in laughter and blushing from head to toe.

'Fair enough,' I say simply. 'How about oranges?'

He makes a face. 'I don't like pulp.'

'Fine. Bananas?'

'I hate the texture.'

'Is there any fruit you *do* like?' I huff, shaking my head at him. 'You are the pickiest prince I know.'

'I am one of the two princes you know, and trust me, Kitt is not much better than I am.'

I give him a pointed look. 'I'm still waiting to hear a fruit you don't find repulsive.'

He's quiet for a moment, pondering his answer while his thumb runs idly over my own. 'Strawberries.'

I blink at him. 'I love strawberries.'

A slow smile tips up his lips. 'And I find them not repulsive.'

'Good.'

'Good.'

'Go.'

The word tumbles from my mouth, and I take advantage of his surprise. Determination drives me as I fight to pin his thumb down, moving my hand and arm in the process. I nearly fall on top of him to finally get my thumb to land on his, though I've broken the rules to do it.

And then I'm suddenly being tugged fully against his body.

He yanks on my arm, pulling me close enough to count the dark lashes surrounding his eyes. 'You cheated, Gray.'

'I did what I had to do to win, Azer.'

'Hmm,' he hums, and I feel it vibrate through his chest. 'I suppose it's my fault for forgetting what a vicious little thing you are.'

'Well, I—'

The words die in my throat when he uncurls his hand from mine and trails his fingers down my arm. I suppress a shiver at his sudden touch, but the smile that lifts his lips tells me it didn't go unnoticed.

'I take it back,' he says softly. 'This game isn't boring in the least bit when I play it with you.' His gaze has dropped to the fingers gliding over my arm, and I still under his gentle touch.

I'm not sure how long we stay like that, listening to the wind rustling the leaves above us as we study one another. And it's only when his fingers trail up my neck to tuck a stray piece of hair behind my ear that I finally come to my senses.

'I should go.'

The unsure words hang between us, barely more than a whisper that the wind nearly steals away.

'That doesn't sound like what you want to do at all,' he murmurs.

I refuse to even puzzle out what it is that I *want* to do, so I say instead, 'One of these days, I'm going to beat you fairly in a thumb war, and then you won't find it so fun.'

He chuckles softly, followed by an equally soft murmur. 'It's not the winning I find fun. It's you, darling.'

After a moment too long, I pull myself out of his hold and sit up slowly. The night has grown colder, and without the heat of Kai's body next to mine, my thin dress does little to keep me warm.

Kai sits up beside me and wraps his jacket around my shoulders. 'You're right. That coat is far too itchy for a prince to wear.' Then his lips twitch into a smirk. 'So, I'll let you wear it instead.'

CHAPTER 46

Paedyn

I clamp my hands over my ears, shielding them from the loud squealing.

'Okay, what do you think?!' Adena is beaming, gesturing wildly to the partially made dress draped across my bed.

'Wow,' Ellie breathes, leaning over my shoulder to get a better look at it. 'It's . . .' she trails off as her eyes trail over the fabric.

'Perfect,' I finish for her. 'Absolutely stunning. You've outdone yourself, A.' I give her a smile, wide and full of wonder at how one person could be so talented.

'Well,' she huffs, snatching the half-made dress off the bed and settling it on her lap again. 'It's not finished yet. I only have two more days until the final ball, and it needs to be absolutely perfect—'

'A.' I give her a knowing look. 'Don't stress, it will be perfect.' Then I snort, shaking my head. 'You could put me in a flour sack and somehow make it look good.'

Adena looks truly alarmed at that suggestion. 'I would *never* put you in a flour sack.' She taps a finger to her lips thoughtfully. 'And not only because it would be hideous, even on you, but because the fabric is much too scratchy, too stiff to—' Her big, hazel eyes dart between Ellie and I trying to suppress our smiles and failing. 'What?'

Her hands are on her hips, eyebrows quirked, legs crisscrossed and covered in fabric. I've never seen someone try to look so stern while looking so innocently sweet at the same time.

It feels good to laugh, to do anything other than train and snoop around the castle in the hopes of finding the tunnel on my own. But it seems that Kitt is the only key, and I'm helpless without him showing me the passage. Helpless if he doesn't trust me. I've spent nearly every day with him, careful not to sound desperate when I casually mention details about Loot, trying to entice him into sneaking away with me.

Nothing.

We are chatting quietly when a knock at the door has us all jumping.

Ellie throws me a look, silently asking if I was expecting anyone, to which I give her a clueless shrug. She scurries to the door and opens it hesitantly, revealing a tall, smiling figure.

Kitt.

Ellie dips into a curtsy and I'm suddenly beside her, a slightly mocking smile on my lips as I say, 'Your Highness, what an unexpected surprise.'

Kitt dips his head gracefully towards me. 'Why, Miss Gray, I hope I'm not intruding?' His amused gaze flicks from Ellie to my bed where Adena sits, wide-eyed and covered in fabric. 'Miss Ellie, Miss Adena, would you mind if I stole Paedyn from you?'

Ellie offers him a shy smile as Adena tries to stifle a shriek before calling, 'No, Your Highness, not at all!'

I duck my head, trying to suppress a smile from both embarrassment and amusement. Kitt is already looking down at me when I peek up at him, his lips quirked in a smile. 'Shall we?'

Their giggling follows us all the way down the hall, and I sigh before asking, 'So, where are you stealing me off to?'

'Actually,' Kitt glances around nervously, 'I was hoping you could steal me away.'

I blink at him, my heart beginning to beat quickly. But I school my features, feigning confusion. 'I'm not sure I follow.'

Kitt slows and leads us into a corner before leaning over me. I'm startled by this sudden turn of events, his sudden proximity, and the sudden scent of spices that washes over me.

His head dips close to mine, his voice dipping to a low hush with it. 'Loot.'

And there it is.

That one word has my heart hammering.

'I want you to take me.'

'Really?' The word comes out breathy and a little too eager for my liking.

Kitt doesn't seem to notice, too busy scanning the corridor to make sure no one can overhear. 'Yes.' His eyes are back on mine, searching. 'I shouldn't, but I . . . I should. What you said was true. All of it. I *need* to see my people. I can't rule over a kingdom I barely know, over people who have needs I haven't learned of.' He pauses, considering something. 'I need to start deciding what *I* think is best.'

He sighs. 'I need to do this. As much as I don't want to go against my father, and as much as I know this is a damn awful idea,' he chuckles but the sound is strained, 'I know if I don't do this now, I never will. And I have you to thank for reminding me of the type of king I never want to be.'

The joy that had warmed me only moments ago is gone, replaced by the frigid, icy fingers of guilt. I'm suddenly reminded of his kindness, his tolerance for me telling him off, his willingness to listen.

And look where it's gotten him. Betrayal.

I swallow the lump rising in my throat. 'You're doing the right thing. And I would be happy to show you my home since you've so kindly shown me yours.'

I smile, trying to look casual and not at all calculating as I wait for him to show me the one thing I have been searching for.

The tunnels.

He nods slowly, looking suddenly serious. 'Are you sure you can get me there and back without anyone identifying me?'

'Do you trust me?'

The words taste like ash in my mouth, and yet they slide off my tongue like silk. My chest constricts, and yet I breathe a little deeper. My knees threaten to shake, and yet I stand a little taller.

You are betraying one man to save the lives of hundreds. To save the lives of your people.

Kitt's smile is soft. 'Yes.'

It's astounding how severely a single word can damn someone.

And then my hand is in his as he unwittingly leads me towards the first step in finding my people's salvation.

I never figured that salvation would be in the dungeons.

Kitt pushes through a large, heavy door connected to one of the corridors before we are stomping down the staircase behind it. The air grows musty and cold with every step we take. He nods to the guards scattered in this damp dungeon beneath the castle, looking completely casual. As if he always brings his lady friends down here to visit.

We pass by dozens of dirty, dingy cells, some of which are still decorated with the bones of their past residents while others are occupied by the living. They watch us as we pass, their eyes prickling my skin, arms reaching through the rusty bars.

'In here,' Kitt says, snapping my attention back to the task at hand. His head sweeps back and forth down the hallway, and after deeming the coast clear, we step into the last cell.

My heart leaps into my throat, and I swallow. The passage is in a *cell*. It's brilliant, really. I would have never guessed that an escape out of the castle would be connected to the one place they don't want anyone to escape from.

'We don't put prisoners in this cell, though they would never be able to get into the passage even if they knew one was in here,' Kitt murmurs as his hands slide across the wall.

He pushes on a large stone just above his head, one that looks completely ordinary alongside the others. It slides back about an inch, and I tear my eyes away from it as I count the stones, marking its spot on the wall.

Kitt has a ring of jingling keys in his hand, shiny metal glinting in the dim light as he grabs hold of the last one and slips it off the ring. It's large and dulled by age with faded raised swirls looping across the top.

Kitt tosses a smile over his shoulder as he shoves the key into a small keyhole that was only made visible after he pushed back the stone. He talks casually as he works on turning the key. 'Like I said, even if we did hold prisoners in this cell, and even if they found this particular stone, they still wouldn't be able to get out. I always have my key ring on me.' I hear a metallic click sound from the wall. 'I figured the safest place for it is on my person.'

I manage a hum of agreement, my pulse racing in anticipation. Kitt drops the key back onto its silver ring before dropping them both into the inside of his pocket.

Then he pushes on a section of the wall, and it swings open in response.

The stones that once looked totally ordinary have now become a camouflaged door. Kitt grabs my hand and pulls me in after him before shutting the door and plunging us into total darkness. The blackness falls over us like a blanket, heavy and pressing.

I can't even see my hand in front of my face, so I jump when it connects with his chest. That same chest rumbles with laughter before flames flare in his fist, nearly blinding me with their brightness.

'Shall we?' Kitt asks with a smile.

We walk down a wide tunnel, damp and slimy, our footsteps echoing off the walls. I think on my next words carefully, knowing I need to craft them as though I'm simply curious rather than desperate.

'Where does this tunnel lead, exactly? And are there a lot of these, like a maze underneath the one that is the castle?' I ask, keeping my voice casual.

My feet falter when we come to a fork in the tunnel where the path splits in two. Kitt halts with me, his answer as casual as my question. 'This actually happens to be one of the main and larger tunnels, hence why it's one of the only ones I have a key to. Several of them are blocked off or too dangerous to use now.'

I keep my face neutral despite the worry weighing on my shoulders. What if the passage leading to the Bowl is one of the dead tunnels? What if it has been blocked off or caved in or—

Kitt nods his head towards the tunnel to the left, cutting through my thoughts as he says, 'That one leads out near the training grounds, but you can't open the door from the outside.' Then he gestures towards the tunnel to the right. 'And the one we are going down leads to Bowl Arena and into the room under the box. The one we stayed in before the interviews.'

I nearly choke. Between coughs, I blame the outburst on the grimy air and not the information he so easily shared with me. The *exact* information I needed.

My head is spinning. I invented the idea of Kitt using one of the tunnels to see Loot in order to learn where the other ones were, and which one led to the Bowl. And here we are, casually going through the exact one I needed to find.

Kitt pulls me down the tunnel towards the Bowl, and I'm flooded with relief after finally discovering the passage. We walk and talk for nearly ten minutes before Kitt's firelight illuminates a heavy door.

There it is. Salvation.

He heaves it open, revealing the dark room beneath the box before propping the door open with a small rock so we can get back in when we return. Then we head to the trapdoor in the ceiling, pushing it open before I'm once again pulling myself up through it. I feel the ghost of his hands on my back before I climb into the glass box. Kitt follows quickly after, and we step out into the empty arena.

'How exactly are we planning on getting to Loot?' I ask, raising my eyebrows at him.

'Since the stable boys can't know that we are quite literally riding off into the sunset,' Kitt flashes me a smile, 'we are headed to the field beside the Bowl where many of the horses graze during the day.'

We make our way out of the arena through one of the many concrete tunnels, ominous even with its absence of a jeering audience. When we finally reach the clearing, the warmth of the sun is blocked by the looming Bowl beside us.

A beautiful white horse canters up to greet us, clearly excited to get away from the Plague-forsaken place as well. I clear my throat and swallow my pride before muttering, 'I don't know how to ride.'

'Then you better hold on tight,' Kitt replies with a grin, his eyes briefly meeting mine.

Without a saddle, Kitt helps me onto the horse before gracefully mounting himself. I don't know where to put my hands, feeling suddenly awkward with my chest pressed against his back.

He turns his head to look at me, his golden hair gleaming in the sunlight. 'Are you sure you can steal me away?'

'Please,' I muse, 'I'm a thief. Stealing is kind of what I do best.'

Kitt hasn't stopped coughing since we arrived at Loot.

'Plagues, it does reek here.' He stifles a cough, trying to clear his lungs of the thick air. '*Damn.*'

I snort, watching as he scans his new surroundings, still trying to take it all in. His gaze runs over the beaten merchant carts scattered across Loot, all decorated with faded banners or torn signs. He takes in the crumbling buildings and shops outlining the wide street, watching as his people meander in and out of them.

His head swivels in the direction of each shout, listening as one man advertises his fresh catch of fish while another haggles loudly with a woman over the price of fabric. Everywhere around us is chaos, a sort of blissful craze. And we are standing in the middle of it, surrounded by a swarm of people going about their lives. Selling and buying. Living and trying to live. Loot seems to buzz with people, and yet, all I see is the buzz of *existence*.

I reach up and tug the cap resting on Kitt's head lower. I snatched that and a beat-up shirt for him to slip on, though I doubt anyone is paying attention to us. He returns my gesture in kind, chuckling as he pulls my own hat over my eyes while silver wisps of hair fall around my face. I huff and readjust my cap with a smile tugging at my lips before leading him farther down the street, dodging laughing children who scuttle around our legs.

Kitt is trying to take it all in, soak up every bit of Loot. Every drab banner leached of color, every person that bumps into us on the crowded street. There is a Veil performing magic for a few onlookers, wowing the crowd and using his power to earn a few silvers. Defensive Elites always do well in this part of the slums, standing out among the many Mundanes.

I watch Kitt while he peers down the smaller alleys and streets jutting off Loot, catching glimpses of makeshift tents and the homeless figures huddling together within them. He stiffens at the sight of lonely, young children weaving between carts, hands clearly itching to snatch any sort of food.

'They'll be whipped when they're caught,' I say flatly.

His eyes are trained on mine now. '*When* they're caught?'

'Yes. When.' I sigh and continue leading him down the crowded street. 'The young ones are reckless and too impatient to be good thieves at that age. And since most Elites in the slums are Mundanes, their powers are likely unhelpful when it comes to surviving. I would know.'

I stop us in front of the bloody post residing in the center of Loot, where thieves and criminals alike are beaten. 'This is where your Imperials will punish those children for their crimes.' I jerk my head towards the guards lining the street, currently scanning the crowd for their next victim.

Kitt steps closer to me, closing the distance between us. His green eyes glisten with emotion he doesn't try to hide. 'Did you ever . . .'

'Yes. I was one of those children once. More than once. And I have the scars to prove it.' The streaks along my lower back seem to tingle at the mention and memory of them. He looks at me with such pain, such pity in his eyes that for the first time since our walk in the garden, I can't bear to hold his gaze.

So, I pull him away before he can say another word. 'Come on. I want to show you something.'

I drag him down the street, holding his hand firmly so he doesn't get swept away in the crowd. No one pays any heed to the future king walking among them, or the Ordinary in plain sight leading him.

I stop at the end of a familiar alley. My makeshift little home is still tucked into the corner where I'm shocked to find it undisturbed. Bittersweet memories claw to the surface of my mind as I step towards the barrier of garbage and rugs I know as the Fort.

Kitt is suddenly beside me, his arm brushing mine as he looks over the mound. 'This is where you slept.' It's not a question.

'Home sweet home,' I whisper, surprised at how strained my voice sounds.

And then my face is suddenly in his hands, and his voice has taken on a soft sort of sternness. 'I'm so sorry. I'm so sorry you had to live like this.' He sighs as his eyes search mine. 'Thank you. Thank you for showing me this. Loot. My people.' He pauses. '*You*. Thank you for entrusting me with the details of *you*.'

My throat bobs when the guilt slams into me again, forcing me to fight to keep my voice steady as I say, 'No, thank you for trusting me, Kitt.'

CHAPTER 47

Paedyn

'What is taking him so long? Plagues, it's freezing out here.' My teeth are chattering thanks to the uncharacteristically cold night, and my thin shirt does little to keep the cool breeze from kissing my skin.

'Patience, Princess,' Lenny mutters beside me. I'm shoving him with an annoyed smile before the words have even finished rolling off his tongue. He suppresses the urge to shove me back and I give him a wicked grin, tempting him to do just that.

And right as I think things are about to get interesting, the door swings open.

'Sorry to interrupt your brawl but it's quite chilly out here and you two should really come inside before you catch a cold.' Calum's voice is laced with amusement as he steps aside to let us into the house.

My house.

We make our way to the study and down the hidden stairs to the basement below. I've been here several times since the night I first ventured back to my home, and I've grown numb to the sight of my father's study. I'm less haunted, but still far from healed. I suppose even trauma grows tired of its endless tormenting, if only for a little while.

A deep, taunting voice greets me when I make it to the bottom of the stairs. 'There she is.'

I wave at Finn from where he sits, ankles crossed over a table and arms behind his head. He smirks in response, and my gaze drops to Leena who is currently residing on the floor littered with maps.

Aside from being different Resistance leaders throughout Ilya, I've come to learn that each of them has a purpose, something they contribute to the cause. Leena is a talented artist, and all our detailed maps are thanks to her, whereas Finn thrives in designing the leather armor and masks. Lenny is their eyes and ears in the castle while Mira is a Silencer, making her obviously valuable.

Leena grins when she sees me and leaves her work behind to join us, Finn following to sit in the circle of chairs. 'No Mira today?' I ask, looking around the large room filled with tables covered in documents and cots covered in messy linens.

'No Mira today,' Calum says quietly. 'She's tending to her mother back home.'

I'm debating asking questions I probably shouldn't be asking when Calum quickly redirects the conversation. 'So, Paedyn, what do you have for us? Anything?' I can hear the same desperation in his voice that has been there every time I've visited and had to admit my failures.

But not today.

'I found the tunnel. Well, actually, Kitt led me right through it earlier today.' I'm practically breathless, finally exhaling the words into existence. They all lean in, eyes wide as I tell them about my plan and the impossibility that it worked.

When I finish, it's Finn who breaks the silence. 'I knew you'd wrap the future king around your little finger.'

'I'm proud, Princess,' Lenny says with a lopsided grin.

With that, I delve into an explanation of everything I've seen and exactly where the passage begins and ends. 'After entering the tunnel through the last cell on the left, about halfway through you'll see a fork in the road. The path to the left leads to the door by the training grounds, and the path to the right leads all the way to the Bowl and the room underneath the box.'

Leena is greedily scribbling down the information, taking in my every word and transferring it onto paper. In a matter of minutes, they know where the passage is, where it leads to, and how to find it.

'There's only one problem,' I add, spinning the ring on my thumb anxiously. 'You need a key to get into the passage, and it just so happens to always be on Kitt.'

Finn snorts. 'Easy. Undress him.'

I throw him a look before turning back to Calum. 'I can get it. At the ball, I'll grab the key and give it to Lenny. Since the Trial is the next day, Kitt won't have time to realize the key has gone missing before then.' I chew on the inside of my cheek before adding, 'I hope.'

'Sounds like a plan to me,' Lenny says with a yawn.

I pin him with a stare. 'Anyone who will be going through the tunnel and into the box needs to enter at the door by the training grounds. So, Lenny, you'll need to let them in since the door only opens from the inside, and from there, you can head down the tunnel towards the Bowl. Understood?'

Lenny gives me a curt nod. 'Understood.'

We talk for at least another hour, discussing the details. And then Lenny and I are standing to leave, stretching our stiff bodies before waving our goodbyes and heading back up the stairs.

When we step outside, the cool breeze bombards me, and I find myself shivering once again. Lenny slings an arm around my shoulder and tucks me close, ruffling my hair with his other hand in the process. I'm laughing, pushing his palm away as I attempt to smooth down the crazed silver strands now tumbling over my shoulders.

'The ball is tomorrow,' Lenny says, almost sounding solemn.

'The ball is tomorrow,' I echo, my voice barely more than a whisper. 'And then it's the final Trial.' He's staring up at the stars looking down on us.

I exhale a shaky laugh, seemingly unable to come up with my own words since I say, 'And then it's the final Trial.'

Lenny looks at me, eyes full of laughter. 'What are you, a parrot or a Paedyn?'

I snort and let my head fall back to look up at the starry sky. My answer is quiet, thoughtful. 'I don't know what I am.'

I feel a squeeze on my shoulder and turn to see Lenny smiling down at me. 'You're Paedyn Gray. Silver Savior, silver-tongued, and quick to shove her silver dagger into people.'

CHAPTER 48

Kai

Screams. Terrible, tortured screams bounce around my skull, echo in my mind.

Her.

It's *her.*

I'm running through the halls of the castle, sweating, searching, screaming for her.

The only response is a cry for help, a beg for mercy.

I throw open her door, burst into the room and scan the darkness.

Something silver glints in the moonlight streaming through her open window.

There.

Her hair. It must be that beautiful, silver hair of hers. But what my eyes land on is not beautiful.

No, it is *broken.*

She is covered in blood, sitting in a pool of it. Tears are streaming down her face, now contorted in agony.

Pain beyond belief. Suffering beyond saving.

I catch sight of that silver glint again, but it's not her hair shimmering like I once thought.

Dagger.

It's her *dagger.*

Its sharp point is pressed against her chest, drawing blood that runs down her body and mirrors the tears running down her face.

What gruesome symmetry.

I'm suddenly beside her, kneeling in a pool of blood. *Her* blood. She doesn't see me, doesn't speak, doesn't do anything but scream. Anguish. I've never seen such anguish.

'Paedyn! Pae look at me!' Nothing. No reaction.

More sobs. More blood.

I grab hold of the slick handle belonging to the dagger she is slowly pressing into her heart.

It's covered in blood.

Blood so sticky it's clinging to my hands, crawling up my arms, coating me in the one thing I will never be able to wash off.

I never wanted her blood on my hands. Never her blood.

Her head turns, ever so slowly, her tear-streaked face now angled towards mine.

'Make it stop.' She's whimpering.

Paedyn doesn't whimper.

'It hurts so much. Just please make it stop. Make it stop. Make it stop!'

Sobs are racking her body, and I'm holding the knife still while she desperately tries to sink it into her beautiful heart.

'My heart *hurts.*'

More sobs. More cries to let her die. This is wrong. This is so very wrong.

Paedyn is too strong, too stubborn, too *special.*

She can't die. I won't allow it. Not by her hand or anyone else's. Her screams are splitting my soul, my head, my heart.

I can't take it. I can't take it. I can't take it anymore.

I feel tears stinging my eyes, streaming down my face.

Now *I'm* begging.

I'm begging her to stay. To live. For me.

I might even be screaming too, sobbing too, shaking too. 'Kai?'

My head whips around, and through my haze of hysteria, I make out a lanky figure looming over me.

There is a familiar boyish grin on his face despite the blood pouring from his chest where a throwing star is lodged deep within.

He falls to his knees, eyes glossy as they bore into mine.

This time I hear the scream rip from my throat as I lunge for him, cradle him, beg him to live.

Footsteps echo off the walls, and I look up to see dozens of bodies surrounding me. All bloody and begging. All victims of mine.

They stare at me, hatred burning in their gazes as they look upon the man who killed them.

I know each of their faces. Each of their wounds that I inflicted. They circle me. Vultures anticipating a death.

Then I hear a sound I know all too well.

The sickening crunch of metal slicing through bone, of tendons tearing apart, of muscles morphing around a blade.

She slumps to the ground – dagger in heart, lips in a smile. I'm screaming.

I'm lifting her into my arms, I'm brushing her bloody hair back, I'm saying something, but I don't know what.

My mind is numb. My heart is numb.

Everything is numb.

She's smiling in death, as though happy to be rid of life. Happy to be rid of *me*.

I am grief. I am sorrow. I am anguish alike.

I think I might also be dead. Just decaying on the inside.

CHAPTER 49

Paedyn

Screams. I've never heard agony in such a raw form.

I had just climbed into bed after making it back from Loot only to throw off the covers and jump to my feet. I'm stumbling through the dark room, tripping over my discarded boots lying carelessly on the floor.

When my fingers finally wrap around the cool handle of my door, I wrench it open and step out into the shadowed hallway.

A cry echoes, and I still at the sound. It's him.

I don't know how I know since I've never heard the future Enforcer cry out before, but something tugs me in the direction of his room. My feet are moving of their own accord, guiding me closer to him with every step.

I halt before his door, dragging my insistent feet to a stop.

What am I doing?

I can't just walk into his room. Right?

Wrong.

This is a bad idea.

Yes, but this is a bad idea I want to do.

Another anguished cry tears from his throat and I don't hesitate before throwing open the door. Darkness engulfs me as I once again

stumble through a room, eyes straining to see, hands outstretched to guide.

The outline of a bed comes into view, along with the outline of the body atop it. I make my way to him, blinking as my eyes finally adjust to the lack of light, only to roam over his exposed chest, heaving and slicked with sweat.

His head is thrown back against a pillow, strands of inky hair sticking to his forehead. He's heaving shaky, shallow breaths, every inch of him taut. I can't even begin to imagine what is haunting his sleep, what is stealing his rest and leaving him so ragged. What nightmare is so terrible that even the prince cannot defend himself?

His lips are moving with murmured words I can't understand, and now I'm truly worried.

I'm worried about him.

I let the thought sink in for a moment before placing a gentle hand on his shoulder and nearly gasping at the heat of his skin. He's burning up.

'Kai,' I say softly, not wanting to startle him. Nothing.

'Kai.' I speak his name louder this time, shaking his shoulder to try to shake him from his nightmare.

He cries out again, and I nearly do the same. Now I'm panting, panicking, pleading with him to wake up so we can go back to bantering instead of begging him to open his eyes.

I climb onto his bed, swinging a leg over his body so he's pressed between my thighs as I lay both hands on his slick chest. 'Kai!' I'm shaking him, hard, willing him to wake.

'Kai!' I'm annoyed that I care so much. Annoyed that I care whether he is hurting or not. Annoyed that I can't bear to see him like this—

And then those gray eyes snap open.

Strong hands are suddenly gripping my waist and throwing me off him. My back is pressed against the mattress as he pins me down, hands crushing my arms, his body crushing mine.

And then something cold is pressed against my throat.

I'd know the feel of a dagger anywhere, so I don't bother looking down at the one he is now pushing against my neck. I'm breathing heavily, keeping my eyes locked on his wild ones and my voice soft. 'Kai, it's me.' His strength is shocking, and I don't think I could wiggle out from under him even if I tried. He's panting just as hard as I am, practically paralyzed above me. 'Kai. It was just a nightmare.' I keep my voice calm while ignoring my thundering heart that says I'm anything but. 'Kai, it's me. Paedyn.'

He blinks. And then he blinks again, over and over as if clearing his head. As if seeing me for the first time. Cool air coats my neck as he pulls the dagger away, his eyes never straying from mine.

'It's me. Pae.' My voice trembles, barely more than a whisper now. 'Kai?' Then my voice cracks and something seems to crack inside him as well.

He takes a shuddering breath, looking at what he's done. Releasing my arm from his startling grip, he slides the dagger back under his pillow while trying to calm his breathing. His cool mask has cracked, crumbled in his panic, and I can see every emotion as it flits across his face.

I've never seen him so disheveled, so disoriented, so disgusted with himself.

His eyes are haunted, filled with horrors as they wander around the room, refusing to meet my gaze. I can tell he is about to get off me without a word, and I refuse to let that happen. Refuse to forget this moment when the prince was merely a boy.

Those ghostly, gray eyes flutter shut at the feel of my hand on his cheek. I cup his face, timidly, tenderly, as I silently marvel at the feel of him against my palm. His jaw is set, and a muscle feathers in it as I slide my thumb across his cheek.

He ducks his head, eyes still squeezed shut so he doesn't have to meet mine. 'Look at me.' My command is both soft and stern, sure and shaky. My other hand is on his face now, helping to guide it back up to meet my gaze. He takes a deep, trembling breath before opening his eyes, the steeliness of them as startling as they are stunning.

'Don't hide from me,' I breathe, suddenly unable to catch my breath with the way he is looking at me. 'Not anymore.'

I want to stare into his face, the one without the mask that I have glimpsed so many times before. I watch as his eyes roam over me, over my body still pressed beneath his, over my hair messily spread across his pillow.

Almost as though he is committing me to memory.

I swallow under his gaze, which only manages to drop his eyes to my neck where I can feel a flush rising. No, not just a flush. My neck stings. Suddenly remembering that my hands are still on his face, I slowly drop them to bring my fingers to my neck.

His swift hand catches my wrist before running his fingers gently over my throat. I barely suppress a shudder at his touch, at the feel of his calluses brushing my flushed skin.

'Look at what I've done.' His voice is rough, still riddled with the remnants of sleep and raw with the cries that ripped from his throat. He pulls back his fingers, now smudged with sticky blood.

He looks so pained by the thought of nicking me with a dagger that I let out a breathy laugh despite the current situation. He looks alarmed by my outburst, which only manages to make me laugh even more.

'Funny,' I huff, 'usually I'm the one pressing a dagger to *your* throat.' I silently wish for a smile to tug at his lips, for those dimples to come out and mock me. But he just stares at me before saying softly, 'You're going to get blood in your hair.'

I might have laughed again at that if it weren't for his fingers at my throat, making me fall silent. He sits up slightly, slowly sliding one hand to the nape of my neck before lifting my head gently off the pillow and brushing my hair back with the other. He takes his time, letting his fingers run through the silver strands while he cradles my head.

'I would braid it back for you again, but you informed me that I'm no good at it,' he says roughly, so at odds with the gentle way he sets my head back onto the pillow. Without hesitation, he grabs the corner of a blanket and begins softly wiping the remaining blood from my neck.

'You just need more practice, that's all.'

We both still, content to let the silence stretch between us.

He looks down at me, and I look up at him. I'm lost in the moment, lost in his eyes. There is no smirk to be seen, no smile to be shared, no sarcastic line to be said. Just the two of us, hearts beating wildly, breath leaving shakily.

I blink, realizing what I'm doing, what is going on, what is happening between us. So I clear my throat, slowly shifting beneath him. He takes a breath, understanding what I want and slowly moving off me. Only when the cool air hits me do I realize how flushed I am, how heated my skin has become.

I sit up, tugging up my tank as I do, and slide to the edge of his bed. I can feel his piercing gaze on me as I stand to my feet, suddenly conscious of the little fabric covering my body.

I take a step away. Another.

Fingers brush the inside of my wrist. 'Stay.'

I still. Time stalls. Breathing ceases.

It's astounding how severely a single word can affect someone. 'Please.'

My heart trips over itself at the sound of that word from his lips.

'Few have the power to make me plead.'

The weight that my next words hold is pressing down on me, crushing my lungs so no sound can come out of my mouth. What I say next could either drive a wedge between us or drive us closer together. Too close together.

Do I stay? Do I go?

My mind is screaming at me to do one thing, but my heart is pounding, pleading with me to do another. Despite the silence stretching between us, my jumbled thoughts are deafening.

Even with my back still to him, I can feel his eyes on me, feel the ghost of his hands on me, feel what he is doing to me.

What if I don't say a thing?

Words can only damn if they are spoken.

So that's just what I'll do. I won't speak, I won't think – I'll feel. I'll drown out the insistent thoughts and simply *feel*.

I turn, slowly, and meet his gaze. His breath catches, his gaze softens. He didn't think I would stay.

He expects everyone to leave him.

And with that heartbreaking thought in mind, I don't hesitate as I lift the covers of his bed. He tracks the movement, watches my hands as they fold back the blankets, my body as I fold beneath them.

I don't think he's breathing, and my head is spinning so much that

I don't think I am either. I sink into his mattress, his soft pillows, the scent that covers them. Him. I'm surrounded by *him*. I curl onto my side, heart racing as I feel the bed shift beside me.

And then I'm *actually* surrounded by him. His chest brushes against my back in question, silently asking if I want him closer or farther. I swallow before leaning back, ever so slightly, in answer.

I want you closer.

He doesn't hesitate. His arm is wrapped around my middle and tugging me against him before I have a chance to catch my breath. I'm pressed to his strong body, tucked between the covers and him. I feel secure and safe and more soothed in his arms than I have in years.

I feel.

Something about this, about us, seems different. Intentional. We both *wanted* this. We weren't forced together because of the cold or because of an injury. I could have walked away, but I chose this. No, *we* chose this. We chose each other.

And that terrifies me.

His thumb is drawing idle circles on my lower stomach and my tank is doing little to stop the heat of his fingers from seeping through. My eyes drift closed, somehow feeling tired yet too terribly aware of his body pressed against mine to let myself sleep.

He rests his head in the crook of my neck, his breath tickling my skin as he murmurs, 'Thank you.'

Those two words startle me enough to make me twist my head to look at him. I wonder how rare it is for the prince, the future Enforcer, to say those words so earnestly.

His face is close to mine, and he studies it thoughtfully, thoroughly, as if he has all the time in the world to do so. He tilts his head to the side, gently tucking a strand of hair behind my ear. My breath hitches when his fingers trail down the side of my neck, and he smiles, soft and sweet and satisfied. So very satisfied in this moment.

A smile he's designed just for me.

'Does it shock you? That I would thank you?' he asks, voice low and quiet.

I study the planes of his face, the perfection that is him. 'It shouldn't. Not anymore.' I swallow as the truth of those words sink in. I've gotten to know him, gotten to see the man behind the many masks who is more than what his father has molded him into.

I'm not sure how long I've been studying him when I realize how heavy my eyelids have become. I'm blinking, trying my best to escape the sleep that is desperately clawing at me, so I can continue memorizing his face a little longer.

He's doing the same, taking in every inch of me with a look of wonder. I blink and my eyelids threaten not to open again, sleep daring to drag me away from this moment.

His lips are suddenly at my ear and that is all I need to have my eyes fluttering open. 'As tempting as it is to watch you stare at me all night,' his voice is a caress, lulling me to sleep with a single sentence, 'sleep, Pae.'

I manage to give him a groggy grin before asking, 'Are you going to sleep?'

'Oh, darling, I'm already dreaming.'

He pulls me impossibly closer, and I turn my head away. My eyes fall closed, the steady beat of his heart a lullaby. I feel fingers combing through my hair, weaving loose strands together as I whisper, 'What are you doing?'

He ducks his head close to mine, and I feel his lips brush against my hair when he murmurs, 'Practicing.'

I drift off to the feel of Kai braiding my hair, vaguely wondering if I should be afraid of how safe I feel with him. If I should be worried that I feel content and comforted in his arms.

I feel happy, I feel words murmured into my ear, and the whisper of fingers stroking my hair.

And then all I feel is blissful sleep.

CHAPTER 50

Kai

I can't tear my eyes from her.

I can't stray my thoughts from her. I can't pry my body from her.

The morning sunlight spilling in from my window is glinting off her hair, the silver strands shining. Her eyes are shut in sleep, dark lashes lying against her cheeks and concealing the ocean blue gaze I know swims beneath. She is breathing deeply, sleeping soundly. She is a mess of tangled limbs and scattered hair.

A messy masterpiece.

I count the faint freckles dusting her nose. Once. Twice. Twenty-eight.

She shifts, and I still as she tucks her hands beneath the side of her face, now covered in strands of silver. Propped up on my elbow, I gently brush my fingers across her smooth skin, tucking her hair away so I can continue admiring the face I'd been in the middle of memorizing.

I blame her for the tiredness settling in my bones. It's her fault I didn't sleep much. I was up most of the night listening to her breathe – breathing her in. Just like I've been doing for far longer than I care to admit. She's captivating, even while crumpled up and claimed by sleep.

Sighing, my fingers run through one last strand of silver hair before I ease off the bed and creep to the door. I leave on my thin pants and throw a shirt over my head before stepping into the hallway, heading for the kitchens. The least I could do is let her wake up to the smell of fresh food, especially after what she did for me last night.

After a nightmare in which I held her cold corpse, waking to find her very much alive and warm on top of me was startling to say the least. And I reacted without thinking. I *hurt* her. Though a little scratch means nothing to the girl who's used to bleeding, it means everything to me. Killing is what I do. Killing and hurting are what I was trained to do, created to do, controlled to do.

But not with her.

I was one swift movement away from holding her very real corpse in my arms, and yet she did nothing to fight back. She held my face in her hands while I held her life in my own. She looked at me like I was worthy of being seen, like she *wanted* to see me. And when she said my name, the sound of it rolling off her tongue finally had my head clearing, heart racing, thoughts reeling.

And then I asked her something I have never asked of anyone before.

Stay.

I'm out the door of the kitchen and balancing a tray of hot food down the hallway in a matter of minutes. The quirked brow Gail gave me makes me smile, and it's not long before I'm leaning against my door and backing into the room, clutching the tray in front of me.

I turn around and—

A shoe is aimed at my face.

She's standing at the edge of the bed, one hand clutching a blanket around her shoulders while the other clutches my dress shoe, a sorry excuse for a weapon. Her arm is cocked back, prepared to fend off the intruder by launching footwear. I see her exhale in relief when she realizes it's me and reluctantly lowers the shoe. But barely.

'Not your typical weapon of choice.' I'm grinning, choking back a laugh.

Paedyn gives me an exasperated look that I've grown very familiar with. 'You scared me.' She sweeps back the curtain of hair shielding her eyes with a smug smile. 'And I'm sure I could do a lot of damage with a shoe.'

'Oh, I don't doubt it.'

I'm in front of her now, though I don't remember moving to get there. Reaching around her back slowly, I place the tray on my bed, juice sloshing over the edge of cups and biscuits rolling. Then I straighten, staring down into eyes that threaten to drown me. 'Good morning, Gray.'

The slightest frown tugs at her lips with the use of her last name. 'Back to formalities, are we?' She says it casually, but her eyes speak a question she will never voice.

What is going on between us?

'Well, you were just about to attack me. Formalities seem fair.' I take a step closer, and she tips her head back to hold my gaze.

'Yes, well, you should be used to that by now.'

'Oh, but I doubt I'll ever get used to you or your violent tendencies, darling.'

She gives me a sly smile. 'I like to think of it as keeping you on your toes, Prince.'

'Yes, because life is far more entertaining when you aren't expecting a knife to the throat or a shoe to the face.' My gaze drops to said shoe still clutched in her hand. 'Speaking of which, still planning to use that on me?'

'Still deciding.'

The smile I give her is a real one, a rarity that has recently become a rather common occurrence when I'm in her presence. She turns her head to nod at the tray on my bed. 'You brought me food.'

I cross my arms over my chest. 'And how do you know that's not for me?'

'There are blueberries on the porridge, Azer.'

Still wanting to play with her, I shrug. 'After rambling about the fruit, you convinced me of how delicious they are.'

She outright laughs at that. 'Then that would mean you're admitting I was right, and that is highly unlikely.'

'You know me so well,' I sigh, smiling at her. 'Of course the food is for you. I wouldn't touch that porridge.'

A smile tugs at her lips. 'Picky prince.'

'Clever Pae.'

We stare at one another, each of us smiling slightly.

My eyes drop to her free hand still clutching a blanket around her shoulders, pulling it tighter when my gaze sweeps over her. 'Are you cold?'

She stiffens slightly. 'No.'

'Then what is this?' I'm eying the blanket before my fingers graze over hers, the ones still fiercely fisted in the folds of fabric. Her gaze trails from my face to my hand that is now trailing over her knuckles, her wrist, her fist and the fabric in it.

The way her breath hitches has my heart halting. 'It's a blanket.'

My laugh is quiet. 'I can see that, smartass.'

My fingers lazily brush down her arm, though the movement has my mind stalling, pulse skipping. Every touch is intoxicating, every look shared is entrancing.

'You look flushed, Gray.' My fingers catch a strand of long hair falling over her shoulder. 'Probably thanks to the blanket.' I can feel the smirk spreading across my face as I say, 'Unless I'm the reason for your blush.'

I watch the emotions flit across her face. First, there is something akin to what I'm sure is reflected in my own gaze – wanting. Then she blinks, and I glimpse shock, realization, and denial before she settles with annoyance.

'No, I'm definitely just overheating.' She's confident as ever despite the strain in her voice.

I tilt my head, eyes dancing between the blanket and her cool gaze. 'Then I suppose I'll help you once again, only this time it will be a blanket dropping to the floor and not your dress nearly doing the same.'

I smile at the thought of the last ball, but before my fingers can close around hers, she lets the blanket billow down around her ankles.

She's standing so close to me, wearing nothing but skimpy shorts and a silky tank. Teasing me, taunting me, toying with me. I hadn't been able to see the black fabric clinging to her body last night, blending in with the darkness around us. But now I can see it, see her, clearly.

There is a fire in her eyes, burning and breathtaking. 'Just to be clear, Prince, I don't need your help – undressing or otherwise.'

'Oh, of course not. Wishful thinking, I suppose.'

She huffs out a laugh. 'And are you unable to help being a shameless flirt as well?'

'Clearly not when I'm with you.'

'Oh? And what else are you when you're around me, hmm?' She has me swallowing, has me *nervous*.

'I'm a fool.'

The smile she gives me is equally amused and alluring. 'Only when you're around me?'

'Only *for* you.'

Her eyes lock with mine as she falls silent, suddenly still. I take a small step forward only for her to take a slight step back, her legs now pressed against the edge of the bed. I swallow, hiding my frown.

Why does she pull away?

'And since I'm also somehow kinder when I'm around you, I should thank you. Again.' I don't think I've ever spoken so softly, so soothingly to someone before. And what scares me even more is that I don't think I ever will for anyone but her.

My hand is suddenly brushing her wrist and I watch it trail up her arm, the ghost of a touch traveling across her skin. Goosebumps follow the path my fingers glide, bringing a smile to my lips.

Then I'm twirling that piece of silky hair around my finger again. 'Thank you, Pae. For last night.'

She shivers, and yet, her flush is still very much present. I can't fight the smile spreading across my face as I murmur, 'Despite my wanting to help, you still seem to be *overheating*.'

'And you still seem to be to blame for that.' She nearly snaps the words, seemingly annoyed with herself.

I tuck that strand of silver hair behind her ear with a lazy grin, letting my fingers linger. 'Are you admitting to me making you flushed? Making you *nervous*?'

'Making me annoyed?' she supplies. 'Because you certainly are doing that.'

I look away, shaking my head. 'Liar.'

'Was it my left foot that gave me away or did you come to that conclusion on your own?' she asks evenly.

My gaze has shifted back to her, blue and bewilderingly beautiful. Then my eyes drop to her lips, soft and pulled into a frown she seems to be fighting to keep on her face.

I step even closer. She leans in.

'I can't take my eyes off you long enough to give a damn about what your foot is doing. So yes, I came to that conclusion on my own.'

Her gaze is burning, boring into mine, begging me to come closer. So I do.

I can't stay away from her.

I don't *want* to stay away from her.

I'm sweeping hair out of her eyes, letting my fingers skim her skin. Simply touching her sends a shock through me, sets my heart racing. And I know she feels it too. Her eyes are flicking between mine and my mouth, lashes fluttering.

I can't do it anymore. I can't stop myself from wanting this. Wanting *her*.

I shift closer, her lips part, and—

And there is something digging into my throat.

What the hell—

She has the damn shoe pressed against my neck.

'I should go.' Her words are barely more than a whisper murmured against my lips as if she is speaking to herself, reminding me of our time under the willow when she uttered those same unsure words.

I clear my throat, untangle my hands from her hair, and straighten. *What the hell just happened? And why the hell didn't something just happen?* 'Right. You'll need plenty of time to get all dolled up for my brother tonight.' I don't bother masking my bitterness, my jealousy, my confusion.

She wants to see me without a mask? Fine. Let her see it all. Let her see my frustration with the feelings she is to blame for.

She flinches.

The girl who has slain wolves, scaled mountains, and survived the slums just *flinched*. I've never seen anything like it. Never thought I would. The sight has my heart sinking, has me wanting to pull her

412

into my arms and hold her there.

But instead, I find myself taking a measured step back, putting space between us. I don't trust myself around her. Don't trust myself not to reach out and touch her, taste her.

She opens her mouth, warring against the words she desperately wants to say. The ones I never get to hear because she clamps her jaw shut, sealing her thoughts from me. I watch her for several, slow seconds. Watch her take a deep breath before leveling me with a calm stare.

'You're welcome,' she says softly. 'For last night. No one should have to endure the terrors of their own thoughts alone. Nightmares can be our worst nemesis. I know what that's like.'

And then she grabs my hand and drops the shoe into it before striding out of the room.

I'm contemplating getting drunk again.

The alcohol swirling in the glass gripped between my fingers is tempting, teasing me to finish it off before following it with a few more. All just so I can get through this last damn ball.

Couples have begun dancing now that the flow of women arriving has slowed significantly. It seems that this final ball will be the only hint of normalcy in this year's Trials.

I traded Blair off to a young gentleman for a glass of wine, and I'm wondering why I hadn't done it sooner. While contemplating whether to down the remaining contents of my drink, I look up to find a group of ladies surrounding me, all clad in varying shades of green. They are all giggles and grins while I nod and talk politely, boring myself with how bland I'm being.

I'm just about to make my exit from the conversation using a mediocre excuse when someone catches my eye.

Someone who has me stunned and staring. Someone who is standing in a sea of black.

Draped in midnight fabric, the faint sparkles dusting her dress wink like starlight. Like a shadow, the fabric clings to her body. Like a second skin, it outlines her curves as she steps down the stairs.

Her tanned arms and chest glisten against the inky fabric wrapped around her. From her waist up, the dress is a detailed corset, cinching her in and displaying her chest and collarbones. The stomach of the corset is see-through, with designs of swirling flowers and beads contrasting against the tan skin showing beneath it. Loose strips of black, intricate sleeves connect to the top of the corset and hang off her shoulders limply. Layers of satin spill from her waist to the floor in a wide pool around her. My eyes trail up her bare legs, exposed through the slits traveling up both sides of the dress and ending high up her thighs. And there, strapped and displayed for all to see is her silver dagger, its swirled handle matching her attire.

Her silver hair is pulled into a loose knot near the nape of her neck, ringlets falling from it onto her back and around her face, tempting me to twirl my fingers through them, tuck them behind her ears.

Every bit of her body is clad in darkness, cloaked in night. I find myself silently thanking the Plague for her different, dark attire because I wouldn't want her blending in. Wouldn't want her lost in the crowd.

Not that she's ever had that problem before.

Not that I've ever had a problem finding her before.

The sight of her in jet black is enough to make me colorblind, make me see nothing and no one but her.

Her legs slide through the slits in her dress as she steps down the staircase, dagger clearly visible. Hundreds of eyes track her every move, and I'm suddenly jealous that everyone else gets to witness her presence with me.

She won't meet my gaze, and for the first time since I met her in that alley, I think this is the most cowardly she's ever been.

She's scared. Scared of whatever it is between us. She always has been. That's why she chose to be my enemy, my rival, rather than let herself feel – which is something I'm not accustomed to myself.

I blame her for it. Blame her for cracking my carefully crafted mask, shattering it to pieces when she is around. I've never felt so much, never feared so much. But if I must endure the consequences that feeling something for her brings, then so does she.

It's like a tangible tether between us, this consuming connection. I will her to meet my eyes, and when they do—

Sparks. Electricity.

Everything beautiful, everything bold, everything breathtaking – that is what I feel in her gaze.

That, and terrified. Terrified of what she is doing to me. She is a vision, a nightmare, a dream.

A grim reaper clad in black, come to steal my soul and my heart.

I've never seen something so beautiful, so bold, so blatantly wrong for me.

She is a devil. She is a deity.

She is a man's downfall in human form. She is *my* downfall.

Then her eyes drift to Kitt. The connection snaps.

And I'm left feeling empty besides the jealousy growing inside of me. Why did I ever think I could have her, ever think she would have me? Because beasts don't get the beauty.

CHAPTER 51

Paedyn

I'm avoiding him. Not the best way to deal with a problem, I'll admit. But Kai is a very pressing problem. A very desirable distraction.

So, I keep myself busy, though I still manage to notice that he is doing the same. Girl after gorgeous girl finds their way into his arms and onto the dance floor, all of them wearing glowing smiles and green dresses.

I bury the emotion I don't want to identify as jealousy, though it claws at me nonetheless.

I have a job to do.

I turn my attention back to my partner for the dozenth time. Kitt smiles, continuing our easy conversation that my mind keeps wanting to wander from. I force myself to focus on his words rather than the thing I need to steal from him. We spin, and I catch a glimpse of the key ring against the inside of his suit coat pocket. My fingers twitch, itching to tap into the thieving instincts I've suppressed while in the castle – for the most part.

'You look beautiful.'

I startle at Kitt's soft words, forcing my gaze up to meet his. He's smiling at the look on my face as he says, 'You shouldn't be so shocked by that.'

We are quiet for a moment before I finally form words. 'You shock me.'

'Do I?'

'Yes,' I answer honestly, 'you are not what I expected.'

His grin looks almost too boyish to belong to the future king. 'Did I disappoint?'

I wish.

'No.' His smile widens at the word, and I hurry to add, 'Not yet.'

Then I'm dipping towards the floor and he's chuckling above me as I suck in a surprised breath. He holds me there, and my opportunity arrives. This is the moment I've been dreading, been planning. His suit coat is open, his eyes are pinned on me, and his thoughts are on anything but the keys in his pocket.

So I do what I do best – thieve.

I fumble, pretending to slip, though it's quite believable in the stilts I'm wearing. I throw my hands out to steady myself, one on his shoulder and one on his chest near the pocket inside his suit.

His arms wrap tighter around my waist as I hold his gaze, smiling even as I slip my hand into his pocket. Smiling even as I betray the boy who has been nothing but kind to me. Smiling even as the key ring opens, and I slide the largest one off the end, feeling the raised swirls that decorate it pressing into my palm.

He pulls me up slowly, strong arms standing me upright. But my hand is already out of his pocket and resting behind his shoulder, innocent and insignificant.

'And here I was, thinking your dancing was improving,' Kitt says with a teasing smile.

'And here *I* was, thinking you would warn me before sending me flying towards the floor.' I blow out a breath, smiling as I add, 'And now I could use a drink.'

'Not too much to drink. You can barely remember the steps as it is.' He tosses me a grin before turning towards the drink table. 'But I'll get you one, nevertheless.'

I let out a shaky breath as I watch him walk into the crowd, my corset suddenly feeling far too tight. The key is slick in my palm, hot against my skin.

'May I have this dance?'

I spin around, my face close to one splattered with freckles. Lenny's usually messy hair is combed, red strands tamed for the evening. He's dressed in a fine black suit, blending in with the rest of the men around us.

'Why, of course,' I reply, forcing a smile to my lips. His hand finds my waist, mine finds his shoulder, and then our free hands meet.

The key is clasped between our palms, and Lenny gives me a wide smile at the feel of it. 'Well done. Easy, right?'

My voice is distant, distracted. 'Yeah. Easy.'

'You remember the plan?'

I sigh. 'Well, I'm not really doing much, am I? Now all I have to do is survive the last Trial.'

'Yeah, well, that may be the hardest task of all.'

I nod once, focusing on the spinning figures around us, spotting Andy dancing with a blushing girl I've never seen before. My eyes wander to where Kitt and Jax are laughing, the former ruffling his little brother's hair with a wide grin. I saw Blair earlier, though it isn't difficult to find her again with her bright green dress burning my eyes. I look away before I find myself searching once again for a certain prince in the crowd.

There are only five of us left.

I briefly wonder how many will survive to see the sun set tomorrow. Briefly wonder what parents will be mourning their child. Death is what these Trials bring – not honor, not glory, not happiness. Only death.

'Are you alright?' Lenny's soft voice washes over me, and I turn my attention back to his big, brown eyes.

'Are any of us alright?'

He gives me a half-shrug. 'Good point.'

The dance ends and our hands drop, but not before Lenny transfers the key into his palm and then his pocket. 'Be careful tomorrow.' His voice is a low whisper, laced with worry.

'Aw, are you worried about me, Lenny?' I croon.

'Maybe a little, Princess.' He almost rolls his eyes. 'Don't die, okay?'

'I can't make any promises, but for your sake, I'll try to stay alive. Wouldn't want you to have to live without me.' He smiles and shakes his head at me, but I catch his arm before he can turn away. 'Hey, good luck. And remember what I told you about the passage. Oh, and—'

His laugh cuts me off. 'Plagues, have a little faith in me, Paedyn. I've got this.'

I sigh and give him a slight nod before he turns and disappears into the crowd.

I smooth a sweaty hand over the thick corset of my dress before running it down the soft fabric billowing beneath. Then I turn on my heel, my legs sliding easily through the skirt's slits I begged Adena to make extra high so I wouldn't feel restricted by fabric. Maybe that's the claustrophobia talking or maybe I simply like to have the option of sending a high kick towards someone's face if need be.

I nearly run into Jax on the dance floor, and he grins at the sight of me. 'Paedyn, hi! Do you want to dance? Andy ditched me. Not to mention that she has had far too much wine, and I don't trust her not to fall on top of me.'

With a laugh, I nod before we begin spinning around the floor. A mellow waltz has started, the type with specific steps and switching partners, the type I typically try to avoid. But I let my feet guide me, trusting myself to remember the correct steps while trying to forget exactly why I can do this at all. Try to forget being held in the dark, led with strong arms and—

Stop.

Plagues, get a hold of yourself.

I look at the boy in front of me, all smiles and excitement. 'You look dashing, Jax.'

His smile shifts into something akin to shy. 'Thank you. Um. You look—'

We spin, and I'm pulled into the arms of a different gentleman. I nod politely to the young man, and he does the same as we step in time. Before I know it, I'm being passed around, held in the hands of men I've never met before. The waltz is a long one, making me regret stepping onto the dance floor.

My feet are killing me.

Then I'm turning into another body, encompassed by arms belonging to a grinning Kitt.

'There you are. I knew I'd get you back.'

I crack a small smile. 'Took you long enough.'

I hear him laugh before I'm pulled flush against a new partner.

'You're avoiding me.'

My heart flutters at that voice, the butterflies in my stomach doing the same as the slight scent of pine washes over me. I blink at the broad chest, very aware of the strong frame hiding beneath the crisp, white shirt. Taking a deep breath, I lift my gaze to meet his.

Oh, and I wish I hadn't.

His eyes are mesmerizing, like melted steel, morning fog. They cut through me as though he is unafraid to see every part of me. His gaze feels right, familiar. And when his eyes lock with mine, I wonder why I ever bother looking at anyone else.

No. No. *No.*

Despite him feeling so right, I feel so very wrong and so very confused.

He hasn't taken his eyes off me, and the weight of his gaze is pressing as he patiently watches me puzzle things out. Puzzle these *feelings* out.

'I wouldn't call it . . . *avoiding.*' I sound very unconvincing, and rightfully so since I have been doing just that. And even though my very life is a lie, it seems my skills of deception have run out for the evening because I'm not fooling him.

The corner of his mouth twitches upwards, and I have to make a conscious effort not to stare at his lips. But just like this morning, I find myself wanting to lean into him. I don't know what would have happened if I'd stayed in his room any longer, and yet, all day I've been kicking myself for not finding out.

It took everything in me to push him away despite how badly I wanted to pull him closer. But then I remind myself of who he is, what he is. Where he is the prince, the future Enforcer, the son of the man I hate, I am a Slummer, an Ordinary, the embodiment of the thing he has been taught to hate.

My thoughts scatter when a dimple catches my eye. 'Then enlighten me. What would you call it, Gray?'

He spins me out with one hand before pulling me back into him, my back connecting with his chest. My hands are crossed over my stomach where he's holding them from behind me, our bodies swaying together to the beat of the music.

'You seemed *preoccupied,* and I didn't want to interrupt,' I say, recalling the women he's danced with. His huff of laughter tells me he does too.

The brush of his jaw against my hair has my heart racing. He leans down so his face is beside mine, lips brushing the shell of my ear. 'Hmm. Do you want to know what I think?' He tugs on my hands, pulling me closer. 'I think you're avoiding dancing with me because you can't handle being so close.'

I nearly choke on the laugh that escapes me. 'Please. I have no problem being close to you.'

Lies. Lies. *Liar.*

It seems my skill for deception is back.

'Is that right?' His lips are against my ear, fingers laced with mine, body pressed close.

I'm hot and cold, yes and no, right and wrong. I'm the embodiment of opposites, a jumble of confusion and contradictions.

I want this.

I don't want this.

He dips his head so his chin rests on my shoulder.

Oh, I definitely want this.

Oh, but I definitely shouldn't.

'Then why do you push me away?'

I still. There was so much emotion in his voice, so much raw uncertainty as the words left his lips. He spins me to face him slowly, not bothering to take a step back or put space between us.

My chest heaves, my heart hammers. His eyes crash into mine and I allow myself to take him in, admire this boy that I have come to know.

He's devastating. Everything about him is stunning and sharp and stealing my breath away. But it's the way he's looking at me that suddenly makes swallowing seem like a struggle, breathing seem like a chore. I've never been looked at like it's a privilege to be in my presence, an honor to hold my gaze, a gift to get a glimpse of me. Not until I met him.

His mask slips, splinters, shatters, leaving only a boy beholding a girl like she is worthy of his wanting.

And what terrifies me even more is that I think I might be looking at him the same way, looking at him with that same longing. Try as I might to fight it, I can't help but long for this boy who has saved my life more times than I care to admit. This boy who is equally calculating and charming, equally cool and caring. The one who's tended to my wounds, learned about my past, been my distraction when I needed it most.

The one who understands me.

And then my heart halts, pulse plummets.

But he doesn't, does he?

He doesn't even know who I truly am. *What* I truly am. And if he did, he would kill me. Because that is what the Enforcer would do. Because that is what the king's son would do. Because that is what he has been created to do.

And for that reason, I push him away. Because if I don't, I'll pull him closer. And if I pull him closer, it will only end in a dagger being plunged through my heart. The heart that beats a little too fast when he is around, breaks a little too easily, and aches a little too much for him.

I stare back at him, not knowing what to say or do or—

I'm suddenly swept from his arms and into another's before I have the chance to answer.

Perfect timing.

'You look beautiful,' Jax spits out, grinning from ear to ear. 'That's what I was going to say earlier.' He puffs out his chest slightly, proud of himself for finally voicing the compliment.

'Thank you, Jax,' I say, smiling at him. When the song comes to an end, I quickly step off the dance floor. I'm eager to get away from the press of bodies as I snatch a drink off a servant's tray and head for the edge of the ballroom. Except that I can't seem to escape the crowd. Everywhere I look is occupied by groups of gossiping guests or silent servants.

My eyes sweep over the packed ballroom, landing on the large windows and the fresh air that awaits just outside of them. I itch for a moment to myself, a moment free from the crowded and closed-in room.

I sip at my wine, watching the whirling guests before I set the glass on the table and head for the hallway beyond the ballroom. I'm forced to slide between bodies, hating the cramped feeling.

I suck in a deep breath as I head towards the giant, grand doors leading to the courtyard beyond. The sound of my heels clicking against the floor fills the silence as I approach the daunting doors.

My hand is outstretched, itching to throw open the exit when a Flash speeds between me and my salvation.

CHAPTER 52

Paedyn

The Imperial's smile is cold as he peers down at me, white uniform crisp and smelling of starch.

'I can't let you do that, little lady.' His belittling tone has me biting back the retort rising to my lips.

I am not in the mood.

'I just need a few minutes outside for a bit of fresh air.' If I were in Loot right now, I wouldn't even bother being polite.

'Like I said, I can't let you do that.' He smirks and a few of the Imperials lining the hallway chuckle with him, apparently a part of whatever hilarious joke I'm missing. 'You don't have permission to be outside of the castle, little lady.'

I clench my fists at my sides, resisting the urge to dare him to call me *little lady* one more time and see what happens. 'All I'm asking for is a moment outside.'

'Really? And what are you willing to do to get it?' He leans in, and the stench of alcohol on his breath is evident as he says, 'What's in it for me?'

Then he slings an arm around my waist, tugging me towards him. Wrong move.

My fingers wrap around the handle of my dagger, feeling the

cold steel I'm about to—

'Careful, she'll press that blade to your throat. I would know.'

I still, turning my head slightly to see Kai standing several feet away, hands casually tucked into his pockets. 'Now let her go and open the door.' His voice is like the steel of my dagger, cold and sharp.

The Imperial only sputters. 'But, sir, we have orders that the contestants are not to leave the—'

'And now you have new orders. So I suggest you open the damn door.'

Kai's blank expression hasn't changed despite his deadly tone. He's even leaning against the wall now, his hands still stuffed into his pockets. The perfect picture of power. 'Oh,' he adds, 'and if you want to keep your job, your hand, and your head, I suggest you release the *little lady*.' I almost crack a smile at that. The Imperial doesn't waste a second before practically jumping away from me. He knows just as well as I do that Kai's threats are never empty.

The Imperial strides swiftly past Kai, but not before the prince's hand grabs his shirt and slams him against the wall. 'I lied,' Kai mutters close to the man's face. 'You'll be lucky if I let you keep your head, let alone your hand for lying a finger on her.'

The doors swing open, tearing my eyes away from the scene I'm not sure I want to witness. Humid, sticky air hits me the moment I begin descending the steps into the courtyard beyond. The sky is dark and thick with heavy clouds that rumble with the promise of rain.

I take a deep breath, relishing the fresh air and open space around me. Something wet splatters on my cheek, and I turn my face towards the cloudy sky that is now beginning to drizzle down on me. I spread out my arms and tilt my head up, loving the feel of rain pelting my skin.

Then the drizzle turns into a downpour. Rain is falling rapidly while I'm smiling stupidly. My head feels clearer than it has in days as cool water coats my skin, my dress, my hair. I spin in place, the skirts of my gown swishing around my ankles, feeling like an idiot and absolutely loving it.

I slip the shoes from my aching feet and pad through puddles like I did as a little girl, reminding me of a time when I was younger and yearning for the love of a father who was no longer with me. When

I was terrified and terribly traumatized. The crowded streets of Loot pressed in on me constantly, making me feel caged and claustrophobic.

But then I would climb up to the roofs of old shops and buildings with only the stars for company. I felt freer in the open air, impossibly more peaceful. I did that for months, years, before my fear fell away and Loot became more of a home and less of a horror.

Laughter bubbles out of me. Hysterical. I am completely hysterical.

Plagues, how much wine did I have?

Rain is sticking strands of hair to my face and dripping down the tip of my nose while I smile through it all, momentarily forgetting about my troubles and simply taking a moment to *exist*.

'I don't know that I ever lived before lying eyes on the likes of you.' I spin, blinking through the steady stream of rain before my eyes find the gray ones blending in with the sheet of water falling down on us. His hair is dripping wet, all wavy and tousled. His white button-down shirt is sticky and see-through, showing off an inked chest and tanned torso beneath.

And the sight of him has me smiling.

'I'm sure you say that to all the *little ladies* who catch your eye,' I say, half-laughing, half-hysterical.

'Oh, but I only have eyes for one little lady, and I can't seem to take them off of her.' His chest is rising and falling just as rapidly as the rain while my heart is thundering just as loudly as the storm.

He's suddenly serious, scanning my face. 'Did you need some fresh air? A break from the crowded room?'

There he goes again, understanding me.

'Yes,' I answer softly. 'I feel much better out here. Freer.'

He bends near the beds of flowers beside the stairs and plucks one from the soggy soil before rising to his feet.

'Good,' he says quietly, 'because I am going to get very, very close to you.'

I let out a slow breath when he takes a step towards me. Then another. And another. He's close enough now that I can feel the heat of his body, feel the heat that spreads through me when he gets too close.

I tilt my head up to meet his gaze, blinking at him as I try to see through the rain. I wipe at my eyes, suddenly aware that there is likely makeup running down my face before deciding that I don't really care.

His lips are tugged into a smile as he holds up the flower to me, drooping and dripping with water. Its small petals are a stunning shade of vibrant blue that hints at purple.

'A forget-me-not, since you always seem to be forgetting who I am,' Kai says with a soft smile, a soft laugh. He lifts his hand, tucking the flower behind my ear before letting his fingers run through my wet hair.

'Oh, I know who you are,' I say breathlessly. 'A cocky bastard.'

He shakes his head at me, his fingers still toying with strands of my hair. 'I don't give a damn if you forget who I am in title, so long as you remember who I am to *you*.'

I stare up at him, and something must be amusing because through my rapidly blinking eyes I watch a slow smile spread across Kai's lips. I open my mouth to say something only to snap it shut when he begins tugging off his suit coat. It slips from his arms, leaving him standing before me in a white shirt completely soaked through.

Well, that's not distracting at all.

He steps even closer, and with the coat draped over his arms, he holds it over my head to cover me from the rain.

'Kai . . .'

The smile that lights up his face stops me short, steals my breath. It's one of those rare, real smiles of his that I confessed I wanted to see more of. One that belongs to me.

Dimples.

Both of them on display. Both distracting. Both devastating.

'What?' I ask, my voice filled with laughter.

He shrugs, a smile still spread across his face. 'I just love the sound of my name coming from your lips.'

I clear my throat that has suddenly become far too dry. 'Well, Kai isn't your real name, now, is it?'

He's silent, nothing but a smile and a sudden intensity in his eyes, daring me to say his full name. *Wanting* me to say his name. And apparently, I want to say it too because when I open my mouth, one word falls out.

'Malakai.'

His eyes flutter shut, his head falls back, allowing the rain full access to his face. The smile on his lips and the column of his neck make me swallow. His head is still tipped towards the sky, speaking to it as he says, 'Only you can make my name sound worth saying.'

'Well, what would you like me to call you? Kai? Malakai?' My voice sounds so breathy, and I almost wish I could blame it on a panic attack.

His answer is simple, straightforward, as he dips his head down to look at me. 'Call me anything you like. I'll never pass up the chance to hear your voice, darling.'

I can feel a smile lifting my lips. 'Alright then, cocky bastard it is.'

I wasn't prepared for the laugh that escapes him. It's a rich, beautiful sound I wish I had the time to commit to memory.

'Careful, Kai,' his smirk grows at the sound of his name once more, 'You're being a gentleman again.' My gaze flicks to the black coat he is still holding above my head to shield me from the rain. 'But you do know I'm already soaked, right?'

'Yes, well.' He sighs and ducks his head so we are eye to eye. 'As adorable as you looked blinking up at me in the rain, I want you to see me clearly when I tell you this.'

There goes that stupid flutter in my chest.

'I meant what I said. I can't take my eyes off you. I can't take my *mind* off you.'

I look away from his burning gaze, shaking my head as I mutter, 'Kai, I—'

'Paedyn.'

I still. I shiver. He says my name like it's sacred, like it's an oath he's swearing.

He tilts his head to the side, eyes roaming over my face. 'Tell me,' he murmurs, 'what do you want me to call you?'

My eyes slowly meet his, confused by his question. 'What do *you* want to call me?'

'I want to call you *mine*.'

We stare at each other. Both of us breathing hard, both of us taking in the other. The rain is still splattering Kai, clinging to his thick lashes and dripping from his jaw.

'I know you feel it too,' he says quietly.

'Feel what?'

'Feel alive. Feel on fire. *Feel*.' There is an intensity in his eyes, his voice, that makes my heart race even faster. He looks away, cursing under his breath before his gaze crashes back into mine. 'Pae, when I look at you . . . I'm devastated. I'm drowning. I'm dying to catch my breath.'

The air leaves my lungs and now my blinking has nothing to do with the rain. His next words are nearly a whisper. 'Look at me and tell me you don't feel the same.'

Silence. And then—

'I don't feel the same, Kai.' Lies. Lies. *Liar*.

He ducks his head, and when he lifts it to look at me again, his smile is crooked. Then he slowly lowers the coat shielding me from the rain and wraps it around my shoulders, fingers lingering against my bare collarbones and sending a jolt through me.

It's far too big, and his hands curl around the fabric before he tugs, pulling me so close that my body is pressed against his. He is still clutching the front of the coat, knuckles brushing my bare skin before his lips are against the shell of my ear.

'Now answer again,' his murmur is amused, 'but without tapping your left foot this time.'

My mouth falls open.

His lips are smiling against my ear, and I'm trying not to focus on the feel of it. 'I . . . I don't—'

His deep chuckle cuts me off. 'God, you're stunning.' Rough fingers have never felt so gentle against my skin as he brushes a strand of wet hair out of my eyes. 'But so damn stubborn.'

I can't do this anymore. I can't *not* give in to the temptation that is him. I'm suddenly unable to think of a single reason why I'm fighting this, why I shouldn't close the gap between us right now. I want to—

His lips meet mine. Barely.

It's the whisper of a kiss, a promise of passion. And yet, I nearly melt at the contact. His hand is cupping my face, thumb stroking my cheekbone and then—

Nothing.

He pulls back.

I nearly gasp, wanting to grab him, pull him closer, press my lips to his. And I'm about to do just that when I suddenly remember a time when our roles were reversed. When I was the one teasing him with touches.

Now I understand exactly how affected Kai was by the lack of my touch during our game of archery and distraction. The feel of something and then nothing is a cruel thing to bestow upon someone, and he's left me burning because of it.

His other hand has found its way around my waist under his large jacket, and the heat of his palm through my corset is a brand. He tilts his head, studying me with a small smile.

He knows exactly what he's doing.

And yet, he's taking me in as though he doesn't want to rush this moment. His thumb has found my bottom lip where it's now trailing lazily, igniting a fire inside of me.

'You promised that I could touch you when I was sober.'

My breath hitches and the corners of his lips twitch in response. I was not expecting him to say that. I was not even expecting him to remember my hasty promise from the last ball.

He ducks his head, his mouth suddenly a breath away from mine once more. 'But I'm never sober around you, Pae. Never not drunk on every detail that is you.'

I'm speechless. Utterly speechless that this boy could feel so much. Feel so much for *me*.

'If I kiss you – really kiss you, like how I've wanted to, how I've waited to – should I expect a dagger at my throat?' His voice is rough, his gaze greedy.

And then I reach up slowly and flick the tip of his nose.

This time, I do take a moment to memorize the smile he gives me. 'I guess you'll have to kiss me to find out.'

430

CHAPTER 53

Kai

She flicked my nose. I never knew a heart could feel so much, could be so affected by the flick of a finger.

'I guess you'll have to kiss me to find out.'

Oh, and I plan on doing just that.

I've barely been able to hold myself back from wanting to hold her.

She's so beautiful I can hardly believe it, hardly breathe. Her soul is stunning. Her very being is bright and bold and so unbelievably better than I am. She is a good beyond my grasp, one that I am not worthy of glimpsing let alone grabbing hold of.

And yet, here she is despite that. Choosing me.

It's a privilege to look into those eyes, to drown in the essence that is her.

Because everything about her is too right and everything about me is too wrong. But I'm selfish. I take what I want, and what I want might just want me for once.

My jacket is still slung over her shoulders, and the rain is rolling down her face, her hair, clinging to her long lashes and dripping makeup. Beads of water join the light freckles dusting her nose, all twenty-eight of them. The steady stream of rain is slapping the cobblestone at our feet, soaking us to the bone.

'I'll take my chances,' I murmur as my fingers catch her chin, tilting her face up towards mine. Her mouth is pulled into a soft smile that only draws my lips closer to hers.

She doesn't pull away.

Perhaps the beast can earn the beauty after all.

Her eyes flutter shut against the rain still relentlessly falling on us, and I don't think I've ever witnessed a more beautiful moment. 'My pretty Pae, what have you done to me?' I murmur, my nose brushing hers.

Is this what it feels like to truly feel?

Closer.

The sparks between us are almost tangible, snaking their way up my body and shocking me.

Closer.

Our lips brush. 'Your Highness.' I halt.

Then I sigh against her lips, making her shudder.

I pull back, barely, just enough to look between her eyes and the mouth I had every intention of lazily exploring.

I don't even acknowledge the Imperial that dared to distract me from her. My eyes are pinned on Paedyn, my voice deceptively calm as I say, 'I hope whatever you have to say is worth losing your tongue over for interrupting us.'

I see the Imperial shift on his feet out of the corner of my eye, equally uncomfortable and concerned. 'Sir, um, you are, uh—'

Paedyn looks like she wants to stab him, and I'm considering letting her do just that. Still not deeming him worthy enough to look at, I speak towards Pae as I say to the Imperial, 'Spit it out before I make you. Or before I let the lady do the honors.'

Her lips twitch and the action has me losing control, has me pulling her face towards mine, completely ignoring the gawking guard.

'It's the king,' the Imperial blurts, no doubt knowing he won't be able to get my attention again once my mouth has met hers. 'It's urgent.'

It was not, in fact, urgent.

And I am, in fact, seriously contemplating carving out that Imperial's tongue because of it.

Even though I know he's not to blame, I need to take my anger out on someone, and that can't exactly be my father.

'I don't need you to babysit me,' I sigh, not bothering to conceal my annoyance.

'Then stop acting like a child and maybe I'll stop treating you like one.' Father's gaze is piercing, pinning me to the spot. Memories of when I was a boy come flooding back, memories of those stern eyes watching as I endured test after test. Watching as he forced me to torture someone for the first time, forced me to fight him.

A cold laugh climbs up my throat only to be lost in the sound of music and chatter filling the ballroom. 'This is bullshit.'

'No, it's necessary.' His voice rises, causing guests to quickly turn in the other direction, avoiding the temperamental king. 'What's bullshit is that my people just watched their prince, their future Enforcer, race off the dance floor after a *Slummer*.' He spits the word like the taste of it disgusts him.

'How quickly you have forgotten that *Slummers* are also your people, Father. *My* people,' I fire back, fists clenched at my sides, so I don't do something I'll regret.

But I certainly don't regret running after her.

He faces me fully, his chest rising and falling with anger, promising punishment. If I were about five years younger and five inches shorter, this look might have frightened me. But not anymore.

'I will not see you throw away your kingdom's respect for a girl. For *that* girl,' he says, voice low and lethal. 'I'll find you a different pretty plaything who isn't a Mundane if that's what you need.'

Once again, I'm puzzling over his clear hatred for Paedyn, and her clear hatred for him. But, knowing he won't answer that question, I ask instead, 'So you sent one of my own Imperials to spy on me? To lie to his prince and say there is something *urgent*?' My voice drops, and I take a step towards him. 'An innocent man will lose his tongue because of the order you gave him.'

'The fact that you don't think this is urgent alarms me.' The king's nostrils flare in a way I've come to associate with punishment to follow. 'I thought I trained you better than this, boy. Perhaps you need some more *lessons*.' At that, he almost smiles. 'Your duties are to these people, your kingdom. You belong in here, a part of this dance, where everyone can see you. See their future.' His lips curl into a sneer. 'Not outside playing with your pretty new *toy*.'

I stare him down, my blood beginning to boil. 'What do you think could possibly happen between you two, hmm?' Father's laugh is cold as he continues, 'Who knows, you might just have the pleasure of killing her in the next Trial.'

Something inside of me snaps.

Power surges through my veins as every ability in the room presses down on me, begging me to release one. When I'm angered like this, it's harder to keep control, harder to suppress all the power thrumming inside of me. The king's words echo in my head, mocking me, making me feel weak for letting my restraint slip away.

'I thought I trained you better than this, boy. Perhaps you need some more lessons.'

A strong hand falls on my shoulder. 'Easy, Brother,' Kitt mutters under his breath before stepping between Father and me. His smile seems to ease the tension like it always does. This isn't the first fight that he has broken up between us.

Kitt clasps his hands in front of him casually, as if he hadn't just seen Father and I nearly ready to rip each other apart. 'Sorry to interrupt. Father, you look like you could use a drink. And maybe a dance or two with Mother.'

The smile he gives him is the same one he's been offering since we were children. The smile that cries out to be called worthy in the eyes of our father. The smile he plasters on, hoping to make the king proud of him. Hoping to live up to the high expectations and fit into the giant shoes he must fill.

He's always craved the approval, the attention, from the king. Kitt loves to be loved, and even he feels a lack of that when it comes to our own father despite the far better relationship they have. So, he will do whatever it takes to earn it.

And I don't fault him for it. Perhaps if I hadn't grown up with a father who tortured me with training, I would love him enough to want him to love me back. But Kitt grew up with a different version of the king, one who instructed and taught with a table of paperwork stretched between them rather than a sharp blade. One who taught him the ways of a king rather than the ways of torture. One who molded Kitt into a man rather than a monster.

Kitt places an encouraging hand on Father's arm, urging him towards the drinks and desserts. They both toss me one final glance, one of them kind and the other quite the opposite.

Fortunately, I've never been one to lust after love. Especially that of our father. I gave up on that the day his blade met my skin for the first time.

I scan the room for Paedyn, already knowing that I won't find her. She's likely been carted off to her chambers to retire early for the night, by order of the king. I almost laugh at his feeble attempts to keep me away from her.

If I can't keep myself away, there is no way in hell he can.

CHAPTER 54

Kai

The Bowl is packed to the brim with people. We could hear their shouts and stomps from the castle as we walked down the tree-lined path towards our final Trial.

For the third time, we face what could be our final day.

At least for this Trial, we weren't drugged before being dragged to a random location first. I awoke to a bang on my door followed by a note slipped underneath it, informing me that the final Trial will be held at the Bowl.

That left me no time to even speak to Paedyn, let alone think of her before I was being silently escorted out of the castle.

We have a live audience this time, and they roar when we step inside of the large arena. Imperials press in on every side, leading us to the rail overlooking the Pit several feet down. I hear a collective intake of breath from my fellow contestants, our gazes locked on what lies below us.

It's a maze.

The entire sandy bottom of the Pit is covered in rows of intertwined hedges and plants. The walls are dense and tall, filling the entire bottom of the oval arena.

It's enormous.

We are ushered down the wide steps descending towards the maze. I'm the last in the line of contestants, and when my feet sink slightly into the sand, we halt.

'Welcome, young Elites, to your final Trial.'

I turn my attention to the comfy glass box sitting at the bottom of the stands, decorated with its three cushioned seats. Kitt sits to the right, his eyes scanning the maze before they seem to land on me. I see his head tip slightly, silently wishing me good luck. After nodding slowly back at him, my eyes slide to where Mother looks elegant as always, legs crossed and face relaxed as she watches her husband standing at the edge of the rail, looking down at us as he speaks.

'Though you have all made it this far,' Father continues, Tealah projecting his voice beside him with a gentle hand on his shoulder, 'there can only be one winner.'

The crowd cheers, the sound like a battle cry I'm all too familiar with. 'Your last Trial is spread out before you. A maze.' Cold amusement contorts his face. 'Though nothing is as simple as it seems.' Then the maze shifts.

I catch the movement out of the corner of my eye and whip my head towards it, watching as the walls of foliage fold and reform. The hedges twist in new directions, altering the paths and creating new ones.

Blooms.

I spot them now, dozens of figures standing along the edges of the maze, arms outstretched. They've created this Trial for us, and they now control it.

'In order to win this Trial, thus improving your chances of winning the entirety of the Purging Trials, you must be the first contestant to make it to the center of the shifting maze.' The king pauses. 'But that is not all.'

There is always a catch.

'Not only do you have to be the first contestant to reach the middle, but you must also kill the person that awaits you there.'

Murmurs skitter across the crowd but Father's booming voice cuts through them easily. 'The person there is deserving of this punishment. They have committed crimes against the kingdom and will pay for them with their life.'

437

I'm not surprised. This way, the king will guarantee at least one kill to entertain the people during this Trial. I mentally shuffle through each prisoner I know to be rotting in our dungeons, wondering which sorry soul will meet its end today.

'May you all bring honor to your kingdom, your family, and yourself.'

The crowd echoes the king's words as an Imperial leads each of us to a separate opening of the maze. My eyes dart across the Pit, scanning the Imperials and the contestants they are escorting.

And then I see her.

Silver hair pinned up, swaying with each stride. Twenty-eight freckles dotting her nose, though I can't count them from here. Lips I have yet to truly taste pressing together, and ocean eyes crashing into mine.

I give her something then – a smile. One that is meant only for her.

There's nothing I can say to her, no time to taunt her with teasing words if only to ensure she will stay alive long enough to punch me in the face when this is all over.

So I don't say a thing.

I raise my hand and flick nothing but the air in front of me as I hold her gaze.

Plagues, the glowing grin she gives me is gorgeous. She lifts her hand, flicks the air, and—

And then she's gone.

CHAPTER 55

Paedyn

Today is the day. In fact, today might be my last day.

The Imperial guides me to an opening near the other side of the maze, leaving me there to stare up at the looming walls of foliage that dare me to enter. Dare me to get lost within its twist and turns.

Just survive today. That's all you have to do.

The sound of snapping twigs and twisting hedges from within the maze tells me that the paths are changing again. The maze is moving.

Movement to my left has my head swiveling towards a young girl, eyes glossy and unblinking as she stares at me with a hand raised above us, projecting what I hope is an emotionless expression onto one of the giant screens for all to see. There must be dozens of them patiently awaiting us in the maze, ready to broadcast the bloodshed.

I keep my face blank as I turn back to the opening of the maze in front of me, though I'm restless to race inside and get this over with.

Everything will change after today. 'Let the final Trial begin.'

I barely hear the king's words echo through the arena before the cries of the crazed crowd drown them out. I blink away my thoughts, blinking up at the opening before me and the walls awaiting.

And then I'm running.

As soon as I step into the maze, I'm smothered by the blanket of

shadows. It's dark and damp but I don't slow my pace. I run through the path of plants and hedged walls, skidding to a stop when I'm faced with my first decision.

Left or right.

I don't have the time to ponder my options, so I hang a left and am immediately faced with the same decision.

Right.

I run and run and— Dead end.

I backtrack, turning left instead of right and pick up my pace despite my slight panting. I fall into a routine of random guessing, retracing my steps, and cursing. Lots and lots of cursing.

'Dammit!' I'm yelling at nothing but the sixth dead end I've had the pleasure of stumbling upon. I spin on my heel and head back the way I came, barely glancing at the Sight who just witnessed, and recorded, my little outburst. I huff, senses feeling dull in this damp maze. The cries of the crowd outside are muffled, muted by the layers of thick foliage separating me from them.

It's eerily quiet in here, nothing but the sound of my pounding feet, pounding heart, and panting breaths filling the silence.

And then the maze shifts.

The path I'm standing in narrows, the hedges on either side of me press in.

I'm about to be squashed.

This is my nightmare. My most terrifying, claustrophobic nightmare. I sprint for the end of the path where another one awaits, one that isn't moving and won't crush me if I make it there in time. My lungs are burning, my feet shifting in the sand with each stumbling step.

Twigs and leaves and thick greenery brush my shoulders on both sides, threatening to swallow me whole as they continue closing in. But I keep running towards my salvation, towards the path awaiting me only a few yards away.

Branches and thorns I hadn't seen before now tear at the exposed skin on my arms, unrelenting as the walls continue to push against me. Any longer and I'll be trapped between foliage, skewered by branches and thorns.

Dead. I'll be dead if I don't get out. *Now.* I dive.

I hit the clear pathway hard, rolling to break my fall. And that's when pain erupts up my leg.

Lying on my side, chest heaving, I follow the stinging sensation to my left foot – the one trapped between the two hedges that have now molded together.

A strangled cry slips from my lips, and I clamp a hand over my mouth to stifle it. Red, hot blood is running down my leg, dripping onto the sand beneath it. I sit up, trying to calm my breathing as I stretch shaky hands towards the ankle that is barely covered by my now shredded boot.

I lean forward and claw at the tangle of twining branches, leaves, and thorns ensnaring my leg. After barely managing to snap off a branch, I've never wished for my dagger more than in this moment.

This maze is the work of Blooms, the work of Elites. Power fills the foliage creating these walls, woven together with the branches and leaves and thorns to make them thicker and stronger and deadlier.

I gulp down air, forcing myself to ignore the flaring pain in my foot. My hands clamp around my calf. I take a shaky breath. And then I pull.

It's like fire. The pain is so hot, so searing. I bite my tongue until I taste blood, watching as I pull more and more of my foot into view while simultaneously pulling the ruined boot off my foot. I stop, gasping for breath and a break from the pain.

Without my boot to protect my foot from the thorns and jagged branches, it is a mangled mass of torn flesh. Well, the part of it I can see, that is. The other half of my foot is still swallowed by the hedges now fused together, refusing to release me.

I swallow my scream of pain when I pull at my foot again. More torn flesh comes into view, bloody and looking like red ribbons trailing deep across my skin. But with one final yank followed by one final yelp, my foot is freed.

I fall onto my back, gasping for air and gasping from pain. I blink up at the sky, allowing myself one more moment to breathe before sitting up and tearing off the bottom strip of my tank. The burgundy fabric blends with the seeping blood from my wound as I wrap it around my foot as best I can.

Adena would be both fascinated and disgusted by how perfectly the colors match.

I push off the ground and stagger to my feet. Pain. Sharp pain and a slew of curses.

I limp forward, trying to ignore the throbbing ache from my foot that's climbing up my leg. But I can walk, proving that the injury could have been much, much worse.

Sweat clings to me, soaking the tank that is now torn dangerously short, displaying a good chunk of skin before the band of my pants wraps under my belly button. And despite the damp, cool breeze blowing through the hedges of the maze, I'm uncomfortably hot and sticky.

I press on, off-balance from pain and the lack of both shoes. The darkness deepens as I head farther into what I hope is the center of the maze and what awaits me there.

And if I make it there first, I will hold someone's life in my hands. *Left. Right. Left. Left. Dead end. Right. Left. Dead end.*

My claustrophobia has me feeling like the hedges are pressing in on me—

I slow to a stop. They *are* pressing in on me.

Panicking, I spin my head in every direction, trying to find a path that isn't attempting to swallow me whole. No luck. I force myself into a stumbling sort of run, skidding down paths at random and finding them all shifting.

This can't be right.

The king wouldn't just throw the contestants in this maze only to crush us for fun, right? Wasn't the fun supposed to be watching us crush each other?

I pause and allow myself to pant, to panic. If the king intends to flatten me with hedges, then there is nothing I can do about it. So, I stop and stare at the walls of greenery closing in on either side of me.

Then I close my eyes, bracing myself.

Looks like there will be one less Ordinary to worry about.

Branches brush my shoulders and I stiffen, suddenly and sadly prepared to greet Death.

I'll see you soon, Father.

442

Nothing.

I peek open an eye only to find that I'm faced with a wall of greenery. I blink. The hedges are no longer moving. I spin around, a branch snagging the fabric of my tank with the movement.

The path is now only slightly wider than the width of my shoulders.

I stagger towards the end and turn down another, finding it just as tight. I swallow, making a sharp left down an equally narrow path.

How cruel and cunning the king is. I almost want to applaud him for this appalling game. I was right. The fun of the Trials *is* watching us crush each other. And he just set the scene for the show.

A scream cuts through the quietness, ringing for a moment before being silenced the next, sending a chill sweeping down my spine.

Once again, we are being forced to fight. And there is only enough space on these paths for one body to pass through.

I take a shuddering breath, feeling the claustrophobia pressing in like the walls brushing my shoulders.

Only one contestant can fit on these paths at a time. So if I run into one—

'Thank the Plague,' the voice behind me is dripping with venom, 'I was worried I wasn't going to get to kill you before these Trials ended.'

CHAPTER 56

Kai

Right.

Right. Left. Dead end. *Shit.*

I tip my head back towards the cloudy sky far above us, seeming even darker from within this dusky maze. Taking a deep breath, I turn and jog back the way I came, choosing to head right this time.

Wrong.

Another dead end is tempting me to drive my fist into it, though I know that will only cause more damage to me than the plants.

I pick up my pace and breeze past a Sight, ignoring him and his unsettling stare. I'm in a pissy mood. Not exactly surprising, considering that I've been running around a maze in the heat, meeting only dead ends, and driving myself mad.

Other than evading being crushed by moving walls and encountering a few dozen snakes slithering out from under them, I've kept myself relatively busy with the constant running. I have no concept of time in here, but with my rapidly beating heart and ragged breathing, I know I've been at this for a while.

Sand shifts under my feet, and then the hedges shift at my sides.

I hear the muffled cries of excitement from the crowd as the maze begins to rearrange itself again, so I dart out of the path and into

another that is also shrinking just as quickly. Turning right, I'm only faced with more closing hedges.

I spin, my eyes searching. Everywhere I look seems to promise death by plants. A pitiful way to die. I stand in the path, watching as the walls close in on me. I've never felt so powerless, so unable to do anything to stop this impending doom.

And then the walls halt.

My shoulders press into the two hedges now threatening to crush me. I step forward, arms scraping against the too-tight walls of foliage on either side.

A bitter laugh escapes me, the sound swallowed by the thick walls. *Clever, Father.*

I sigh, pressing onward through the maze, knowing that if I come across another contestant, there is only one way to get around them.

Left. Right. Right. Jaguar. I blink.

That was not what I was expecting.

The jaguar blinks back, its coat the color of deep wine, its eyes the color of sweet honey.

'Hello, Andy.'

She cocks her head to the side, her mannerisms mirroring that of a cat toying with a mouse. And that worries me. I don't know how long she's been in her animal form, but I can see it's been long enough for her to lose herself in it.

Andy's ability is just as dangerous to herself as it is to others. The longer she stays shifted, the harder it is to keep her head. This is the exact reason she's trained so much with her ability, and the exact reason why I don't use it very often. When we were children, she would be in her animal form for days at a time, unable to shift herself back until finally waking up as a human again with no memory of what had happened.

Over the years, she's learned to control it, learned to stay in her right mind even while being in a different body. But with all the adrenaline pumping through her jaguar form, her control seems to be slipping. Which is exactly why she's staring at me like I'm a piece of meat.

'Easy, Andy.' I raise my hands slowly in the air, taking a step back. She takes a step forward. No, she *prowls* forward.

Shit.

This path is so tight that there's no way she could get peacefully around me even if she wanted to. Not that there is anything peaceful about the way she's looking at me, the way she's crouching low in the sand.

I don't want to hurt her, but hell, she wants to hurt me. She's eying me like a predator would, promising their prey a painful death.

I reach out for an ability close by like I've done multiple times since stepping into this maze. Plague knows I've tried to grab hold of a Bloom's power so I could flatten these walls and walk straight to the center of the maze. And that's exactly what I would do if they weren't so deliberately staying out of my range.

The thrum of Andy's ability is overpowering, the only one close enough to feel—

Wait.

There's a faint tickling in my veins, the feel of a power coming closer. I grasp at it and—

Andy lunges.

Claws outstretched towards my throat, razor teeth bared, a blob of burgundy flashing towards me.

And then I'm standing behind her.

Andy crashes into the sand where she intended to crash into me. She lets out a roar of frustration and is barely able to spin around in the narrow pathway. Only the agility of a cat could fold itself to face me with such little room.

With another roar, she lunges at me again. And with another Blink of Jax's ability, I'm behind her. Again. She follows the same pattern of spinning around to try and sink her teeth into me all over again.

And then Jax's power coursing through my veins falters, flickers.

No, no—

And then it fails.

He's too far from me now, lost in the maze and taking his ability with him.

Well, that leaves me no choice.

With only one ability available to me, I finally take advantage of it. I shift.

Plagues, I forgot how much I hated this. There is a flash of light before my bones begin shifting, muscles stretching, every part of my body achingly aware of every change. I'm close to the ground, body sleek and strong and slicked with a shiny coat. I feel my canines elongate, sharpened to deadly points. My eyesight sharpens with them, narrowing on the smaller jaguar before me.

Keep your head. Keep your head. Keep your head.

With the little training I've had compared to Andy, it's far easier for me to lose my mind to the animal I have just become. So, the faster this fight ends, the better.

Andy seems only slightly surprised that I have gone from human to jaguar, matching her, mirroring her. But she recovers quickly, and the sudden swipe of her claws catches me across the side of my face. She slashes upward, barely missing my eye.

I grunt in pain. No, *growl* in pain.

I leap towards her, slashing out with my own razor-sharp claws. I swipe her across the chest, and she lets out a cry of pain before leaping on top of me.

This might be the strangest fight I've ever been in. And that is saying a lot.

And yet, it feels so natural in this body. My claws and canines know exactly what to do as I slash at her. Red blood blends into her burgundy fur as we roll over one another, growling and slicing each other's flesh anywhere we can.

We are quite literally fighting like rabid animals.

I let instinct take over, let myself tap into that animal side a little more.

Keep your head. Keep your head. Keep your head.

She's on top of me and my teeth snap, meeting the soft skin of her neck. She yelps, and I throw her off me, watching as she tumbles into the sand and crashes into a hedge. I slink towards her, paws padding silently as I close in on my kill.

No. Not my kill. My family. Andy.

She's trying to get up, trying to slice me with her claws and teeth as I approach. I crouch over her, this small jaguar who dared challenge me. My teeth are bared, and a growl grows in my throat.

I am Kai Azer, prince and future Enforcer of Ilya. I am Kai Azer, prince and fu—

Pain.

Jagged teeth are clamped around my shoulder, tearing at flesh and fur. I roar and raise my uninjured arm, ready to finish this with one swipe.

A flash of light momentarily blinds my sharp eyes and I stagger back, stunned as I'm returned to my senses.

I was about to kill her.

I need to change back. Now.

Blinking, I look down at where Andy should be lying beneath me. But there's nothing there. A sudden shadow looms above, drawing my attention up towards the sky. Well, where the sky would be if I could see it.

Vines and thick foliage have created a barrier over the top of the maze, a dome of greenery enclosing us completely. I hear the rustle of feathers and a flash of wine-red wings flapping against the thick ceiling.

She's shifted into a falcon, trying desperately to fly up and over this maze with no luck. A valiant effort, but one that the Blooms cannot allow. Andy screeches, trying to claw at the branches trapping her in this cage. Then she's diving back towards the sand, blinding me with a flashing light. I blink and she's back in her jaguar form, not giving me a second glance before limping away.

I don't waste another second before shifting back. My clothes are still intact, if not soaked with blood. I'm covered in deep gashes, the one on my face stinging as blood streams down into my eye. But it's the bite mark that draws my attention. It's deep and dripping blood, the outline of a set of sharp teeth imprinted into the skin of my shoulder.

And it hurts like hell.

I rip off a strip of fabric from the hem of my shirt and wrap it around the wound, trying to stop the steady flow of blood. My very bones seem to ache as I head off again through the maze, having wasted far too much time clawing at my cousin.

Right. Left. Left. Screams. I still.

Another cry. Right.

Left. Right.

I stop, suddenly.

The faintest tingle of power bubbles in my veins. I focus on it, willing it to grow stronger. It does. And I don't hesitate to grab hold of it.

A smile splits my bloody face.

Looks like a Bloom got too close.

CHAPTER 57

Paedyn

'Don't worry, I'll make this quick. Sadly, I don't have enough time to play with you.'

I spin around slowly in the narrow path, facing the owner of that cold voice and even colder brown eyes. 'Blair,' I say stiffly.

She steps towards me with a smile twisting her lips. 'Hello, Paedyn.'

'Are you sure you want to do this?' I ask coolly. 'Have you already forgotten what I did to your nose the last time we fought?'

'No,' she practically snarls, 'I haven't forgotten.'

I take a step back, branches clawing at my arms, foot protesting in pain. I open my mouth to spout off another remark to buy me more time, but nothing comes out. In fact, air isn't getting in.

And then my feet leave the ground.

I'm gasping, clawing at my neck though I know there isn't a hand constricting my windpipe. No, this is the work of nothing more than Blair's twisted mind. Her signature move. I'm dangling in the air, several feet off the ground, choking.

'Just because I'm going to make this quick, doesn't mean it won't be painful.' She gives me a pout. 'Sorry, Paedyn. We don't always get what we want, do we?'

My vision blurs, making it difficult to see the hand stretched

towards me or the wicked smile curving her lips. I can just barely breathe. Despite her promise to make this quick, she's drawing this out.

Think. *Think.*

I need to get close enough to her to land a blow. Our spar after the ball taught me all I need to know about the lack of physical fighting she does. If I can just get close to her . . .

If I can just *breathe.*

'You would know a lot about not getting what you want.' My voice is a croak, a pitiful excuse at sounding passive. Just using the limited air I have to speak those words has my head spinning, has me praying that she'll take the bait.

Her hold loosens. Barely.

There is a question in her eyes, one I intend to answer. 'Kai.' His name tumbles out of my mouth, breathless.

Blair's stare is sharper than my dagger I so desperately wish I had right now. 'The princes,' I continue with a cough. 'Kai and Kitt both. You can't have either of them.' I pause before choking out, 'Because they don't want you.'

I slam into the ground.

The little air I had whooshes out of me. I'm left panting, my face half-buried in the sand.

Get up.

I lift my head and push shaky arms underneath me, slowly making it to my feet. And alarmingly, Blair lets me. A fit of coughing laughter escapes me when my eyes meet hers.

I hold her gaze, now burning with anger.

That's it. Get mad enough to hurt me with your own two hands.

'Tell me, what's it like? Being rejected over and over and—'

I don't even get the chance to finish my sentence before I'm thrown through the air and crashing back into the sand. Coughing, catching my breath, I begin rolling over onto my back.

Blinding pain shoots through my ribs.

I curl into myself, my only defense against the hard boot connecting with my stomach. I crack an eye open, catching sight of Blair's livid face above me, contorted in rage.

'*Never forget that your wit is a weapon to be wielded, if only your mind can be as sharp as your blade.*'

I smile despite the pain.

I have her right where I want her.

Her foot drives into my stomach again, and this time, I catch it. I hear her gasp of surprise when I twist it terribly before yanking it towards me, sending her crashing to the ground.

I've knocked the wind out of her, something I know she isn't used to feeling, not when she's always had her power to hide behind. I'm crawling on top of her in an instant, pinning her arms down beneath my knees. She growls up at me, her gaze filled with guttural rage.

I know I only have time for one hit before she recovers and throws me off with her mind. So I make that hit count.

I slide my father's ring onto my middle finger and send a hard right hook to her temple, hitting that sensitive spot on her head with very little sensitivity.

And just like that, she's out cold.

But not for long. She'll wake within the next couple of minutes, and by then, I'll be lost in the maze and hopefully far away. Because next time we meet, I have a feeling she'll crush my heart on sight.

I stumble to my feet, body aching. Every inch of me screams in protest, staggers with each step. But I force myself forward, force myself to pick up speed.

I'm lost in the madness of the maze again, second guessing each path I take, wondering if the other would have led to my victory.

Left or right?

Left. Definitely left.

Definitely not, seeing that it's a dead end.

Every few minutes I hear a cry of pain or sounds of a struggle blending with the shouts of the crowd far beyond these walls. Sights stand in the paths, startling me so much that I nearly punch half of them. But as soon as they see me coming, they move out of my way as best they can. I feel sorry for them, sorry that the things they have witnessed have been permanently burned into their brains.

The maze rearranges itself for the dozenth time, forcing me off my closing path and onto a new one.

I want to scream.

I turn right down a path at random before skidding to a stop. There, at the end of this narrow path, is a sandy, open circle. The center.

The victory.

My victory.

CHAPTER 58

Kai

The very earth is under my control. One could say I hold the world in the palm of my hand, though it's a very dramatic interpretation of my power. Well, the power I'm borrowing.

The maze wall before me collapses. The vines and foliage that make up the hedge sink back into the ground, slipping beneath the sand. I run forward, reaching out with the Bloom's power to tear down walls or split them in half.

I'm destroying every bit of the maze near me, unraveling vines and branches.

I create a clear and wide path all while hoping I'm running in the right direction. And I don't slow. Hedges melt apart for me to run through while others slither back into the earth where they sprouted from.

The shouts of the crowd amplify with each wall I tear down. The sound of my name echoes through the audience but I ignore it, focusing on my ability.

Focusing on the ability that is flickering. The power inside of me dims.

The Blooms have finally figured out what I'm doing and are no doubt running away from the maze, trying to get out of my range.

I split a wall in front of me, creating a path for me to run through. It grows and grows and then—

Stops.

The ability seeps from my bones, leaving me powerless and pointlessly holding an outstretched hand at the hedge. I push my way through the hole I created, thorns and branches clawing at me.

I hear the maze rebuilding itself behind me as the Blooms try to fix the damage I've done. But it's too late.

I've already made it to the center.

I step into the open circle, filled with nothing but sand and the two figures within it. The first came from a path in the maze opposite mine, and the flash of silver glinting in the light tells me exactly who it is.

Paedyn is limping. Her whole body seems to drag even while she pushes it to run. Her leg and body are bloodied, bruised.

I start forward.

But her gaze never finds mine. No, those blue eyes are fixed on the figure at the center of the circle. Paedyn's steps falter, fumbling as though she's back in my bedroom where I taught her how to dance.

And then she's sprinting towards the criminal who's destined to die.

CHAPTER 59

Paedyn

I suddenly can't breathe again, and I vaguely wonder if Blair is back, squeezing the air from my lungs with her invisible grip.

I sway on the spot, feet sinking into the sand beneath me at the edge of the circle.

I'm seeing things. I must be seeing things.

I stagger forward, tripping into a run. I force myself to go faster, ignoring the protest of pain shooting up my foot.

'Adena?'

This can't be right. This can't be happening.

Her beautiful form is broken and bleeding. Her knees sink into the sand, and her hands are tightly tied behind her back. Tears streak down her once glowing, dark skin, now dull and drenched with blood.

A shuddering sob escapes her, and my heart threatens to fail me at the sound. I've never heard Adena cry. Even after losing her parents as I had, after being beaten for attempting to steal those sticky buns she loves so much, after shivering on the streets – nothing has ever broken her. Nothing has ever dulled the light that is *her*.

She's *my* light.

I'm stumbling towards her, numb and nauseous all at once.

This isn't right. This can't be right—

'Paedyn!' Her voice cracks and I think my heart does the same. She struggles to stand, trying to walk towards me even with her feet bound. Panic laces her next words, fast and frantic. 'Pae, I'm so sorry. I—'

Time seems to stall.

The scene seems to slow, unfolding so vividly, so violently.

And I know in this moment that I will see it every time I shut my eyes. All it takes is one brutally blunt branch.

One single, broken branch to break her.

The gnarled wood flies, guided by an invisible force before it meets her back, skewering her right through the chest. The scream couldn't even tear from my throat fast enough.

'Adena!'

She sways, blinking down at the bloody branch protruding from her chest. Then her gaze slowly climbs up to mine as I stumble into a sprint, tears blurring my vision.

The sound of screaming fills my ears. I think it might be coming from me. She crumples.

And when she does, I catch sight of the leering smile and lilac hair at the other side of the circle, hand outstretched. The hand that guided and granted the gift of death, using nothing but her mind to meet the target.

'No!' My scream is raw, ripping from my throat.

I reach Adena before she hits the ground, gathering her into my arms as I gently lower her into the sand. I'm cradling her head while her bloody body is draped across my lap. Tears are streaming down my face. Screams are crawling up my throat.

Her skin is sticky with sweat as I push the dark curls out of her face, smoothing the uneven bangs from her eyes that she had me cut in the Fort with unsteady hands. Those wide, hazel eyes are staring up into mine, watery with unshed tears.

'You're going to be fine, A.' My hands are shaking as I tenderly touch the wound, my voice shaking as words spill out of me as quickly as my tears. 'You hear me? You are going to be fine and when you are, I'm going to get you so many sticky buns that even you will grow sick of them. Okay?'

I look up frantically and scream, 'Help! Please, somebody help!' But my cries are drowned out by the cheers of the crowd, leaving me to whisper my pleas. 'Help her. Please. *Please.*'

I look down at Adena through the tears in my eyes. 'You have to stay with me.' My voice breaks. I break. 'You have to promise me you'll stay— '

Adena draws in a sharp breath, weak and wavering. 'Pae.'

The sob I've been smothering slips past my lips when she says my name, so soothing and sweet. As if I'm the one who needs to be comforted.

'You know I don't make promises I can't keep.' Her voice grows softer with each word, her energy spent. And with another wheezing breath, she pulls her cracked lips into a smile. Even in the face of death, she smiles.

Death.

She's *dying.*

'No, no, no . . .' My words are a sob, a shaky cry. 'Don't say that. You're fine. Everything is going to be fine!'

She's still smiling at me as the tears slip down her face from those warm, hazel eyes now slightly unfocused. 'Promise you'll wear it for me?'

I blink at her, only blurring my vision with more tears. 'What?'

'The vest.' Her voice is barely a whisper, forcing me to lean forward to hear her as she says, 'Th-the green one with the pockets.' She takes a wheezing breath before ragged coughs rack her body. Blood stains her lips and slips from the corners of her mouth, but she continues, determined as ever. 'The stitching took me ages and I'd hate for all my . . . h-hard work to go to waste.'

An equal part sob and hysterical laugh escape me. 'I promise, A. I'll wear it every day for you.'

She smiles the kind of sad smile one would think the sun does when setting. Warm and wonderful. Worn out and weary. Ready to say goodbye, to take a break from having to be a constant source of light. Relief at the prospect of rest.

Her eyes flutter shut, and I'm suddenly so terrified I'll never get another glimpse of that hazel gaze again. 'Please,' I whisper, pulling her closer to me. 'Please don't leave me, A. You're all I have left.'

She's the only person who *knows* me. My heart *aches*.

Death is too dark for Adena, too bleak for her brightness, too undeserving of her dazzling soul.

Her eyelids crack open, revealing a sliver of those hazel eyes for me to memorize one last time. She struggles to speak, struggles to take shallow breaths. 'This is not a goodbye . . . only a good way to say bye until I see you next.'

My body shakes with sobs as I stroke her beautiful face, remembering those words as the same ones she had said to me before I left Loot. Only then, her phrase was accompanied by smiles and waves, so sure that she would see me again.

And now she never will.

It should have been me. It was *supposed* to be me. I was the one meant to die in these Trials, not her. Anyone but her.

A wave of guilt crashes over me, threatening to drown me like my tears. This is all my fault. She's only here because of my forgetfulness, my selfishness. I brought her here after I had *forgotten* about her. I brought her to her death.

'I need you to know that I will never forget you, A,' I choke out through my sobs. 'Not in this lifetime or the next.'

Never again.

She barely manages a nod before her eyes flutter shut.

I sob, my body slumping over her as I press my forehead to her own. 'You're my favorite, A.'

With lips pulled into a soft smile, I hear her take a shuddering breath.

Take her final breath. Leaving me shaking. Leaving me screaming. Leaving me sobbing.

Leaving *me*.

CHAPTER 60

Kai

Utter anguish. Utter agony. Utterly alone.

That is what I hear in her cry.

I'm rooted to the spot, unable to tear my feet out of the sand or my eyes from her crumpled form. I barely saw the branch before it ran the criminal through.

No, not a criminal – Adena.

Confusion clouds my thoughts as another one of Paedyn's cries cuts through the air. Adena shouldn't have been here. She was no prisoner of mine, and she certainly was no criminal worthy of this death.

Paedyn is sinking into the sand, rocking back and forth as she clutches the lifeless form of her best friend against her chest. I heard countless stories about the two of them together during the first Trial. Paedyn's love for her friend was evident then, but now it's written all over her face, riddled with each cry. I never imagined I would see her weep, but even the strongest among us break down, burdened and buried by grief.

I want to go to her. Want to wrap my arms around her, distract her, comfort her in the way I know I should but am unsure how. Hurt is what I know how to do, not what I know how to help.

The crowd has erupted in cheers and chants. Blair steps farther into

the circle, grinning at the gruesome act she's committed. She's just won this Trial and the crowd praises her for it.

It's over.

It's all over.

I step towards Paedyn and farther into the open ring. I glimpse Jax's head peek out behind a wall before he Blinks several feet into the circle. Out of the corner of my eye, I catch sight of Andy staggering into the circle, fully human and coated in blood. She's clutching her head, disoriented after finally being able to shift back. The pain from the wounds I inflicted most likely jolted her mind, allowing her to think clearly enough to turn again.

I'm close enough to Paedyn now that I can see the tears streaking down her face, trailing through the dirt and blood coating her skin. Her forehead is pressed against her friend's with her eyes squeezed shut and sobs shaking her body.

The cries of the crowd are deafening as I deftly make my way to her, ready to drop to my knees and—

Something about the stomping crowd *shifts.*

The shouts of elation and excitement turn to hideous screams of horror. I was too focused on Paedyn to hear it earlier, but now the sound crashes into me, confuses me.

I hear the shout of a panting Imperial nearby, sounding winded as though he ran here. 'The tunnels! They came through the tunnels into the box!'

I swivel around, nearly as frantic as the crowd filling the stands. They are all shouting at once, trapped in their seats by black-masked figures blocking the exits from each of the stands. And with the Mute covering them, the people have no power to fight back. My eyes sweep over their scared faces before they land on the glass box where my parents and Kitt reside.

And then I see it. See *them.*

The Resistance.

A man is standing beside my father wearing a black mask and pressing a knife to his throat. There are other members of the Resistance in the box, surrounding the king and queen and Kitt. They are holding them almost lazily, all gripping daggers in their hands though they don't look like they intend to use them. Which can only mean one thing.

They are Silencers. Maybe even other Fatals.

Otherwise, my father would have torn their limbs off by now, Kitt would have lit them on fire, and Mother would have helped by electrocuting them if it weren't for their powers being suppressed or controlled.

I can barely make out their twisted faces, grimacing with the weight of a Fatal's power crushing them. But I know the agony all too well. The agony of everything you are being suppressed as the very power you possess is stripped away from you. I know that face they are wearing because I've worn it many times before.

They are being smothered by Silencers. And then so am I.

CHAPTER 61

Paedyn

'Please.' I keep muttering the word, over and over again like it can bring her back to me. Like a prayer, a plea. 'Please, please, *please*.'

I barely hear the cheering crowd over the roaring grief in my head, my heart. I clutch her against me, my forehead resting atop her soft curls. I can still smell the faintest scent of honey on her, sticking to her hair and body. She always smelled like honey. She always smelled like home.

My face feels numb, and I can no longer feel the tears rolling down my cheeks. I lift her up gently, cradling her back so I can hold her closer. My blurry eyes snag on her bound hands tucked behind her back, and the sight of them sends a shuddering sob through me.

They broke her fingers.

They are bent at odd angles, bleeding, bruised. Those small and slender hands are mangled, a mockery of what they once were, of what they could do. Before death, the thing that made her feel most alive was taken from her.

Her sewing hands. Her talented fingers. Broken.

Then they broke her.

A wave of white-hot anger sweeps through me, washing away the

guilt and sorrow to replace it with searing rage.

She broke her. Blair.

I'm going to kill her.

I blink down at Adena's lifeless form. Even in death she is beautiful, brilliant, breathtaking. Just the sight of her so still, so silent, fans my fury, redirecting it towards another murderer.

He broke her. The king.

He brought her here to be killed. Adena is – Adena *was* – no criminal. My hatred for him flares. He did this on purpose. He warned me I wouldn't win these Trials, made sure of it. Not when I had to kill my best friend to do so.

This man has taken everything from me.

This king has killed the only family I've ever known. First my father, and now Adena.

Screams from the crowd finally reach my ears, pulling me out of my pathetic state for a moment. I look up to see that the walls of the maze have vanished, leaving me sitting in the center of the sandy Pit.

The other contestants are standing close by, all looking equally confused. The crowd is crazed. Elites are yelling and pointing and—

'The tunnels! They came through the tunnels into the box!' I stiffen.

They're here.

My eyes scan the crowd for anyone familiar before landing on the glass box. Sure enough, I spot Calum leading the king out, one hand clutching a dagger to his throat while the other clutches his arm. A man I've never seen before, whom I can only assume is a Silencer, follows closely behind to the rail overlooking the Pit.

'—came through the tunnels!' I hear another Imperial shout through the crowd, barking out other orders along with it. But there are few guards who aren't trapped by the Mute-encased stands where members of the Resistance are blocking the exits. And the handful of Imperials that are free make no move to rush to their king's side. They can't. Not without fear of their leader's throat being slit if they get too close.

For once in their life, Elites feel truly powerless. And then I feel his eyes burning into me.

They are like green emeralds, sharp and cutting from where he meets my gaze inside the glass box. How wrong I was to think their eyes weren't similar.

Because when his gaze pierces mine, I don't see him. I see his father. The future king knows this was my doing.

He knows because he showed me that tunnel and its key. He knows because he trusted me with that information. Kitt knows that I betrayed him.

He holds my gaze, looking so hurt, so horrified, so full of hatred. His eyes are so cold that I nearly shiver under his stare. The boy glaring down at me is devoid of every bit of warmth, every bit of charm I've come to know. He is cold. He is callous. He is like this because of me.

He is his father.

I hear sand shifting beneath feet and rip my eyes away from Kitt to find four Silencers walking towards us, hands outstretched, power pressing.

Grunts echo from the contestants near me and my gaze lands on Kai only a few paces away, eyes squeezed shut against the pain. My heart constricts at the sight of him clutching his head, sinking to his knees in the sand. Blair, Jax, and Andy do the same, grimacing with the pain of their powers being silenced, smothered, subdued.

'And this concludes the sixth ever Purging Trials.' Calum's voice booms over the arena, stilling and silencing everyone with a single sentence. Tealah is beside him, looking terrified with her hand pressed against his arm. The king, on the other hand, looks almost deceptively calm as he tries to seem completely unaffected by the dagger at his throat and the Resistance surrounding him.

'Many of you may not know who we are,' Calum continues, voice clear, eyes roaming over the crowd. 'And that is because we are your king's most deadly secret. His dirtiest secret. We are Ordinaries. We are Fatals. We are the Resistance.'

A collective gasp echoes through the stands, shock settling over the crowd. They can do nothing but watch the scene unfold with their powers suppressed by the Bowl and Resistance members blocking their escape.

'Today, we come out of the darkness and show you who we are. What we want to change.'

I can't move, eyes glued to Calum as he turns to look at the king now. Every guard, every citizen watches in stunned silence, unable to stop this. 'This could all be over. No more death, no more fighting.' He gestures to the crowd now, waving a hand. 'We are everywhere. We are not extinct from this kingdom, despite what your king has you believe. We have never stopped growing, never stopped fighting against the injustices that the Purging brought. And we have gathered here today.'

The people seem terrified at the prospect of so many *diseased* Ordinaries living among them. It's clear that Elites will do anything to keep their powers, to survive, and if they continue to believe that Ordinaries will kill them off, then they will only continue to kill us off first.

I silently plead with Calum to tell them the king's lie, tell them we are healthy and whole. We may not have proof, but the fact that we've lived among them for decades with no outbreaks of disease or loss of Elite powers will have to be enough for now. Although, it seems that most of the kingdom doesn't care enough about Ordinaries to even consider that. They just blindly trusted their twisted king.

Calum's gaze shifts between the future king in the glass box and his future Enforcer grimacing in pain beside me. 'We can peacefully come together, or we cannot. I would think the lives of your only heirs would be enough to persuade you to set your pride aside and reunite all of Ilya's people together.'

My heart stops before sputtering back to life.

They are going to kill the princes if the king does not relent. They are gambling with the future of Ilya. Gambling with lives.

They didn't tell me that.

No, no, *no.*

The crowd's response is a roar of rage. This was not how it was supposed to go. Threatening the princes' lives will only lead to the people's anger being directed at us, at our cause. It's harmful, not helpful.

My head is spinning while Ilyans scream in protest.

Calum's voice is stern. 'People of Ilya, welcome us home. We are no threat to—'

A sharp intake of breath from behind startles me, pulling my attention from Calum and the king. The Silencer standing before Kai stiffens. His eyes are wide, sweat slicking his brow. He opens his mouth as if to shout something, a warning. And then—

Kai erupts in flames.

CHAPTER 62

Rai

My mind feels muffled, my head hazy. *This can't be happening.* Four Silencers stand in front of each of us, smothering our powers.

Every contestant but Paedyn is feeling like their head is splitting. I know she isn't affected by the Silencer's power, but why is no member of the Resistance even touching her, guarding her, getting close to her?

The thought slips my mind when another wave of what I can only describe as *heaviness* crashes into me.

The ache and agony of it is hardly bearable, even with all the training I've been doing with Damion. My pounding head is making it hard for me to focus on the man beside Father, his face swimming in my vision.

From what I can hear through the ringing in my ears, his speech consists of how the Ordinaries want to live, even despite the disease they will spread to the Elites.

But if there are as many Ordinaries living among us as he says, then why have we not felt the effects? The loss of power?

My head throbs even more as I try to puzzle it out. The man keeps talking but I bare my teeth and block him out. I take a deep breath, pushing aside the pain to focus on the feeling of power beneath it. I

focus on the man currently silencing me as the tingling thrum of his ability grows under my skin.

I shut my eyes, reaching out towards that power just as I had done so many times before with Damion. Of course, I'd never actually been able to do it—

Not. Helping.

Adrenaline mixes with that faint feeling of power, so feather-light beneath my skin.

I latch onto it.

It's odd to think that the very same power the Silencer is using to suppress my ability is still my power, nonetheless.

Clinging to the Silencer's ability, feeling it flood my body, I throw it back at him.

His eyes go wide at the sudden feel of his own power battling him. He was not prepared for this, not expecting this. He let his guard down.

Only a Silencer can beat a Silencer.

And that's exactly what I do.

I beat him with his own ability.

The weight of his silence slips from my shoulders. And then I consume them in flame.

CHAPTER 63

Paedyn

Screams fill the air. Silencers are doused in flame, and the smell of burning flesh has me gagging.

The Silencers are rolling around in the sand, trying to smother the flames licking at their skin, burning their clothing. Their smothering silence over the contestants has snapped, setting them free.

I still have no idea how it happened, how Kai suddenly broke free of the Silencer's control and took on Kitt's Dual ability. His blast of fire, his brutal attack, has sent the whole arena into chaos once again. My eyes dart to the stands where the crowd is beginning to push back against the Resistance, and a struggle ensues.

Imperials are suddenly pouring into the arena to join the fight, and I'm shocked by how many have arrived so quickly. I whip my head around, aware that the number of black-masked figures is dwindling.

We weren't expecting this. We weren't prepared to fight, to lose.

I need to get out of here. Now.

The idea of running at a time like this makes my stomach churn, but the future king knows what I've done. The thought pounds through my skull as I scan the arena for him. He's currently pushing through the crowd now gathered around the glass box after they overpowered the Resistance and scattered from their stands. Flames lick up his arms

as he fights anyone who comes near him.

Kai has run to join the fight, his movements precise, perfect, as he drops Resistance members left and right. The sight of it makes me sick. I have no idea where Jax is, but I spot short burgundy hair in the sea of people and know immediately that it belongs to Andy.

And for her sake, Blair is lucky I can't seem to find her.

Oh, but I will. And I'll enjoy killing her.

I move to stand to my feet and abruptly stop at the feel of a heavy weight on my lap.

Adena.

Tears prick my eyes yet again, but I blink them away, forcing myself to keep my head. I look from her calm, motionless face to the chaos around us and the bloody battle that is raging. I try to lift her up with me, but she's heavy – dead weight. Literally. I choke at the thought as I push her off my lap and settle her onto the sand.

I can't take her with me.

She will never get a proper burial. She will never get the goodbye she deserves.

'I'm – I'm so sorry, A,' I whisper, kissing her forehead. 'I'm so, so sorry.'

I stand to my feet, wiping at the tears I tried to stop from falling. I start to turn away from her lifeless body, unable to bear the sight of it any longer.

'I love you.'

And then I'm running.

Coward. Just like with Father.

The symmetry in their deaths is sickening. Both run through in the chest.

Both bleeding out before me.

Both left lying on the ground, left to rot without a burial. Both deaths ending in me *running*.

I want to scream.

At myself. At their killers. At the world.

I push through the throng of people, through the massive mob fighting in the Pit, the stairs, the stands. Black and white masks clash as Resistance members battle Imperials. But the fight isn't fair. There are so many Imperials, and even with the power of the Fatals beside the Ordinaries, the Resistance is outnumbered.

I weave between bodies and duck under punches as I shove up the crowded stairs leading out of the Pit and onto an equally crowded pathway above. My many years of dodging and slipping unseen through Loot serve me well as my feet fall into a familiar rhythm, treading softly, swiftly.

Shouts wash over me, cries echo through the arena. The fight is a dull roar in my ears, but I force myself to follow the flow of people trying to get away from the fight rather than join it.

I want to turn around. I want to fight with the Resistance, with my people.

What good would you do?

Those five words snake their way into my head, wrapping around me so tightly I feel like I might suffocate. The choking hold of that thought only tightens when nine little letters string together, creating a word equally as devastating as the last five.

Powerless.

In every sense of the word.

The human current I've allowed myself to be swept away in finally dumps me outside the Bowl. Wind whips at my hair when we emerge, all of us spilling out into the long, wide path lined with trees. The path that leads to the palace.

The Ilyans around me scatter. They dart, running around the outside of the Bowl until their feet find another road heading in the opposite direction. The road that leads to the city.

I start to follow them, my legs moving of their own accord, leading me to Loot. Leading me home.

And then I stop.

Something in my chest is aching – my heart.

Adena's vest.

I spin, staring at the castle that holds the promise I made.

'I'll wear it every day for you.'

The promise pounds in my head, and it's all I need to start sprinting down the tree-lined path. The pink flowers and dainty petals that rained down on me the first time I walked this path are long gone.

They are now dead and trampled on the ground, leaving only empty buds and leafy branches swaying above me as I race beneath them.

Bloody foot and injuries be damned. The few Imperials that chased me back in Loot for stealing could have never gotten me to run so fast, so far.

When my feet hit the cobblestone courtyard, I don't bother slowing. I race over it as raindrops begin to prick my skin and slick the ground beneath me. I scramble up the stone steps leading to the giant, gilded doors of the castle.

Get inside. Grab the vest. Get out. Make it to Loot and—

'Miss Gray!'

I startle, looking up to see four Imperials stationed outside the heavy doors I had been too busy sprinting towards to see. An older man rushes down to meet me, concern crinkling his eyes around the white mask he wears.

'Miss, are you alright? Has the fighting stopped? Has the Resistance been defeated?' His eyes search mine, looking for answers.

So they clearly know what is going on inside the Bowl's walls, and yet they are stuck here. They've no doubt received specific orders to stay and guard the castle, along with the many other Imperials I'm sure are prowling inside. The ones I need to get past to get to my room.

'Yes, I'm—' I need a plan. Fast.

And the one that comes to mind is one I'm not proud of.

I let my body go limp as I stumble forward on the steps. I throw out my hands to catch my fall, but the Imperial beats me to it. He wraps an arm around my middle to steady me, and I suppress the urge to snap it in half.

I reach down and clutch at my foot and the blood-soaked cloth carelessly wrapped around it, now nearly falling off with all the running I've done. I plaster on my best grimace, though it's not difficult to do with the adrenaline slowly seeping from my body to be replaced by pain once again.

'You're hurt.' The Imperial's eyes dart to my foot when I hiss in pain.

How observant.

'Yes, but I'm fine. I just—' I place my foot back on the step and gasp dramatically in pain. I'm really milking this for all it's worth. My fingers curl around the Imperial's starchy, white uniform, my eyes pleading. 'I could barely make it out of there. It's chaos. And I'm—' I take a shaky breath. 'I'm so scared and my foot hurts so badly and I don't know what to do—'

Plagues, I cannot believe I've reduced myself to this.

I sound hysterical, and that is exactly what I was going for. The Imperial glances up to his friends at the top of the steps before returning his concerned gaze back to me. 'Why don't we get you back to your room so you can rest and get that foot healed? This will all be over soon.'

A tear rolls down my cheek as I nod fervently at him, hoping I look scared and stunned, though I am neither of those things. I just need him so I can get to my room without looking suspicious. Without drawing attention from the other Imperials who will ask questions I don't have the answers to. But if I have an Imperial as my escort, the problem that is me will already be handled and under control.

Another two things I am neither of.

'Ranken, take Miss Gray to her room. Then inform a Healer that she needs assistance.' The Imperial gestures to a broad man with bulging muscles that are evident even through the stiff uniform he wears.

Brawny.

He nods and saunters over to me, saying in a deep voice, 'This will be faster and far less painful for you if we do this my way.'

Apparently, his way involves scooping me up and carrying me like an incompetent child. His hands are under my knees and around my back, easily holding me against him as we step through the large doors and into the hallway beyond. My first instinct is to swing my legs over his shoulders and lock him in a chokehold before flipping him to the ground. But that was before my smarter, more strategical instinct reminded me that this is what I want, what I need to do.

So, I swallow my pride and let him carry me. Let him stride down each hall with me in his arms and dozens of Imperials buzzing around us. I fight my smile when they barely bat an eye in our direction.

Before I know it, the Imperial sets me on my bed, grumbling

something about sending for a Healer. I wait until the sound of his footsteps grows distant before bolting off the mattress and throwing open the doors of my wardrobe.

I tear through the dresses and fancy training gear to a shelf in the back. Pants and comfy shirts are neatly folded there, the work of Ellie and her constant cleaning. Reaching under a stack of cotton shirts, my fingers brush against familiar rough fabric.

My heart squeezes as I pull out the vest I've kept hidden away. Its olive fabric is dull, and yet, I've never seen anything more perfect. I run my fingers along the pockets lining both the inside and outside of the vest, making it the ideal accessory for a thief.

I take a deep breath before slipping it on over my cut tank now slicked with sweat. Then I grab a new pair of boots and am about to slip them on when the door creaks open, revealing a stout man who can only be the Healer. 'I heard you were injured?'

'Yes,' I blurt before putting on a show of stumbling towards him. 'It's my foot.'

'I see.' The man waddles over, gesturing for me to sit on the bed. I consider knocking him out before deciding to take advantage of his quick healing first. He gently takes my foot in his hands, and I watch as his fingers dance over the jagged cuts crawling up my ankle. The sight of my flesh knitting back together sends memories of my father flooding into my thoughts, paining me more than the injury.

I blink them away when the Healer finishes, leaving only faint pink lines as evidence of my wounds. 'Well, if that is all—'

I slip my dagger out from under the pillow beside me, and the Healer is out cold when the hilt of it connects with his temple. I try my best to soften his fall, but he nearly crushes me as he comes crashing to the floor. I step over his body, slipping on my boots and whispering my thanks though he will never hear it.

I silently slip into the hallway. The Imperials think I'm safely in my room, whining about my wound, and though that image infuriates me, I'd like to keep it that way. If I'm seen, my cover is blown.

Luckily, I have lots of practice at going unseen.

I'm on the balls of my feet as I creep down the hallway, prepared to jump into a room or change directions at any sign of movement.

I dart down halls, avoiding the large, more frequently used ones as best I can.

The few Imperials that happen to cross my path are distracted and easily evaded as I head towards my escape – the gardens. It's the closest exit to where I am, as well as the only one that is likely unguarded. With the current chaos causing the castle to be undermanned as it is, I'm betting that the exit will be far from every Imperial's mind.

And I was right.

I reach the door leading to the beautiful landscape beyond and swing it open. The rain is relentless, continuing its fall from the cloudy sky above. I hurry through the paths lined with flowers of every color, size, and shape. Then I'm breezing past the fountain where Kitt and I nearly splashed half of the water out at each other—

Kitt.

I push the thought of him and my betrayal away, focusing all my attention on making it back to Loot as quickly as possible. Which won't be quick at all, considering I'll have to make it there on foot.

I'm back on the path leading towards the Bowl, making my way to the one leading towards Loot. I'm panting, legs pumping, as I sprint once more down the tree-lined path. Grief and anger mix with adrenaline, making me feel equally energized and exhausted all at once.

The Bowl looks more daunting than ever before. Metal beams and concrete tower over me, and the shouts and sounds of the struggle within only add to its intimidating presence. Every citizen who hasn't joined the fight must be long gone by now, leaving the Resistance and Imperials to battle within the arena.

I pass a tunnel leading into the Bowl. And then another.

I keep my eyes on the road home as it draws closer and closer.

The broad figure of a man staggers out onto the path I'm so desperately trying to get to. He's clutching at his head, though I can't make out any of his features as I blink rapidly in the rain.

All I know is that he is in my way.

He turns, hand still pressed to his temple, and spots me. I don't bother slowing my pace. Whoever this man is, I won't hesitate to take him down if he tries to stop me.

I'm running, getting closer with every step, all while squinting through the rain as I try to get a clear view of his face.

He's smiling at me.

It's the kind of smile that sends a shiver down your spine. The kind of smile that is anything but kind. The kind of smile that tells me this man knows exactly who I am.

My feet falter. Less than a dozen yards separate us now. And that's when I see it.

I see green eyes, colder than the rain soaking through my thin clothing.

I see golden hair, duller than the cloudy sky.

I see lips twisted in a smile, wickeder than the storm raging above us. 'Ah, Paedyn Gray,' he calls to me over the whipping wind, his voice sharp and silky all at once. 'Or should I call you a Resistance member? An Ordinary? A betrayer?'

I step closer, though I already know exactly who stands before me. I see the king.

Anger isn't a strong enough word for the emotion coursing through me when I look at this man – this monster, this murderer.

His eyes are crazed, his hair bloody from a deep gash near his temple still dripping blood. How he managed to get away from the fighting mob inside the Bowl is beyond me. And yet, here he is, stumbling right into my path. Stumbling alone.

The king is completely alone.

I almost want to thank the Plague for this gift. Almost.

I continue striding forward, refusing to run from him, from this opportunity. The sound of sliding steel sings through the rumbling thunder as he draws a sword from the sheath at his side.

'Oh, don't look so shocked that I figured it out,' he croons, causing my blood to boil. 'I knew this was coming. You wheedled your way into my naïve son's head, his heart, and got what you needed for your little Resistance. And as for knowing you are an Ordinary, well, I've known for quite some time now.' A smile twists his face at the look of shock on mine. 'Not to mention that I knew who your father was, what he was a part of. I knew many things about him before his *unfortunate* end.' His smile is evil incarnate. 'Stabbed through the chest, was it?'

I go rigid, every part of me filled with rage. But I force a cool mask over my features, ignoring his last statement and referring to his first. 'And what should I call *you*? King or coward? Liar or murderer? All would be appropriate, don't you think?'

He barks out a laugh, and I can barely control my anger at the sound of it. My hands shake as I ball them into fists at my sides, nails cutting into my palms. Words fall out of my mouth before I can stop them. 'You killed her.'

He huffs as if this amuses him. 'Who, your little friend?' His eyes flash, betraying the anger he's kept buried. 'No. *You* killed her. I warned you about the Trials. I warned you to stay away from my sons. You've made my kingdom look weak. You've made my heirs look *weak*.' He spits out the word, disgusted with his own flesh and blood. 'You had Kai helping you in the Trials, running after you during a ball. You had the future king wrapped around your finger, spilling every secret and bit of information you needed. *You* are the murderer, Paedyn.' He takes a step towards me, and I'm rooted to the spot, shaking my head. 'You forget what you are, *Slummer*. An Ordinary doomed to die. You are *nothing*.'

'Then why didn't you kill me?' I yell. 'If you knew what I was then why not kill me like you have with every other Ordinary?'

'Because I needed you alive,' he says simply. 'But now you are of no use to me, and since the Trials didn't kill you, I get the pleasure of doing that myself.' He pauses and a sneer twists his lips. 'Can you *read* what I'm going to do next with that *Psychic* ability of yours?'

A sudden flash of silver blends in with the rain. A sword is swinging at me.

CHAPTER 64

Kai

A knee connects with my spine. *Well, someone has a death wish.*

I spin, easily burying the knife I nicked off the last man I killed into this one's chest, pushing through the tough leather encasing him. I feel the familiar spray of blood splattering my clothes, my face. I'm covered in it. I yank out the blade, letting the man fall to the ground with a thud.

They all have a death wish.

The arena is utter chaos. Imperials and Resistance members clash, one in white, one in leather. Ordinaries, Elites, and Fatals fight side by side.

It's bizarre.

It's also the only reason this fight isn't over yet. If it weren't for the Fatals and Elites joined with the Resistance, this would have been a bloodbath. But they are still significantly outnumbered against all the Imperials that now fill the Bowl.

A black-masked figure comes charging towards me, leather armor soaked with both blood and the rain pelting down on us. I plant my feet on the slick concrete, letting him come to me. The hardest part of this fight is not knowing whether you'll be facing an Ordinary, an Elite, or a Fatal. I barely have enough time to reach

out with my power before he's on me.

I feel nothing. Ordinary.

But not to be underestimated.

He flashes two knives at me, deadly sharp and skillfully swung. His daggers slash with quick movements, forcing me back. I duck under a swipe that was intended to slice my neck and send a quick jab to his open abdomen. He grunts, but the leather covering his chest and stomach helps to absorb my hit. I sift through the powers that surround me, feeling dozens buzzing under my skin.

Why does it feel wrong to fight an Ordinary in an extraordinary way? So far, I've used only my own strength to kill them, avoiding the use of an ability. It feels like cheating for some reason, and I like to win my fights fairly. I haven't even touched any of the Fatals' powers, though I feel them, potent and powerful. To use one of their abilities correctly could take years of training, so I stick to what I know, killing with my hands and the familiar abilities around me.

He stabs his knife towards my chest.

Predictable.

I catch his wrist and twist, vaguely hearing his cry of pain as the other dagger plunges upwards, aiming for my heart. I turn, barely missing the fatal stab, and instead earn a shallow slice along my ribs.

Still holding his twisted arm, I bend the blade back towards him while grabbing his shoulder. Then I yank him forward. His own knife buries deep into his chest, his eyes widening as he stares down at the hilt in his hand and the blade now buried in his chest.

Staggering, he falls towards the concrete path, but I've turned away before his body hits the ground. Pressing an already bloody hand to the new gash across my ribs, I scan the throng. My gaze lands on Kitt, watching as he douses those around him in flames.

Something isn't right.

I've never seen my brother like this before. So bloodthirsty, so brutal. Usually, those words are reserved for me, the future Enforcer, and not Kitt, the kind and caring future king. But right now, he looks enraged, feral in a way I've never seen before.

I continue fighting through the crowd, trying to get a glimpse of Father and Mother. I'm both relieved and worried when I don't, hoping that Imperials got to them first and escorted them back to the castle.

It's only then that I notice how much the crowd has dwindled. My eyes dart to a figure running out of a tunnel and beyond the Bowl. Another follows, clad in leather and masked in black.

They are trying to escape.

And I intend to follow.

CHAPTER 65

Paedyn

Sharp steel slices deep across my forearm. I had jumped out of the blade's way, though I still earned a searing slash across my arm for my efforts. I bite back a cry of pain and crouch low, pulling my dagger from my boot and gripping it in my sweaty palm.

The king laughs, taking another swipe at me with his sword, forcing me to dance around and avoid being sliced into ribbons. It's clear he has the advantage with his longer weapon to accompany his Brawny ability. But despite that, he's unsteady on his feet thanks to the wound at his temple.

So I do exactly what he mockingly suggested: I *read* him.

He sways with each swing, having to steady himself slightly before trying to land another blow. His right foot steps with each swipe of the sword, followed by a small half step from his left. He's holding the sword with his right hand, but he has two sheaths at his side, telling me he had another weapon at one point and can fight left-handed as well.

He swipes again, high this time, forcing me to duck and roll to the right. We circle each other, his twisted smile visible even through the steady stream of rain.

I need to get close to him. I need to distract him.

Because I am not leaving here until I murder this murderer. Maybe that makes me no better than him.

'You killed him! You killed my father!' I shout over the thunder rolling above us.

I step closer, and his sword swings down in a wide arc that would have cleaved me in half if I hadn't dodged in time. He sways like I knew he would after a strike like that, and I use the opportunity to send my dagger sweeping across his chest. It carves a line through his shirt, his skin, leaving blood blooming in its wake.

Something hard meets my temple and my vision bursts with spots. I stumble back, blinking. Through my blurry gaze, I see the king's bloody chest and the sword he's holding, the handle still outstretched after sending it slamming into my skull.

He laughs. But I hear the tremor in it. He's worried. He hates that I – a Slummer, an Ordinary, a no one – just left my mark on him.

Oh, I'm going to do far more than leave a scar.

'Yes, well, a friend told me of his intentions and this *Resistance* he was a part of.' His voice is filled with laughter. 'So, I did what I had to do.'

Another swipe of his sword catches me off guard and slices a shallow line across my abdomen before I dive away. 'Don't worry, Paedyn, I didn't just kill your father simply due to some gossip, though I've killed men for less. I killed him to ensure my Elite society remained.'

I can't seem to comprehend what he's saying, but that may only be due to the rage clouding all reason. 'Admit it,' I spit, 'you lied to create your Elite society. There is no disease spread by Ordinaries. We don't weaken the Elites or their powers.'

'I did what was necessary, and you have no proof.'

'You're a monster,' I choke out.

The gesture he makes is something like a shrug. 'A monster? Maybe. The most powerful king Ilya has ever had? Most definitely. No city is like Ilya, no people like my Elites. And I intend to keep it that way.'

I lunge at him, knife slashing. The steel of his sword meets the much shorter steel of my dagger, hard. Very hard. Even when weakened, he's a Brawny with strength that is far greater than my own. My dagger flies out of my hand, knocked to the ground by the force of the blow.

I don't even hesitate, don't even give myself time to panic before grabbing hold of his outstretched wrist and driving my knee up to meet his elbow. The sickening crack of his bone breaking blends in with a clap of thunder rumbling above us.

His sword slips from his hand and hits the ground as he cries out. And then the earth is racing up to meet me.

He's thrown me to the ground using every bit of Brawny strength and raw rage he can muster. The back of my head smacks the packed earth and I'm suddenly seeing spots again.

I can't see.

I'm blinking ferociously, desperately trying to clear my vision. My head is pounding, feeling as though it's splitting into two, and maybe it is. Something hot and sticky is oozing from the back of my head, and even in my hazy state, I'm certain that isn't a good sign.

My vision slowly begins to return, clearing enough for me to see what is looming over me.

The king, sword clutched with his unbroken arm, a smile curling his cracked lips.

No.

I struggle to sit up, but a heavy weight pushes me back to the ground. His booted foot is crushing my ribs, pinning me beneath him helplessly.

Not like this. I refuse to die like this.

'Is that all you care about?' My voice sounds foreign in my own ears, scratchy and scared. 'Power? Ruling over an Elite kingdom? Does human life mean nothing to you?'

'Ordinaries are a weak excuse for life. An embarrassment,' he growls. 'They should have died with the Plague but instead they plague us. I've planned for this day a long time, waiting until I could rid myself of this Resistance. And I suppose I have you to thank for their downfall.' His smile is twisted, and my head is pounding as I try to understand what he's saying.

'Only the strongest, the most powerful, will prevail.' He leans down slightly, his cold gaze boring into mine as he says, 'It's survival of the fittest, and the fittest are the Elites.'

He straightens, his boot still crushing me beneath it. 'So, where were we?' He laughs like he's said something humorous. 'Ah, yes. I was ridding my kingdom of one more worthless Ordinary.'

He points the tip of his sword down at me, and I squirm under his boot. He's so strong and I'm so weak—

'Unfortunately, Kai has grown more skilled than I am when it comes to playing with his kills. He was quite the quick learner. I taught him everything he knows, did he tell you that? He has me to thank for his cruelty.' I shudder when the sharp tip of his sword meets the skin of my cheek, just above my jaw.

And then he drags it down.

I might have screamed – I'm not sure. All I know is the slow, slicing pain trailing from my jaw and down my neck. Hot blood is pouring from the cut and pooling on my skin as rain stings the open wound. I feel my mouth moving but I don't hear anything coming out, only the ringing in my ears.

He's smiling when he finally drags his sword to a stop at my collarbone. 'This is very entertaining. But maybe I should have let Kai do the honors, hmm?'

I feel sick, and all I smell is the metallic scent of my own blood. Cold steel meets my skin again, stilling me and my churning stomach. He's chosen the spot right beneath my other collarbone – right above my heart.

He clucks his tongue. 'I'm almost impressed that this pathetic little heart of yours is still beating. What, with all the betrayal, heartbreak, and near-death experiences you've somehow endured as an Ordinary.'

'Everything I've endured was because of *you*,' I snarl, lifting my head off the ground despite how heavy it feels.

'Hmm.' He sounds almost thoughtful. 'Very true.'

Blinding pain jolts through my body once more when his sword carves a line above my heart. A strangled scream escapes me, nearly drowning out his soft words. 'Then I will leave my mark upon your heart, lest you forget who's broken it.'

His slices are deep and disgustingly slow. He goes over each line he's carved again and again as screams tear from my throat. I close my eyes against the grin twisting his face, unable to bear looking at this man any longer. No, not a man. A *monster.*

Tears slip down my cheeks against my will, mixing with the rain and blood splattered across my face. I know exactly what he is carving into my skin, can feel it with each swipe of his sword. He is branding me before death, and it's almost more painful than the agony racking my body.

I don't know how much time has passed when he finally lifts the sword to admire his handiwork. 'There.' Casual. He sounds so casual, so cruel. 'Something to remember me by in the afterlife.'

Then he lifts his sword, aiming the point down at my chest.

No. No, no, no—

He smiles. 'Stabbed through the chest. Like father, like daughter.'

I cannot die.

The king towers over me, gripping the hilt of the sword, raising it up, up—

I will not die.

I'm desperate, driven by madness. Even lifting my arms sends shooting pain through my body but I ignore it as my fingers claw at his boot atop my chest, one hand clamped around his ankle and the other around the leather toe of the shoe.

And with every bit of strength I have left, I twist. He grunts in pain, swaying unsteadily.

Perfect.

I yank his foot forward, hard. The injury to his head combined with the injuries I've so graciously gifted him have made him weaker, made him wobbly.

And he lands with a hard thud on the wet ground.

I don't hesitate before scrambling towards the sword that slipped from his hand. I crawl, pain and adrenaline mixing to create a dangerous concoction of recklessness. A rough hand closes around my ankle, dragging me backward through the mud.

I scream, frustrated and fearful, as my fingers brush the hilt of the sword before I'm pulled away. My head whips around to see the king's face contorted with fury, equally bloody and muddy. I kick back as hard as my broken body will let me, and when I hear a crunch, I know my heel has found its mark.

The king cries out, the sound gurgling as the blood streaming from his crushed nose runs into his mouth. I wrench my ankle free from his grasp and dive towards the sword, finally folding my fingers around its hilt.

I drag myself to my feet, every movement painful. I'm soaked in blood, soaked to the bone by the pouring rain. I stagger towards the king, breathing raggedly as I drag the sword through the mud behind me.

Now *I'm* hovering over *him*. Funny how quickly our roles have reversed. Me, about to take a life. Him, about to be the life I take.

The teeth he bares at me are stained red with blood. 'Don't you want to know who it was that killed your father, Paedyn?'

That one sentence stalls the sword I'm about to shove through his chest. He rasps out a laugh before choking on his own blood.

'I already know who it was,' I bite out through clenched teeth. 'I saw you drive the sword through his chest.' I turn my attention back to the weapon gripped in my hand, unable to bear this anymore and ready to—

'Wrong.'

I still before echoing, 'Wrong?'

He lets out another wheezing laugh, and I don't wait for him to stop coughing up blood before digging the point of my blade into his chest as I slowly say, 'It was *you*.'

He coughs out his next words. 'Funny how the mind can make us see what we wish to. You already hated me for what I did to your kind, so it must have been easy to convince yourself it was me who drove that blade through your father's chest.' A bloody smile stretches across his lips. 'But it wasn't.'

'Liar,' I breathe, pressing the sword deeper into his chest.

His next words are little more than a hysterical whisper. 'Let's just say that your first encounter with a prince wasn't when you saved Kai in the alley.'

No. *No.*

'It was when he killed your father.'

The world spins around me, threatening to throw me to the ground.

This can't be happening. He's lying. He's a liar. He's—

'His first kill, too.' The king continues with a bloody, reminiscent smile. 'It was the first mission I sent him on, and I think the boy may have even cried after. Look at how far he's come. Look at how well I've trained him. Now he kills at my command and barely bats an eye at the dozens of deaths delivered by his hands.'

I can barely breathe. The boy who taught me how to dance, healed my wounds, asked me my favorite color under the stars—

'You're lying,' I choke out.

He lets out a raspy laugh. 'No, you're lying to *yourself*, Paedyn.'

The memory of the night my father died suddenly seems so fuzzy, so unfocused. Where I once thought I saw the face of the king, I now see a blurry body. I can't make out any of the details, can't seem to recall anything about my father's killer.

I shake my head. I can't think about this now. I refuse to let my reeling thoughts of Kai distract me from the task at hand.

Because now I will kill *his* father.

Once again, I find symmetry to be a sickening thing.

I will not fail.

The king's smile is bloody.

I will not falter.

Hysterical, mocking laughter follows.

I will not feel remorse.

'Weak. Just like your father—'

The sword I drive through his chest shuts him the hell up.

My next words are hollow, horribly calm. 'This is for my father.'

He lets out a weak, wheezing gasp as he lifts his head off the ground to stare at the damage I've done. His eyes widen at the sight of his own sword buried deep in his chest. A gurgling noise follows his gasp, blood spilling over the corners of his mouth and gushing from his wound.

Nothing – I feel nothing for this man dying at my feet, dying by my hand.

'And this,' I twist the hilt of the sword, drawing a scream from the king as more of his flesh rips and shreds, 'is for Adena.'

He lets out a strangled sob when I yank the sword out, throwing it to the ground. I spin around, finding my dagger lying several feet away. Each step towards it has me feeling stronger despite every wound weakening my body.

The silver swirled handle of my father's dagger is slicked with rainwater, blood, and mud – matching me. Drops of water stream down my face, stinging my open wounds as I turn the dagger over in my hand. I flip it once, twice, feeling its familiar weight.

'And this is for me, you son of a bitch.' I let the dagger fly.

CHAPTER 66

Paedyn

The blade finds its target, guided there by my hatred, my heartbreak, my heartlessness. It sinks into the center of his throat, instantly ceasing his raspy breaths.

I'm shaking all over, staring at the corpse of a killer who's staring back at the creature who just became one.

The king's head is lolled to the side with my father's dagger lodged in his throat, his eyes wide and watchful. A tear slips down my cheek, mingling with the beads of rainwater rolling down my face. I wipe it away with bloody hands, unsure why I feel like crying.

Is it regret?

No. Not regret. Not remorse. Not anything remotely close to guilt. It's relief.

I take an unsteady step towards him, intending to grab my dagger and bolt.

Something catches my eye.

I spin towards the movement despite my body screaming in protest. My eyes land on glossy, unblinking ones. The girl is small with dark skin and even darker hair. She blinks, her eyes clearing before a look of horror settles on her face.

And then she's sprinting.

A Sight.

I blink in the rain, staring after the retreating form of the girl who likely just recorded me killing the king. I barely have time to process this before I hear heavy footsteps echoing down the stone tunnel to my right.

I hesitate. My dagger.

I need it. I have to have it. I—

Whoever is heading through that tunnel is coming fast. I need to get out of here now. I have no idea whether this person is friend or foe, and I have no intention of finding out.

I don't have a moment to spare. Not a single second to grab my prized possession, and my breaking heart is my most painful wound right now.

Then I'm running.

Every part of me is on fire. My body is screaming, streaked with blood, staggering with weakness. But I can't stop. Once I make it farther down the road, there will be woods to my right and—

A knife whizzes past me, skimming my forearm with its sharp blade. I whip my head around and stumble to a stop at what I see.

Every bit of his body is covered in blood. His hair is a mess of inky waves, sticky with sweat and streaked with blood. A thin blade is gripped between his fingers, his hand raised and ready to send it flying towards me.

And something snaps into place at the sight of him.

I'm suddenly back in my old home, hidden behind a cracked door as I watch a sword plunge into my father's chest. The sword held by a boy with wavy black hair, a boy with gray eyes full of fear, a boy who just became a murderer.

I shudder as my eyes sweep over that same black hair, those same gray eyes, and the same murderer before me. The sight of him now suddenly makes the memory of that night clearer than it ever has been before.

Pieces of the puzzle that is my scattered memory begin to fall into place.

That night so long ago, my mind made me believe it was the king who killed my father, made me blame the man I already hated. And in a way, it was the king who killed him, just not by his own hand. It

491

was his son who sunk the blade into my father's chest.

My breath shudders as I stare at him. It suddenly all makes sense.

The attraction. The connection. The *familiarity*. I was so easily drawn to him because deep down I knew him, recognized him, remembered him. He was familiar to me.

And now my father's murderer is going to murder me.

We stare at each other, and I see the boy who's been the king's instrument of death his entire life, commanded and controlled to be a killer. He was made this way. Made to mirror the monster his father is – *was*.

But that doesn't make him any less a murderer.

It's his eyes that are more startling than his ragged, enraged appearance. That gray gaze is like smoke billowing from the hottest fire, and yet, cold like chips of ice, piercing like the tips of icicles. Those eyes betray the horror he feels, looking like they did the night I saw him take his first life.

I did this to him. I killed his father.

But he killed mine first.

He knows what I've done. I doubt he would forget the distinct look of the dagger I've pressed against his throat so many times – the same dagger that is now protruding from his father's throat.

And yet, his knife missed me.

Kai doesn't miss. Not unless he wants to. 'What have you done to me?'

His words are almost lost in the storm, but they chill me to the bone more than the streaming rain ever could. I've heard those exact words fall from his lips before, when they were brushing my own. I've felt this rain cool my heated skin when we were inches apart. I've had his gray gaze on me before – when it was heavy with heat rather than hatred.

'My pretty Pae, what have you done to me?'

How can a single moment mirror another in such a morbid way? Was it only yesterday that his lips formed those words with longing, and today with loathing?

But the only similarities between last night and this moment are the fire and fortitude of feelings filling his eyes. With his mask gone, he's unguarded, allowing me to clearly glimpse the grief gracing his features. His hand holding the knife, ready to strike, shakes in the air. I can almost see the pieces falling together in his mind, the realization of what I am and what I've done snapping into place.

He cocks his arm back farther, ready to bury his blade in my chest.

My eyes flutter shut, and I plant my feet, accepting my fate.

I *hurt*. Everything hurts. Maybe I deserve this death. Maybe I even desire it—

My pitiful thoughts are interrupted by a strangled cry of frustration that has my eyes flying open. Kai's hands are dragging through his hair, his head bowed. When his eyes finally meet mine, cutting through the rain and distance separating us, I see the battle raging within them.

He knows what he needs to do, and yet he *isn't*.

Kai's voice trembles like his hands. 'I should bury this blade in your throat.'

And he could easily do it too. I have no weapons, no will, no energy to try and stop him.

My voice sounds as ragged as I feel. 'Then do it.'

He's shaking his head at me, looking just as disgusted with himself as he is with me. 'I will. I *should*.'

He grimaces as he grips the dagger aimed right at me. Another frustrated sound tears from his throat. He runs both bloody hands through his hair, shaking his head at the ground.

'Then why can't I do it?' Now he's staring at the weapon in his hand, at the weapon he could easily take my life with. 'Why is it that when it comes to you, I'm suddenly a coward? Why is it that when it comes to you, I suddenly *care*? Why is it that I can't throw this damn knife at my father's *killer*!?'

His chest is rising and falling rapidly with each ragged breath. I, on the other hand, think I've stopped breathing altogether when he says, 'I told you I was a fool for you, and it seems I was right.' His laugh is biting. 'I'm a fool when it comes to you.'

The next words out of his mouth are damning yet deceptively calm. 'Maybe when I rid myself of you, I'll find my courage. So I'm giving you a head start.'

I blink at him. My feet seem to be rooted to the spot. I don't move an inch, too shocked and startled to do anything but stare.

'At least you kept your promise. You stayed alive long enough to stab me in the back.' He laughs bitterly, remembering the attack after the first ball when I tended to his wound. 'And now I promise to return the favor.' His voice strains with emotion. 'Run, Paedyn. Because when I catch you, I will not miss. I will not falter. I will not make the mistake of *feeling* for you.'

I'm frozen, still standing in the freezing rain.

'Go!' he yells, his voice breaking. 'Go before I find someone who isn't a coward, someone who isn't a fool, and let them bury this dagger in your back right here, right now.'

I stumble, tripping over uneven ground before turning away from him. And then I'm running again like I've found myself doing all day, all my life. I throw a glance over my shoulder, glimpsing Kai dropping to his knees beside the king with his eyes trained on me.

I swallow the emotions clawing their way up my throat, threatening to leak from my stinging eyes.

I don't look back.

CHAPTER 67

Kai

How could I have been so blind, so oblivious?

I watch her retreating form grow smaller, watch her escape me – escape a killer.

Except, I didn't act like the one thing I was born to be. I didn't act like the murderer I've been molded into.

I let her go.

I let her go.

I look down at her dagger clenched in my fist, its sharp blade slicked with blood.

My father's blood.

My eyes drift to his lifeless body, to the eyes staring glassily at where Paedyn must have thrown her knife from. I reach out with trembling fingers and close them, unable to stand seeing Kitt's eyes so lifeless.

I haven't shed a single tear. I feel numb.

I feel shocked. I feel betrayed.

Was anything real to her? Was it all a lie? All pretend?

I know my thoughts should be on the dead king I'm kneeling beside, but they keep wanting to wander back to her.

I could never sense her power. She was untouchable to Silencers.

The Resistance didn't lay a finger on her when they attacked.

Because she is an Ordinary.

Because she is part of the Resistance.

Well, she *was*. There is not much to be a part of anymore after today. How could I not see it before?

I shake my head, already knowing the answer to that question. Because I was blinded by everything that is *her*.

She killed him. She killed the king. She killed my father.

And yet I let her go.

But not for long.

I stand to my feet, looking down at the dead king before my gaze snaps back up to the speck that is her, now barely visible through the rain.

The title of Enforcer has never weighed so heavily on my shoulders. I'll have to find her.

And when I do, I'll have found my courage.

CHAPTER 68

Paedyn

I don't stop running until I stumble into the woods beside the road leading home. Running is soon replaced with tripping when roots catch my ankles and rocks stub my toes. The rain hasn't slowed its attempt to drown me yet, pelting each of my open wounds.

My finger finds its way to the gash trailing from my jaw and down my neck, tenderly following the torn and bloody path that I know will never look the same. Then my fingers fumble across my chest, stopping only when they meet the shredded skin right above my heart. I wince, and I wish it was because of the pain.

O.

I trace the jagged lines that form that single letter. That single letter that will forever scar, marring it with the memory of *him* and what I am.

O for Ordinary.

The brand is just as mangled as the heart barely beating beneath it.

I stagger onward, hand pressed against the *O* carved into my skin and every meaning behind the seemingly simple letter.

A pop of color catches my eye, bright against the dark foliage of the damp woods. My heart splinters at the sight, lungs squeezing and legs shaking. It was only yesterday that the sight made me smile, that the

symbol was slid into my hair by strong hands, sure fingers.

'A forget-me-not, since you always seem to be forgetting who I am.'

I stare at the bundle of blue flowers, mocking me with the memory of stolen touches, silent promises.

Now all that's left are shouts of revenge, steely eyes that promise no mercy, and a stolen silver dagger so dear to me, yet so likely to be the blade that's stabbed through my heart.

'I don't give a damn if you forget who I am in title, so long as you remember who I am to you.'

I open my mouth to laugh only for a sob to slip past my lips instead, my body deciding to shake with hurt rather than humor.

Oh, I remember who he is to me.

How could I forget my father's murderer?

I stumble forward, blinking through the constant stream of rain and tears.

Thick, hot liquid runs down my brand, my body, my very being.

Honey.

That's what I tell myself.

It's just honey.

EPILOGUE

Kitt

It's been three days since I saw my father lying dead in the mud.

Three days since I last slept.

Three days since I could close my eyes without seeing his bloody body.

Three days since the Resistance attacked at the final Trial.

Three days since the girl I trusted, the girl I grew to want, became a murderer and a betrayer.

Three days since I became king.

The crown atop my head is heavy, much like my eyelids have grown, and much like the weight of the kingdom now thrown onto my shoulders. I blink awake, reminding myself of what I will see if I give in to the fatigue.

My only true parent, dead. The parent I have been trying to please, make proud, my entire life. Lying lifeless beside me. My knees sinking into the mud as my tears fall onto his bloody chest, his severed neck—

I silence the screaming thoughts that have echoed in my skull for dozens of hours. My gaze makes its way back to Father's favorite chair, brown leather worn from years of sitting. I find that I study it quite often, even when he was alive and sitting in it, signing treaties and strategizing. I studied everything he did. *Before he was brutally murdered.*

'Kitt.'

Kai.

My Enforcer.

He steps into the study after a light rasp of his knuckles on the open door, sounding almost timid. I nearly laugh at the sight of Kai trying his best to be cautious around me. It's a valiant effort, though I didn't ask for his pity.

I'm not like Kai. I'm not cool and collected and constantly wearing a carefully constructed mask around most. My emotions are on full display, my heart on my sleeve. I'm Kitt, the brother who is supposed to be kind and charming. Said to become the kindest king Ilya has ever seen.

Wrong.

I feel anything but kind. I feel *everything* but kind.

I feel rage and grief. Inadequate and hollow. Despair and—

'You wanted to see me?' My brother's words are soft, sounding slightly concerned.

And he should be. Kind Kitt doesn't act crazed. Kind Kitt is caring, not a killer.

Kind Kitt has changed.

Grief is a bitch.

'Yes. Take a seat.' I gesture casually to Kai's usual chair. His eyes flick to Father's worn one before he sits, crossing an ankle over his knee.

He leans forward, eyes searching mine for answers he won't find. 'How are you doing, Kitt?'

The concern filling his voice cracks something in my heart—the one that has become so cold over the past seventy-two hours. My gaze softens slightly, momentarily shifting into more of Kitt and less of the king. He's still my brother, the only flesh and blood I have left. Maybe even the only person I have left.

'I'm . . . doing.'

I'm doing? What the hell kind of answer was that?

I clear my throat. 'How is,' I hesitate, 'Mother doing?'

She's not my mother. My mother is dead, just like my father.

'She's . . . doing.' Kai gives me a weak smile. 'She won't leave her room. It's like the grief of losing him is slowly . . .' he trails

500

off, turning his attention back towards Father's worn chair to distract himself from the unspoken words.

'I see.' I *did* see. I understand how she feels. How it feels to be so swallowed, so smothered, by grief.

My eyes shift to Kai, taking in his stiff shoulders, his bruised and bloody knuckles.

I pity the who or what he hit to take his mind off things.

I almost cluck my tongue at him, wanting to chastise my little brother for wearing that cool mask of his around me. He never does that, never shuts me out of his feelings like he is doing now.

I'm not sure what Kai felt for our father, but I know he never cared for him like I do – like I *did*. Perhaps it was a mix of love and loathing he felt for the man who made him into what he is. The man who was a king to him, not a father.

But to me, Father was my foundation. He was who I strived to be, who I longed to be loved by. But now he's dead, and I'm still willing to do whatever it takes to make him proud. I've been walking through my whole life waiting to follow in his footsteps, and here I am, suddenly trying to fill his shoes. And I will do what needs to be done, so that in death, he will be proud.

I glance at my brother, knowing he feels the grief too. Despite their rough relationship, Kai still lost the man he called Father, if only in title alone. I can glimpse that grief peeking out in the hard set of his jaw, the constant crinkle of his brow, the bounce of his knee.

But I know he's mourning more than one person.

I know I am.

'Kai.' His attention snaps to me. 'My coronation is completed, Father's burial has been dealt with,' I pause, needing a moment to clear the emotion from my throat, 'and you are now my true Enforcer.' He nods slowly, knowing all this information already. 'So, it's time for your first mission.'

He nods again, just as slowly. It's a formality. We both know he couldn't refuse even if he wanted to. He has sworn his services to me despite how damn awkward our dynamic has become. I knew I would be ruling over my brother one day, I just didn't think that day would come so soon, so suddenly.

I school my features into neutrality. 'Find her.'

And there goes Kai's mask. It slips, flooding his face with feelings that flit by too fast for me to interpret. But I'm not blind. I saw the way she affected him. Saw the way he let his guard down around her, something he used to reserve only for me. It seems that she got the best of both of us before stabbing us both in the back by stabbing Father through the chest and throat.

My only true parent, dead. The parent I have been trying to please, make proud, my entire life. Lying lifeless beside me. My knees sinking into the mud as my tears—

'I want you to find her,' I speak over the shouting sorrow in my head, 'and I want you to bring her to me.'

Kai doesn't look at me as he dips his head in a single, solemn nod. 'Yes, Your Majesty.'

The title on his lips sounds foreign, but I find I like the ring of it. I stand from my seat and stride over to the one with faded brown leather, filled with the memory of a dead king.

And then I sit down, slowly.

'Bring me Paedyn Gray, Enforcer.'

Acknowledgements

Before I begin gushing about the people who helped make *Powerless* possible, I would like to first take a moment to formally freak out over the fact that I even made it far enough to *write* an acknowledgements page in the first place. The journey to the end of this manuscript was a long one, an adventure I was terrified I wouldn't be able to finish. And for that very reason, of all the thousands of words I wrote before this, typing acknowledgements at the top of this page may be the one I'm most proud of.

With that being said, I will now begin gushing my gratitude.

Most importantly, and most obviously, I want to first attempt to express my thankfulness and appreciation to my patient parents. Mom and Dad, you have supported me every step of the way through this crazy journey, and I truly could not have accomplished this dream without the two of you. Thank you for believing in me, I love you both dearly.

Following the family theme, there are three other people I'm related to who deserve my thanks. Nikki, thank you for not only listening to me rant about plot holes, but for helping me find ways to resolve them. I owe you big-time. Josh, I couldn't have asked for a better fake agent. Thank you for your willingness to help and wisdom throughout this process, Foo. Jessie, the love and support you've graciously given me means more than you know. Your enthusiasm for me and my dream is truly contagious.

For once, it seems I'm at a loss for words when it comes to expressing my immense appreciation for my incredible editor, Michelle Rosquillo. I am so unbelievably thankful for all the dedication and hard work you poured into *Powerless*, Michelle. Your guidance and wisdom helped make my manuscript what it is today, and I could not have asked for a better woman to tackle the task of editing this lengthy book. Thank you for making this process fun and exciting, including the four-hour phone calls I would put you through. Simply put, you are the best.

The breathtaking cover before you is all thanks to Stefanie Saw at Seventhstar Art. You are truly magic, and I will be forever mesmerized by your work. As for the gorgeous map in the front of this book, we all have JoJo Elliott to thank for that. I am blown away every time I admire how the both of you brought my world to life.

To the incredible team at Simon & Schuster, it is truly an honor to get to work alongside you. And as disgustingly cheesy as it sounds, this is very much a dream come true. If only little Lauren could see me now. In short, thank you for believing in me. I am forever grateful for this opportunity, as well as unable to properly express my excitement to continue this journey with you all. I cannot wait to see what the future has in store.

Now, if I were to write about every person who helped get me to where I am today, whether by encouragement or aid, I fear we'd have another book on our hands. With that in mind, I'd like to give a general and ginormous thank you to my incredible friends. Your excitement for me and willingness to listen to me ramble about my writing is more than I could ever ask for. Thank you for putting up with me – that task alone is not for the faint of heart.

Alright, it's about time I thank a few thousand people who have played a *huge* role in not only the writing of *Powerless*, but also in my life. To the chaotic family I am blessed enough to have through TikTok, you all are the reason I even got to write this page. *Powerless* wouldn't exist if it weren't for the support and love I've been shown since posting my very first video on BookTok. You are my favorite menaces, and I will never be able to thank each and every one of you enough for giving me this opportunity. You're all the main character, and don't you ever forget it.

I'd like to now thank the One who gifted me my love of words and desire to write. I truly would not be where I am today without my Lord and Savior, and I thank God for the opportunity He has given me.

Okay, I'm almost done being sappy. This is a thank you to you, dear reader. I simply cannot fathom a world in which people want to read my ramblings, so thank you for spending time in the world I created with the characters I am unhealthily attached to. You are my inspiration, and I hope I have the privilege to continue writing for you.

Now, pretend I'm giving you a hug.

XO, Lauren

About the Author

When Lauren Roberts isn't writing about fantasy worlds and bantering love interests, she can likely be found burrowed in bed reading about them. Lauren has lived in Michigan her whole life, making her very familiar with potholes, snow, and various lake activities. She has the hobbies of both a grandmother and a child, i.e., knitting, laser tag, hammocking, word searches, and coloring. *Powerless* is her debut novel, and she hopes to have the privilege of writing pretty words for the rest of her life. If you enjoy ranting, reading, and writing, Lauren can be found on both TikTok and Instagram @Laurens1library or her website laurenrobertslibrary.com for your entertainment.

Turn the page for a sneak peek of the second book
in the epic and sizzling Powerless trilogy
by Lauren Roberts.

Coming May 2024!

Paedun

My blood is only useful if it can manage to stay inside my body. My mind is only useful if it can manage to not get lost.

My heart is only useful if it can manage to not get broken.

Well, it seems I've become utterly useless then.

My eyes flick over the floorboards beneath my feet, wandering over the worn wood. The mere sight of the familiar floods me with memories, and I fight to blink away the fleeting images of small feet atop big, booted ones as they stepped in time to a familiar melody. I shake my head, trying to shake the memory from it despite desperately wishing I could dwell in the past, seeing that my present isn't the most pleasant at the moment.

. . . sixteen, seventeen, eighteen—

I smile, ignoring the pain that pinches my skin.

Found you.

My stride is unsteady and stiff, sore muscles straining with each step towards the seemingly normal floorboard. I drop to my knees, biting my tongue against the pain, and claw at the wood with crimson-stained fingers I struggle to ignore.

The floor seems to be just as stubborn as I am, refusing to budge. I would have admired its resilience if it weren't a damn piece of *wood*.

I don't have time for this. I need to get out of here.

A frustrated sound tears from my throat before I blink at the board and blurt, 'I could have sworn you were the secret compartment. Are you not the nineteenth floorboard from the door?'

I'm staring daggers at the wood before a hysterical laugh slips past my lips, and I tip my head back to shake it at the ceiling. 'Plagues, now I'm talking to the *floor*,' I mutter, further proof that I'm losing my mind.

Although, it's not as if I have anyone else to talk to.

It's been four days since I stumbled back to my childhood home, haunted and half-dead. And yet, both my mind and body are far from healed.

I may have dodged death with each swipe of the king's sword, but he still managed to kill a part of me that day after the final Trial. His words cut deeper than his blade ever could, slicing me with slivers of truths as he toyed with me, taunted me, told me of my father's death with a smile tugging at his lips.

'Wouldn't you like to know who it was that killed your father?'

A shiver snakes down my spine while the king's cold voice echoes through my skull.

'Let's just say that your first encounter with a prince wasn't when you saved Kai in the alley.'

If betrayal was a weapon, he bestowed it upon me that day, driving the blunt blade through my broken heart. I blow out a shaky breath, pushing away thoughts of the boy with gray eyes as piercing as the sword I watched him drive through my father's chest so many years ago.

Staggering to my feet, I shift my weight over the surrounding floorboards, listening for an indicating creak while mindlessly spinning the silver ring on my thumb. My body aches all over, my very bones feeling far too fragile. The wounds I earned from both the final Trial and my fight with the king were hastily tended to, the result of shaky fingers and silent sobs that left my vision blurry and stitches sloppy.

After limping from the Bowl Arena towards Loot Alley, I stumbled into the white shack I called home and the Resistance called headquarters. But I was greeted with emptiness. There were no familiar faces filling the secret room beneath my feet, leaving me with nothing but my pain and confusion.

I was alone – have been alone – left to clean up the mess that is my body, my brain, my bleeding heart.

Wood groans. I grin.

Once again I'm on the floor, prying up a beam to reveal a shadowy compartment beneath. I shake my head at myself, mumbling, 'It's the nineteenth floorboard from the *window*, not the door, Pae . . .'

I reach into the darkness, fingers curling around the unfamiliar hilt of a dagger. My heart aches more than my body, wishing to feel the swirling steel handle of my father's weapon against my palm.

But I chose the shedding of blood over sentiment when I threw my beloved blade into the king's throat. And my only regret is that *he* found it, promising to return it only when he's stabbed it into my back.

Empty blue eyes blink at me in the reflection of the shiny blade I lift into the light, startling me enough to halt my hateful thoughts. My skin is splattered with slices, covered in cuts. I swallow at the sight of the gash traveling down the side of my neck, skim fingers over the jagged skin. Shaking my head, I slip the dagger into my boot, stowing away my scared reflection with it.

I spot a bow and its quiver of sharp arrows concealed in the compartment, and the shadow of a sad smile crosses my face at the memory of Father teaching me how to shoot, the gnarled tree behind our house my only target.

Slinging the bow and quiver across my back, I sift through the other weapons hidden beneath the floor. After tossing a few sharp throwing knives into my pack, joining the rations and water canteens I'd hastily tucked inside, I struggle to my feet.

I've never felt so delicate, so damaged. The thought has me swelling with anger, has me snatching a knife from my waist and itching to plunge it into the worn, wooden wall before me. Searing pain shoots down my raised arm when the brand above my heart pulls taut with the movement.

A reminder. A representation of what I am. Or rather, what I'm not.

O for Ordinary.

I send the knife flying, plunging it into the wood with gritted teeth. The scar stings, gloating of its endless existence on my body.

'. . . *I will leave my mark on your heart, lest you forget who's broken it.*'

I stalk over to the blade, ready to yank it from the wall, when the board beneath my foot creaks, drawing my attention. Despite knowing that flimsy floorboards are anything but foreign to houses in the slums, my curiosity has me bending to investigate.

If every creaky board were a compartment, our floor would be littered with them—

The wood lifts and my eyebrows do the same, shooting up my forehead in shock. I huff out a humorless laugh as I reach into the shadows of the compartment I didn't know existed.

Silly of me to think that the Resistance was the only secret Father kept from me.

My fingers brush worn leather before I pull out a large book, stuffed with papers that threaten to spill out. I flip through it, recognizing the messy handwriting of a Physician.

Father's journal.

I shove it into my pack, knowing I don't have the time or safety needed to study his work. I've been here too long, spent too many days wounded and weak and worrying that I'll be found.

The Sight who witnessed me murder the king has likely displayed that image all over the kingdom. I need to get out of Ilya, and I've already wasted the head start *he* so graciously gave me.

I make my way to the door, ready to slip out and onto the streets where I can disappear into the chaos that is Loot. From there, I'll attempt to head across the Scorches to the city of Dor, where Elites don't exist and Ordinary is all they know.

Reaching for the door and the quiet street beyond—

I halt, hand outstretched.

Quiet.

It's nearly midday, meaning Loot and its surrounding streets should be a swarm of swearing merchants and squealing children as the slums buzz with color and commotion.

Something's not right—

The door shudders, something – *someone* – ramming into it from the outside. I jump back, eyes darting around the room. I contemplate ducking down the secret stairwell to the room beneath that held the Resistance meetings, but the thought of being cornered down there makes me queasy. That's when my gaze snaps to the fireplace, and I sigh in annoyance despite my current situation.

How do I always find myself in a chimney?

The door breaks open with a bang before I've barely shimmied halfway up the grimy wall, my feet planted opposite me while bricks dig into my back.

Brawny.

Only an Elite with extraordinary strength would be able to smash through my barricaded and bolted door so quickly. The sound of heavy boots has me figuring that five Imperials have just filed into my home.

'Don't just stand there. Search the place and convince me that you're useful.'

I stiffen, slipping slightly down the sooty wall. A shiver runs down my spine at the sound of that cool voice, the one I've heard sound like both a caress and a command.

He's here.

The voice that follows is gravelly, belonging to an Imperial. 'You heard the Enforcer. Get a move on.'

The Enforcer.

I bite my tongue, whether to keep myself from letting out a bitter laugh or a scream, I'm not sure. My blood boils at the title, reminding me of everything he's done, every bit of evil he's committed in the shadow of the king. First for his father, and now for his brother – thanks to me ridding him of the former.

Except he's not thanking me. No, he's come to kill me instead.

'Maybe when I rid myself of you, I'll find my courage. So I'm giving you a head start.'

A lot of good his head start has done me.

I can't risk being heard scrambling up the chimney, so I wait, listening to heavy footsteps stomping through the house in search of me. My legs are beginning to shake, straining to hold me up while my every wound has me wincing in pain.

'Check the bookcases in the study. There should be a secret passage behind one,' the Enforcer commands dryly, sounding *bored*.

Once again I find myself stiffening. A Resistance member must have confessed that little secret after he tortured it out of them. My pulse quickens at the thought of the fight after the final Trial in the Bowl when Ordinaries, Fatals, and Imperials clashed in a bloody battle.

A bloody battle that I still don't know the outcome of.

The steps of the Imperials grow distant, the sounds of their search softening as they head down the stairs and into the room beneath.

Quiet.

And yet, I know he's still in this room. Only a feeble amount of feet separate us. I can practically feel his presence, just as I've felt the heat of his body against mine, the heat of his gray gaze as it swept over me.

A floorboard creaks. He's close. I'm shaking with anger, revenge coursing through my blood and desperately wishing to spill his. It's a good thing I can't see his face because if I were to catch sight of one of his stupid dimples right now, I wouldn't be able to stop myself from trying to claw it from his face.

But I steady my breathing instead, knowing that if I fight him now, my fury won't be enough to beat him. And I intend to win when I finally face the Enforcer.

'I imagine you pictured my face when you threw that knife.' His voice is quiet, considering, sounding far more like the boy I knew. Memories of him flood my mind, managing to make my heart race. 'Isn't that right, Paedyn?' And there it is. The edge is back in the Enforcer's voice, erasing Kai and leaving a commander.

My heart hammers against my ribcage.

He can't know I'm here. How could he possibly—

The sound of a blade ripping from splintered wood tells me he yanked my knife out of the wall. I hear a familiar flicking noise and can practically picture him mindlessly flipping the weapon in his hand.

'Tell me, darling, do you think of me often?' His voice is a murmur as if his lips were pressed against my ear. I shiver, knowing exactly what that feels like.

If he knows I'm here then why hasn't he—

'Do I haunt your dreams, plague your thoughts, like you do mine?'

My breath hitches.

So he doesn't know I'm here, not for certain.

His admission told me as much.

As an Ordinary who was trained and tailored into a *Psychic*, I was taught by my father to read people, to gather information and observations in a matter of seconds.

And I've had far more than a matter of seconds to read Kai Azer.

I've seen through his many masks and facades, glimpsing the boy beneath and growing to know him, care for him. And with all the betrayal now between us, I know he wouldn't declare dreaming of me if he knew I was drinking in every word.

I hear the humor in his voice as he sighs, 'Where are you, Little Psychic?'

His nickname is laughable, seeing that he and the rest of the kingdom now know I'm anything but. Anything but Elite.

Nothing but Ordinary.

Soot stings my nose and I have to clamp my hand over it to hold in a sneeze, reminding me of my many nights thieving from the stores lining Loot before escaping through cramped chimneys.

Cramped. Trapped. Suffocating.

My eyes dart across the bricks surrounding me in the darkness. The space is so small, so stuffy, so very easily making me panic.

Calm down.

Claustrophobia chooses the worst times to claw to the surface and remind me of my helplessness.

Breathe.

I do. Deeply. The hand still clamped over my nose smells faintly of metal – sharp and strong and stinging my nose.

Blood.

I pull the shaky hand away from my face, and though I can't see the crimson staining my fingers, I can practically feel it clinging to me. There's still blood crusted under my cracked nails, and I don't know whether it's mine, the king's, or—

I suck in a breath, trying to pull myself together. The Enforcer looms far too close to me, pacing the floor, wood groaning beneath him with each step.

Getting caught because I start sobbing would be equally as embarrassing as getting caught for sneezing.

And I refuse to do either.

At some point, the Imperials stomped back into the room beneath me. 'No sign of her, Your Highness.'

There's a long pause before *his highness* sighs. 'Just as I thought. You're all useless.' His next words are sharper than the blade he flips casually in his hand. 'Get out.'

The Imperials don't waste a single second before scrambling towards the door and away from him. I don't blame them.

But he's still here, leaving nothing but silence to stretch between us. I have a hand clamped over my nose again, and the smell of blood combined with the cramped chimney has my head spinning.

Memories flood my mind – my body caked in blood, my screams as I tried to scrub it away, only managing to stain my skin a sickening red. The sight and smell of so much blood made me sick, made me think of my father bleeding out in my arms, of Adena doing the same.

Adena.

Tears prick my eyes, forcing me to blink away the image of her lifeless body in the sandy Pit. The metallic stench of blood fills my nose again, and I can't stand to smell it, to look at it, to feel it—

Breathe.

A heavy sigh cuts through my thoughts. He sounds as tired as I feel. 'It's a good thing you're not here,' he says softly, a tone I never thought I'd hear from him again. 'Because I still haven't found my courage.'

And then my home bursts into flames.

Hunted. Hunter.
Destined for each other.

Powerless

LAUREN ROBERTS

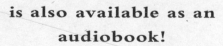

**is also available as an
audiobook!**